CHARLOTTE FEATHERSTONE

PRIDE & PASSION

HQN™

Recycling programs
for this product may
not exist in your area.

ISBN-13: 978-0-373-77617-7

PRIDE & PASSION

Printed in U.S.A.

To all the readers who fell in love with Sussex—
here's your man! Hope his story doesn't disappoint!

PRIDE
& PASSION

PROLOGUE

"BEYOND THE MIST, the darkness and shadow, he waits, reaching out through a veil of gossamer threads—'your future,' he whispers, 'your destiny.'"

Heart fluttering like a trapped bird, Lucy swallowed hard as she focused on the swaying piece of silver.

"He has been there all along, waiting for you. Now is the time to reach out to him, to pull him out of the depths and into the light."

Slowly Lucy nodded, understanding the words, hoping with every beat of her heart and pulse of her blood that the mystic's words were true.

Occultism, spiritualism, mysticism...whatever one chose to call it, one fact remained true—it was sweeping through Victorian England, a dark presence that resided over soirees and salons, spirit meetings and private clubs.

The dark arts were an invitation to evil. Or so many a mere mortal believed. But Lucy Ashton knew them to be a door to another world—a world of darkness and mystery, a realm where demons and angels—the fallen—roamed free, selling their secrets for the price of a soul in need.

As she sat surrounded by golden candelabra, coated with layers of dripping, drying wax, with nothing but the sound of the autumn wind howling and the crackling of a log being engulfed by flame, Lucy knew she was that soul. One who needed—deeply.

The woman who sat opposite her held a silver pendulum in her hand. She knew how to find what Lucy so desperately searched for.

"Your lover," the woman said in a voice that seemed so far away the longer Lucy followed the swaying pendulum with unblinking eyes. "He will come—*soon*."

She dearly hoped so. Eight months it had been since she had last seen him—gone without a trace, taking with him any warmth, any feeling she possessed. The heady sensation of that warmth had been too brief—much too brief.

"You were right 'ta come to me, m' lady," the woman whispered. "I can find 'im. Bring 'im to you. Keep watching," she encouraged. "Follow the pendulum and let yer thoughts drift 'ta him, the man who shall fix yer future."

Lucy's lids were heavy, and the flickering candle-light made shadows leap on the wall, a macabre dance. The mystic's heavily wrinkled face grew shadowed, half of her cast in darkness, the other half yellowed in the candles' glow.

"Yes, yes…" she murmured excitedly. "That's the way, lass."

The room narrowed and rippled; the absinthe Lucy had taken moments before the mystic produced the pendulum had found its way into her bloodstream, filling her veins with a strange sensation—one of heightened awareness meshed with a dreamy quality. *Like floating on water,* she thought as her body relaxed and sunk deep into the velvet chair. Watching that swaying pendulum, Lucy felt her spirit and inhibitions leave her.

"Where are ye now?"

As if in a trance, Lucy answered, "A room. It's dark, with only bits of light filtering through gauze curtains."

"Yes? Go on."

"I am not alone," Lucy whispered. "I can sense another."

"Close yer eyes, and see 'im with yer mind, luv."

Obeying, Lucy allowed her lids to close fully. Immediately she saw herself, masked, her back pressed against the filmy gauze that separated her from the other person. Sliding her hand out, she slid her palm along the curtain, feeling an answering slide from the other side.

"He is there," the mystic whispered. "The premonition of yer future."

Yes...

She sensed the heat, the passion. Her body remembered it—*him*.

At last she had found him. He had come to her. His touch was hot, warming her instantly. She pressed back, felt the hard, solid body of a man.

"Now tell me what ye see."

Opening her eyes, Lucy jumped up from the chair she occupied, a suffocating scream lodged in her throat. The mystic followed her, snapping her fingers before Lucy's eyes, breaking the spell that held her.

"M' lady?"

Perplexed, Lucy stared at the woman who claimed she could show Lucy what awaited her future. The Scot-

tish Witch, with her fading red hair and wild golden
eyes stood before her.

"You, madam, are a fraud."

Snatching her reticule, Lucy left the coins on the
table she had given to the crone when they had begun.
The woman's expression was stricken, and Lucy curled
her lip in disdain. "You may enjoy fleecing others, but
I will not be fooled. This is the last time we will meet.
You needn't attend me next week."

"But…" The woman, just Mrs. Fraser now, no longer
the Scottish Witch, or the occult mystic Lucy had once
believed her to be, followed anxiously behind her.
"What did ye see, lass?"

Lucy whirled on her. *"Not my future!"*

Mrs. Fraser's gaze narrowed, replaced by a knowing look. "Oh, aye, yer future indeed, lassie. Just no'
the one ye desire."

"Good day, madam," she answered in a clipped tone.
Thrusting her hands into her soft leather gloves, Lucy
left the drafty parlor and took the rickety steps down
the three flights of stairs, out to the back of the building where her carriage awaited.

That is what she got for visiting a charlatan in the
theater district, she thought mulishly. A first rate performance in fraudulence.

Future indeed, she scoffed as the carriage jolted forward, leaving Mrs. Fraser's rental flats and her occult
babblings far behind.

Gazing out the window, Lucy hardly saw the scen-
ery passing her by, for the images of that trance would
not leave her in peace.

Yes, the dark arts were an invitation to a mysterious

and dark realm. One of secrets and danger, and forbidden yearnings. A world of sensual pleasure and hedonistic pastimes.

She had seen that world in the vision, felt the heaving pulse surrounding her. She heard the words, whispering to her, wrapping around her like a lover's touch.

Why did you forsake me?

His answer had been soft, a mere whisper. Their palms had touched through the gauze, his heat singing her just as his words did. *I have been here all along, waiting for you to see me beyond the veil that separates us.*

She had turned then, breathless with anticipation. She saw her pale hand reach for the curtain, its trembling strength barely able to grasp the filmy material between her fingers. But with one tug, the fabric that separated them fell, pooling between them. She had looked up from the black mound, up along a body that hers recalled with such visceral pleasure. To a set of eyes that were so…wrong.

Gray eyes.

There was something about those eyes that pulled at her memory—a different time; a past that caused pain when it was recalled. No, the possessor of those eyes was definitely not her future!

CHAPTER ONE

"MY DEAR, YOU have been looking forlornly out that window for half an hour now. Why do you not go and call on Lady Black?"

Lucy tucked the bit of lace she held in her hand between the voluminous folds of her rose-colored silk and velvet skirts, as she gazed over her shoulder at her father. It was early November, and the day was gray with drizzle that promised to turn to sleet. She pulled the fur shawl a little tighter about her shoulders. The fire that had been laid was crackling, the amber flames flickering with warmth, filling the room with the comfort that only a roaring fire in late autumn could bring. But still Lucy was cold. She had been for months. Nothing seemed to warm her.

"It is early yet, Papa," she answered. "Too early for calls."

"Nonsense, the new Lady Black is your cousin—I daresay almost your sister. It's never too early to call on family. Besides, I'll be leaving now for my club, and I would like to know that you're not at home, hanging about at loose ends."

A wry smile escaped her as she cast her gaze once more out the window, to the mammoth black iron gates that stood across the street. How strange it was, that after all these years—decades, actually—her father cared about what she might—or might not—be doing. Her loneliness, and it had been substantial, had never mattered to him before.

The Marquis of Stonebrook was neither a heartless nor an intentionally cruel man. Lucy could not say that about her father. Only that he wasn't mindful of others and their needs. He was emotionally absent—not mean or quarrelsome. Just…absent. There was no other word for what her father, and her mother, had been. Although, perhaps *uninterested* might be a close second. The long-held adage of "seen and not heard" did not pertain to her upbringing. For her parents had seen very little of her, and heard her? Not at all.

Her parents had been more concerned with their own lives than that of their child. She had been of little consequence to them, bringing to them little enjoyment. Her conception had been an obligation to further the title, and when she had turned out to be a girl, and no other children followed her, her parents had resigned themselves to the fact that their legacy would live on through the husband they would choose for her.

And Lucy knew without a doubt who her father wanted her to take for a husband. The passionless and priggish Duke of Sussex.

The duke was a sedate, dull and frightfully proper man—nothing like the man she dreamt of when she imagined a husband. Nothing like those dreams she had entertained when she was younger, when the butcher's boy would come round with his master and keep her company in the kitchen while the butcher haggled with Mrs. Brown, their old housekeeper. Those had been silly, girlish fantasies of what it might be like to follow one's heart and dreams; those fantasies had swiftly been dashed by her father, and she soon learned what being a marriageable woman in her world truly meant.

And such was the essence of her life. Until eight months ago when she had taken her future into her own hands, seeking out what she felt her life lacked in the arms of an artist. The warmth and acceptance she had found with him would not exist with the duke. Their union would be an alliance, not a relationship.

"Come, my dear, I've been watching you for a while now, sitting on that window box, lost in thought. Surely whatever it is you're hiding there beneath your skirts isn't so serious for one as young as you?"

A bit of Brussels lace, that's what she had buried beneath the folds of her skirts. It was embroidered with her initials, and given to her lover on the night she had offered herself to him. And then he had died. Or at least, she had believed he'd died in the fire that had consumed his rented rooms.

She had grieved, wept and despaired over never feeling alive again, until a fortnight ago, when the lace had been resurrected and delivered to her hand. That it had been his grace, the Duke of Sussex, who had delivered the handkerchief to her never ceased to perturb her. Why he had been the one to return it to her was still something she mulled over during the long, lonely nights spent alone in her father's town house. She did not care for the notion that Sussex knew of her dalliance with another man. She didn't care what he thought of her, or what he made of the handkerchief—or if he thought her fast and immoral, and so far beneath him for indulging in base pleasures.

It did not matter what his grace made of it all, for Lucy cared about only one thing: Thomas was alive, she was sure of it. He had made her promises. He'd spoken to her of their future together. She had believed that future burned to ashes in the fire, but the lace that she rubbed between her fingers told her that everything she believed was about to change.

"You're frowning. Your mama always said it would give you creases about your eyes."

Lucy found herself smiling. "Yes, she did say that. But I haven't gotten the wrinkles yet."

It was her father's turn to frown. "Dare I hope the reason for your deep rumination might be the subject of marriage, especially after you have witnessed the marital felicity between your cousin and her new husband?"

"I am afraid not, Papa."

"I thought not, but one can hope, and I haven't given up yet."

Her father would never give up. It was his desire to see her wed to the duke, and nothing less would do.

"And that is all that you intend to say on the matter, is it? Well, then I shall let it rest for now. Come then, Lucy, I must be off. I shall escort you across the street."

"Really, Papa, there is no need for concern. I am quite all right at home."

"Alone?" he guffawed. "Absolutely not, you're still recovering from your illness."

There was no fighting him on this. A fortnight ago she had been gravely ill—her own stupidity, which she refused to think on—and ever since, her father made certain that she was never left alone, although it was not him who was a constant presence, but Isabella, whose task it now seemed was to hover about and mind Lucy's activities.

Lucy thought back to those months ago, when, in an attempt to appease the loneliness left behind by the imagined loss of her lover, she had turned down many a dark and dangerous path, one of séances and scribing, and bargaining in her dreams if only she could find her lover once again. There had been that awful sense of incompleteness, having never had a chance to say good-bye. To see him one last time before he faded forever onto the other side, where breathing mortals could not follow.

Dabbling in the occult had been a way of idling her time away—and perhaps a somewhat foolish and desperate measure to find him in the ethers of the spiritual realm—it was then that she had come across the mysterious Brethren Guardians and their sacred relics—a relic she had stolen and used for her own purposes. The result had been disastrous, and nearly deadly.

It had terrified her father, and now he was hovering about, foisting her onto her cousin, and generally distrusting her, treating her like a child.

"Come, Lucy. I insist," her father muttered in that voice that would brook no refusal. "There is no moving me on this. You will join Lady Black today and attend to those things that ladies do during morning calls."

"I will just change," Lucy sighed, quite resigned in the matter.

"Balderdash! You are quite appropriately attired. There is no need to waste time on changing your wardrobe."

Her father wouldn't hear of it. He was in something of a hurry to get to his club, and therefore, she was escorted out of the salon, and into the hall, where Jennings, their butler, assisted her with her cloak and umbrella.

"Damn this weather," her father grumbled as he reached for her elbow and ushered her down the stone steps to the waiting carriage. "We'll drive across the street, for there is no telling how long it will take Black's footman to open the gates. I have no desire to wait in the rain for the gates to open. Don't know why he needs them, anyway." *Because he was a Brethren Guardian.* But she couldn't very well inform her father of such a fact. She herself should know nothing of it. Lucy barely understood this strange Brethren that Sussex and Lord Black belonged to, but it didn't matter. During her study of the occult, she had stumbled across it, discovering not only who the Brethren were, but the relics they kept hidden. She had sworn an oath of silence, promising never to speak of their little group to anyone. And in return, her own shocking secret would be kept from her father, and the microcosm that was their world—the ton.

She knew only bits and pieces of the Brethren Guardians' secrets; it was an esoteric society made up of three influential peers: Black, Sussex and the Marquis of Alynwick.

Their business was mysterious and secretive, and dangerous. From what she knew of their secrets, there existed an onyx pendant, which was the very essence of evil, and some sort of chalice that they protected. But what they represented, she could not say, and could not find out.

Black, who had recently become the husband of Isabella, Lucy's cousin, had been shot a fortnight ago during what was termed *Guardian business*. Well on the mend, Black pretended that naught had happened, and Isabella, a true and honorable wife, would not speak of it. Lucy had tried, but Isabella had remained stubbornly tight-lipped. And the pendant…it had belonged to Black and his family, and purportedly contained seeds with magical powers. Lucy had taken it, ingested a seed inside the pendant and wished with everything inside her in the hopes she might once more see her lover and say her tearful goodbyes.

Of course, the rash action had caused her days of vomiting, and a strange feeling of possession, not to mention the fact that her actions had both alarmed and angered not only Black but Sussex. But in the end, her goal had been achieved. Thomas was alive…

And the Brethren Guardians were not only looking for him, but watching her as well to see if Thomas would come to her. When Sussex had delivered the lace to her he had also informed her that the man who had dropped it was a man he and the Brethren were hunting. He was their enemy, Sussex had claimed, and that man, Lucy knew, was Thomas. Her lover from the past. And Lucy knew with every cell of her being that she must protect him from the duke and his two fellow Guardians, for they were powerful and influential men, while her lover was an artist, without influence of a title or the power that both peerage and money could wield.

Yes, those iron gates that surrounded his lordship's

home, standing sentry like a castle drawbridge against marauding knights, was a security measure—one Black would never abolish.

Her father cleared his throat several times, while glancing sidelong at her, all indications that something was weighing on him, something he felt compelled to speak of. "I'm afraid I cannot allow our previous conservation to lay fallow. I must speak plainly, Lucy. I've noticed, my dear, that Sussex hasn't been by for some time. Two weeks, at least, I believe."

Lucy refused to take her gaze from the rain-streaked carriage window. She would not talk of his grace, and she would not have this conversation with her father.

"I hope you have not had a falling-out."

"I wasn't aware that we had a falling-in."

That quip made her father glare at her. "You don't make it easy on the poor fellow. You hold him at arm's length. He's trying to court you, but you're too obstinate to see it."

"I am well aware of the fact, Father. You have made it too blatant for me to misunderstand. You wish me to marry the duke."

"You say it with such disdain, as though he were a common laborer, when he is the furthest thing from it."

She thought back to her young friend Gabriel, the butcher's boy, and realized that they had shared something remarkable—the same sadness, the same loneliness, despite their stations being so opposite. "I am not at all opposed to a common man, if he were to feel a genuine sense of affection for me."

"Affection!" Her father's thick mutton chops twitched in irritation. "Good God, child, are we back to that?

Those fairy-tale thoughts were amusing when you were twelve, now they are downright mortifying. Marriage is an institution—"

"Rather like one of those asylums for lunatics," she mumbled, unable to help herself. She didn't want an institution. She wanted a marriage. A friendship. A loving partner.

Her father sighed deeply, but did not bother to address her thoughts and instead began to talk to her as he had so many years ago, as she lay on her bed, sobbing into her pillow after he had turned away the only friend she had ever had—Gabriel. Depriving her of that friendship had destroyed her, frozen part of her heart and soul. How wretched her father had been— how horrid it was to see her friend leave, and never, ever return. Internally she had railed against the injustice of it all, but she had been powerless then to take charge of her life, and her future. And now, here she was years later, still just as powerless, still enduring the same lectures on duty and the responsibilities of a female of her class.

"Now, Lucy, must I remind you that every station in life has its obligations, and the daughter of a marquis's obligation is to marry well, furthering their nobility, and riches. You were put on this earth, girl, to marry a duke."

How many times had she heard that particular lecture? Her entire existence in the world was based on matrimony and breeding. A harrowing thought, one that made her feel pity for all the other unborn daughters of the peerage.

"You won't find a better man than Sussex. His reputation is impeccable. His bloodlines impeccable. He is well-respected, connected, titled and as rich as Croesus—"

"And as cold as the Arctic."

"The man is conscious of propriety is all. As all gentlemen should be," he reminded her.

"He only looks at me to pick me apart and draw attention to my flaws."

"The man is a paragon, he can't help it."

"No, he cannot, but I don't have to marry him. After all, I would not suit his ideas of an ideal wife."

"Of course you would. You come with an enormous dowry, from a long and noble title. Your son will inherit not only a dukedom, but my title as well. Not to mention the fact you are a very lovely young woman. What more can a man want in the way of a recommendation for marriage?"

Finally she forced herself to meet her father's eye. "Is there anything other than commodities to recommend our union, Papa?"

Stonebrook flustered and gripped the head of his walking stick with his gloved hand. "Come now, it's time you gave a serious thought to marriage, Lucy. I won't live forever, you know, and I would like to meet my maker knowing you've been set up in a proper home."

"With someone to love me? Someone who will give me solace when you are gone?" she asked quietly, which made her father grumble and shift his weight on the seat.

"With someone who will keep you safe and fed, and well in hand," he growled.

Of course. Well in hand. Someone to control her, to make her live in the confines of polite society, just like her parents had done all her life—like her father continued to do. To Stonebrook Sussex was the ideal candidate for her husband. It didn't matter that they had not a flicker of attraction, or affection for one another. Why, Lucy still recalled the night Sussex had informed her of the fact that once they were married, there would be no more séances or anything of the like. Then he had kissed her, and she had felt nothing but his firm lips pinched into a straight line as they mashed up against hers. It had not been the stuff of dreams. In fact, his grace had been stiff and rigid as he held her, leading Lucy to believe that he had felt the same thing she had—distaste.

"I'll have Sussex and his sister to dinner, and you shall see, my dear. His grace will make you a fine husband."

"And am I to have any say?" she asked.

"No," her father answered, "after that debacle two weeks ago we cannot trust your judgment. You will marry Sussex just as I wish. And you'll be happy. You'll see, my dear. Ah, here we are," her father said with a great air of relief. "I see the footman is already opening the gates. Good," her father muttered as he pulled his pocket watch from his waistcoat and flipped the lid open with his thumb.

"Father, we are not done with this conversation, and I am perfectly capable of walking up the drive," she said, annoyed by the fact her father kept glancing at his watch.

"Nonsense. Won't be but a minute and I'll be on my way."

"I am not a child," she mumbled as she watched the rivers of drizzle snake down the carriage window. From the corner of her eye, she saw her father turn his head. He was watching her from beneath his bushy white brows, and the thick mutton chops he was so fond of twitched with aggravation. While watching her, his lips thinned, and she could almost hear his thoughts. *Yes, you are, or you wouldn't have gotten yourself into trouble a fortnight ago.*

Trouble, Lucy mentally snorted, wasn't the beginning of what she'd gotten herself into. She'd been impulsive and headstrong, and yes…childish.

"My dear, I worry for your health is all," Stonebrook said as the horses pulled the carriage up the sloped drive of Black's town house. "You've not been yourself for months now, and while I know you would wish to have your mama here for these sorts of discussions, surely you must know that Lady Black would listen and help you with anything that might be troubling you. If it is Sussex, then may I suggest you talk with your cousin about it? Isabella will affirm what I've always believed, that you and the duke will get on well."

Lucy hid her grimace. Her father had no idea what had happened all those months ago with Thomas, and she prayed he never would. He would never understand, never credit the notion of love and unbridled passions. That he was fobbing her off onto Isabella was very typical of the sort of parent he had always been.

"Ah, look, there she is now, waiting for us."

Sitting forward, she saw Isabella standing just inside

the covered alcove of her new home. She was looking
radiant, and carried the expression of a woman well-
loved—and loved passionately. A bitter tang of envy
resonated through Lucy's soul. She wanted the very
same thing. And she would have it.

"Uncle. Lucy," Isabella called as the footman opened
door. "Come in."

"I daresay I cannot, Lady Black," her father returned
as he ushered Lucy through the door, and out into the
chilly drizzle. "But Lady Lucy is more than eager to
take up your generous offer."

Seconds later, Lucy found herself ushered up the
steps, and into the warm entrance hall. Billings, the
butler, was taking her bonnet and cloak, and Isabella
was tugging her along, into the private salon she used
to entertain Elizabeth and herself.

"When was it arranged that you would child-mind
me for the day?"

Isabella's lovely eyes widened with feigned shock.
"Oh, Lucy, how can you say that?"

"Very easily, you've been my companion—I daresay
my governess—for the past two weeks. And no doubt
my father's coconspirator in arranging my marriage to
the Duke of Sussex."

Flopping down onto the settee, Isabella began toying
with the thick fringe of tassels that decorated a pillow.
"Your father wants only the very best for you, and
after you…well, after you were poisoned he became
consumed with worry. He knows something is wrong,
Lucy."

"I don't know how. He's never home, and when he

is, he spends hardly any time engaged in conversation. He's perpetually buried in his study."

"Do not be cross with his lordship, Lucy, for he is not the only one who is worried about you. I am, as well."

Isabella reached for her hand; her smile was kind and filled with sympathy and it made Lucy want to run away and hide. She didn't want to be pitied. "Is there anything I might do for you, Lucy?"

"Well, you might start talking some sense into my father."

"About?"

"His dimwitted idea to thrust me onto Sussex as his duchess."

"Dimwitted? I think it brilliant."

"You wouldn't say that if you were the one that was being forced to marry him."

Isabella glanced at her slyly. "The duke is very handsome, I dare say."

Lucy glowered. "Handsome is only enticing when you are eighteen and a naive ninny." Or twelve, and experiencing the pleasures of your first crush, and yes, absolute adoration if she must be honest with herself. She'd never forgotten Gabriel, and the sad, haunted look in his lovely gray eyes that were always a little too sunken from hunger.

"Lucy, handsome is an attribute appealing to any female, of any age."

"I am afraid my requirements in a husband are rather more lengthy than just being handsome."

"But you do agree he is handsome?"

"Among other things," she muttered.

"Like?"

"Boring, staid, proper, passionless—"

Laughing Isabella held up her hand in defeat. "Lucy, you are unfair! How can you surmise the duke passionless? You aren't even betrothed—well, not formally—ergo you cannot reasonably believe Sussex devoid of… well, the more amorous emotions."

"Oh, and the lack of a formal betrothal stopped Black from acquainting you with his 'amorous emotions'?"

"That's different," Issy sniffed. "And you know it."

"No, Issy. That is touché."

"We are not talking about myself and Black. We are talking about you."

"Well, then, allow me to inform you of what I desire. I know that I want a man like Black, who looks at me with blistering heat, as your husband does you. I know I want a marriage based on love and trust, and a deep, abiding passion. Like yours. Would you so willingly deprive me of it, Issy, after tasting such bliss for yourself?"

Lowering her head, Lucy watched her cousin nibble her bottom lip. When she looked up, Issy's eyes were bright. "I would never deny a woman what I have—it is what every young girl, young woman and spinster dreams of—and deserves. But," Issy cautioned, "I cannot deny that I sense a very good match with Sussex. If you would but give it a chance," Isabella said, raising her voice to be heard over Lucy's grumbling.

"Are we finished with this discourse?" Lucy inquired. "I have already spent the better part of the morning with Father on this very topic. I am quite worn down by it, and any more time spent dwelling upon it shall put me in a mood most foul!"

"Very well. Our discourse on Sussex and his merits as a husband is tabled—for now."

Lucy curtsied mockingly. "Why thank you, your ladyship. I am so grateful for the reprieve."

"It will be short-lived, you know. Since having Black, I have become a shameless matchmaker, nearly rabid in my need to see all my loved ones as happy as I am."

Lucy felt at once happy and envious for her cousin's obvious adoration of her husband. An adoration that was all the more envious by the knowledge that her husband reciprocated Isabella's feelings.

"Well, we were cooped up in here all day yesterday. I cannot stomach another day of listening to rain pattering against windowpanes. What shall we do?"

Isabella brightened, although Lucy saw the hesitation in her eyes. Her cousin wasn't fooled but she was prepared to let it go—for now. "I had Billings send a missive to Elizabeth. We're going to Sussex House for lunch—and gossip."

Sussex House. The duke's town house. The very place she did not wish to go. But then, she did wish to see Elizabeth again. The drizzle had turned to rain, which in fact sounded very much like icy pellets tinkling against the windows. The sound would drive her to bedlam, and the dreariness of the day would send her into even deeper melancholy. She did not want to be a morose little waif, taking to her bed consumed with grief and sadness. She wanted to be strong and tall, someone Thomas would come back to. Something dif-

ferent. She so desperately wanted to be rid of her old
life, and become something—*someone*—else. A but-
terfly emerging from the chrysalis.

"What do you think, Luce?"

Standing, Lucy smiled—a genuine one. "I think it
a sound plan. Lunch with Elizabeth is just the thing to
bring some sunlight to this horribly dreary day. Besides, you will never believe the juicy tidbits I garnered
at the Moorelands' soiree last night. Positively shocking, and I know you will wish to hear all about it as you
sip away on a hot cup of Darjeeling."

"Oh, do tell," Isabella said with a tiny pout. "Black
hasn't let me out of the house since our wedding. I'm
in great need of a little bit of gossip."

Lucy could well imagine what sort of activities kept
the reclusive Earl of Black and his lady occupied. And
while she was the tiniest bit envious that her cousin was
married to a most passionate man, the feelings of happiness for Isabella far outweighed her jealousy.

One day she would have the same sort of passion.

"Well, you shall have to wait to learn of it," she
teased.

"Lucy!" Isabella chastised as she followed her out
of the salon. "You cannot mean to make me wait until
we reach Sussex House to hear the news! You fiend!"

"That is precisely what I mean to do! Thank you,
Billings," Lucy murmured as the butler helped her with
her cloak.

"What shall I tell his lordship, your ladyship?"

Isabella slipped into a black velvet wrap, and reached
for the bonnet Billings held out to her. "Tell Black that

we shall be at Sussex House. We're having lunch and indulging in gossip, Billings."

Billings smiled ruefully before bowing. "Do enjoy, madam. Lady Lucy."

Lucy shot Isabella a smile. Suddenly the day didn't seem as miserable as she first thought. And maybe, during the course of lunch and gossip, she might find something useful that would aid her in finding Thomas—and keep him safe from Sussex's hands.

CHAPTER TWO

SOMETIMES A SOUL was just born fortunate. Sometimes they weren't. Adrian York, the Duke of Sussex, firmly believed that. Some men were lucky enough to bring themselves up and change their fortunes.

Himself, he was something of an enigma—and a fraud. He'd been born a damn unfortunate, and then something had happened. The stars and planets had aligned, and something in the cosmos had shone down on him, making him the most fortunate soul that had ever graced the ballrooms of London. He'd been gifted, not once, but twice. Something more than an enigma, he thought with a sardonic smile, but a downright lucky bastard.

He'd given thanks to his maker, had glanced up at the black velvety sky nearly every night and stared at the twinkling stars, wondering why it had been him they'd decided to favor with such fortune and luck. For him, it was always a question of why—the unanswered question leaving behind the bitter taste of guilt in his mouth, when there were so many unfortunate souls who would never experience such blessings. Fortune had shone down upon him, despite his being a fraud, despite knowing that he was wrongfully gifted by the Fates.

For the last twelve years he'd walked with Lady Fortune. Everything he had touched had turned to gold.

The ton admired him, his peers tried to emulate him and the stars had never failed to shine down upon him. That was, until a fortnight ago, when he had trudged down the front steps of Lord Stonebrook's London town house, utterly defeated and numb after returning a lace handkerchief belonging to Lucy that had been in the possession of a man whom he had witnessed kill another in cold blood.

The memories of that day still ate away at him. He had wanted Lucy to deny any knowledge of the man, to show outrage that the scrap of lace had found its way into the stranger's possession. But she had not, and it only confirmed what he did not care to think about—that she was not only involved with the Brethren's enemy, but also that she had an intimate connection with him.

"So cold-blooded," she had murmured as she looked up from her lap and the piece of lace he had placed in her hands. He had made it clear then that the man was his enemy, and that he would find him—and destroy him. "There is not an ounce of warmth in you," she said. "No heart. No passion."

If she only knew how those words pierced him, haunted him during the darkest, coldest hours of the night. He could still see her, sitting on the window bench looking small and sad—and pale. How he had wanted to hold her, to show her that he had just as much passion—probably more so—than she could imagine. But she did not want him. She wanted someone else. His enemy. The enemy of the Brethren Guardians. It was his penance for the years of taking what Fortune had bestowed upon him, taking what he didn't deserve.

She had vowed to stand between them, her lover and him. To protect Thomas, not him. He had warned her that any attempt to do so might, regretfully, make her an enemy of the Brethren as well, but she hadn't flinched at that. In fact, she seemed to already know and understand what would happen if she chose to cast her lot in with this shadowy figure he and his two fellow Guardians hunted.

Nothing had ever distracted him from his duties as a Brethren Guardian. Theirs was an ancient order, handed down for generations. In his, Black's and Alynwick's blood surged the blood of crusaders, who had kept three sacred relics safe from the world. There was nothing that had ever persuaded him to abandon the cause he had sworn an oath to keep secret, and sacred—until now. Until Lucy.

Damn if he wouldn't sell his soul—and the relics—to the Devil himself to have Lucy in his bed for just one night. Gone was his honor. His moral compass. She had tied him in knots, and still he allowed her to pull the strings tighter and tighter.

He should be repulsed by the thought of himself as a helpless marionette, moved and manipulated by her slight hands, but he could only smile in mocking amazement. He'd lived his life controlled and ordered, never once allowing the passionate nature that lurked within him to surface. For years he feared someone discovering his secret, and his controlled aura had been the only way to ensure it was kept safe. But now, after all these years of honing the skill, he'd let it all go down to the cesspool.

"Adrian, it is downright frigid in here. How can you bear it?"

His private thoughts shattered, he looked up from his desk, and the journal that lay open, in time to see his sister, Elizabeth, stroll carefully into the room.

"I hadn't noticed the chill. I'll stoke the fire."

She fumbled over the turned leg of a table, her hands outstretched before her, searching for obstacles. Rosie, her liver and white springer spaniel pressed against her, her muzzle nudging Elizabeth's wrist, steering her away from danger. Tamping down the impulse to go to her and help her, he rose from his chair and turned his back, his attention on the fire.

Elizabeth was a proud woman. And damn stubborn, too. Two traits they shared, inherited from their tyrannical father. Elizabeth was blind, and because of it her pride and stubbornness had grown twofold. Lizzy would not thank him for his help.

"There!" she said, letting out a loud sigh. "We've made it, Rosie." The spaniel gave a little whimper as she struggled up onto the settee. "Poor love, you're getting as big as a barn."

Tossing a glance over his shoulder, he couldn't help but grin at the spectacle the spaniel made as her hind paws scratched and pawed for purchase against the leather. Rosie was having her first litter, and Adrian hoped to the devil her offspring would be as intelligent and trainable as she. It had been his very great desire to breed her and train her offspring to assist the blind, like Rosie assisted his sister.

Rosie finally made it onto the settee and set her head in Lizzy's lap. Lizzy's fingers brushed along the dog's long ears and a deep sound of contentment—a little growl, really—filled the room. It was followed by the sounds of Rosie burying her head into Lizzy's damask skirts, and the subtle snore of self-satisfaction.

Lizzy laughed and continued to stroke the dog's fur. "Now, then, will you cease having the maids move that table, brother? I am forever banging into it."

"My apologies, Lizzy. But it's me moving it. I like to watch the moon at night, and the table seems to follow it."

He turned in time to see his sister's exasperated expression turn to one of longing. "Oh, the moon. Is it big and fat and hanging low in the sky? I just loved a November full moon."

This was a side of Lizzy no one saw but him. In society she was put-together, so seemingly in control. She never let on that her sightlessness bothered her, but at home, when they were private, he saw her frustrations, and wiped away the tears of sadness. He, of all people, understood what it was like to live in a world full of cruelty and distaste when one was not, in polite society's estimation—desirable. Neither he nor his sister had been what their father wanted, and Adrian had been forced to live with that knowledge, to suffer the harsh realities of life. Lizzy, too, had been forced to endure her lot in life, with the same cold, demanding father. Adrian's childhood shaped him, had given him sympathy for those less fortunate, for those who were born to circumstances beyond their control. He cared for things that no other duke would concern himself with. For the lives of those left to struggle without help.

It was moments like this when he realized his role

in society gave him power, power that he didn't waste on flaunting his wealth, or using his name to gain admission to clubs, parties and liaisons with beautiful women. No, his power went to protect those who, unlike him, had never been blessed by anything but hard times. When he worked diligently with his cause to emancipate the poor in the East End from their daily suffering, he was not unworthy. Nor a fraud, nor an impostor in this world he had never understood and never wanted.

"Adrian," Lizzy said, amusement ringing in her voice. "You're brooding about something. I thought you had outgrown that particular pastime years ago."

"My apologies, Lizzy. You were saying?"

"The moon. Is it full?"

"No, it is not," he murmured as he came to sit beside her. "It is just a little crescent."

"When it's full, I expect you to invite me into your study and you can describe it to me—*vividly*," she clarified. "I swear, Adrian, you have no gift for words."

"No, I do not."

Perhaps if he did, he could seduce Lucy with them. But words had never come easily. Twelve years ago, he had learned to guard well what words he used. Being too free with his words could cost him everything he loved, his position within the Brethren Guardians, his sister and Lucy.

"Ah, that feels nice," his sister whispered as she lifted her feet up and toward the heat that was now blazing in the hearth. "I thought my toes might drop off."

"Well, your tootsies shall be warm momentarily."

"I wonder how you didn't feel the chill?"

He was inured to the cold. Growing up, he had forever been cold, and he had strengthened his mind around it. He could not tolerate any weakness in himself. Just like his father could never tolerate any weakness in his son, or daughter.

"Your lack of skill with words aside, you've been inordinately quiet of late. Do you care to share your troubles? And don't deny you have them," she commanded. "I may not see your sullen expression, but I can sense it. Your melancholy shrouds every room you've been in."

He laughed. "Damn frightening what you can sense."

Smiling, she titled her head until she found his shoulder, and let her head rest against him while she continued to pet Rosie. "Is it this Brethren business, Adrian? I thought the investigation was getting somewhere."

"It is getting somewhere—deeper and murkier. Thank God we found the chalice in Wendell Knighton's office at the museum. How the bastard discovered its hiding place, and the importance of its existence, I would dearly love to know, but it's unfortunately a secret he took to his grave."

"Well, at least it's back in your possession, and Black has the pendant. All three artifacts are safe and sound."

"But who took them is still a mystery," he muttered. "However, we have some leads. Black's wound has healed and he'll begin searching through the Masonic Lodge for more clues of this mysterious Orpheus, and Alynwick and I have taken over the investigation of the House of Orpheus. Although, being allowed admittance into the secret club is proving more difficult than either of us had anticipated. Still, Alynwick won't let it rest."

"Alynwick," Lizzy snorted. "You'll only find him of use if you can keep him out of the bedchambers."

Frowning, he realized his sister was right. Iain, the Marquis of Alynwick, was a rake, and little induced him to be anything but.

"If Alynwick would put his head into it—and not the one he's so fond of using—you might discover the identity of Orpheus much faster. Alas, the marquis is selfish and only interested in what amuses him. And it is not, I am afraid, Brethren business. Oh, if only I had been born a male, I would have kicked Alynwick in his rear end, and forced him to remember his oath."

Smiling, he thought of Elizabeth as a boy—and a Brethren Guardian. She was brave, smart and so disciplined—not to mention she was the eldest child. She would have made an excellent Guardian—better than him—and she certainly would have given the marquis some much needed grief.

"Alas, I am only a poor helpless female, concerned only with fashion and fiction. Speaking of that—Lady Lucy and Lady Black are due here any moment. They're bringing the new penny dreadfuls."

Adrian hid his groan. Lucy in his house. He could hardly bear it. But he would, for Elizabeth's sake. She had very few real friends, and he would never think to deprive her of Isabella and Lucy's companionship.

"Now, you know that I don't condone this…this snooping about, but should I question Lucy about anything?"

Elizabeth could not see the surprise on his face, but she sensed it.

"You didn't think I knew, did you? Adrian, really, she's my friend. And you're my brother. I want to help you find the man responsible for stealing the pendant and murdering Mr. Knighton. I want also to keep Lucy out of danger, if indeed she is in danger."

"She is," he growled, "believe me, she is." He thought of the murderer who had been carrying Lucy's hand-kerchief. What the devil had she been about giving a man such as that any token of her affection? A strange sense of betrayal filtered through his blood but he shook it off, determined to try to think of other things.

"Why don't you tell me what it is, so that I may aid both of you?"

He'd kept the secret well-guarded, deep in his heart. It haunted him at night, and he wanted to be purged of it, to forget he had ever discovered it. But was telling his sister the thing to do? Was it betraying Lucy?

"Adrian?" she asked. "There is no need to war with yourself over this. I just thought, well, sometimes se-crets are a burden when one must shoulder them alone."

Suddenly he was speaking, not thinking it through, only knowing he needed this, the ability to talk to an-other soul who might have some wisdom to impart to him.

"The man who shot Knighton," he began, recall-ing the scene a few weeks ago when the pendant, one of the relics the Brethren Guardians were responsible for keeping, went missing, and Isabella's—now Lady Black's—former suitor, Knighton, had been found with it. "He was involved with Orpheus. Hell, he might even *be* Orpheus."

Orpheus was a rogue Freemason. Adrian was certain. This Orpheus had an uncanny knowledge of the Brethren Guardians. Their existence was a secret. No one but the three of them and their families knew of it. No one knew that the relics they protected even existed. But Orpheus knew. And so had Wendell Knighton. The urge to find and unmask this Orpheus positively seethed and festered inside him. It should have been because of his oath—the liege he owed to the generations of his family who had successfully kept the chalice and the secret of the Brethren Guardians carefully hidden. But it was not. It was the knowledge that Lucy was intimately acquainted with the bastard that ate at him, made him want to discover Orpheus's identity, and tear at him—destroy him. For what, he had asked himself? And the answer was always there, whispering in his mind. *For taking the woman he loved, for turning her away so that she could not see him, or his need; for making her unable to accept anything he offered her.*

"You're woolgathering again, brother," Lizzy murmured. The touch of her fingers pulled him out of his reverie and escalating anger, and helplessness that had been his constant companion these past weeks.

"This man who shot Knighton, he obviously didn't want us to capture Knighton alive. Before he shot him, I spotted him on the roof of the lodge. I ran to the back of the building and gave chase, but he had quite a head start on me, and when he was out of sight, I stopped, deciding it prudent to return to Black who had been shot. And then I saw it. A lace handkerchief, with three initials."

The memory made his stomach fall to his feet, just as it had when he'd picked up the lace and saw what he held.

"Lucy Ashton's initials, I presume."

"Yes."

"I think I know the rest. She had given this man her favor—and he is the lover that she's trying to connect with on the other side, via all the séances and soothsayers she's been visiting."

Adrian could no longer deny the truth to himself. "She loves him," he said on a breath that he knew sounded pained. "She believed him dead, and when I gave her back the handkerchief, it told her that he was indeed very much alive and not killed in the fire as she had assumed. She doesn't seem to give a damn that he's a murderer, and my enemy, and also the enemy of her cousin's husband. She's obsessed with finding him," he snapped. Lunging up from the settee, he paced the room like a caged lion.

"She's determined to find him, even knowing that we search for him. She's resolved to stand in our way, and if it makes her an enemy of us, so be it."

"Then we must protect her for her own good."

"How? She won't do or say anything that might help us."

Rising, Elizabeth held out her hand, and he grasped it, steadying her. "She won't tell you, brother, but she'll confide in a friend—I am sure of it. Now, I hear a carriage…that will be them. Take yourself off, Adrian. Your expression, I'm quite certain, is rather ferocious.

It will hardly induce poor Lucy to share her confidences with me."

He stood there, stunned. "You would do that?"

"Betray Lucy's confidence?" She shrugged, and reached down to where Rosie, now off the settee, placed her head against Elizabeth. "Only so far as it might help you. Anything she says that is of no consequence to this case, or Orpheus, I will not share. I like her, Adrian. And I could not live with myself if she were to be hurt by this man."

"Thank you, Lizzy."

"There is no need to thank me, yet. I haven't gotten her to confide in me—and I won't if you're standing around."

"All right," he said, kissing her on the cheek. "I'll head out to Blake's. I'm meeting Black and Alynwick there."

"A good idea. Be back for tea and I shall share what I learn."

CHAPTER THREE

IF IT WASN'T for Elizabeth's excellent conversation and friendship, Lucy wouldn't dare step foot inside the huge town house. Despite its size, there was every possibility she might very well run into the duke—whom she was presently arduously avoiding.

"Ah, good day, ladies," Elizabeth said as she breezed into the foyer with the help of a footman, her pet spaniel at her side. "You have brought the contraband, I hope?"

Isabella held up a stack of leaflets. "The penny dreadfuls. Hot off the press. I made Black run out early this morning to get them."

"How fortunate for us that you have the ability to persuade your reclusive husband to leave his home, and at so early an hour."

"There are some inducements his lordship is unable to resist," Isabella murmured. Laughter filled the entry, and the footman struggled to hide a crooked smile.

"Well, my brother has gone to see Lord Black, so we have the house to ourselves. We may eat as many scones as we like, and drink pots of tea, without any tedious male intrusion."

Lucy let out a sigh of relief. While she had been looking forward to visiting Elizabeth, she dreaded the thought of running into the duke. To know the house was devoid of him was something more than a sense of relief. It was gratitude.

"Come. I've decided to use the yellow salon in the hopes it might make the day brighter. I've been told it's cold and dreary, and quite dull outside."

It was. And Lucy despised it. Too many days and nights she passed by herself in weather such as this. Since Issy had married Black and moved out of the house they had once shared with Lucy's father, Lucy had found herself at loose ends—and alone—again.

She had quite thought of Isabella as a sister, not a cousin, and was just getting used to having her about, when Lord Black had dashingly and passionately swept Issy off her unsuspecting feet.

It was rather uncharitable of her, but Lucy was resentful at times of Isabella leaving her. It wasn't fair, of course. Issy deserved to have a life, and a loving husband. Lucy just wished she hadn't had to leave her behind to have it.

They lived across the street from one another, and still it was not close enough for Lucy. The lonely nights, and the empty days seemed to be growing, and the sadness she had felt as a child and young woman seemed to be coming back—although darker and more ominous than before. Isabella claimed it was the effects of the occultism Lucy had begun studying, but Lucy knew it was something else entirely.

Refusing to sink further into her thoughts, Lucy shoved them aside, and followed Elizabeth and the footman down the long stately hall of Sussex House. Despite the gloom of the weather, the hall was bright and airy owing to the pale colored walls, and the enormous

domed window that filled the ceiling. At the end of the
hall was a glass conservatory that looked out onto the
back gardens. Tall green palms and brilliantly colored
hothouse flowers drew her eye, making her think of a
warm summer day, although, behind the crimson petals
were rain soaked windows and a bleak gunmetal-gray
sky.

Still, what a lovely spot it would be in the spring,
when the grass was green, and the trees newly leafed
out. Hyacinths would be particularly pretty in that
room, giving it a rich, feminine floral scent. Hyacinths
always reminded her of a warm spring day. She gave
the conservatory one last longing glance before turning
the corner. She had always wanted a conservatory, but
Papa had never been one to be pleased by gardening.
He was even less pleased by the prospect of improving
a house that was part of an entailment. Even though,
that entailment might very well one day come to her
own son, and his grandson.

"There now," Elizabeth murmured as she allowed
the spaniel to nudge her gently away from a chair that
stood directly in her path. "Is this not nice? I can almost
feel the sunshine."

Indeed it was. The sitting room was bright and
cheery; small, but warm, and with the fire that crack-
led in the marble hearth it was rather cozy. It was also
very feminine and Lucy could easily get lost in the
comfort of the room. Lemon-yellow walls with ornate
white plaster cornices and mullions gave the room a
light, but aristocratic flare. The curtains were a billow-
ing concoction of white silk, edged with the palest of
green fringe. The furniture was light and delicate, up-

holstered in shades of yellow and pink and pale green, with chintz pillows, and a thick carpet. Lucy could not help but imagine the imposing duke sitting down on the delicate rosewood settee that was patterned with big pink cabbage roses, sipping away at his tea. She could imagine what it must be like for a visitor to sit opposite him, to have those mysterious brooding eyes watching for faux pas, while he systematically stripped each layer away in his search for imperfections.

Those eyes…a woman could either be intimidated or besotted by those gray eyes. Thank heavens, Lucy was neither.

"Thank you, Maggie," Elizabeth murmured as her companion, who seemed to come out of the ethers, took her by the hand and helped her to lower onto the very settee that only seconds ago Lucy had been imagining the duke sitting upon.

"Will there be anything else, my lady?" the portly but kind companion inquired while Elizabeth settled herself and arranged her skirts. With a gentle pat on the cushion beside her, she called her dog up, and Lucy could not help but grin at the sight of the very pregnant Rosie struggling to get her hind legs up onto the settee. Once the spaniel was settled and curled up by Elizabeth, she and Isabella took the chairs opposite their host.

"Thank you, Maggie. I believe we shan't stand on ceremony and all the little rules to tea today." She smiled, and her gray eyes began to shine with mirth. "I am quite certain that my companions will see to it that I do not take it into my head to play hostess and pour."

Maggie sent Elizabeth a scowl, while Lizzy patted the companion's hand. "Truly, Maggie, I am fine. Take the afternoon with my blessing. Lady Lucy shall act as hostess today."

Surprised, Lucy straightened her spine just a fraction. She expected Isabella to have been given the honors. After all, she was married now—to an earl—and was the only married lady at the table.

"Will that do, Lady Lucy?" Elizabeth asked.

"I would be honored, of course."

"Well, if I might dispense a measure of advice, Lady Lucy, it would be to watch that one," Maggie said while pointing to Elizabeth who sat grinning. "Far too stubborn for her own good. Right then, I shall be on my way, but I won't leave the house. Call if you need me."

"She's right, you know." Elizabeth sighed as the salon door clicked quietly closed behind Maggie. Settling back onto the cushions, Elizabeth allowed her hand to rest affectionately on Rosie's pregnant side. "I am far too stubborn. But I shall not repeat my performance of yesterday. I nearly scalded poor Sussex. My brother—" Her words were whispered as she smiled fondly. "What he won't do to make his blind sister happy. Even make her believe she could play hostess and pour tea."

There was warmth and a true sense of affection in Isabella's voice when she spoke. "His grace seems so very nice. I cannot tell you how welcoming he has been to me since marrying Black."

"He wasn't always so indulgent," Lizzy said. "He was rather spoiled and selfish as a child—quite mean, as well. In truth, I didn't really like him, and he was horrid to Mama. Like me, she was afflicted with dwindling sight, and I think Sussex feared it might happen to him…he hid that fear by belittling her—a trait he learned from my father."

"How horrible, Lizzy. To see you both together, one would never know the troubles between you. The duke seems, well, quite the perfect model as a brother," Isabella observed.

"No, I agree. Sussex is an ideal brother. I don't know what caused his change—one day he was insufferable, and then he fell ill and was removed from London to an estate that Papa rarely frequented in Wales. It was above a year, I think, before I saw him again—Papa wouldn't allow me, you see. I was kept away for fear of my own health. When we next saw each other I was completely blind, but I could tell he had changed. His voice was softer, his pattern of speech slower, more defined. In all, he was quiet. Composed…given to contemplation and silence—so unlike his prior proclivities."

"I suppose he became a man in that time spent away from you," Isabella offered. "Little brothers, I should think, have a terrible tendency to grow up into men."

Lizzy smiled. "Indeed they do. And Sussex's transformation was quite welcomed. My mother, you see, had just died before he took ill, and I think it might have had a lot to do with the change in him. I know from experience when one is confined to bed, one has a great many things to think about—to ask forgiveness for." Lizzy straightened then shrugged a little. "Well, then, enough about my brother, let us have some tea."

Lucy reached for the teapot. "It's milk and sugar, isn't it?" she asked Elizabeth.

"Yes, please. And one of Cook's lemon scones, with extra lemon curd. There's no unearthly reason why we should let her delicious lemon curd go to waste. Slather it on, if you will, Lucy, and I shall instruct my maid to tighten my corset laces."

"Oh, how I loathe tight lacing," Isabella said with a shudder. "How does one take a proper breath?"

"I've never found any assistance from it," Lucy murmured as she tipped the teapot and watched the amber liquid spill into the delicate cups. "One needs something of a bosom for tight lacing to be effective."

Elizabeth tutted. "Well, when one possesses a figure like mine, tight lacing only makes you look like a sausage casing filled with too much meat!"

"Scandalous!" Isabella laughed.

"But true," Lizzy said with a smile. "I can have enough bosom showing without the aid of tight lacing, thank you very much."

Smiling, Lucy watched Lizzy and marveled at how composed and at ease she was. She was a beautiful woman, with long shining black hair and the most lovely gray eyes she had ever seen. Lizzy was blessed with pale, smooth skin that reminded her of moonstone. And her figure… Well, Elizabeth York was rounded in all the right places, and possessed a bosom that Lucy felt quite envious of. Nothing ever spilled out of her own necklines, despite the fact she had taken to making her own clothes.

Once the tea was poured, and the scones cut and swathed in lemon curd and clotted cream, they sat back with a collective sigh and kicked off their shoes, while assuming positions of comfort that no lady of gentle breeding would dare consider during an afternoon call to tea.

"I adore it when the house is devoid of men," Elizabeth said on a sigh as she bit into her scone. "One can eat as much as they desire without speculation, and sit in the most unseemly positions. Do put your feet up, ladies, if you're so inclined."

Isabella moaned as she bit into a pink iced cake that oozed custard from its flaky sides. "This is to die for, Lizzy, the little square cake with the pink icing. What do you call it?"

"I have no idea what its proper name is, but Cook likes to refer to it as 'the bit of sweet his grace adores.' It's Sussex's favorite. All almond paste and marzipan and thick custard. What I wouldn't give to see him sitting here with a delicate pink square in his hand."

Laughter erupted as Isabella agreed, while wondering aloud what her husband would look like indulging in the fancy pastries, and little thin sandwiches. Try as she might, Lucy attempted to picture the mysterious Earl of Black, but instead of his image, a set of haunting gray eyes appeared, and she blinked it away, and instead finished off her scone.

"So, what news is there to be had?" Elizabeth inquired.

"As you know, I haven't been out of the house in a fortnight," Isabella grumbled, "but I do know that Lucy has some gossip to share."

Elizabeth sat up a bit straighter, jostling Rosie in

the process, who gave a little grunt of displeasure then stretched out onto her back. "Gossip? Oh, do tell!"

"Well," Lucy hedged, "I don't know if I should be repeating this. Gossip, you know, such a nasty thing."

"Oh, hang it," Elizabeth said on a laugh. "Regale us with it, Lucy, because like Isabella, I've been cooped up here, and Maggie absolutely refuses to read the gossip rags to me—she thinks she's keeping my mind from being poisoned, but I assure you it's far too late for that."

"All right, but I warn you, it's positively indecent, and I only know about it because I happened to witness it when I came out of the ladies' retiring room. So it's not really gossip, more like an eyewitness account."

"Oh, better and better!"

"As you will recall, I was forced out of the house last night."

"Oh, that is right—you went to the Moorelands' soiree last night. How was it?"

"Dreadfully dull, but Mooreland is one of Papa's closest friends, so I was somewhat obligated to endure it. But it was made all the more delightful by what I saw."

"And that was?" Isabella purred as she finished off the last of the pink square.

"The Marquis of Alynwick caught red-handed kissing Lord Larabie's new wife. And his hands… Well, I can tell you, his hands were really quite busy—one was beneath the lady's skirt, and the other was wandering quite wildly over the bodice of Lady Larabie's pink frock."

"No!" Isabella gasped. "I cannot believe it. The

marquis…" She swept a glance between Elizabeth and Lucy. "Why, I thought him a gentleman."

The excitement that seemed to glow in Elizabeth's gaze dimmed. She tried to hide it, Lucy saw, by sitting forward and gently reaching for her teacup.

"I've never known Alynwick to be anything but an egotistical rake," Elizabeth answered. "I see his shocking way of living his life has not changed."

Elizabeth's face was pale, the pink of her lips all but drained away. Lucy had done it now. She had shocked poor Lizzy with the gossip. It was rather scandalous for a man to be caught with any woman in such a way at a ball, but a married woman—one who was not his wife. Well, it was rather unseemly and to repeat it at tea, really was very common. And Elizabeth was the daughter of a duke, after all, whose manners were quite above reproach.

"And Lord Larabie?" Isabella asked, cutting into Lucy's worries.

"Oh, he came charging down the hall and they fought. Fists flying, tailcoats waving in the tussle. Lord Pickett and Mr. Downing had a devil of a time separating them, and Lady Larabie stood there screeching like a cat that had its tail caught in a mousetrap."

"My word, I had no idea that Alynwick was such a rake!" Isabella gasped.

"Believe it," Elizabeth whispered, her voice so soft, her gaze distant, and perhaps a touch unfocused. "He is a disreputable heartbreaker."

There was pain and sadness in Elizabeth's eyes, and even though she could not see, she raised her chin high and gazed straight ahead of her, right where Isabella and Lucy sat.

"If there is anyone who knows how much of a rake the Marquis of Alynwick is, it is me."

"Tell us!" Lucy demanded as she set her teacup and saucer down onto the table. "All of it, Lizzy, every sordid detail!"

Elizabeth smiled, and Lucy could not help but feel that something strange had shifted between them. "The day is dull and dreary, so let us make the most of it by playing a game, hmm?"

"What kind of game?" Isabella inquired.

"Truth or dare, shall we? Now then, for the price of my story, I shall extract either truth or a dare from…" Elizabeth paused for a moment as her fingers raked through Rosie's soft white fur. "Yes, I think I shall require that from…Lucy."

Nothing good would come out of this game. Lucy could sense that much, and what was more, she was certain that Elizabeth knew she was hiding something. She didn't want to play, but knew that to disagree to it would cast more speculations. Besides, she dearly wanted to know how the very proper Elizabeth knew the Marquis of Alynwick was a wicked rogue.

"Very well," she agreed. "I will accept your truth or dare."

CHAPTER FOUR

SUSSEX FOUND BLAKE'S CLUB to be, thankfully, empty at this time of the afternoon. Servants buzzed about, preparing tables in anticipation for the crowd that would shortly arrive and not leave until well into the early-morning hours. Soon, he and Black would depart before they could be observed by anyone who might know who they were, or might find interest in seeing them together.

Part of being a Guardian was not to let anyone know you were one, and that meant keeping a polite distance from one another. As far as anyone in the ton suspected, Sussex, Black and Alynwick were acquaintances through their Masonic Lodge, and through the nature of their peerage. Anything closer would not be assumed, for they took great pains to never be seen socializing outside of any tonnish or Freemasonry events. They especially did not meet at any of the fashionable clubs in Mayfair. For them, it was Blake's in the remotest part of Bloomsbury. Mostly the clientele were poets and writers, and the odd actor. People whose thoughts were altruistic, not peers who were plagued by ennui and the constant stream of gossip that made the monotony of a title bearable.

"Where the hell could he be?" Sussex snarled before taking a sip of strong, bitter coffee which had grown cold in the half hour they had waited for the recalcitrant Marquis of Alynwick. The brew needed more sugar—he adored sugar. Having never been allowed it as a child he had developed something of a sweet tooth in adulthood. Dumping more spoonfuls into the mug, he stirred it, took a sip and slammed the cup down onto the table once more.

"Where is he?" he growled irritably.

The pressed news sheet across the table from him rolled down, and Black's blue-green eyes peered out at him from beneath heavy brows. "He's always tardy. Why are you surprised?"

"Because one would think that the matters we need to discuss would be a bit more important than his damned beauty sleep!"

Black had the nerve to grin before folding the paper and slapping it down onto his thigh.

"Damn him! Does Alynwick treat everything in his life with such indifference?"

"He informed me yesterday afternoon that he had planned to do a bit of reconnaissance work last night. Perhaps it was a late evening."

Sussex snorted in indignation. "There can be nothing worth exploring at a ball that will aid us in our case to find Orpheus."

"Oh, I would most certainly disagree with that."

Sussex glanced up in time to watch the debauched and unshaven Marquis of Alynwick flop inelegantly into a leather club chair. "Coffee," he groaned as the waiter approached the table. "God, yes. Nectar of the gods, isn't it?" he said as the waiter poured his cup full of the black brew.

"Cream or sugar?"

"Just black, if you please."

With a nod, the servant was on his way, leaving them alone.

"Devil of a headache, I take it, then?" Black asked as he raised his own cup to his lips.

"Devil? And a few more metaphors that aren't fit for priggish ears." He gave Sussex a meaningful glance. Apparently he was the prig. The thought bristled, especially when he thought of Lucy and her accusations that he was a cold, boring aristocrat with no fire in his soul. What did the bloody pair of them know, anyway? His breast was on fire for want of her, and his soul…it was filled with an unholy lust that would never be satiated. Lucy Ashton would never discover for herself the amount of passion he kept hidden beneath his proper facade.

"You're late." His coffee cup hit the table with more force than he intended, but damn it, he was in something of a mood today, and could not shake it. One would think that after being shut out of Lucy's life for the past two weeks, one would be somewhat more civil. Yet as each day passed he was becoming increasingly more intolerable—and short-tempered.

Alynwick, he surmised, must be used to his outbursts, because he merely raised his dark eyebrow and made a grand show of leisurely sipping away at his coffee. "You have pent-up lust, Sussex. Get yourself a woman. You'll be right as rain after it, I swear it."

As usual, Alynwick's answer to everything was sex.

"I have no need of your solicitation, Alynwick."

"No?" the marquis said with a grin. "Come now,

Sussex, you're a healthy male, living like a monk. It can't be healthy."

He didn't need any reminders that he hadn't bedded in a woman in...good God, months! Almost a year, he reminded himself. When Lucy Ashton and her flamered hair had flitted past him, robbing him of breath, speech and rational thought. She'd been a compulsion to him ever since, and every woman he'd seen or met since paled against her.

"Well?" he asked irritably, when he could no longer stomach the marquis's antics, or his pitiful one-sided longing for Lucy. "What did you find out on this supposed reconnaissance mission of yours?"

Alynwick shrugged and crossed his leg over his knee, while his fingers fiddled with a loose thread on his sleeve. "That the new Lady Larabie has the mouth of a pinched fish, and her bosom, which has been much touted, is nothing but the sham of a rather imaginative, yet very hardworking corset."

Groaning in frustration, Sussex sent a pleading glance to Black in hopes the earl could knock some sense into Alynwick. Everything was such a damned jest with him. He cared for nothing but frivolities and women, and to hell with anything else.

"Really?" Black drawled. "A feigned bosom? Poor Larabie. To be drawn in and duped by an artfully arranged décolletage."

"Hang Larabie, and bosoms," Sussex snarled. Alynwick, with that devil's twinkle in his eye, slunk deeper into his chair and stared at him.

"Bosoms, Sussex, are the sustenance of the world.

How can you not be a devoted follower? I myself find I can be led quite merrily about by a fine pair of—"

"Alynwick…" he warned.

"Is this strange aversion of yours to the discussion of breasts in particular, or is it because the ravishing Lady Lucy has but a rather modest bosom?"

"You ass!" he hissed, and jumped up from his chair with his hand fisted, and his arm pulled back, ready to plant a facer on the marquis. Laughing, Alynwick held up his hands pleading with mock horror.

"My God, you're like a baited bear. Sit, you oaf, before you spill my coffee. I swear you've lost your sense of humor. This girl has all but sucked it out of you—well, not sucked per se—"

"Watch your tongue," Sussex growled in a deep voice, "or I'll pull it out of your mouth for you."

"My, such a strong reaction. I see you're still moon-faced over the girl. Disgusting what love does to a perfectly healthy and virile man. And what are you smiling about over there?" Alynwick asked, making Black's grin vanish. "You're no better, the way you've been barricaded in your town house with your new wife."

"Mmm, yes, and if you dare say anything about my wife's bosom, I will flatten you right here. Understood?"

"Good Lord, I'm surrounded by prigs."

"You'll be surrounded by a pool of blood—your own—if you don't get on with it, Alynwick," Sussex growled. He was in no mood for this type of banter before, and he certainly wasn't now. How dare Alynwick have sized up Lucy, and found her lacking? Damn the man, she had a perfectly lovely bosom, and he should know, he'd spent months staring at it, and wondering how perfect her breasts were beneath her tight-fitting bodices, and if her nipples were coral or pale pink, and how they might tighten with the graze of his thumb, the tip of his tongue…

God, he was unraveling. The sooner he could quit the conversation, the better. Alynwick had always been a terrible influence on him.

"Once more, Alynwick. What was it you discovered?"

With a sigh, the marquis shoved away his irreverence, and fortified himself with another large gulp of hot coffee. Wincing at the bitterness, he set it down. "False bosom aside, Lady Larabie has a surprisingly naughty nature. Between heated kisses in the hall, she invited me to join her at a special Wednesday nightclub. Any guesses what it might be?"

Black pressed forward. "The hell she did!"

Alynwick grinned. "I keep telling you, Black, it's the sweet, innocent-looking ones that are really hellcats in the bedroom. Yes. It's true. The new Lady Larabie slips out on Wednesday evenings when her husband is gambling with his cronies. She's been going to the House of Orpheus for weeks, and she's offered to drag me along."

"In exchange for what?" Sussex demanded.

Alynwick looked at him as though he were sporting two heads. "Dear me, your grace, has it really been that long?"

Sussex felt his face flame. "You do not need to sell your soul for this, Alynwick—we can get information about Orpheus in other ways."

"Kind of you to think of my soul, Sussex, but I assure you, I sold the thing years ago. It was of no use to me. I gave it to the devil in a two-for-one bargain, my soul and conscience for a tidy little abode in his realm when I expire."

To hear him say such things in such a cavalier tone chilled him to the core. Was there nothing Alynwick held sacred?

"So, you will carry on an affair with Lady Larabie in order to gain entrance into this mysterious House of Orpheus?"

"A little more than just an entrée, my friends. I intend to be introduced to this shadowy Orpheus, thanks to the lady's generosity."

Black sat back and studied the marquis. "And if Larabie takes it into his head to pursue his wife's activities?"

Alynwick shrugged. "He won't. We're going to settle it tonight in a duel. I'll need a second, of course, and then it will be all over and done, and his lordship can have his peace of mind that he has fought for his lady's virtue. His honor will be placated, and he'll be too arrogant to believe that the lady would continue to carry on with me behind his back. And then, every Wednesday night thereafter we will meet and I will try my damnedest to find out what I can about Orpheus, and how the devil he discovered anything about the Brethren Guardians."

"You're insane. A duel with Larabie? You'll get yourself shot—and most likely killed," he snapped. "Especially since you cannot seem to pass away a night without getting roaring drunk."

"I do not need a cataloguing of my sins, Sussex. Believe me, I'm well aware of them all. Trust me. I know what I'm doing, and this plan will work. Lady Larabie is entirely indiscreet. I'll have her spilling what she knows about the club and about Orpheus himself within a week. There is nothing else to be done. Wendell Knighton did not act alone in his attempt to steal the artifacts—there was someone else pulling the strings, feeding him information. We cannot just let it rest now the relics are safe and Knighton is dead."

"You're right, of course. We need to follow the leads we have, and every single one of them return to this Orpheus fellow."

"I trust neither one of you have a better plan to find him?"

"No," Sussex grumbled.

Alynwick was many things, a dissolute roué, an amoral, unfeeling clod, but he was on their side, and he always, *always* kept his word. His oath to the Brethren Guardians would never be broken, Sussex knew that much. He also could not fathom a guess of what price this mad scheme was going to cost Alynwick.

"This is most dangerous," Black murmured, "but the fact is, we really have no other recourse. Orpheus has withdrawn into the ethers of London since Knighton's murder, and we can't afford to have any more lost time. We need to find him. What really matters is, this Orpheus knows about us, and we can't have that—we *must* ascertain how he discovered our existence, and those of the artifacts."

True. Sussex hated to admit it, but at this moment Orpheus had the upper hand. There was no telling what he might do with the knowledge he had gained of their order, or when he might decide to strike again and attempt to steal the relics—or worse, expose them and what they hid to the world. Orpheus needed to be stopped, and they had no other way, or information.

"All right. It's settled then. Tonight, you and Black will go to the Masonic meeting, I'll get ripping drunk and meet you at Grantham Farm, where one of you will be my second. I'll say that I ran into one of you, and that my usual set was too drunk to be of any assistance. It shouldn't raise too many questions, especially with one of you doing the honors. Everyone knows you won't gossip about it. Should be all right, I'd think."

Black shook his head. "I don't like this. Anything could happen, especially with Larabie. The man is a fool, and with a woman's involvement, he's likely to be even more foolhardy than usual."

"We're all fools in love, aren't we?" Alynwick drawled, and Sussex glared at his friend as the marquis's amused grin focused on him.

Yes, he was a fool in love. He'd already tried to wrangle his way out of it, but Lucy Ashton had an unholy grip on his heart. She would not let go, and he didn't think he could let her, even knowing that she loved another. That was the damnable thing. If it were only lust he felt for her, this entire debacle would be behind him. But it wasn't simply a case of desire, but love. Or at the very least the stirrings of a true and abiding love. How he wished he could get her alone and discover her, the true woman she was. Not the society miss she pretended to be, but the woman she hid from the world. But there was little chance for that now. She'd made it perfectly clear that she loathed the very sight of him.

"Well, then, I think I'll be off. I need a new waistcoat. Something dashing and debonair, something befitting the field of honor."

"Wait, I have news. We have a new ally."

"Do we?" Alynwick drawled. "How did this come about?"

"Elizabeth."

Alynwick frowned. "I don't see how your sister can be of any use to us."

"She is going to discover what Lucy knows about Orpheus and the club."

"And how would Lady Lucy know anything about such matters?" Alynwick asked through narrowed eyes. "Damn it, Sussex, you're a liability around that girl."

"It's a private matter, Alynwick. All you need know is that Lucy Ashton does indeed have some involvement that goes beyond her knowledge of the pendant. The particulars of which are of no concern to you."

"Bah," he grunted with a wave of his hand. "Elizabeth would never betray a friend. Whatever Lucy Ashton tells her will remain with Elizabeth until her dying day. I would not wait about with bated breath to discover what Elizabeth learns from Lucy."

"Lizzy is concerned enough about Lucy to share what she discovers. Even now they are at Sussex House discussing matters. I have no doubt that Elizabeth will be able to discover what we need to know."

"No doubt. Your sister has the unnatural ability to discover one's most carefully hidden secret, doesn't she? I wonder how she'll accomplish it, making Lucy part with her secrets?"

"The way females always do," he answered. "By telling her one of her own secrets."

The loss of color in Alynwick's face was comical, and puzzling. So was the way he jumped up from the chair and left as though the devil were on his heels.

"Secrets," Black murmured as he reached for his hat. "Damnable things aren't they?"

Black didn't know the half of it, Sussex thought, or the secrets he harbored. God help him if the world was to learn his. It would ruin everything.

IN THE SHADOWS, Orpheus waited—and plotted his revenge—a retribution that would be beautiful and painful. Much like that of a spider's web—an intricate, glittering thing of exquisite beauty, but treacherous, offering a slow, suffocating death to those caught in its silken tendrils.

His web was no less complex, or less beautiful, but it was infinitely more dangerous. And the Brethren Guardians…well, they were wrapping themselves into the delicate silken weaves, just as he had planned. Soon, they would be cocooned, and their little group and the ancient artifacts they hid from the world would be his.

There was no stopping him, not even death could, for he had seen death and had battled his way back from its grip. There was nothing left now but to succeed, to lure and entice and destroy the three men who had destroyed him and everything he might have been.

But a spider is a clever thing, and constructs his web in a most abstruse manner. And while he was busily lying in wait for his prey to draw to his web, he needed something else—a bait of sorts—to lay upon the silk to lure the Guardian he wanted most.

He watched this victim from the dark corners of his club—his house—the House of Orpheus. She was the adhesive his web needed to draw and hold his enemies. She was the one he could so easily entice into his silken world of mystery, beauty and forbidden passion. She was the next step in his plan.

He signaled his accomplice across the room, who moved through the crowd with predatory grace, compelled by the same soul-destroying need for vengeance that ruled him.

"It is time to be resurrected," Orpheus murmured, and his minion's breath stilled for a fraction of a second, then resumed with heat and excitement. Yes, this man had waited so long—so many months for this very moment. Now that it had arrived, Orpheus could sense the taut strength, the scent of bloodlust that suddenly rushed free from within the cold confines of his subordinate's soul, which was consigned to hell—just as his was. "Do what you must, but bring her to me."

"As you wish, Orpheus. It shall be done. But what of the pendant and the chalice?"

Anger seethed through him, and his body vibrated with the barely controlled shaking of that rage. Damn Wendell Knighton! The man had proved to be useless, and selfish. He had made a grave error by bringing Knighton into his fold. Weeks ago he had possessed one of the sacred three relics of the Brethren Guardian—the pendant—only to miscalculate the extent of Knighton's own greed and thirst for power. Now it was gone, and so, too, the chalice—which Knighton, curse his rotting soul, had managed to find and steal. No doubt by now, Sussex and the other two Guardians had both relics back in their possession. Leaving him with none.

But he had the upper hand. He had something the Guardians wanted—or at least one of them did.

"My lord?"

Gnashing his teeth, he growled, "The girl, bring her to me, and I assure you, the rest will follow."

Through darkness and shadows, Orpheus heard the retreat of his minion. The loss of both pendant and chalice was a momentary setback, one easily overcome. Soon, he consoled himself, soon he would have the woman in his web, and all too soon, the proud Duke of Sussex would follow the lovely bait, and thereby meet his greatest weakness—and his ultimate demise. And in the end he, Orpheus, would take his rightful place in the world. No longer would he be a footnote in time, but the leader he was born to be. And the world would bow at his feet.

CHAPTER FIVE

ANTICIPATION AND NERVOUSNESS coursed through Lucy as she watched Elizabeth elegantly sip her tea. What would Lizzy ask her in return for the secret she was about to shed? Perhaps she should take a dare instead? After all, there were some secrets she wanted to fiercely guard—like the one about Thomas.

Silly game, she thought. She should not have allowed herself to be drawn in so easily. It was a game for children, not grown women who needed to keep their secrets protected and buried.

Except the lure Elizabeth had dangled so temptingly before them had made her weak. Not that she desired to know anything more about the Marquis of Alynwick, but because she dearly wanted to know Elizabeth better. On the outside, the duke's sister was a vision of loveliness. Despite her blindness, Elizabeth carried herself with pride and confidence, and a cool, sophisticated elegance that Lucy would never be able to achieve. Lizzy was refined, demure and proper. Lucy couldn't imagine her stepping one toe out of place. But upon occasion, Lucy saw something more complex in Elizabeth's gray eyes. A shadow of sadness, a flicker of deep pain. She had seen the same in her brother's eyes. What did they share? What trauma from the past did they try to hide from the world?

Elizabeth cleared her throat, and Lucy saw how her pale fingers trembled slightly as they raked through Rosie's silky fur. Whatever she was about to share with them, it was meaningful and, Lucy sensed, painful. In truth, there was nothing like the shedding of secrets to bring females together.

"Twelve years ago— No," Lizzy said with a small smile that conveyed only sadness, "I must go farther back than that. Almost from the moment I became aware of the male species, I have fancied myself in love with Alynwick."

Lucy found herself biting her lip as she watched Elizabeth gather her self-control. What she wouldn't give to take back her words. She had hurt Lizzy with the gossip of Alynwick and Lady Larabie.

"Twelve years ago, I gathered the courage to tell him. He confessed that he reciprocated that love, and we…" She swallowed hard, and her grays eyes began to well with tears, tears she held back with a ruthless determination. "We began an affair. It was the summer my father took my brother to the continent for his grand tour after convalescing, and I was left home alone with only the servants to keep an eye on me. Alynwick's ancestral estate abutted ours, and we spent the entire summer together. I was already losing my sight by then, but he claimed he didn't care. He persuaded me that it didn't matter, and I believed him. I…" She lowered her head, her eyes closed. "I gave him my virginity, and the next day—Sunday—his wedding banns were read at church."

Lucy and Isabella both gasped, and a small sound like a strangled sob was wrenched from Lizzy. "It appeared that his marriage had been arranged for years—yet I had never heard of it. Of course, I behaved like a simpering chit, I was barely eighteen and he was only nineteen. Oh, when I think of how I clung to him, crying and sobbing. But to no avail. While I pleaded and begged him, and spoke of my love, he was… remote. He claimed he thought me amusing, and in truth, my impending blindness disturbed him. It took some time for me to reconcile it all, but I finally came to the conclusion that I had been a fool. I was nothing to him but a diverting interlude to while away the summer days."

"Black and I shall cut him dead!" Isabella announced with outrage.

"You cannot, what would you say? What grounds would you give? No one but us knows what happened, and until today, I've never told a soul what transpired that summer."

"Lizzy," Lucy murmured as she reached out to grasp her friend's hand. "I had no idea. Had I, I would never have told you about what I saw last night."

"If it had not been you, Lucy, I would have heard it from another source. The marquis does attract gossip, and there are no ends to the females who are willing to create it with him."

"How you must have suffered," Issy murmured as she reached forward and rested her palm on Lizzy's arm.

"Endless nights of wailing into my pillow," Lizzy said with a deprecating smile, "only to be followed by hours of humiliation whenever I thought on my actions after. I vowed then never to make a spectacle of myself ever again. And especially over a man."

"If only we had known each other then, Lucy and I would have boxed his ears!"

Elizabeth's laugh was soft and genuine. "Time heals all wounds. However, I do upon occasion allow myself to reflect upon that summer, and remember those days when he had been everything to me."

"He's not worth it," Isabella sniffed. "To be so careless with you, Lizzy, he doesn't deserve you, or your love."

"Oh, I haven't loved him in years. But tell me," she asked quietly, "what does he look like? I haven't dared ask another soul that, for fear of how it might be taken. But I would be a fool if I did not admit that there are some nights, when I lie awake in bed, and wonder about him. Is his hair still dark?"

Lucy felt her own eyes well with tears, and she glanced to her right, to discover that Isabella was discreetly blotting the corner of her eyes with her napkin.

"Yes," she answered Lizzy. "His hair is dark, like coal—"

"And when the light hits it, does it have the blue of a raven's wing?"

"Yes, I think it must, for it is black as jet, and given to curl. He wears it unfashionably long, to his shoulders, and when he talks with Black and your brother, he occasionally brushes it behind his ears."

Elizabeth's eyes closed, as if she were savoring the images of the marquis. "And his eyes? Are they still dark blue? I always thought the color reminded me of the sky at twilight."

"I…I don't know, Lizzy. I thought his eyes dark. There is a hardness to them, and when he looks directly at you, well…one cannot help but to think that he is looking directly past you. There's coldness there, nothing soft or comforting."

"Eyes consumed by sin," her friend whispered. "How sad, for the man I thought I knew that summer was not hard or cold, just…lost and hurting. But then, I didn't really know him, did I?"

"Sometimes, our hearts won't allow our eyes to see what is really there, Lizzy."

Where those words had sprung from, Lucy had no idea. She only knew how right they felt. For it was true, the eye was blind when love and desire was involved. Or was it only blinded by lust? Did the eye truly see love, or was it just for the heart to feel it? Thomas had claimed to love her, had made the same sort of promises to her that Alynwick had made to Lizzy. Only Lucy was certain that but for the fire, Thomas would not have left her the way the marquis had left her friend.

The bit of lace in her pocket reminded her that Thomas was indeed alive. There could be no other explanation for the reappearance of the handkerchief, and for the identical description of Thomas that the duke had given her of the man who had dropped it.

He was alive, and because of those very promises he had given to her, Lucy knew without a doubt he would find a way to come for her.

Squeezing Lucy's hand, Lizzy replied, "Yes, one can be blind, can't they, even when they possess the gift of sight. I was young and naive and I learned a difficult lesson."

"What happened to the woman he was supposed to marry?" Isabella asked. "I hope she made him utterly miserable. He deserved no less after what he did to you."

Lizzy shrugged. "I do not know the particulars. Only that the marriage did not come into being, and after their broken engagement, he went to the East with Black. Upon his return home, he was changed, much as he is now, irreverent and uncaring, consumed with pleasure and gain. There is nothing left of the man I had given myself to."

"He didn't deserve you," Lucy said, truly meaning it. "One day, you will meet with the perfect gentleman."

"I have given up on that. Besides, I believe that once given, the heart does not easily love again. Especially when it's been betrayed."

For some reason, Lizzy's words struck fear inside her. Gray eyes flashed before her, and she startled, not understanding where the image had sprung from. Only knowing she had no wish to see them, or to be drawn in by the ghosts that looked out at her. She thought of her young friend and her father's cruel treatment of him. She had been betrayed then, and she was quite certain that although she had been very young, her friend had quite captured her idealistic heart. It had not been easy to allow someone in, after that. She had mourned his loss for quite a while, and still did.

"Oh, love, what a burden it can be. How can something so heady and perfect cause such deep-rooted despair?" Isabella asked.

How indeed? She had only ever known that love led to despair. The two were synonymous to her. "I suppose," she answered, "it is because there is such a fine line between passion and despair."

Elizabeth looked up, and in that brief second, Lucy could have sworn her friend glimpsed inside her soul. "You have felt despair while in love?"

Glancing quickly at Isabella, Lucy struggled for an answer. Isabella knew her secret—most of it at any rate. She would know if she lied to Lizzy.

As if sensing her inner turmoil, Elizabeth inched forward and reached out her hand, which Lucy took in hers. "Tell me, Lucy, have you ever given up everything you are, everything you believed in, for one moment of passion?"

Truth or dare…at last, the dreaded moment had arrived.

SAVED BY HIS GRACE!

Never in her life had Lucy been more delighted to see the large-bodied presence of Sussex lurking in the doorway. With typical cool indifference and ducal autocracy he strolled into the salon, his high glossed boots ringing against the marble floor. His gaze swept over her as he prowled closer to them, and Lucy fought the urge to give in to a tremble. The last time she had seen him he had been handing her the lace handkerchief, and warning her away from her lover. She had refused to listen, and now…now she suspected they were enemies.

There was no denying that his grace would make a formidable one. What he lacked in passion, he more made up for with a determined tenacity, some-Lucy knew he would use to discover Thomas. She could almost find herself admiring that trait in him, if it wasn't for the fact that he was now her—and Thomas's—enemy.

With an elegant arch of his dark brow he stood before them. "Am I interrupting something?"

"Of course you are, brother. Off with you!" Elizabeth drawled as she shooed him away with a wave of her hand. "You have the most inopportune timing."

"Don't be silly, your grace, do come in," Lucy said a little breathlessly as she avoided Isabella's astonished gaze. "The tea is still hot, and there are plenty of sandwiches left."

She saw the way Elizabeth frowned and the speculation in Isabella's eyes. Even though the duke really was the last person she wanted to see, at the present he was the lesser of two evils, the greater evil being the question Elizabeth had asked her.

Truth or dare…well, she dared not give the truth, and if suffering through tea with Sussex was to be the reprieve from having to answer, then so be it.

Taking the vacant cushion between Elizabeth and Rosie, the duke slouched deeply onto the soft settee and reached for a plate. With a glance, he peered up at them from a veil of thick lashes. "You don't mind, do you?"

Swallowing hard, Lucy bit her lower lip and thought back to that evening when she had visited the Fraser Witch and the feelings she had experienced. They were the same ones she felt now—in the duke's presence. And it was damned inconvenient, she thought churlishly, especially since she sought to dislike everything about his grace.

She couldn't understand it, this new reaction in her body whenever Sussex's cool gray eyes locked with hers. Every nerve ending seemed overly sensitized and raw; her spine tingled with warning and a sense of foreboding she had never once experienced in the presence of another man. Sussex had a way of looking at her that made her think he was peeling back her carefully placed layers and peeking into the core of her. It was disconcerting, his way, and no less now, when his gaze briefly flickered along her face. For Lucy knew that despite that deft sweep of his eyes, the duke missed nothing.

For all his propriety, his grace never let on that they had drawn their respective lines in the sand. Lucy found herself wondering if the duke ever thought of that afternoon, and what he had discovered of her past. No doubt it riled his sense of propriety and surely he now found her lacking and utterly unsuitable in the role of his duchess.

There was relief in that thought. Now if only her father would accept the fact that his grace would no longer be calling upon them.

"For heaven's sake, Sussex. Take your sweets and go along with you," Elizabeth muttered, which made Sussex grin. And that grin…what it did to his normally somber face. Lucy found herself blinking in surprise, and…no, not wonder. She would never admire his grace in that fashion. Yes, he was tall, dark and very handsome. But there wasn't anything about the duke that tempted her. He was rigid and controlled, stuffy and proper. Aloof and cool, which only made her realize how very much like her father he was. And that sort of man was the furthest kind she desired. She craved warmth, and emotional intimacy. Never would she marry the sort of a man her father was. Her mother may have chosen her cold, polite matrimonial bed, but Lucy would not endure the same in her marriage.

From across the tea table, the duke studied her, and Lucy suffered beneath that heavy, watchful stare. How he looked at her…there was something vaguely familiar about that stare, but of course she was being fanciful. His were not the eyes she had seen in her vision when she visited the Scottish Witch. She was sure of it.

"Are you quite finished pillaging our tea tray, Adrian?" Lizzy demanded. "We have a pressing matter of business yet to discuss."

"Dear me, Lizzy, your mood has turned sour since I left. What has transpired to make you so irritable?"

"How can you be so obtuse, brother? Your arrival has put a damper on our conversation."

His dark brows rose in question, causing a scar that bisected the left one to be more noticeable. "What then were you discussing when I arrived that I might not listen to now?"

"Nothing that need concern you," Elizabeth muttered.

"Ah, gossip, then," he said then focused his attention on Lucy. "Do you enjoy it?"

"Enjoy what, your grace?"

He didn't blink, but kept his cool, steady gaze upon her. His mouth was set in a grim, disapproving line. "Gossip, Lady Lucy. Do you enjoy indulging in such pastimes as spreading tales about others?"

The censure with which he had asked his question

did not dissuade her from answering. "You would be hard-pressed to find a tea table devoid of gossip."

"But it is not others I am inquiring about. I am asking about you. Do *you*, Lady Lucy, enjoy gossip?"

She met his gaze head-on, refusing to be intimidated by his blatant reproof. Obviously he held himself above the lesser mortals who found tittle-tattle a tempting sin. Such a virtue he was! Lucy could not admit that she was of a like mind. She had found gossip much too helpful to disregard it altogether.

"Well?" he asked again.

"I, like so many people, find it vastly amusing, your grace."

Cocking his head, he studied her through narrowed eyes as though she were a new species of beetle stuck to a felt board by a stickpin. "I don't think you do. You merely partake of it because it is an expected requirement at such gatherings, as well of your station. Your heart, I think, is never fully in it."

She flushed, but forced herself to stay steady and still. "I wonder why you asked then, in the first place?"

"I am merely trying to make out your personality, Lady Lucy. There are so many sides to it, one wonders who you truly are. Or indeed, if *you* know who you are."

"Your grace, you are too bold."

"Insufferable, isn't he?" Elizabeth said as she glared to where Sussex sat next to her on the settee. "Very bad manners, Sussex."

"Apologies. It is just that I cannot imagine that you take joy in laughing at another's expense. To be amused by someone else's misfortune or folly? You are too soft-hearted for that."

She sniffed, despising him for making her feel things she did not care to admit to, for seeing that beneath her aloof facade to the soft core she had tried to harden through the years. She didn't want him to know she was soft and kind and so easily hurt. She would rather he think her a lofty, snobbish woman who had fallen low for the sins of the flesh. Far better to be considered a cold woman than a weak one. One could not be timid and easily damaged when one moved about the ton. It was as deadly as a three-legged gazelle amidst a pride of lions. With such an obvious weakness, they would run her to ground and devour her whole. Far better to possess the hide and horn of the rhino.

The facade of the uncaring society lady was her favorite and most often employed shield, and to have his grace take it from her, really was rather harrowing. Having him peek deep inside her was downright frightening. She had not shared herself with another since she was twelve—not even Thomas had been given a look into her soul.

"I am right, aren't I?" he asked, his voice dropping to a husky purr. He spoke as though they were alone, as if his sister and Isabella were not present. He was far too familiar, and she didn't like it. How he seemed able to command the room, the conversation, and even more frightening, her emotions.

Gathering her courage, and stiffening her spine, Lucy prepared to meet his challenge. "I suppose you think you're always correct in your assumptions and estimations, your grace. But in this matter, I must strike a blow to your vanity, for you are indeed wrong."

His smile temporarily disarmed her. "No, I don't believe I am. You talk of gossip because it is expected. Not because you enjoy it, and the pain it causes others."

She was right. The duke did see far too much—she could not run from the truth now. "Well, it is vastly more entertaining, and I suppose ego sparing to talk of another than our own follies, wouldn't you agree, your grace? It at least allows one a moment of reprieve from the prying eyes of others," she snapped, while shooting him a meaningful glare.

"You use gossip as a shield, then?"

Lucy was conscious of the way Isabella's head seemed to volley back and forth between their increasingly heated banter. If she were thinking clearly, Lucy would back down, but there was something about Sussex that riled her. She would never bow to him, never let him needle her. Therefore, she would continue this strange, far too familiar conversation. "Who does not use gossip as a weapon, or defense, your grace?"

"And what secrets have you to hide that you would not wish others to pry into?"

"Adrian, you beast!" Elizabeth scolded. "I vow you are merely toying with my guests, much like a cat with a mouse. Pay him no heed, Lucy. He enjoys these little debates, you see, and has quite forgotten that he is in polite company, and not the men of his club."

Sussex blatantly ignored Elizabeth, and kept his gaze trained on her. "Or do you use it to keep others at bay, Lady Lucy? From straying too close to what you do not wish them to discover, which would be you, and who you truly are?"

How had he guessed? she wondered. Everyone who looked at her believed her to be a spoiled, shallow society miss who cared for nothing but fashion and parties. Certainly no one had ever thought she might have a heart and conscience. Yet with one sweep of his storm-gray eyes, Sussex had seen to the core of her, and what she kept hidden.

"Sussex, stop this at once," Elizabeth demanded. "You cannot come in here and start such a bold discussion without first at least inquiring as to our company's health and spirits."

"Absolutely. It was unpardonable of me. Forgive me. Now then, how are you ladies today?" he inquired politely as he placed four of the pink custard squares on his plate, but not before his gaze flickered to hers and he grinned. Such a cheeky grin, she thought as the hair on her arms stood straight on end.

CHAPTER SIX

"OH, WE ARE very well, your grace," Isabella replied as she stole a perplexed glance at Lucy. "Now, if only the weather would cooperate and allow the sun to shine, if only for a few hours, we would be much better off."

Sussex glanced over his shoulder and out the tall window that was behind the settee. "Mmm, yes, it is gloomy. Makes one long for the comforts of bed."

Isabella flushed delicately, and Lucy struggled to swallow the mouthful of hot tea she had just taken. The word *bed* was one she would have preferred not to hear coming from Sussex's mouth. It was far too familiar, and she could not put aside her fears that when he said it, he was recalling the moment between them when he had returned the bit of lace to her, and discovered her most carefully guarded secret.

How she wanted to quit this house, to leave Sussex and his strange conversation behind. She was on tenterhooks, she realized. Disconcerted by every glance, and word. She could not endure this, not while trying to stay polite and removed.

Studying Lizzy, Lucy looked for any signs from their host that the tea was over, and they should take their leave. Unfortunately Lizzy had only managed to appear more comfortable on the settee, as if she were settling in for a much longer conversation. Even Isabella, who had looked extremely uncomfortable during their discussion of gossip now looked at ease, and was even in the process of pouring herself more tea.

Traitor, Lucy wanted to shout at her friend. Did no one understand how horrid it was to sit across from his grace and suffer through his stare? Of course they did not. Because neither Lizzy nor Isabella knew what had transpired between them. Only Sussex knew, and Lucy could not help but imagine what thoughts were running rampant in the proper duke's mind. "Oh, yes, I adore afternoon naps," Elizabeth said on a sigh, "especially in the rain. Just lying there, listening to the raindrops rattle against the windowpane is so soothing. Don't you think, Lady Lucy?"

Determined to ignore Sussex, she focused her attention on answering Elizabeth. "I am afraid I am not a fan of rain, but I am rather fond of the feel of cool grass beneath my feet on a warm spring day. I like to hear the chirping of birds, and see the swelling of flower buds. I like the wind not to be cool and bracing, but warm and scented with the aromas of the sun and earth."

Sussex met her gaze, allowed it to linger, then slowly he slid it away, down to his plate where he picked up a custard slice, and popped it into his mouth.

"Oh, I enjoy that too," Elizabeth said wistfully. "When I was younger I could lie in the grass for hours and stare at the sky and imagine the clouds were all kinds of fanciful shapes, and animals."

Lucy knew her expression was not one of rapture at Elizabeth's description, and the duke noticed and said, "Do you not approve of the pastime, Lady Lucy?"

She was forced to raise her gaze from the teacup and

saucer that was balanced on her lap and look at him.
That stare…it made her tremble once again, and she despised how easily he could disconcert her. No one had
ever had that ability, she'd made certain of it, but when
the duke came into her life, he had torn down those safe
walls she had erected.

Now here she was, feeling vulnerable and cornered,
held hostage by eyes that bored deeply into hers as he
patiently awaited her answers. And he would wait. She
had learned that about Sussex, he was the most patient
man on Earth—maddenly so—and she knew he would
sit there all afternoon, his plate of pink sweets balanced
in his palm while he watched her with his eyes that
saw too much. Nothing dissuaded him when he wanted
something; she had learned that much about him.

"Stonebrook wouldn't have allowed it," he replied
for her, his gaze unwavering. "Your father is a difficult
man to please, not given to gaiety or lenience."

Yer papa will tan my hide if he finds ye getting yer
'ands dirty wit the likes o' me. I'm yer lesser, or so Mr.
Beecher says. No lady of Gov'ner Square will look at
a little street urchin the likes o' me.

Lucy recalled that day in the kitchen, as she and
Gabriel sat at the table and talked. She had made it
her business to be in the kitchen on Tuesdays when
the butcher made his deliveries. It had been curiosity
at first—the quiet, sullen boy who had accompanied
Mr. Beecher had captured her interest. But after a few
visits, and some shared stories, it became something
more than curiosity, but infatuation. They had become
friends, borne out of common circumstances, their dif-

ferences ignored as they shared whatever treat Cook had left at the table for them.

"I don't care about such trivial things such as stations in life," she had boldly stated. *"Are we not all created equal?"*

"No, Miss Lucy, we ain't. Ye were made better 'n me. And that's why I'm to leave ye be and not look at ye. I'm beneath ye."

She had glared in the direction of the butcher, then. *"Never mind him,"* she'd ordered. *"We're friends, are we not?"*

"I ain't never 'ad a friend."

"I ain't never, either."

They had dissolved into a fit of laughter, which had died as suddenly as it sprung up when a dark shadow emerged in the kitchen...

"He would have had you kept inside the schoolroom," his grace continued on, pulling her from her memories, making her confront a reality she had no wish to contemplate. "A young lady meant to remain pale and unmarred, her mind filled with useful information, her days occupied with learning tasks that would set up her future. He would have frowned upon frivolous pursuits such as daydreaming and cloud watching."

She swallowed, and he followed the action of her throat, his long, dark lashes shielding the expression in his eyes and the thoughts behind them. How Lucy wanted to rail at him for it.

"Is my brother right?" Elizabeth asked sympathetically. "He paints a rather bleak picture of your childhood."

"Yer just as lonely as me," her friend had once told her. *"I guess it don't make no difference if you live on a pallet of straw before a fire, or in a great big palace like this one. I'm a prisoner of St. Giles parish, and yer a prisoner of this world. We are what we are, so different because ye have money, I have nothin'...but that's just the outside. Inside I think we're more alike than any two people could be."*

That was when their connection had been made, when she realized there was someone else like her, who felt the same way, who was trapped in a world they did not want, and did not choose.

"Promise me, then," she had pleaded with him, *"that you'll always think this way of me. That when we're grown you'll come back and rescue me from this life."*

"All right, then, after I own me own butchery and get meself set up. I'll come back for ye, and ye can be me wife."

In her innocence she had believed it possible. That was, until her father had shown her just how impossible it truly was. How futile it was for her to believe a world where young girls' dreams might one day become reality—where the world and everything was treated equally.

Bristling, Lucy set her cup and saucer aside, struggling to shield the emotion she knew would be brimming in her eyes. She loathed talking of her past, and especially her parents. She especially despised speaking of it knowing it was the privileged Duke of Sussex who had brought it up.

"Well?" Elizabeth gently prodded. "Is Sussex correct in his estimation?"

"My parents held particular views when it came to child rearing," she said carefully. "Neither of them was possessed of a frivolous personality."

"In other words," Sussex drawled as he finished another custard square, "they were all work and duty, and no play."

Lucy felt herself sneering, the memories of her lonely, isolated childhood tasting like acid in her mouth. "Succinctly put, your grace. Indeed, my parents found not much in life amusing. My mother lived to advance my father's goals, and to uphold his hallowed title. My father existed, and still does, in the sanctity of his very male domain. As an only child, and a female at that, my parents' goal for me was simple—to marry well, and to manage my husband's home with dignity, decorum and efficiency, while providing him with the requisite heir. An heir that would not only inherit his father's title, but my father's as well. I was always very conscious of my role, and the inferiority—and disappointment—of my sex."

"And that did not sit well with you," he said, his voice dropping to a husky whisper. "I can see the truth in your eyes. You can hide nothing beyond those emerald depths, Lady Lucy."

Nervously she glanced over and noticed how Isabella was trying her best to study the painted flowers on the delicate china cup. The air was quite thick with a new intimacy that was completely inappropriate. Such intimate discussions were not to be borne at tea, and Lucy tried her best to deflect the conversation to a more tactful and less revealing place.

Casting a gaze about the room, she sought an ap-

propriately benign topic, and remembered that she had
wanted to invite Elizabeth to an evening out.

"Before your untimely arrival, your grace, I was
about to ask Elizabeth if she was interested in accompanying me to the Sumners' musicale this evening."

There was a flicker of amusement in his eyes, before
he sat back against the settee, his plate in his lap, his
long fingers wrapped around the rim of the teacup. He
thought her a coward, she knew, but she didn't care. He
touched too close to the truth, and she would run from
it. No one came to know her so intimately. Isabella was
possibly the only person in the world who had ever
come close, but even still, her cousin did not know all.

Even Thomas, through their shared encounter of passion had never known her so well. She shared her body
with him, but nothing else.

"Oh, I would love to," Elizabeth said. "I haven't been
to a musicale in years. Adrian despises them."

"You mistake me, Lizzy," he said silkily as he rested
his cup on the arm of the settee. He met Lucy's gaze,
and she noticed the coolness was back in his eyes. "I
am inclined to enjoy them, if the company is agreeable.
I would be delighted to escort you ladies."

Like a fish out of water, Lucy floundered for a way
to deny the duke. She did not want him with her this
evening, did not want to sit in a carriage, or make conversation with him. She didn't want him looking at her,
and seeing her, seeing the things she tried so hard to
hide.

Thankfully she hit on something that Sussex would
not be able to refute. "But what of your lodge meeting
tonight?" she inquired. Thank heavens her father had

thought to remind her of his Freemasonry meeting. As part of the Grand Lodge, Sussex would be obliged to attend, thereby forcing him to forgo his attendance to the musicale.

Lucy gave a small smile of triumph, which faded as the duke perused her slowly.

"I think your friend would like it if I were not to attend," he drawled, making Lucy's face flame.

"Oh, Adrian, do not tease. Lady Lucy means nothing of the sort…she only seeks to remind you of the obvious. Tonight is lodge night."

"Ah, yes, but one only has these special opportunities arise so infrequently. The lodge can wait, I believe. Yes," he murmured thoughtfully as he watched her. "I think I shall send word around to Mrs. Sumner that the three of us shall be attending. If you'll excuse me, ladies."

And that was the end of it. Of course, Mrs. Sumner would be ecstatic to receive the Duke of Sussex. The man was a paragon in society, and every matron swooned at the thought of having the duke attend their gathering. There was no possible hope for it now. She was committed to an evening out with Sussex. And she knew very well what everyone in the ton would be speculating come the morning—that she and Sussex had an understanding.

Blast him for so easily commanding the upper hand!

"You are in for it now," Isabella whispered into her ear. "Here is the end of your avoidance of his grace."

Refusing to acknowledge Isabella's outrageous, but truthful, claim, Lucy stared out the window, wondering what dreadful illness she might concoct to relieve her of the night's invitation.

"I cannot say how excited I am," Lizzy said with a smile that was beaming. "I adore music. One doesn't need the gift of sight to enjoy it. And it's been such an age since I left the house to do more than shop, or visit Isabella. Thank you, Lucy, for inviting me. What wonderful friends you and Isabella have become."

How could she do this, deny Elizabeth an outing? Lizzy was a good friend, and Lucy was being a poor one, thinking of nothing else but her own discomfort. No, she could not do this, hurt Elizabeth. One insufferable night with his grace. She could tolerate it, if for nothing else but the enjoyment of her friend.

"Lucy and I feel very much the same, Lizzy," Isabella added.

"Well, then," she said, while checking the door. His grace had left for his study, and Lucy wanted to be far, far away if he decided to return to the salon. "Shall we go upstairs and choose your gown for the evening?"

"Oh, yes, yes, of course. You and Isabella have such a way with descriptions. I can almost see when you two are around."

Lucy dearly wished her knack with descriptions worked with words of denial. Because she truly wished she would have found the right words to say to make the duke leave before their conversation had even started.

"But first, Lucy, I think you must take a few minutes to peruse the conservatory. We had planned on it during your last visit, and time got away from us, if I recall."

The idea of a few stolen moments of silence and

solitude lured her to agree. That was what she needed, a moment or two to gather her spiraling thoughts, and set herself to rights.

"If that would be agreeable, I would love to. There was a beautiful, bright pink flower that needs further investigation, I believe."

"Oh, the lily. Yes, yes." Lizzy nodded. "And wait till you smell them. Gorgeous scent—heady and exotic. I've asked Sussex for an accurate description, but I shan't bore you with what he told me."

"Well, then I am convinced that I shall give you a better description, Lizzy. I won't be long, however."

Together they rose, and Lucy watched as her cousin escorted Lizzy from the room, grateful for a few minutes of peace to gather her thoughts.

CHAPTER SEVEN

SILENTLY, LUCY ALL but tiptoed past the duke's study and entered the room that was designed in the shape of an octagon. With its glass walls and ceiling, Lucy could see the gardens outside from every angle. Inside, the room was filled with a dizzying array of colors and scents, from miniature orange trees, to exotic palms. A water fountain, with its gentle cascade of water upon stones lured her, and she sat down on a rock as she trailed her fingers through the cool water, while capturing a delicate pink water lily in her palm.

Despite the gentle patter of rain against the glass ceiling, and the melancholy sky, the room was bright and uplifting—and smelled like a warm, sunny spring day. With a little sigh, Lucy allowed the quiet to blanket her, and soothe her jangled nerves.

It was the perfect place for contemplation, and she decided that if she were ever fortunate enough to be mistress of her own place, she would build such a room as this.

"You look like a woodland nymph sitting beside an enchanted pool."

The lily dropped with a little splash, and Lucy found herself gasping in surprise, and jumping up all at once.

"I didn't mean to frighten you." Sussex stood against

the wall, his legs crossed as he studied her with his disconcerting gaze.

"I didn't hear you come in."

"That's because I was already here when you arrived."

Glancing away, she watched the cascade of water stream over the stones, and into the fountain base. "You should have said, should have announced your presence. I...I would have left you to your privacy."

Shrugging, he glanced away and plucked a brilliant pink lily from its stem. "It is not an unwelcome presence."

Their gazes met across the room, through the display of flowers and shrubs and gently waving palm fronds.

Waving his hand, he indicated the room. "What do you think? A labor of love that was the pride of the previous duchess."

"I think it lovely," she answered truthfully. "If I had a room such as this, very little would tempt me from it."

He smiled, and Lucy found herself momentarily disarmed by the beauty of that smile—of him.

"Perhaps one shouldn't be tempted from this room, but tempted in it."

This did not sound like the duke. It did not look like the duke, either. His cravat was loosened, and his hair was rumpled, as if he had been running his fingers through it. He was still wearing his dark jacket, and silver waistcoat, but she could see the wrinkles in the fine wool, the way it hung not quite as immaculately as it had when she had first seen him.

She had never seen Sussex looking anything less

than immaculately groomed and dressed. Standing before her like this, he was no longer the lofty Duke of Sussex, but just a man. While she took in his dishabille, he studied her. His gaze swept over her, taking in the pink-colored dress, the dusty rose velvet edging that swept the dark floorboards, and up, to her hair, her face. Resisting the urge to run a self-conscious hand along her body and hair, Lucy instead fisted her hands, and hid them in the folds of her full skirts.

"*You* look lovely today. But then, you always do."

She blinked at the compliment, immediately felt her cheeks heat with embarrassment and discomfort. "Your grace—"

Stiffening, he pushed away from the wall, and began to slowly walk the perimeter of the room. "There is no need for such formality between us, is there?"

"I think it best, do you not? We are not exactly... friends."

Cocking his head, he studied her. "Ah, you refer to that afternoon between us, then?"

"Have you forgotten our last private meeting?"

His expression turned dark. "I have not."

"You didn't tell anyone what you had found. Why not?"

"How do you know I haven't?"

"Because Isabella would have mentioned it, would have alluded to the fact Black was looking for the man who carried my handkerchief."

He paused, half turned and looked at her queerly, which made her pause, made her stare back at him. "Does Isabella know all your secrets, then? Have you shared them all?"

Stiffening, she decided to be prudent and stand confidently before the duke. "Not all, but she knows of Thomas. And she's said nothing of you searching for him, or the fact that you found him carrying my token. She would not betray Black or your order, but she would tell me if she thought you knew something that might damage my reputation."

"I have no designs to ruin you, Lucy," he whispered quietly.

"Why didn't you share what you discovered about me, and this man you claim killed Knighton? Why do you still keep it hidden?" she asked, wondering aloud.

"It was not important."

"You led me to believe it was when you returned the handkerchief to me."

"I am still investigating the matter. When I am confident I know everything there is, I shall confide in Black and Alynwick. You may be assured of my discretion, I will not name you."

"Your investigation will not lead you to the man you think I am connected to. Thomas would not kill another."

"He carried your handkerchief. You agreed the man I chased bore a resemblance to the man you believed had died. Tell me, Lucy, how does one suddenly become re-animated?"

"If you think to tease me, your grace, about my interest in the occult, then you can be assured I do not find your barbs amusing. I allow that the similarities in their appearance is strange, but I am sure once I have a chance to speak with Thomas, it will all be revealed, and we will learn that the man you hunt, is someone else entirely."

"You play a very dangerous game, believing in a man who has allowed you to believe him dead and gone."

Lucy was aware the moment the energy in the room changed to something dark and dangerous—and barely contained. That energy, she realized, emanated from the duke, the man who was always in control, always proper. But he was no longer.

"Tell me, then, have you seen him? Has he visited you, written to you? Have you met clandestinely, an assignation at a ball, or the theater?"

He was being purposely rude—and hurtful. Stiffening her spine, Lucy tried to make herself appear taller—and stronger. "What business is it of yours, if we have met?"

He glared at her, and she noticed how a muscle in his angular jaw twitched. "I have every right to know—his existence, his presence, his every movement is *my business.*"

"If that is so, then you must already know the answer to your impertinent questioning. You are, after all, a Brethren Guardian."

"Just answer the question!" he growled dangerously. "Has he come to you?"

"Your line of questioning shocks me, your grace. It tells me that you have had limited success in running your quarry to ground, and you seek answers about him through me."

He laughed despairingly, the mirth not quite reaching his eyes. "I seek many things from you, Lucy, but answers to any questions about your past liaison with a murdering bastard are not among them."

She flinched at his tone, at the unfounded statement that Thomas could have caused a man's death. "You wrongfully accuse him! And I shall not hand him over to you until I know the truth."

"Please do not trouble yourself. I prefer the chase, the *hunt,* if you wish to discuss it in such terms. Why should I wish to have him deposited on my doorstep? It would only deprive me of the pleasure of running him to the ground and skewering him like the reptile I believe him to be."

Fisting her hands at her sides, she fought for control. "You are so gravely wrong about him, and I shall not stand by and allow it."

He shrugged, cocked his head to the side. "How will you stop me?"

"By any means necessary."

"Such steadfast loyalty," he murmured. "One wonders what he did to deserve it."

"That is none of your concern."

"You are, of course, correct. It is not my concern, but it is a question that I cannot help myself from asking. I am always left wondering how he accomplished it, when I have been so unfortunate as to inspire in you nothing more than glares, and looks of disgust. He seduces you and leaves you alone, to bear whatever consequences might have arisen from your liaison—and he is awarded with your protection. I compliment you on your beauty, and wish to offer you an honest courtship, and you glare at me as though I were a rat nibbling on your hem."

Thomas had promised her everything the duke hadn't. Angrily, she tossed out the first thing that came to mind. "He was at least sincere in his compliments."

His dark brow arched, his eyes darkening dangerously. "And I am not?"

"You are determined to press your suit, to further the plan you and my father have so coldly undertaken together. I believe you capable of saying anything if it suited your purposes."

"You find me mercenary, then? The villain to his hero?"

"I do not find you anything, other than completely wrong for a choice in husband."

"You've cast your lot with the wrong side, love," he said, his voice softening, whispering evocatively with his upper-class accent. "I mean to destroy him—utterly."

"So, you have decided, in your own words, to 'run him to ground' because I hold an affection for him, and none for you." He flinched. Almost imperceptibly, but she saw it, and the way he recovered with remarkable speed. "That is really the issue in play, isn't it? You've taken offence to the knowledge that I have, in the past, cared for someone—"

"Cared, not loved?" he asked, his gaze acute—watching.

She chose to ignore him, and continued on. "This is your way of bullying me, isn't it, your grace? You have made plans with my father, and both of you assumed that I would comply like an obedient young woman should. But you have made a grave error—both of you. I am not complacent. I will not bow to the dictates of

you or my father. This isn't at all about your precious
Brethren Guardians—this is about bringing me to heel
by using my affection for another man."

"It has everything to do with the Brethren Guardians."

"And your pride!"

He glared at her. "And what of your pride? You purposely protect someone who callously took your innocence, then left you, only to reappear from God knows
where to murder someone—and still you protect him.
But only because your pride is hurt because your father
arranged to have you courted by a man who would
make you a duchess. The audacity," he mocked, "such
a brute your father is, wanting to see you settled and
secure—and safe."

Crimson rose to consume her cheeks, and she forced
herself to meet his eyes. "You would make me nothing
but miserable!"

"And he will make you happy, then, this furtive
lover of yours, who comes and goes as it pleases him,
taking what he desires, and leaving you with nothing
but heartache and regrets?"

Her chin rose defiantly. "I have no regrets. Besides,
you know nothing about him, about the truth of what
has happened. He is innocent, I know it. I am a good
judge of character, and his is the very best. He would
never kill anyone, and he must have had good reason
to do what he did. He wanted only my protection, he
told me that. I believed him then, and I still do."

"He won't have you," Sussex vowed, his voice nothing but a feral growl. "Of that I can promise you."

"What shall you do, your grace? Blackmail me? Will

you spare his life if I consent to marry you. Is that what you are trying to say?"

"No. I will spare him nothing."

"And what then?"

"You'll be mine. Of that I have no doubt."

"I cannot believe that. You said we were enemies."

"No. I said *he* would be my enemy. Never you, Lucy."

"It is one in the same, is it not?"

"No, it is not."

He finished his stroll and came to stand before her. Reaching for her hand, he gently uncurled her fingers, exposing the smooth skin of her palm, then he placed the pink lily he had plucked into her hand. When their gazes met, she noticed the duke's eyes had warmed. The cool gray was now warm silver, the black pupil bigger, dilated as he stood so tall above her, his face angled down, creating a heated intimacy between them. When he released her hand she exhaled with a sense of relief, only to catch her breath as he cupped her cheeks with his large, warm palms.

"No, it is not the same, far from it. But if you insist that we must be enemies, then I must be honest and inform you that I believe in the old adage, that one must keep his friends close, but his enemies closer. I know what I saw that morning on the rooftop—I saw what he did, and I intend to prove it you, to find him, to hunt him down and make you see him as I saw him, if it's the last bloody thing I do."

The tension in the room swiftly shifted from danger, to a mesmerizing intimacy, and Lucy was powerless to brace against the effect. Her voice, when she spoke, was soft, barely a whisper. "How do you plan to do such a thing, your grace?"

Angling her face up to his, they were now eye to eye, mouth to mouth. She could feel the warmth of his breath—scented, not with tea, but the spicy hint of brandy, brandy he must have imbibed when he went to his study. It had a curious effect on her, making her stomach flutter, and her pulse speed up.

His gaze roved over her face, and when he began to talk, the deep, rich timbre of his voice and the feel of his strong hands wound deeply into her, causing the strangest sensation in her—a feeling of acute need, of recklessness. He was robbing her of thought, of breath, of the very dislike and disdain she had always believed she held for him. He was changing the rules of their little battle, this cat and mouse game they had somehow found themselves playing, and she didn't like it, couldn't take the control back to where it needed to be—in her hands.

"How will I accomplish such a thing?" he said, and her lashes fluttered closed as his bottom lip scraped gently up the curve of her chin. "I'll be everywhere you are. Your very shadow."

His voice was a whisper now, deeply masculine and erotic. His mouth… Good God, he was making her fall apart, with just a brush of his bottom lip and the warmth of his breath caressing her skin. Behind her closed lids, she could see him, dark hair in disarray, lush mouth parted as his lips covered her skin.

"Everywhere you are, I will be. Everywhere you go, I will go. I will follow you into your dreams, stay while you sleep, watch while you eat."

That sinful bottom lip touched hers, then played with it, brushing it, tugging on it, parting her mouth as if he had all the time in the world to play and coax. "I will be the very air you breathe."

Slowly she opened her lids, only to see the duke staring deeply into her eyes.

"You threaten with that which you cannot possibly carry out, your grace."

His mouth brushed hers in a whisper of a kiss, barely a brush, the faintest touch, like the tips of a hummingbird brush the leaves of a honeysuckle bush.

"No. I promise. I vow. I pledge and commit myself to the task."

"I won't allow you to do this. To destroy my hopes. My dreams."

"I only want to be part of them, Lucy."

That telling sentence was far more intimate than his mouth against hers, his breath on her face, his palms on her skin. And she tried to fight it—his hold, on both her person and deeper inside, to the place where she had always felt cold and removed. A place where she had allowed no one, not even Thomas, to see or touch. But Sussex wanted more, he saw more, and he would ask for something she did not know if she could give—if she even possessed. She had buried her softer emotions, those girlish fantasies of love everlasting, and the white knight come to rescue her from the villains for so long she had forgotten she had ever believed in love.

She had indulged that dream once, until her father had cruelly destroyed it, taking it away from her. That was when she had learned that the pain that hit one's heart was far more powerful and painful than the stroke of a leather strap.

It was then, after the tears had been shed and dried, that Lucy had somehow allowed her fanciful dreams of love to die, only to be resurrected as something harder, and less painful. It became a pursuit not of love, but of passion. Passion was a physical thing, separated from the heart, mind and spirit. When passion ran its course it was over, leaving only pleasant memories. Love, on the other hand, when it deserted you, it left your soul shattered, your spirit unrecognizable.

As she looked up into Sussex's eyes, she was fleetingly thrown back to that moment, when she had believed in the fairy tale, that love lasted forever, that it endured all things, only to find its way back to her. And then it dissolved, leaving her with the sensation of a broken heart, and shattered dreams.

"Lucy," he whispered, his mouth so close. "Let me in."

And it was for that reason that she could never marry him. Passion—on her own terms—was the only consideration. For once, she was ruthlessly honest with herself. Part of her dislike of Sussex stemmed from the realization that she would never be in control with him. He would look deep inside her, into the secret places she hid, and refused to glimpse at. She had known, almost at once, that Sussex would not be satisfied until he completely broke down her defenses, leaving her that shattered and lonely girl, whose dreams had been dashed away by a father who dictated what her life would be.

Never again would she be that pathetic creature,

forced to obey. She would rebel against his wishes, and his wish was an unfulfilling union with the duke.

"Let me go," she whispered, struggling. But it was weak and ineffective, and Sussex would not obey. Only held her tighter, gazing down into her face with the same type of eyes that had once stared at her with the same disconcerting effect.

She tried to protest, to beg him to unhand her, but she was struck mute, and immobile. And then suddenly, he was releasing her, and she was left feeling, not grateful, or relieved, but slightly disappointed. The moment had been fraught with tension, with the temptation of a forbidden kiss amongst the flowers, and the distant trickle of water.

But the duke did not make use of it. His passion, whatever miniscule amount he possessed in his breast was locked up tighter than the crown jewels in the Tower of London.

"Good afternoon, Lady Lucy," Sussex said, as he bowed before her. "I shall be anxiously awaiting this evening."

"Well, I will not," she snapped as she made a brilliant exit—full of feminine hauteur and indignation.

"Nevertheless," he called after her, "I shall be there. Remember, *the very air you breathe…*"

CHAPTER EIGHT

"MY HEAVENS, THAT was the oddest conversation with his grace, wouldn't you agree? Highly peculiar and verging on improper, as well."

"Hmm?" Lucy murmured as she gazed out the carriage window. It was late afternoon, and Grosvenor Square was bustling with carriages. Through the window, she saw the familiar faces, women who had once been friends with her mother.

Even though the Season was completed, many families with unwed daughters stayed in the city, and the pale faces of those daughters stared back at her. These were the same girls who should have been Lucy's friends, but were not.

She didn't have friends, not in the true sense of the word. At least not until Isabella and Elizabeth had come into her life.

"I said, verging on improper, cousin. The duke... being improper? Queer, isn't it?"

"Hmm?" She shook her head to clear her thoughts. "I'm sorry, Issy, my mind is wandering. You were saying?"

Lucy saw the way Isabella was watching her—studying her, more like.

"The duke."

Lucy rolled her eyes. "I would rather not talk of him." *Infuriating, perplexing man!*

"I'm worried. That discussion of gossip was rather opportune, don't you think? Do you believe his grace overheard us talking of Alynwick?" Isabella asked, her voice laced with concern.

"I don't care if he did," she replied irritably. "His grace can go hang for all I care."

"Lucy!"

Reluctantly Lucy tore her gaze from the rain-streaked window to where Isabella sat in shadow, the brim of her feathered bonnet casting dancing shadows across her pink cheeks. Even after marriage, there was still an air of innocence about her cousin. Lucy marveled at it, and wondered what Isabella saw when she looked upon her. Unbearable sadness, in all likelihood.

"About Sussex—"

Lucy thought back to their brief encounter in the conservatory, and the same strange—and perplexing—feelings flared once again. She would *not* think of Sussex. She would not attempt to understand him, or to recall those seconds, when he had held her face, and stared down into her eyes. She would not recall how she had stood helpless—*breathless*—waiting for him to kiss her. Instead she said, "I hope this is not the point in our conversation where you attempt to change my feelings about the duke, Isabella."

"Well, it would serve you right, especially since it was not quite a month ago you forced me to think about Black, and his scandalous pursuit of me. If you ask me, I owe it to you, a little taste of your own medicine."

"Ha! Lord Black was perfect for you, as you have only discovered."

"And his grace is not, is that right?"

Lucy scoffed at the absurd notion. "Of course he is not. He is a pompous prig, and I want nothing to do with him."

"One cannot help but notice how much he looks at you, Lucy."

"It is only to pick me apart, to discover the bits he finds lacking."

"He kissed you once."

"It was like kissing a fish dragged out of the Thames," she sniffed.

"What happened between you two?" Isabella asked. "It was not like this before. This…simmering tension between you. Lucy?" Isabella watched her from beneath her bonnet brim. Her head was tilted so she could study her through the gloom of the carriage. "Please tell me what is wrong. I know something is. You are not yourself. I know you've been heartbroken by the loss of Thomas, but I cannot help but believe it goes deeper than that. There is a melancholy to you that wasn't there weeks ago."

"Too many séances," she said, trying to make light, but she could tell that Isabella would not let up her line of questioning. She was in earnest, and concern and love shone in her eyes.

"Perhaps," Issy answered quietly. "The occult is an invitation to darkness, as far as I am concerned, and you've been dabbling in it for months now."

"Lizzy, my mood has nothing to do with the occult, I assure you."

She could not confide in Isabella now. Her cousin

was married to Black. Black was a Brethren Guardian, the Brethren were hunting for Thomas, whom they believed killed Wendell Knighton and who might even be this mysterious Orpheus they talked of. It would put Issy in a terrible place, and Lucy couldn't do it. Besides, all these revelations were too fresh. She needed time and solitude to sort them.

She knew so little of the facts, only this: she had given her embroidered handkerchief to Thomas, and then he had disappeared, believed to have died in a fire. Then he had been seen on the rooftop of the Masonic Lodge and witnessed to have shot Wendell Knighton. When Sussex had given chase, the lace had been dropped. Sussex's description had led her to believe it was Thomas.

Despite dabbling in the occult, Lucy didn't believe a man who was supposed to be dead could simply appear alive and well. Obviously Thomas had never died, if indeed the man Sussex had chased had been him. And because he had never died, she had to face the fact that for some reason, Thomas had wanted her to believe that he had. And that didn't sit well with her. She had trusted him. He had promised to make her his wife. She'd believed that, but now…well, there were things that needed to be explained before she could make complete sense of this whole business. And there was still the matter of Sussex and his refusal to see Thomas as anything but his enemy. And she couldn't even bring herself to think of the other concern with Sussex—that her father wanted her to marry him. *That,* she could not bring herself to think on.

"Ah, Lucy, you make me worry, cousin."

"Issy," she said, smiling as she reached for her cousin's hand. "Truly, I'm fine."

With a doubtful glance, Issy sat back against the squabs. "I shall not let this rest, you know. I can be as tenacious as dog with a bone."

"I know. Trust me, I know your faults as well as my own."

"Will you not at least think on the matter of Sussex? I know…that is…well, I have a feeling that Sussex has developed a rather strong attachment to you."

She let out a loud, irritated sigh. "Isabella, you are a woman hopelessly in love, with a man who is just as hopelessly in love with you. Think on your marriage, now think on Sussex and myself. Do we appear to be anything more than barely civilized acquaintances?"

"One can feel that there is more between you than meets the eye."

"In this you are wrong, Issy. Sussex wishes an alliance, and since he has Papa's heartfelt approval, he's focused on me to take to wife. It's nothing short of a business transaction between Sussex and my father. And I won't be a part of it."

"How will you manage then tonight?" she asked. "Spending hours in the duke's company?"

Closing her eyes, Lucy tried to forget the impending hours of torture that awaited her. "I will try to remember the expression on Lizzy's face, that's how. It is for her that I'm doing this."

"She was rather enraptured by the idea, wasn't she? What did you think of her story?" Isabella asked, quickly derailing their conversation. "I was completely shocked by it. The nerve and utter callousness of Alynwick!"

"Yes, how she must have suffered," Lucy murmured. She recalled the trembling of Lizzy's hands, and the way her eyes had filled with tears that would not spill.

"To abandon her because of her impending blindness. Oh, the cruelty. I won't be able to look at him the same way again."

There had been such sadness in Elizabeth's gray eyes. Such pain. Lucy had felt an immediate connection with her friend at the moment, realizing that they shared the same sort of bond. A love most painful.

Lost in thought, Lucy continued to gaze out the window as the carriage made slow progress down the street to where Black's and her father's town houses stood across the road from one another.

The fashionable hour was approaching, and although it was November, those that remained in town still made the daily jaunt to Hyde Park to see and be seen.

The carriages blended into a sea of black; the sound of carriage wheels splashing into puddles mesmerized her. Isabella was chatting away. Lucy heard her voice in the distance, but couldn't seem to focus on the conversation. Her mind was caught up in thoughts, and memories, and the beginnings of a plan for tonight.

Dipping to the right, the carriage made its turn down Grosvenor, her street. The streetlights had come on, and the misty rain was now becoming a heavy blanket of fog that wrapped itself around the lampposts. Her gaze, caught by the haunting beauty of the mist, lingered over a post, and a man who stood tall, his head bent, his silhouetted figure so familiar. Pulse quickening, she pressed against the side of the carriage, her gloved hand thrust against the window. Every nerve in her body stood to attention, and her breath froze in her lungs, as his head slowly raised, and a pair of dark eyes peered out at her from beneath the brim of his hat.

My God...

She gasped, and Isabella asked what was wrong. But how could she speak? What words did she say?

Arm lifting, he took the tall hat from his head, revealing the golden curls she remembered so well.

Thomas?

"Come to me..."

She saw him mouth those words, read them so easily as they spilled from his mouth. With a cry, she moved closer to the window, pressing up against it, as the carriage pulled away, tearing him from her field of vision. She wouldn't allow it. She tried to call out to stop the carriage, but her voice would not work. Instead her entire being was frozen, trying to absorb everything, to recall this moment so she could think on it.

This was no vision or trance she was seeing. Not a dream, or a dead man walking amongst mist. He was real, and he was alive...and he had come for her.

Everything sharpened to clear focus. He was very much alive, and he was looking at her like he used to. No, Sussex was wrong about him. He was not a killer. But there were questions to be asked and answered.

Soon. She would find a way to him, and then her mind would be put to ease.

Wait for me, Thomas...

"YOU'RE NERVOUS."

"Whatever gave you that notion?" Adrian grumbled as he struggled to cease fidgeting in the coach. He had already dispensed with his hat and greatcoat, yet sweat trickled down his neck, making his linen shirt stick to his skin. Despite the chill in the night Adrian felt hot and uncomfortable, the confines of the carriage nothing short of a cage that he felt compelled to prowl inside.

He was on edge, strung high and tight, and ready to explode with the energy that was tightly tethered inside him. He had been in a simmering rage ever since his meeting with Lucy in the conservatory. To finally have her feelings for him laid out before him was demoralizing—and anger-provoking. Never before had he felt like such a charlatan, an actor in a play he no longer wanted to perform. He wanted to be who he was, who he was born to be, not who his father said he must be. But he risked too much revealing his true self. He couldn't show Lucy the truth inside him, and as a result he was left feeling like a rampaging boar.

Damn the woman, did she not have an inkling of his feelings? That he wanted her not only as his duchess, but his wife, his lover? Any other woman would have at least softened the blow, but not Lucy. She made damn clear her feelings so there would be no misunderstandings.

She did not want him. But he would bet his fortune that despite her feelings, she had wanted that kiss he teased her with.

"Good Lord, I can feel you flopping about over there like a rat with its leg caught in a trap."

"Lizzy," he said on a sigh, which of course made her laugh.

"Adrian, I have never known you to suffer from nerves. Shall I fetch my vinaigrette from my reticule?"

He glared across the carriage, not that it did much good. "You are the last woman in the world to suffer from swoons, Lizzy. I happen to know you would not be caught dead toting a vinaigrette."

Her smile was brilliant in the dim light of the carriage lamps. She looked radiant tonight, with her thick black hair piled high in an elaborate style. The mother of pearl clips she had used gave her a mystical, almost otherworldly aura. And the twilight-blue gown she wore was the perfect color to rest against her pale skin. How he wished she could have seen her own reflection in the looking glass.

"Lizzy, your beauty is dazzling," he said as he reached for her hand. "Truly, I cannot imagine a more lovely woman."

"Yes, you can, Adrian. Lucy Ashton."

He groaned, unable to stand the torture of hearing her name. For weeks now, he had thought of that morning when he had cornered her in her father's house. His thoughts had been consumed by her, and the way her green eyes had been flat and sad. He'd cut her to the quick, he had realized that, but the need to see deeper into her mind, and her secrets, ate at him like a poison that coursed through his blood.

She was not what she would have people think of her. She was not the aloof society miss who cared for naught but her own selfish needs. He knew that, just couldn't understand why she sought comfort in such a thing as being thought of as selfish and indulged. But then, he had learned through his father's "lessons" that there was nothing more repugnant than a weak man. The ton ate the weak for afternoon tea. He had seen it firsthand. Perhaps Lucy had learned that lesson as well, that a soft heart was easy prey for the vicious appetites of society.

Whatever the reason, she had not been distant that afternoon. No, she had softened as he held her, cradled her delicate face in his hands. By God, it had taken every ounce of self-discipline to keep his mind—and hands—in check. He had wanted to kiss her senseless, punish her lips with his own. And what was more, there had been a fleeting flash of her eyes that told him she had been waiting for his kiss. Or had he just wished it there? he wondered, not for the first time.

"It was very kind of Lucy to think of me," Elizabeth said as the carriage rocked them in a slow, comforting sway. "She has become a very dear friend to me."

He had hoped, at one time, that Lucy might be more to Elizabeth. A sister in marriage, as a matter of fact. But those plans had gone awry. But there was still hope. Still a plan that could be executed. It had not been a jest, what he had said that afternoon to her. He *would* become the very air she breathed, because he would not malinger, waiting for fate to tug him along. He was taking matters into his own hands, and those hands would not allow Lucy to discover and protect her lover. Fate would not take her away from him.

"It has become my mission to ensure her safety, brother. I can't bear the thought that she has somehow gotten mixed up with this Orpheus fellow."

There was no need to reply. Lizzy knew full well how he felt. Lucy's safety was paramount. But so was finding Orpheus, and destroying him. His desire and affection for Lucy could not change that, or what he was—a Brethren Guardian. Lucy would be his, and Orpheus, despite her attempts to shield him, *would* be his as well.

"Oh, how I wish you hadn't arrived home when you did," Elizabeth murmured. "I suspect I was this close—" Adrian watched as Lizzy held up her thumb and index finger, spacing them so that they were almost touching each other "—to having Lucy spilling her secrets."

"I'm sorry."

"Are you, I wonder?"

Uncomfortable with the obvious underlying question, Adrian cleared his throat and gazed out through the window at the gathering fog. The prudent thing to have done was to leave the ladies to their own devices. But one look at Lucy had left his brain devoid of every proper—and discerning—thought. He'd wanted to be near her, and he had thought of nothing else but fulfilling that goal.

How lovely she looked taking tea in the salon—a part of his house, his family, *him*. He couldn't keep from staring at her, mesmerized by her flawless skin, her beautiful eyes, the way her throat worked as she swallowed. He had been consumed by images of his dark head covering her, his lips pressed to the expanse of delicate flesh. He imagined his tongue gliding up the fragile column of her throat, lingering over her pulse.

He'd been hard as steel, and disgusted with himself. Dukes were above base desires. Or so his father had drilled into him. With a snort, he mentally mocked his sire, who was nothing but a damn hypocrite of the highest order.

He wasn't a hypocrite, but he was a fraud. He was a duke, but he was also a man. And he most assuredly was not above the carnal desires that ruled his mind and body when Lucy Ashton was near.

"What were you about this afternoon, brother?"

"I don't know what you mean."

She laughed. "Yes, you do. That talk of gossip! It was rather unorthodox."

"My curiosity got the better of me, that is all."

"I think Lady Black might have been scandalized."

He snorted. "You know Black as well as I, Lizzy. Isabella is married to the man. I daresay, very little must scandalize her."

"Still, you made a rather large muck of my plans, brother. Now I will have to rack my brain for another scheme in which to get Lucy to share her secrets."

"You are excellent with stratagems, Lizzy. I'm quite certain you will devise a nefarious plan to have Lucy part with her treasured secrets."

And he for one didn't want to hear them. He didn't think he could bear it. Many a night he had thought of another man's hands on Lucy, and it had nearly driven him mad. He only wanted one chance with her—that was all it would take for her to see the man behind the title. But Lucy, it appeared, was not going to be generous, and allow him to court her. She might have wanted his kiss that afternoon, but kissing and courting with the intention of marriage were two vastly different objectives.

Strangely he wondered at her stubborn refusal to think of him as anything other than infuriating. Especially when she had allowed the man who called himself Orpheus to deflower her, then abandon her. Him? He was barely tolerated for a waltz. *But she had wanted his kiss....*

"You never said—did you discover anything when you met with Black and Alynwick this afternoon?"

The intrusion of Lizzy's voice was welcome. He was dwelling too much on Lucy, and the unabated desire that always seemed to seethe inside him. "Nothing much, I am afraid. Alynwick has found a lead that should aid us in getting inside the House of Orpheus, but other than that, there is not much news to tell."

"Alynwick," his sister snorted with derision. "I would not put too much stock in his leads," she warned, "for they only wind up leading to one place, some woman's boudoir."

He glanced across the carriage at his sister who was sitting serenely composed. He knew she had no love for Alynwick, but lately she was much more vocal about the marquis. For some strange reason he felt defensive of Alynwick, and dearly wanted to share with her what he had learned today. But it was not the sort of topic one discussed with a lady of good breeding. Something told him that Elizabeth would not look fondly, or favorably upon the marquis's involvement with Lady Larabie. Even if it was a good faith gesture to aid the Brethren Guardians.

"I am hoping that Lucy and I might find some time alone this evening to discuss matters. I feel she trusts me enough to share her very great secret. More than that, I sense she actually desires the chance to talk about it. There is a very unsettled feeling within her, I think. One I hope I might be able to appease."

He didn't reply. He'd seen the look in her eyes, the sadness and pain, and had wanted to take her in his arms, and kiss it away.

"That is my very subtle way of telling you, brother, that I do hope you'll not attempt to monopolize her company all evening."

He scowled. "I do not monopolize her," he snapped. "Quite the contrary."

Elizabeth broke into a brilliant smile. "And this afternoon, what was that, then?"

"Discourse," he snapped.

"One does not need eyes to see that you will have to work very hard to gain not only her trust, but her heart."

"Perhaps I don't want her heart," he growled as he folded his arms over his chest. He was sulking, he knew, and was uncharacteristically grateful that his sister couldn't see him. Him, a grown man—a duke— sulking like a ten-year-old in ruffles and short pants.

"That is like saying a man imprisoned in a dungeon does not crave light. Sussex, you're a fool if you think you can make me believe that you've changed not only your mind, but heart, toward Lucy Ashton."

"Lizzy," he warned, "you're beginning to act like all the other females of the ton. You talk too much."

She smiled, and he glanced away despite the fact she could not see him, or the emotion and thoughts in his eyes. "The course of true love never did run smooth. That is the quote, isn't it?"

"Shakespeare didn't know what he was talking about when he wrote that."

"Really? You presume to know what the bard did or did not know?"

With a groan, he laid his head back against the squabs. "You are the most maddening female I know."

"Really? What a wonderful compliment. It is nice to learn I can be provoking."

"It wasn't a compliment."

"And I'm not fooled. You do not find me provoking, you find this topic, and Lucy's cool reception of you, provoking."

Thankfully the carriage rounded the corner and began to slow, preventing him from answering. "We're here. I won't be but a minute."

Lizzy held out her hand, halting him. "Lucy needs time, Adrian. And…" Elizabeth flushed, and Adrian could only stare at his sister in wonder. "Perhaps some gentle persuasion. You know, you don't have to be a duke all the time, brother. Sometimes it is perfectly acceptable to a lady for you to be just a man."

Closing his eyes, Adrian thought of how those words were going to haunt him for the entire evening. *Just be a man…* If only he could, but the weight of his title and reputation would not allow it; neither would the secrets he carried with him.

CHAPTER NINE

"Look, she's come, the Ice Princess herself. The Sussex Spinster."

"She is at least thirty now. Quite past any hope of marrying."

"Haughty creature, isn't she? Look at the way she holds herself, above everyone, as though she were the highest ranking here. Everyone declares her an angel, but angels are not filled with hauteur."

"Blind to the world as well as her own failings," someone snickered behind them.

They had been in the Sumners' music room less than five minutes, and already Lucy could hear the whispered taunts, filtering around them like a poisonous cloud. Alone, Lucy was forced to listen, and endure. She had thought it providence when Sussex had promptly abandoned them upon entering the room. She hadn't cared a whit, that by leaving them alone, he had left them standing on the peripheries of the crowd, watching, as if they were on the outside, not permitted amongst the ranks of the ton. But now, she wished him back, his steady, cool eyes glaring iced daggers into the harpies behind them.

"Plump as a hot buttered bun," a woman with a rasping voice whispered nastily. "Not so grand a lady as she once thought herself. Quite lost any beauty she might have once possessed. And those eyes…eerie, aren't they, seeing them open and perfect and knowing she can't see a blessed thing out of them?"

Lucy stole a glance at Elizabeth who stood tall and proud beside her. She was serene, not even a faint blush to mar the perfect porcelain of her cheeks while Lucy's fair complexion was growing red and hot with indignation. A redheaded failing. She possessed the temper, and the skin tone that impeded any sense of serenity when riled.

"Acts as though she were the daughter of a royal duke," the rasping voice said once again. "Her mother was nothing but a generation removed from a disposed French aristocrat. French," she spat, "not even good-quality English blood."

"I'll wager she rues the day she turned down that young viscount. Look at her, plump and blind, and a spinster, while he is happily married with a lovely wife and a passel of beautiful children."

"Thought herself too good for him, just a lowly viscount. Well, serves her right for being such a snob. Look at her now, firmly on the shelf. No one would want her for a wife, or the mother of his children."

Lizzy raised her chin a fraction higher, the only movement Lucy could discern as they stood side by side waiting for the hostess to announce it was time for them to take their seats. Lucy, unable to bear it any longer, turned to send the gossiping biddies a scathing set down, but was stopped by the feel of a leather glove on her bare arm.

"Pay them no heed," Lizzy whispered. "It is naught but the hateful words of empty-headed women."

"How can you bear it?" Lucy snapped. "I am livid with them for what they're saying."

"I bear it, because I am better than them. I would never dare disparage another, unlike them. I won't stoop to their level, and I would not have you do so, either. Let us annoy them by not remarking upon their comments. Indeed, they've said them loud enough. One could only surmise that it was purposely done. The best and most exasperating thing to do is to ignore them completely. Act as though they and their thoughts are utterly insignificant, that they are beneath our contempt."

"Lizzy—"

Her friend merely patted her arm. "I feel pity for them, that they must occupy their time being so vengeful and hateful. Imagine how empty their lives must be. How unhappy. Imagine taking delight in cruelty as they do."

Gripping Elizabeth's hand, Lucy tried to stem the flood of anger that threatened to spill over. How dare they, those gossiping fools, say such things about Elizabeth? Elizabeth who was everything that was kind and pure.

"You're vibrating like a tuning fork," Lizzy murmured. "Pray, let it be, Lucy."

"I cannot. If you could only see the self-satisfied expressions on their faces. It...it quite makes me feel violent."

Smiling, Lizzy kept her unseeing gaze straight ahead. "That is possibly the nicest thing anyone has ever said to me. And I do wish to thank you. But I have a very thick hide, and their taunts no longer have the sting they used to. But I would like to clarify one thing. The viscount—Newbury, it was. I refused him not because he was merely a viscount, but because there was no affection between us. He was down on his luck, and needed a fortune. He was one step away from running to the continent in an attempt to flee his creditors. I suppose he felt that the blind sister of a duke would be easy prey."

"But he discovered something else?"

"Yes. How formidable a blind woman can be, and how enraged her brother can become. Sussex tossed him out after planting his fist into Newbury's nose."

"Sussex?" Lucy gasped. She could not imagine the proper duke engaged in fisticuffs. Why, it was positively undignified.

"You sound astonished, Lucy. I assure you, Sussex can be very unducal at times. Beneath the title, he is just a man."

Just a man.... Lucy couldn't countenance it. The duke was everything that was proper, but she could not deny that he had possessed a certain edge she had never seen in him before.

"Now tell me, how is the room decorated?"

Lucy stole a glance behind her, sent the rasping voice woman a lethal glare before turning her attention back to her friend. "It's really rather glorious, Lizzy. The room is circular, and the ceiling is domed glass—the sky beyond the glass is like rippling black velvet, the stars, silver gems twinkling amongst the folds.

"Oh, how nice."

"There is a bank of French doors and between each

set of doors are Corinthian columns, made, I do believe, out of marble."

"Not too bad for the youngest son of an earl, is it?"

Lucy smiled and squeezed Lizzy's hand. "Not bad at all, I would say. Now, the walls are a very pale blue, with white plaster work. The ceilings are high, crowned with thick plaster moldings that contain images of fruit and flowers. On the walls, family portraits hang, and the pianoforte dominates in one corner. On top of the piano is a large bouquet of white lilies and pale pink roses in a gilt vase. Overall, it feels stately and elegant, but not at all stuffy."

"I can picture it, Lucy."

"It's grand, truly elegant. And there are so many people here. Quite a crush."

"I can feel the heat," Lizzy said. "It is quite a crush. Now, the gowns, if you please."

Lucy glanced around the room, her gaze skimming from person to person, taking in the array of colored gowns, the velvets and silks, and the elaborate edgings. She saw one gown that caught her eye, and she began mentally sketching how she might take the style and make it more becoming for her figure.

"Nothing that stands out, hmm?" Lizzy said, a smile sounding in her voice. "Then let me ask, who are we listening to tonight? I assume Mr. Beethoven and Mr. Mozart?"

Lucy glanced down at the program she held. "And Mr. Schubert. The queen adores Schubert, I understand. It was said Prince Albert courted her to Schubert."

"Mmm, yes. I rather think that must have been a very romantic courtship, don't you?"

Just as Lucy looked up from the program, her eye caught the fleeting image of a tall blonde woman in an exquisite dark blue gown. Lucy didn't know who she was, only that she was the most stunning woman in the room, and she was headed directly toward the Duke of Sussex.

Curious, she followed the woman's progress through the room; the swath she cut; the appreciative smiles—and leers—of the men; the glares—and cut—direct from the ladies.

When the woman's gloved hand slid down Sussex's arm, he turned, and the change in his expression gave rise to a very strange, very disagreeable feeling inside her, one that came swiftly out of nowhere.

Rude as it was, Lucy could not stop herself from watching the two of them, of thinking how perfectly matched they were. The woman was tall, and Sussex did not have to incline his head to talk with her. Not like how he had to with her.

The woman then lowered herself into a deep and sensual curtsy, the dark blue of her silk gown glimmering in the gaslight. Lucy could not help but notice how the woman's ample bosom was showcased to the greatest effect by her position. The duke reached for her hand, helping her to rise then lifting her gloved knuckles to his mouth, where he smiled so enticingly before kissing her hand. There was some mysterious, unspoken message in his gaze, and unconsciously, she crushed the delicate vellum program in her fist.

Lucy was certain that her mouth gaped open like a floundering fish, and quickly she snapped it shut then cast her gaze around her, hoping no one was watching her. Thankfully no one was. Who would be, she wondered, when the duke and his lady were commanding their curious glances?

After so narrowly escaping embarrassment, the prudent thing to do would be to look elsewhere, but her eyes were drawn to the spectacular couple like a moth was to a flame.

The woman was draped in jewels; the long diamond ear bobs reached her delicate shoulders, which were bare. Lucy watched how the diamonds grazed her skin, how they twinkled in the light, giving the woman a seductive radiance. She saw, too, how the duke's gaze dipped to the earrings, then the bared shoulders, and lower, to the voluptuous bosom that was barely contained beneath blue silk.

The gown, while very plain, was elegant in its simplicity, tailored to showcase the woman's figure. Her golden hair was piled high, showing off her long, slim throat, and the diamond pendant necklace that nestled provocatively in her décolletage.

Courtesan… The word screamed at her. This was a woman of the world, sensual, sophisticated, and she had Sussex eating out of the palm of her hand.

"Who is that woman that Sussex is talking to?" she blurted out in a somewhat peevish tone, before she could help herself.

With a quiet chuckle, Elizabeth said, "As I am quite blind, Lucy, I have no idea."

Flushing, Lucy stiffened beside her friend. The woman was inching closer to Sussex; he was dropping his head as the woman reached up and whispered something in his ear. What would those gray eyes be like now, she wondered, with that sinful creature's lips whispering against his ear? No doubt his gaze was fixed on the expanse of flesh the woman seemed intent upon showing him.

And what did she care? she asked herself.

"If you would describe her, Lucy," Lizzy suggested, "I might be able to help you."

No, she didn't care to—she did not want to look at the woman any longer than she already had. But then came the dawning horror: she could not seem to make herself look away.

"Perhaps it is Dorthea Abernathy? She has made somewhat of a nuisance of herself lately."

"He doesn't appear to be annoyed by her presence," she grumbled.

"Is she dark-haired? It might be Lady Greaves. Recently widowed, and looking for a new a husband."

"No, the woman is blonde." A very beautiful, very sensual, *very* skilled blonde, quite at home in her own skin…

Lizzy frowned. "Well, then, I have no notion who it could be. Sussex barely leaves the house, unless it is to go to his lodge, or his club."

Or Brethren business.

"It is of no consequence." Lucy winced, hearing the superfluous tone she'd used. Lizzy was smiling now.

"Is it not?"

"No. It is absolutely not."

The dynamic couple parted, and she stiffened as the duke turned his head and found her watching him. Willing herself not to blush, she looked at him as though she were seeing right through him. She would *not* give the man the satisfaction of thinking she thought anything about him, and the little scene that had just played out with the woman.

And he claimed to be sincere in his compliments. *What utter rubbish!* Raising her chin, she looked away, conscious of a strange trembling that had somehow taken over her hands.

"Ladies."

The duke's velvety voice swept over her from behind, and she jumped, not realizing he had even moved from his spot.

"Shall we find a seat?" he asked. "I would be honored to escort you both."

Lucy fought the urge to search the room for the woman. Would Sussex find a seat close to her, so he could watch the mysterious woman during the performance? Would she then be forced to bear witness to the nauseating scene?

Really, there was nothing more revolting than a man of Sussex's stature and reputation slobbering over a beautiful woman. She had thought him better than that, above the sort of base temptations that rule so many of the men of their sphere.

Perhaps you were wrong, a wicked voice inside her taunted. *You thought him devoid of any passion at all, but perhaps...*

Oh, do shut up! she wanted to shout. She was becoming quite unglued, her mind a rambling collage of idiosyncratic thoughts! *You do not like Sussex*, she reaffirmed. *You do not care who he speaks to or who he spends time with. In essence, you don't give a damn about the Duke of Deliciousness.*

"Shall we?"

Reluctantly Lucy placed her gloved fingers on the duke's left arm. Lizzy curled her forearm around his free one, and they then proceeded to the chairs. Sussex haughtily claimed the best seats in the room for them. She noticed the blue goddess was nowhere in sight.

"Champagne? Punch?" he asked.

"No, thank you," Lizzy replied. Lucy merely shook her head.

She was in a devil of a mood now, and she couldn't reason out why. She had been relieved at the duke leaving them to their own devices when they had first arrived. Hadn't she? She didn't want to be with him, to have to make conversation with him, and play the part of a polite well-bred young lady. Right?

Oh, where was Isabella at these moments, to inflict her calming, rational influence upon her? She was utterly befuddled, and she didn't like it. Frowning, she felt the duke's body brush against hers, and she didn't like the sensation that shot down her flesh at the contact.

"Is the seat not satisfactory? You're frowning." He was seated between her and Lizzy, and when he inched to his left to whisper that, she was overwhelmed by the cloying scent of perfume. The blue goddess's perfume. Well, she would not give him the satisfaction of knowing what she thought of him and his goddess. Like Elizabeth, she would rise above, and provoke him by ignoring the fact he had made a spectacle of himself with that woman.

"The seat is perfectly fine. Thank you."

His brow furled, and he pulled away. Lucy kept her

gaze focused straight ahead, wondering when the music would begin. She wanted to get lost in the mindless minutes that would follow. She wanted not to think of Sussex and his paramour, but of her lover. Thomas. Who she had seen that afternoon. Who she intended to make plans to meet.

How had she almost forgotten the event? How, when the last eight months had been consumed with finding a way to be with him once more.

"You look lovely in this shade of crème," Sussex whispered. "Champagne silk and pale pink," he murmured, and to Lucy's horror she saw how he discreetly rubbed his fingers along the nap of fabric. "Exquisite. Your modiste is very gifted. She's designed the most beautiful dress here tonight."

More lovely than the blonde's blue dress? she wondered sourly. It wasn't like her to be petty, but suddenly the emotion took hold of her. In reality she should thank him, and glow at the compliment, for she was the modiste who had designed her gown. But something irked her about that brazen woman saddling up to the duke. She had always found it quite easy to ignore him, but lately…lately she had found her thoughts were more and more drawn to him, and that gloomy morning in the parlor when he had returned the handkerchief to her. They had become enemies that morning, but it was a strange sort of opposition, one that seemed to be drawing them closer to one another, not pulling them apart.

Perhaps that was his plan, like a spider drawing its prey into its web. Perhaps it was the method of the Brethren Guardians to keep those they distrusted the most within arm's reach. Whatever it was, this new…

acquaintance that had unwittingly been forged between them had to stop.

Lucy was aware of the way Sussex's gaze stayed focused on her, aware the moment his gaze lowered, lingered over the tiny rise of her bosom, and the decadent Irish lace she had used for a flounce along the neckline. He would be sadly disappointed if he were looking for the same sort of voluptuousness his blonde goddess possessed. *Greatly* disappointed, she reminded herself, for Lucy had been shortchanged in that department, by being given two small, firm apples for breasts.

"You really do loathe me, don't you?"

He'd murmured that, and she wondered if she was meant to have heard it. Turning her head, she studied the man seated beside her. Normally his gray eyes possessed a chilly tone, but now…they were downright glacial. Something compelled her to honesty—perhaps it was the flicker of pain she saw in those cold depths. "Loathe is a very strong word, your grace."

"As strong as your dislike of me?"

Cocking her head, she tried to understand this perplexing exchange and her response to it. "Is this a continuation of our discussion this afternoon? If so, I have no desire to finish it. I thought we said everything that needed to be aired out between us."

"Everything? Hardly," he rasped. "All that was said was that you will not countenance the idea of a marriage between us because you despise me."

"I never claimed to despise you, your grace. That's a rather strong feeling."

"Then, may I ask what it is you feel? If it is not contempt, or loathing, or ambivalence? What is it?" His fingers rubbed against her skirts while his gaze stayed pinned on her face. "What have I done or said that makes me so abhorrent?"

She flushed, glanced nervously about her. But the guests were all talking amongst themselves, and it was impossible that they would have heard him. "Can this not wait until another time?"

"No, I don't believe it can. You see, it has been the most frequently asked question in my mind, ever since that night I escorted you to that séance. Do you recall?"

Inwardly Lucy groaned. He would have to bring up that night.

"I made it very clear that I desired you, and when I kissed you, you slapped my face. What have I done to make you feel this way?"

Biting her lip, Lucy flicked open her lace and pearl fan and began beating the air vigorously. Using the fan as a decoy, she whispered fiercely, "You most certainly did *not* inform me of your desire, your grace. In fact, you alluded not at all to any of the higher, more romantic sentiments. You informed me, *sir,* that when we were married you would curtail my interests, keep me at home, under your thumb, and then you importuned me with a kiss that possessed all the finesse of a dead fish!"

Abruptly Sussex pulled back and glared at her. "A dead fish? Is that what you compare me to?"

"Yes."

"And this is your opinion of me, that I am a prig? A boring, staid duke who lacks the warmth and skill to properly incite a woman's passion? Well?" he growled when she refused to answer.

"Lower your voice. People will hear."

"Then answer the question, Lady Lucy. Is that your opinion of me?"

"Yes, your grace. That is precisely what I think. You are a dead bore, and the last man in the world to tempt me into marriage."

Immediately she bit her lip, sought to apologize, or at least find a way to make her assessment softer.

"I see."

Oh, she could not bear to look in his eyes, to see their flinty depths. There was hurt there, pain... It reminded her of another day long ago, when another pair of eyes had looked at her with such suffering, and it caused her to feel remorse for her words. "I...I..."

"No, say nothing more. I fully comprehend now."

Why now did she feel pain? Because she had admitted the truth, she found him dreadfully dull and uninspired? That was the truth. It had always been her assessment of Sussex. He was the shining archangel, and she was most certainly not attracted to bright and glittering—dark was her lure. And Sussex was certainly no dangerous fallen angel.

As if by divine intervention, their hostess for the night quieted the crowd and introduced their entertainment for the night—a Mr. Dubuque, who was currently all the rage in the most fashionable salons in Paris. As the gathered guests clapped their approval, and Dubuque took to the stool, Sussex leaned over. Those around them continued their applause.

"You have not given me sufficient opportunities to be anything but proper, Lucy. And I'll have you know that I will not consider this matter between us over until you do."

"And what is that supposed to mean?"

"That I have just drawn a new line in the sand, and I will not hesitate to bring you across to my side."

CHAPTER TEN

"Oh, THAT WAS most enjoyable," Lizzy said happily as Sussex escorted them over to the punch bowl. "Don't you agree? Dubuque has such a way with interpretation."

The duke's response was little more than a grunt, leaving Lucy to pick up her end of the conversation. "Delightful! It has been a long time since I've enjoyed myself so much. And thankfully there was no screeching soprano to join him. The last musicale the Sumners hosted had a most dreadful singer."

"Oh, yes. I remember a musical I attended at Lady Branwell's years ago. Her daughter sounded quite like a cat being skinned, and the others who joined her were not much better!"

They laughed as the duke steered them in the direction of the refreshment table.

"You are unusually quiet, Sussex," Lizzy announced.

"Merely taking it all in," he muttered.

"No doubt he's wishing he had abandoned his plans to escort us, and is now fondly thinking of his lodge meeting," Lucy teased.

"No, thinking of other things, I'm afraid. And formulating a plan." When he gave her a pointed look, Lucy darted her gaze away.

"Sounds diabolical," Lizzy said dryly.

"Oh, it is."

"What did you think of the music, brother?"

"Adequate."

"What a scintillating conversationalist you are!"

Sussex frowned as Lucy and Lizzy both grinned.

"He's scowling, isn't he?" Lizzy asked. "I can almost see it, his glare boring into my person!"

"Indeed he is," Lucy answered, "most fiercely."

Which made Sussex's scowl deepen. "I am not frowning or scowling—or anything of the kind. Perhaps you two—"

"Your grace, what a wonderful surprise to see you here, tonight."

Half turning, Sussex stuck out his hand in greeting. "Ah, Lord Sheldon, how are you?"

"Very well, your grace. And you?"

"As well as can be expected after enduring forty-five minutes of Mozart."

The newcomer laughed and rocked on his heels. "Decidedly so."

"And here I thought I was the only one in the room bored to tears."

"No, misery loves company, I'm afraid, but it *is* rather selfish of you to claim boredom when you have been seated between two of the loveliest women in the room."

Lucy felt a gentle tug on her hand, pulling her back, away from the gentlemen. "Who is this?" Lizzy whispered discreetly. "He has a voice as thick and smooth as honey."

"I have absolutely no idea. I've never met him before."

Lord Sheldon and the duke continued to converse,

oblivious to the fact Lucy and Lizzy had discreetly taken another few steps back and were now hurriedly whispering back and forth.

"Lizzy, *honey?* Really!"

Lizzy gave up a beautiful smile. "Do describe him, Lucy."

Lucy glanced at the man. "He is tall."

"Yes?"

"And excellently dressed."

"Yes?" Lizzy asked, sounding breathless.

"And he seems very polite, and amiable."

"Oh, do get on with it, Lucy!"

"Get on with what, Lizzy?"

"Is he handsome or no!"

Lucy smiled, and reached for both Lizzy's hands giving them a big squeeze. "Very. And he keeps stealing peeks at you while Sussex is droning on about something or other."

"Oh dear, my brother droning on? He'll have the poor man running away in horror." Lizzy's face suddenly lit up like the dawn. "Oh, how do I look?"

"Stunning and ethereal, as always."

Lizzy pulled a face then seemed to recover. "What color is his hair?"

"Sandy-blond, with streaks of… Is that honey, I detect?"

Lizzy's scowl was quite reminiscent of the one she had seen only moments ago on the duke's face. "Make fun of me if you will, Lucy. I will bear it, if only you'll go into greater detail. You're capable of it, you know. *Make me see him!*"

Heart softening, she took a surreptitious glance at

the man, and saw how his gaze lingered over Lizzy.
"Tall, lithe, but not skinny—his shoulders are quite
broad. He looks quite stunning in his dress clothes,
very gentlemanly with a hint of wildness. He's tanned,
in fact."

"Tanned?" Lizzy asked with a frown. "Is he English? No Englishman possesses a tan in the middle of
November."

Lucy let her gaze slip once more to the handsome
gentleman. "Definitely tanned, Lizzy. His hair is, I
think dark brown, but with honeylike streaks running
through it—" she could not suppress the smile at her
taunt "—which I'm certain are sun-streaked strands.
His hair is given to wave, I think, but he's brushed
it back and tamed it for the night. His eyes…hmm, I
cannot see them well, but I think them dark, and they
are framed with a very lush amount of dark lashes. His
lips…well, I think they must be perfect."

A masculine cough interrupted her, and she looked
up to see the duke arching his brow in annoyance.
"Ladies, may I introduce the Earl of Sheldon? Sheldon, this is Lady Lucy, the Marquis of Stonebrook's
daughter."

"Delighted, Lady Lucy."

"And this…" Sussex delicately took Lizzy's hand
in his and brought her carefully forward. "This is my
sister, Lady Elizabeth."

Lucy watched the way the duke elegantly placed
Lizzy's hand in Sheldon's gloved one. She also noted
the way the earl's gaze roved over Lizzy as she dropped
into a perfect curtsey. *Smitten.* That was exactly what
the earl was.

"Lady Elizabeth, an honor."

"Why thank you, Lord Sheldon."

"Your brother has spoken very highly of you, and none of it has been exaggerated, I assure you."

Lizzy's smile was one of beauty, and Lucy had to hold back the impulse to clap her hands together with glee.

"Would it be permissible, your grace, if I escorted Lady Elizabeth around the room?"

"Not at all, as long as my sister has no objections?"

"None at all."

Sheldon placed Lizzy's fingertips on his arm, and carefully led her away from the refreshment table. Sussex watched them like a hawk circling a mouse for a very long time before he spoke. "What do you think of him?"

Lucy was startled by the question. "I beg your pardon, your grace?"

"Sheldon. What is your opinion of him? He is new to his title, spent the majority of his life abroad in the Middle East, but he's been back now for months. He's been hinting for almost that long about desiring an introduction to my sister."

Lucy watched the pair as they strolled the perimeter of the room. They stopped before a painting, and it was clear that the earl was taking his time to describe it to Lizzy. And by the expression on her friend's face, she was in raptures over the earl and their conversation.

"He seems very caring, and not at all surprised at her infirmity."

"I made it clear," Sussex said before taking a sip of his champagne. "He's known all along. And still he has made his wishes known. He's rich—I checked. No bad habits, or any sordid secrets—I checked that, as well. There was a hint of trouble, though, back in the East that I haven't been able to ferret out yet. But there is a story there, somewhere, and most likely a scandal. I can sense it. No one in our world is clean and free of secrets."

The duke's gaze darkened at the last, that Lucy could not help but goad him. "Gossip, your grace? How unlike you to indulge in the pastime."

He grunted, but his cool gaze stayed focused on the pair. "Where there is smoke, there is fire. Something happened and has been swiftly, and quite safely, brushed beneath the carpet. I intend to discover what it was."

Lucy couldn't help but look at him. He wasn't paying her any mind; his full attention was focused on Lizzy. There was a very great love there, she thought wistfully, wondering what it might be like to have a sibling care for her. It was very apparent in the way Sussex watched Lizzy, protecting her from anything or anyone who might wish to harm her. No man, Lucy realized, would be free of Sussex if he wished to court Elizabeth. In fact, Lucy was beginning to fear that no man was good enough.

"You cannot keep her tucked in the house all the time, your grace."

He glanced down then swiftly found Lizzy. Once more, there were ghosts in his eyes when he spoke. "You don't know what it was like growing up as we did. She had no one—I had no one. We are all the other has, and I would do anything to see her safe and happy. My father…" He swallowed. "He had no use for anything he perceived as weak and ineffective. He all but abandoned her when she began to lose her sight. I *won't* do the same." His vow warmed her despite the fact she was trying to stay cool and indifferent. How could she? "I think, your grace, that you have done everything in your power to ascertain that Elizabeth will be quite safe with this man. Now it is up to fate."

"Fate?" He looked down, studied her face. "I never leave anything to chance, Lucy. You should know that."

"And why do I need to know such a thing?"

"For the future. I won't leave my future, or yours, up to some whimsical fit of fate, or chance, or any other esoteric nonsense."

The way he looked at her gave her pause, made her study him, before she shook her head. There was something there, when he looked at her just so…but she could not place it. She tried to pull away, but he reached for her, held her by the wrist. When she looked up, the strange familiarity was gone, replaced by eyes that were warm, heated with the effects of the champagne, and perhaps something else? Passion? No, his grace did not succumb to such things. Passion was a foreign word to him—a forbidden concept.

"Your grace," she whispered, her voice chastising. "It is not done to touch me so forwardly. You'll cause a stir."

"Did you think our conversation from before finished?"

"Emphatically."

"Well, it is not. Quite the contrary. I have had forty-five minutes to think of the things I want to say to you."

"I hate to disappoint you, your grace, but I am not in the frame of mind to indulge any priggish sermons you have mentally dictated. I have had my fill of sermons and lectures to last me a lifetime and into the next. My father, you see, is quite fond of them, my mother was as well. I don't need you," she spat, "plaguing me with them, either. Let us be enemies, as we had mutually agreed upon a fortnight ago. This, whatever this is—" she waved her free hand between them, indicating the way he was holding her wrist, and how close they stood together "—is far too complicated. Being enemies is much easier, and simpler."

"For you, perhaps. For me? It's utter agony."

He held her tighter, leaned closer, and she could smell that woman's perfume on his clothes, and it sent her emotions scattering like the petals of a rose in a gale. Surely she could control these frightening emotions that seemed to flare so violently inside her whenever she recalled the duke with that woman.

"You would make a spectacle of us, sir, please, release my hand and step away."

"Now who is the prig, concerned only with rules and etiquette?"

The glare she shot him could not be misunderstood. She wanted to do serious damage to his grace.

"You should never underestimate me, Lucy—especially when I want something."

"One would hate to deny a duke anything, it would be social suicide. But I don't care."

He smiled, showing his teeth, and his eyes crinkled at the corners as if he were enjoying himself immensely. "I will have you, Lucy. Make no mistake about it, and it won't be by clandestine fate, or chance. I assure you."

As they stood toe to toe, the duke's fingers wrapped around her wrists, their gazes locked, the Sumners' majordomo announced in a ringing voice, "The Marquis of Alynwick, and Laird of the Clan Sinclair."

Appearing in all his Highland regalia, complete with kilt and sword, Lucy watched the marquis stroll into the room. His gaze roved over the guests, jumping from person to person, searching for someone.

With a groan, Sussex reluctantly released her hand.

"What is it?" she asked, stepping on the tips of her slippers, in an attempt to see over Sussex's shoulder.

"An inconvenience we don't need."

"Who doesn't need?" she asked.

"The Brethren Guardians," he growled as he glanced at her. "Damn it," he muttered, swinging his gaze back to the marquis, "there is going to be more than one duel tonight. I'm going to blow his head off for this stunt."

"I beg your pardon? A duel? Your grace—" She could hardly breathe, her corset squeezing her lungs so tight she felt light-headed. *Thomas?* Was the duke going to drag him to some lonely, fog-shrouded field and murder him in cold blood?

Sussex glanced at her, looked deeply into her eyes for the briefest of seconds and discerned her worries. "Not *him*. Not tonight."

Her relief was audible, and it sent a muscle in his jaw clenching.

"Truce, Lucy, for the next few minutes?"

It was against her better judgment to grant such a

thing, but she found herself nodding despite herself. "Very well."

Holding out his arm, he offered it to her. "Stroll with me."

She did, and allowed Sussex to maneuver her effortlessly through the throng of guests who were busily chatting away, and watching the marquis with marked interest.

As they promenaded closer to where the marquis stood surveying the gathered crowd, Lucy was aware the instant Alynwick sighted what he was looking for. When the marquis's gaze fell to Sheldon, who was holding on to Elizabeth's hand, Alynwick's expression turned violent.

"Sussex," Lucy hissed, "look."

But it was too late. In one swift move the marquis had parted the couple and had the earl pressed against the wall, his arm lodged against Sheldon's throat. With a thrust, he slammed the earl back hard. Words were shared, and Lucy feared for her as Alynwick reached for Lizzy's hand and proceeded to all but drag her out of the room. The crowd went silent; nothing could be heard except the fall of shocked, slackened jaws.

"There is keeping our presence a secret," Sussex growled. "Goddamned, hotheaded Highland brute!"

"What now?" she asked, fearing for Lizzy. What would that beast Alynwick do to her?

"Damage control, I'm afraid. Get Lizzy for me, and I will take care of Alynwick. Then be ready to depart immediately."

"Of course." She was already moving when the duke reached for her hand.

"Lucy?" Sussex paused for a beat then took a step closer. Lowering his head, he whispered to her, "This isn't over. I always get what I want. And by God—" he paused, brushed his mouth against the loose curls she had left dangling down her temple "—how I want you."

As the duke pulled away, Lucy was left with an odd warmth flowing through her veins. Immobile, she watched Sussex weave through the guests, his tall form easily seen between the swelling crowd that was eager for a glimpse of the spectacle Alynwick was creating.

Poor Lizzy, she would be devastated by such a scene—and Alynwick's callousness.

Stepping back, Lucy inched back toward the periphery of the room. Everyone was too busy looking to the opposite side; no one would notice her as she carefully and unobtrusively made her way to the exit, where Sussex was calmly separating his sister from the marquis.

She had almost made it, when a voice came from behind her. Her wrist was snatched up and she was whirled around. She froze when she saw a footman with her gloved hand in his.

"My master bids me to give you this. He awaits you. Tonight."

Lucy followed the footman as he swiftly melted out of sight and disappeared amongst the crowd. She glanced down at her palm, and immediately closed her fingers around the gold circle. Her gaze found Sussex, who was still heading toward the door of the music room with Alynwick alongside him. He was not paying her mind. He had not seen.

Carefully she uncurled her fingers and stared down at the coin, with its lyre and laurel leaves.

The House of Orpheus...Thomas.

Excitement mixed with dread. She did not want to discover any connection between Thomas and Orpheus. She wanted there to be no question of his innocence in Sussex's mind, or in hers.

There was only one way to know the truth. She must go to him, and Sussex must never discover that fact.

ALL THE WAY HOME, as the carriage rocked and swayed through the dimly lit streets of Mayfair, Lucy wondered—and worried—what the remainder of the night would bring, considering the duke's strange mood. The coin was pressed against her palm, inside the glove, and she felt it, a reminder of what the night would bring.

She worried that perhaps Sussex would discover her plan, but he was preoccupied—with thoughts of the marquis, no doubt.

Stealing a glance at her friend, Lucy could well believe that it was not only the duke who was brooding about the marquis, but it was evident that Elizabeth was, too.

Lucy had found them in a darkened hall, Alynwick looming over Lizzy like a menacing shadow. Reluctantly he had pulled away, but not before he'd leaned down and whispered something that had caused Elizabeth's delicate pink flush to drain from her face. Something had passed between them—Elizabeth firmly denied it, but Lucy had seen the lie in her friend's eyes. Something had transpired to make Lizzy quiet—too quiet—and worried, too. Her friend was still biting her lower lip and clutching her reticule tightly in her hands. Lucy had tried numerous times to draw Lizzy from her thoughts with talk, but her friend seemed oblivious to her attempts. The only thing left to do was to reach out and grasp Elizabeth's hand, holding it tight in her small gloved one. With a gentle squeeze, Lizzy recognized the small comfort, but still did not speak.

What had that brute Alynwick done or said to her? Any number of vile things, she supposed. The marquis was known for such things, and he had hurt her friend before… Well, she would not stand for it this time. Brethren or no, Alynwick would not be allowed to further hurt Elizabeth.

Before she knew it, the magnificent ducal coach pulled up before her house. Sussex, without any sort of pretext, handed her down from the carriage, and escorted her up the tall steps of her home. When Jennings opened the doors, the duke bowed and bid her good night, then turned and disappeared into the fog-shrouded night.

"Good evening, miss, I trust your evening has been an enjoyable one?"

Jennings took her cloak, and waited for her gloves, which Lucy had no intention of giving up. "Very enjoyable, Jennings. And my father?"

"Not at home, miss. Lodge meeting tonight."

That's right. She had forgotten.

"Well, then, Jennings, I think I shall retire. I am tired tonight."

With a bow, the butler withdrew. "Very good, miss."

Lucy forced herself to climb the curved staircase with dignity and decorum. She could feel the austere stare of the butler following her progress. When she was out of sight, she lifted the hem of her dress, running down the long corridor, the silk of her gown making a rustling, sifting noise as her heeled slippers, muffled by the thick carpet, tapped against the floor.

At last she was there, slightly winded as she threw open the door then slammed it behind her. Tossing her reticule and gloves onto her dressing table Lucy rushed to her window, pulling aside the heavy brocade curtains, she saw that the Sussex coach was already rolling down the street.

She tried to think of the coin pressed to her flesh, the excitement that was to come. But she caught a glimpse of the ducal crest emblazoned on the carriage door and it made her think back on the events of that evening.

By God, how I want you...

Dratted man.

It had been uttered in the deepest, darkest, most velvety voice she had ever heard, and it had made her whole body shiver. It was most definitely perfect, and full of passion, and quite the most arousing thing ever said to her—and it would have to be the duke who said it.

"Well, to hear this door slam, it can't be good news."

Lucy turned to see her maid, Sybilla, enter the chamber. Every time she saw her, the effect was the same. Sybilla was breathtaking, with dark, thick hair, and exotic almond-shaped eyes. Her skin was the color of amber honey, and her faint accent most alluring. She had come from France with her last employer, who had died not long after arriving in London—succumbing, no doubt, to the damp weather. Lucy had immediately snatched her up—not because Sybilla was beautiful, or gifted with needle and thread, or heavens above, pins and brushes, but because she shared a very unique interest with her.

The occult.

Lucy's interest had only been budding when Sybilla came into her life. Now, and with Sybilla's uncanny ability to discover the most diverting occult gatherings, and séances, Lucy could definitely say that her interest was far more than merely fleeting.

Sybilla knew most of the details of Lucy's affair, and it had been her maid who had suggested they use the occult as a way of communing with her dead lover.

With a sigh, Lucy let the drapes fall back into place. "Elizabeth had a wonderful time. And that is the most important thing."

"And you did not?" Sybilla asked as she picked the discarded gloves up from the table and smoothed them out. Lucy still held the coin in her tightly curled fist.

Sinking to the chair that sat before the dressing table, Lucy sighed once more and gazed into the mirror. "I don't know if I did or didn't. Does that sound strange?"

Sybilla smiled, and started pulling pins from Lucy's hair. "It sounds like a man was involved for you to give such an answer."

"Mmm," she mumbled as she picked up a pearl hair clip and started twirling it mindlessly. "Have you had a chance to get those books at the library I requested?"

"*Oui*, I put them on your nightstand. They were very heavy, and dusty, I might add."

"I don't doubt they are all dusty old tomes. I highly

doubt there are many readers in the city eager to read up on the crusades."

"Then why are you?"

Their gazes met in the mirror, over a mound of Lucy's red hair that looked wild and untamed as it was released from the pins. "Something compels me," she replied. "Something I feel I must know."

"About what?"

Lucy didn't dare breathe a word about such things to her maid. Not that she didn't fully trust her, but because she had given her word to Black, and by extension to Sussex. She had sworn not to speak of the Brethren Guardians, or their Templar lineage. She had promised not to reveal that the three of them—Sussex, Black and Alynwick—were linked by something beyond anyone's imagination. And for that reason alone she kept her council, stating only, "I had heard that they dabbled in the occult, and I wanted to do research on the matter, that is all."

Sybilla nodded briskly, telling Lucy she accepted the answer, but the maid's dark eyes said something completely different.

Despite this, Lucy knew what must be done. She must learn more of the Guardians, and she must tell Thomas about them—tonight.

"You are in blue spirits, I think," Sybilla muttered.

"Nonsense," Lucy replied. She was just… She didn't know what was wrong with her. She had had a very steady, very sure course set for herself, until tonight. Until the duke had given her a surprising—and shocking—glimpse of another side of him. And it was far from polite—or dead boring—and she couldn't stop thinking of it, despite the fact the coin she held was warm in her hand. *Thomas...think of him.* Eight months of being parted was about to end....

"Mrs. Fraser sent her card around," Sybilla announced as she pulled the remainder of Lucy's pins from her hair. "I did not send a reply, as I was uncertain of your thoughts."

She had thought never to call upon the Scottish Witch ever again, but that had been weeks ago, before Sussex had returned the handkerchief, before everything had seemed to blur and change.

"I think I'll leave it for now," she murmured, unsure of what to do. Ever since that night she had visited the mystic, she had been possessed by dreams of her vision, and those gray eyes, and the portent it might mean. She had thought of her childhood friend more than she had in years, and she didn't like how it stirred up the old feelings that she had tried to suppress.

"I think I have something that will make you happy."

Lucy looked up into the mirror, and saw that her hair was not hanging free of the pins, but rather had been redressed. Curiously her gaze found Sybilla who was once more reentering the room, carrying a missive.

Passing it to her, she smiled secretively. "This will bring a smile, *non?*"

Tearing open the wax seal, Lucy breathlessly read the words she had prayed for and longed to hear these last long months. The coin fell from her hand, and Sybilla picked it up, holding it for her until she had read the missive.

A carriage will await you at the corner of Mount and Green at one o'clock. Bring the coin and show it to the footman, who will direct you to me.

 Yrs, as ever,
 Thomas

"It is from him! I told you, Sybilla, that I had seen him, that he hadn't died at all!"

"You must go to him, but when?"

"Tonight! *Now!*" Lucy cried, jumping up from the chair. "I'll need a heavy cloak, a bonnet—with a thick veil." She paused, met Sybilla's gaze. "My father—"

"I will tell him you are indisposed."

"That will arouse his suspicions, and he'll come to check on me when he gets home."

A glint reflected in the maid's dark eyes. "Not if I tell him it is female in nature."

"Oh, how clever, he'd never dare enter after learning that."

"Most men won't."

"You are brilliant, Sybilla."

Lucy ran from the room after her cloak and bonnet had been carefully secured. The gold coin was safely in her palm, back beneath her glove. "My lady, you will have a care, won't you?"

"Of course. There is nothing to fear. I will be back by morning, safely in bed, with none the wiser."

CHAPTER ELEVEN

THICK FOG SWIRLED around the lampposts, a gray spec-
ter mingling and coiling in the dim light of the gas lan-
terns. Senses alert, Adrian prowled down the cobbled
street, his fashionable walking stick with its concealed
knife at the ready for anyone who might wish to make
a rush at a gentleman, prowling the empty streets alone
at this time of night.

It was an impulsive, not to mention foolish, decision
to walk to the little house he kept on Mount Street. Had
he been in control of his faculties and not still reeling
from his evening spent with Lucy, and the perplexing
arrival of Alynwick, he would have seen the plan for the
reckless, foolhardy idea it was. But his temper and considerable lust were charting this particular course and
once either of those emotions were aroused, not much
persuaded him to ignore his inclinations. He was in a
strange mood, dark and brooding, his thoughts leading
him to things he hadn't allowed himself to dwell upon
in years. Engrossing himself in such thoughts only
made the fear come back. The feeling that he deserved
nothing of what he had been given rose up like bile. The
fear of discovery had always been there, his constant
companion. He had learned to cope with it, to accept it
as a part of himself and the life he lived. Secrets were
a Guardian's companion, his secrets no less so.

"Damn it to hell," he muttered, stabbing the cobbles with the end of the stick, if it wasn't the secret he tried to keep buried, the one thing that could ruin him in the eyes of everyone he cared for, it was Lucy driving him stark raving mad.

One minute he wanted to ravish her, the next he wanted to shake her till her teeth rattled and she couldn't think clearly enough to toss out her impeccably placed barbs.

She thought him boring, staid—and passionless. If she only knew how his gut burned with unabated passion, if she could see inside his mind and realize that he was not just a stuffed shirt, but a flesh-and-blood man. But she refused to see it, and worst of all, she would refuse him the right to be alone with her, so he could show her just what sort of passion he was capable of.

Of all the gall, he spat, shooing away a stray cat that was stopped on the cobbles staring at him with its watchful green gaze. Had he any reasoning at all, he'd put any thought of Lucy and her lovely eyes and fiery temper right out of his mind and fix himself on other more willing, and far more accommodating, company. He could have any woman he desired, not just as a mistress, but as a wife. But he had fixed on Lucy. His heart would countenance no other. If it were only a matter of speaking from his heart, he would have done so by now, but he was quite certain that Lucy would not listen— and if she did, she would not believe that he had fallen irrevocably in love with her. She would think it yet another scheme to force her into marriage.

Besides, she had made her thoughts quite clear, and a man's heart was a fragile thing, despite what women thought. It was difficult enough for a man to admit he loved someone; he didn't need to say it knowing the feeling was not reciprocated. That did smack of pride, but he was only human after all.

Perhaps what he needed to do was to show her, through action and deed, the proof of his love. It was too soon for the words; she wasn't ready to hear them. But there were other ways to make her understand that he meant to have her as his duchess—and it had nothing to do with an arrangement made with her father.

God Almighty, he would make her more than willing; he'd make her burn as hot for him as he did for her.

A cat hissed at him, arching its back as he motioned with his stick for it to move aside. In a state of distemper, he hissed back, sending the animal racing for cover in the gutter. If only he could send Lucy scurrying with his bared teeth and bad temper. But the damnable woman had risen to the challenge, had refused to back down and let him win their joust of words.

A smile flitted across his lips despite his foul mood while he fished around his pocket for the key to the house. Hell, he had to do nothing more than think of her and his unruly cock came to life. No courtesan, no matter how beautiful or talented, had ever done that to him.

Never had a woman challenged him so. Never had he endured so many sleepless nights due to unrequited passion and longing. He was utterly smitten and it was all one-sided.

Fitting the key into the lock, he let himself into the darkened hall; Adrian knew emphatically Lucy was going to be the death of him. There was nothing healthy about the feelings she aroused in him. He needed her, and he had never needed anything or anyone before, not like this.

What he wanted above all else was Lucy's good opinion—for her to see beyond the title to the man. He wanted her to come to him of her own volition. He cared about what Lucy thought—cared a great deal.

Stalking to the study, he opened the door, thankful that the man he paid to look after the place was not about to hover over him or see him in his present state of confusion. He liked letting himself into his home. He enjoyed the solitude, the feeling of being nothing but a man in his own home. He'd purchased the little house as a means to meet with Alynwick and Black in relative secrecy when it was necessary. But tonight he was meeting someone else there. Lord, he hoped he could put on a better face than he now presented.

The door to his library was already opened, and the soft shadow of gas lighting seeped into the hall. Quietly he entered, surveyed the room, his eyes instantly drawn to the sideboard where a decanter of good Scotch whiskey sat awaiting his arrival. Ah, that was what he needed—that would banish any lingering thoughts he had about Lucy, and the beastly mood he found himself in.

"Good evening, your grace," a woman purred behind him, her voice a mixture of husky female entreaty and an Eastside London accent was rather alluring. It conjured up all sorts of titillating images, and possibilities.

He straightened; why, he had no idea. They had planned to meet here, at precisely this hour. She had her own key, for God's sake. But still, he jolted. Trying to hide it, he glanced at her, saw her sprawled on the leather settee, her long, dangling diamond ear bobs scraping against her shoulders, the soft lighting making them as brilliant as prisms.

"Anastasia," he mumbled. Acknowledging her with a curt nod, he moved to the sideboard, poured a whiskey and tossed it back in one long swallow. The burn down his throat felt good, settling him. He poured another, and proceeded to swallow it like before. Normally he did not drink to excess, but tonight he didn't give a damn. He felt reckless and wild...maybe even feral. He had not felt like that in twelve years—he thought he'd curbed that distasteful tendency. But old habits die hard, and he had acknowledged reluctantly that he had never really been completely civilized. The image society saw, and bought into, was nothing but a sham, a fraudulent image of a duke.

"You are not yourself tonight," his guest observed.

He glanced at her as he poured his third whiskey. "Am I not?"

She smiled, and he blinked, temporarily taken in by her beauty. She had dazzled many a man, not only with her beauty, but her confidence and knack for knowing what men desired—in and out of the bedroom. She shrugged, making her breasts nearly spill from her low-cut gown. "I have known you a long time, Adrian. You can't hide from me."

Sighing, he ran his hand through his hair as the whiskey warmed in his hand. "I suppose not." She knew too much. Knew what he was.

"We have known each other for so long," she murmured as she tilted her head to study him. "Will you not confide in me?"

Lowering himself into a comfortably stuffed chair, he let out a groan and tossed his head back, resting it against the scrolled wood carved frame. Closing his eyes he sought the words. "It's nothing. Pay me no mind."

The rustle of satin made him look up, and he saw Anastasia glide across the library, a goddess in blue satin and diamonds. He had thought her rather lovely a few hours before when they had met at the Sumners', but now he thought her utterly ravishing. Any man would be fortunate to have her.

"Adrian," she said, her voice a soft caress as she ran her bare hands through his hair. "You have too many secrets to bear the burden alone."

Closing his eyes once more, he laughed, a mocking sound from deep in his chest. "You have already shared too many with me, Anastasia, I won't burden you further." To do so would make the guilt insufferable. He loathed the feeing it gave him, and tried not to think of it, like he did every other night when he was alone, staring up at the ceiling in the ducal chamber, contemplating his life and what it was.

He stood, and she moved silently, like a cat, surprising him, making him jolt as she slid her palm up his chest, till she could skim the tips of her fingers along his cheek. She was looking at him with such an intense expression that he wanted to look away, but he couldn't. Somehow, he needed this tonight, needed to unburden his soul to another, someone who would understand what he endured. He wanted it to have been Lucy, but he could never share this secret with her. She would turn from him in disgust—horror, repulsion—and that, he knew, he could not live with.

"This is how he would have looked," she whispered, her gaze skating over his face, "without the cruelty. So beautiful, so virile and strong."

They both knew who she was talking of, and he stiffened even more, not wanting to think of him.

"You are so much like him, Adrian," she said, cupping his cheek. "Tall and proud. And those eyes…"

"Don't," he said, his voice sounding hard and broken. "I am nothing like him. You should know that. You know what he was like."

"Mmm, yes. I know. How strange it is, that when I look into your haunted gray eyes that I am reminded that, in a way, he made us both, didn't he?" Stepping closer, her bodice brushed his waistcoat. "He took us both, and made us what we are—a high-class whore and a dutiful, proper heir. Despite all that, I loved him."

"My father—" he began, then suddenly choked on the word. "He was never satisfied with anything until he got his hands involved, sullying and destroying, and making a creation that fit his ideal of perfection," he growled as he took a sip of the whiskey, which Anastasia suddenly snatched from his hand, before resting the crystal glass on the table.

"All those years with him, I gave him my fidelity while watching you grow into something he could never aspire to be—a good, honest man, concerned with things that few of your world see as they go about their lives. He never saw the good in anybody, Adrian, only in himself. And you are so unlike him in that respect. You see the good in everything that surrounds you."

He swallowed hard, watching as Anastasia pressed in closer. Remorse for all his lies flooded him as he listened to her words. When he looked in the mirror, he did not see what Anastasia saw. He did not see a man worthy of respect or redemption.

"It is time you put the past behind you. Put *him* behind you. Perhaps it is time for both of us, hmm? Despite loving him, I wanted you." Her fingers reached for his cravat, began to slowly untie the knot. "But you knew that, didn't you? But you were too dutiful, too proper to be tempted, too honorable in your own sense of right and wrong."

He tried to protest, but she raised her finger to his lips silencing him.

"One look from you is all it would have taken. All it would still take."

Alcohol was infusing his blood, but no amount would make him accept what she offered. Gently he cupped her shoulders in his palms and pulled her away. "You're lovely, Anastasia, you know that."

Her smile was at once sad and amused. "But not lovely enough to entice you."

Turning from her, he strolled to the fireplace. Leaning against the mantel with a raised arm, he stared down into the hearth, which was left unlit. "No." His answer was quiet, but firm. "I can be tempted by only one woman, and she will not have me."

"More fool her, then," she said, and he sensed that she was walking across the carpet, back to the settee.

"She could have no idea of how lucky she is to have captured your attention."

"Heart," he clarified, and he looked over his shoulder in time to see her golden brows arch in surprise.

"Lucky girl. I would have given everything I had for a chance to gain your father's heart."

"My father had no heart, surely you realized that?"

"You're right. He gave it all to you, didn't he? Whether he knew it or not. You are everything he wasn't." She tipped her head, studied him. "And everything he was. The power is there, the ruthless determination. The strength and beauty—the animal lust, too, I think. But your eyes lack his cruelty, your hands..." Her gaze slipped to his palms, and her voice grew soft, almost reverent. "Your hands could touch with benediction, just as well as possession."

"Anastasia," he warned, but she smiled, and glanced away.

"Your lady will weep with pleasure, Adrian, with just one brush of those strong, loving hands. And you deserve nothing less than a woman who will treasure you. I have long hoped that perhaps, in time, I might be the woman to fulfill your needs."

"I am sorry, Anastasia."

She waved away his apology. "I did not wish to meet here tonight for that," she said. "Although, I would be a liar if I did not hope it might happen."

"It has nothing to do with your—"

"Age?" she supplied.

He shook his head. "I remember the day he introduced us. I was sixteen, and you were—"

"Your age now—eight and twenty," she said with a grimace. "Now, I am forty."

"I thought you rather beautiful, but now...you are simply stunning."

Smiling, she glanced down at her hands. "It is only because you have taken such good care of me, Adrian."

"You were good to my father, despite the fact he was nothing but a bastard to everyone—including you. You were good to me, too, and I could not see you return to that world of—"

"The demimonde?"

He nodded. "A plaything for men. I cannot stomach the notion, I never could."

"How I wished I was fifteen years younger, Adrian. I would not give you up to any woman—not without a very great fight. You are the sort of man a woman should fight for."

He snorted. "If only that were true."

"Oh, it is, darling. I always told you that, didn't I? How truly worthy of the title of duke, and gentleman you are."

Indeed she had, and he had never believed it. Still didn't.

"I have no plans this evening," she said. "And I have a very good set of ears, despite the fact they are weighted down with these outrageously beautiful earrings you bought for me. Make use of my listening skills, and talk to me, Adrian."

He glanced at the jewelry he had purchased for her the day after his father's funeral ten years ago. He had set her free from his father's grasp, buying her a small house in Mayfair, supplying her with a pension and monthly allowance, allowing her to keep the small bits and bobs his father had purchased for her. He'd bought the diamonds as a thank-you, not as prelude to anything more than that. He kept her in style, befitting what she was used to when she was his father's mistress, because she had been his friend. His confidante during those horrible years when his father decided to make him into a Brethren Guardian.

"Well, then, if you have no desire to talk of your lady, then perhaps we might carry on with what brings us here?"

Mentally shaking himself, he downed the remainder of his whiskey, and turned to face her. "Yes, we should get on with things. I have a dawn appointment to attend."

She gasped, her eyes growing large with alarm. "Adrian—"

Waving off her concern, he said, "Alynwick. Who else?"

Shaking her head, she settled back into the settee. "He will be the undoing of your little group."

"I know it. I think father knew it, too. Always thought the Alynwicks were a reckless bunch."

"Your father was a superstitious man, but he was as smart and cunning as the devil. I admired him for that."

Anastasia Lockwood was the only nonmember of the Brethren to know anything about the Guardians, and he and she were the only ones who knew that. Neither Black nor Alynwick knew of Anastasia's existence, or her knowledge of their order. By means out of his control, his father had included his mistress, telling her all. It proved just how much his father had trusted her. It proved how faithful Anastasia could be. After ten years without his father, she was still carrying their secrets.

"That little East End whore won't tell a soul if she knows what's good for her. I made her into what she is, and I can break her and bring her back to the little hovel I found her in."

The previous Duke of Sussex deserved nothing out of the woman he had "made." Regardless, Anastasia knew Adrian's most damning secret of all. She would keep it. He would trust her with his life—in fact, he already had.

"Adrian?"

"Apologies, woolgathering, I'm afraid." He should stop drinking. His mind was getting muddled, and he didn't like the feeling, the sense he was giving up control. But he confessed he liked the numbness he felt. He hadn't thought of Lucy for at least…two minutes.

Strolling to the sideboard, he splashed more whiskey into his snifter, watching as some of the amber liquid sloshed over the rim of the glass, landing on the polished rosewood. When he turned around, Anastasia was studying him intently.

"When we met two weeks ago, you shared some troubling news. I trust you have made progress in your search for this Orpheus?"

Nodding, he started to pace the room, indulging in the movement, the way the alcohol numbed him, filled his veins with a sensual lethargy. "Aye," he slipped, and he shook his head, avoiding Anastasia's raised brow. "Yes, we have. Black and Alynwick are doing more than I am, I'm afraid."

"Too busy investigating other things, I imagine?" she said with a laugh, and he joined her.

"Yes, you would be right."

"Well, since you take such good care of me, and I have had little interest in entertaining offers of male companionship, I have found myself at loose ends."

"Oh?" he asked, surprised. "What of shopping or going to balls?"

She glared at him. "I have never been one to be amused by an excessive amount of fripperies, Adrian. You know that, but I will forgive you. Yes. In a plain manner of speaking, I've been bored to tears. But—" she reached to the side for her reticule and pulled it open, drawing something shining out of it "—there was one heady meeting at a ball last week, a perfectly delicious stranger who found me in a darkened corner. He presented me with his."

She tossed it at him, and when it landed in his hand, it took everything he had not to drop his full snifter onto the carpet. What he held in his palm was a gold coin, with laurel leaves and a lyre. "The House of Orpheus."

She smiled triumphantly. "Indeed. I've been twice. My companion is…well, let us just say he is rather high up in that little club, and he tends to speak rather freely during the art of amour."

"Ana," he ground out. "This is dangerous. It is no game for you to play."

"Adrian, really, that is quite enough. I won't have you scolding me like a child. I know what I am doing. Helping you. Like I used to assist your father."

"Stop it at once."

She jumped up from the settee, settling her hands on her hips. "Oh, don't you dare!" she snapped. "Do not think to tell me what I can and cannot do. I know the risks, and I accept them."

Anastasia had come from the rookeries of St. Giles parish. She knew danger, and had an uncanny knack for avoiding it. She was tough and smart, and if anyone could infiltrate the club for them, Ana could. But as a gentleman he couldn't allow her to do so. As a Brethren Guardian, he needed her to.

"While you think of appropriate excuses to curb me from going, allow me to tell you what I know."

Rubbing his thumb over the raised markings of the coin, he drank from his snifter as he watched her.

"Now then, my man's name is Eros." She winced. "The Greek God of Love he is not, but he believes himself to be, and I play along—it quite loosens his tongue."

Adrian winced. He preferred not to hear anything along these lines, but he would endure it if only to discover what Ana had learned.

"The club is a reincarnation of the old Hell Fire Club. There's food and music and debauchery. Plenty of debauchery, but it's mixed with the new sensation for dabbling in the occult. There are soothsayers and séances, opium and absinthe to make the visions and séances more compelling—and other things, as well."

When he was going to interject, Anastasia held up her hand. "There is an initiation ceremony two nights from now, and I have been invited to join. Orpheus, the leader of the club, is the master. He's the one who inducts all the new members."

Adrian saw where this was leading. "You'll have a firsthand account of him."

"And his weaknesses, plus any secret passages that might be of use to you and the other Guardians. I suspect that I shall even be able to get you in."

He shook his head, glanced down at the coin. "I don't know, it's not safe."

"Life is always a gamble, Adrian, and I believe this is a cause worth risking life and limb for. Don't you?"

He had vowed on his life to hide the chalice, to uphold the order of the Guardians, to protect the world from an evil they had no idea lurked amongst them.

"Never tell what you know. Never say what you are. Never lose faith in your purpose for the kingdom to come will have need of you and your sons," she said, repeating the Brethren oath.

"I remember," he muttered, thinking of the oath, the way he had been held down by his father, the old Marquis of Alynwick and Earl of Black. Their sons had been there, too, Alynwick with his unreadable gaze, and Black with his eerie blue-green eyes.

He still felt the burn of his flesh as he was branded with the image of the Brethren Guardians, the way his body had twisted and lifted from the stone slab. He had screamed, the sound echoing off the coved ceiling of the Masonic Lodge, the hallowed place where the Brethren Guardians had initiated their sons for centuries.

"Keep it on his flesh longer," his father had growled, "until he ceases to scream like a child and bears it like a man."

He could still smell his burning flesh, feel the

way his father's big hands anchored his wrists in a steely hold.

"You disgust me, weakling," his father had later said as he came to the room where Black and Alynwick had been adding salve to the burn in preparation of bandaging it. That was the way it went: the old order caused the pain, the fledglings, as they were known after initiation, were left to the menial task of soothing and bandaging. "Did you think it was only me that noticed the tears in your eyes? God, you humiliate me, boy!"

His father had swatted him across the head, and he had sat there, cold, unmoving. Numb. A poor reflection of a man and heir in his father's eyes.

"You had better prove of use to me," he'd growled, "or you'll pay for it."

"Think of something else," Iain had suggested after his father had left in disgust, and the salve burned its way through the tender, singed flesh. "It always helps."

"Think of what you'll get out of this," Black had said. "Think of the power."

And he did. He thought on it, what he would obtain after the ordeal. It had sustained him; it still did.

The world of the Brethren Guardians was cold and isolated. Only the sons and fathers were to know of it. His father had broken a centuries-old silence by bringing his mistress into the fray—and to a certain extent, his daughter, who had discovered the truth through his drunken rages. Their world was at times violent and dangerous—like now.

But things were changing. Isabella knew of Black's involvement, and Black took solace from his wife when he needed it, when he needed to talk. Now Ana, who had always been involved, was standing before him, wanting to help.

"You know, I will never listen to what you think, Adrian. I am determined."

Closing his fingers over the coin, he gazed at her. "Then we welcome your assistance, Anastasia."

A smile lit up her face. Hugging him, she pressed herself closely to him. "I will aid you in any way I can."

"First, you can promise that you will stay safe, and come to me if you suspect you're in any sort of danger at all."

"Agreed."

"And you will report daily, do you understand? Even if you have nothing to report. I want to know you're safe. And damn it, Ana, send word whenever you go to that godforsaken club."

Pulling away, she smiled and kissed his lips—like a mother with a son, or perhaps just two friends parting. When she moved back, she ran her fingers through his hair, tilted his face so she could look deeply into his eyes.

"Everything but the cruelty," she whispered once more. "Lucky girl."

She moved past him, reaching for her cloak that was draped over the arm of the settee, then her reticule. He tossed her the coin; she caught it and smiled. "It's the ticket in," she said, studying the coin. "You show it to the doorman at the Adelphi, and he has a footman escort you up to the club."

Slipping away, Adrian watched her walk to the door, where she paused and glanced back at him.

"Thank you, for allowing me this opportunity to repay you for all you have done for me."

He growled. "There is no need. I've told you—"

She waved off his remark. "Till we meet again."

CHAPTER TWELVE

SWIFTLY, LUCY maneuvered herself down the street, the heels of her half boots clicking in time along the cobbles, echoing against the bricks of the fog-shrouded town houses that loomed around her.

A dog howled, making her shiver as she cast her gaze left then right, searching through the misty gloom for any sign of danger. She must be mad to be out here at this hour of the night. What fool would risk her reputation, and her very life, by walking the streets of Mayfair at one in the morning? It wasn't even the Season, after all, when Mayfair would still be bustling with carriages and elegantly dressed couples strolling from ball to ball. No, it was November, and the West End was all but deserted, its residents at home, tucked warmly before their hearths, or beneath their down bedding.

And here she was, on a fool's errand. Or so many would believe.

Come to me tonight. Walk to Mount Street and round the corner, where a carriage will await you at one.

There would be no better timing. Papa had not been home, out as he always was. More and more, her father had taken to spending his nights at the old Lodge, for what purpose she could not fathom.

Ever since her mother had died, Stonebrook had taken to spending his days and nights away from their

home. They had not even left the city for the country
and the Stonebrook seat. But then, in the country, her
father would be obliged to adhere to country hours,
and country living, which meant he would be home—
in proximity to his daughter. The child he had nothing
in common with. The one person in the world he had
no clue how to talk to.

It did not take any amount of brilliance to reason out
that her father chose not to be at home for any length of
time because he wished to avoid her.

Painful as that admission was, Lucy had forced herself to admit the truth. By the age of ten she had realized she was alone in the world, and this little jaunt
tonight, walking the dim gaslit streets with nary a soul
around, only served to reinforce the sentiment. And it
was that very thought that had propelled her into action
tonight.

Thomas was alive and he wanted her to come to him.
She needed answers, to know why he'd allowed her to
believe him dead. Surely he would have thought she
would grieve for him. That she would, at the very least,
be upset by the news. And she also needed to hear that
Sussex was wrong, that Thomas was the not the man
he hunted for. The only reason Sussex believed that her
former lover was Orpheus was that he carried her lace.
It was only a coincidence, and she would prove it.

"And where would you be off to at this time of
night?" The voice reaching out to her in the quiet was
like a lance down her spine. "Who's there?" she asked,
searching the shadows, careful to remain beneath the
light of the lamppost. She wasn't far now from the
corner. Just feet to go, then she would round the corner

and find the carriage Thomas had sent for her waiting there.

Nothing but the rhythmic tapping of rainwater dripping from a drainage pipe met her question, and she hurried on, clutching the braided strings of her reticule tighter between her gloved hands, while her hurried stride sent the velvet skirts of her gown swirling around her boots as she moved quickly down Mount Street.

She sensed the man following her, and she picked up her pace, her lungs burning in her chest as her rapid breaths blew against the black veil she had used to disguise her identity. Tightening her hand on the strings of her reticule, she strove for composure even as her nerves took flight in the darkness.

Casting a fearful glance over her shoulder, her gaze caught something golden, a fleeting flash, and she stopped, stared into the darkness, her gaze narrowed as she tried to peer deeper into the inky blackness.

"Thomas?"

Something reached out of the darkness—for her—and she shrieked, the sound muffled by a large hand encased in leather. Pulling her into the shadows, Lucy felt her body held in place with something viselike around her midriff. Behind her, through her woolen cloak, she could feel steel beneath skin, a tower of unyielding muscled flesh that pressed unmercifully into her small frame, while the hand across her mouth stayed frozen.

"Is that who you're meeting? I'd wondered."

The voice was deep, husky in the darkness as the villain lowered his head, allowing his breath to caress her throat.

Frozen, she could not process what was happening. She was terrified as she was pulled deeper into the shadows between two houses. In the silence, she heard the distant echo of horses' hooves clopping along the thoroughfare followed by the clacking of carriage wheels. The sound became fainter, telling her that the carriage was moving away, not coming to her rescue.

The reality of what was happening to her began to sink in, and she struggled, only to be held tightly—and oh so easily—by one thick arm.

"Don't think to struggle," the voice growled, and she tried, through her terror and panic, to place the voice. Different, yet somehow familiar. Even the scent of him was familiar, but fear fogged her mind, and she found herself stilling in his arms, if for nothing other than self-preservation. Good God, she was terrified!

"Please, sir," she mumbled beneath his hand. "Pl-please don't hurt me."

The body which had been so stiff, so unforgiving in its strength suddenly yielded the slightest bit. She was no longer held rigidly against him, but rather more softly, as if he were molding her body into his.

"Never," he said, his voice still husky, but filled with a deep sensuality. His breath was warm against her cheek, the scent of whiskey strong, yet strangely, not at all offensive, but rather…alarmingly enticing.

Time stood frozen for what seemed like minutes, but then, through the tendrils of fog, she saw the image of a man, tall, dressed in black, carrying a torchlight, and realized it was the night watchman making his rounds. Invigorated by the sight of safety, Lucy whimpered, kicking and flailing, fighting her assailant with everything she had, but he subdued her with his arm, pulling her tighter against him so that she was lifted up from her toes, to press along the length of his body.

His palm, she realized, was just beneath her breast, his hand, so large that the tips of his fingers touched her other breast. He could crush her, she realized. Do unspeakable, horrifying things to her in this alley…

"Who's there!"

The night watchman's gravelly voice echoed between the houses. She saw his arm rise, preparing to lift his torch and sweep the alley with the light. He would find her there, held in the brutal arms of her assailant, her eyes wide with terror, as the brute's hand covered her mouth.

"I hear ye," the watchman growled. "Come out, now."

To her horror, Lucy found herself lifted effortlessly against him as her assailant pulled her deeper into the bowels of the narrow alley. She reached out, her arm outstretched, pleading in muted silence for the watchman to see her—to save her. But his light did not reach this deeply, and she was being pulled back as if everything was in slow motion.

She would die tonight. She knew it. But it would be a painful, agonizing death, for she knew what the villain wanted from her. She could feel it, the hardness of his body pressing insistently against her.

Well, she would not be a victim—not without a fight.

Lucy waited until the right moment, the second when he found a wall and turned her to face him, bracing her against it. In the darkness, she could not see him—only smell him, the scent of linen and wool, and the freshness of mint, and rain. The warmth of whiskey as his mouth came closer to hers.

She did not fight him then, she was too small. Too weak. She waited…waited until he was closer, until his leather-encased hand caressed her chilled cheek, then down to her jaw, where his fingers curled gently around her throat, and his breath rasped in excitement. She waited until his mouth was descending, angling…until she raised her arm up between their bodies, a show of submission and desire, as she curled her fingers into the breadth of his shoulder. And then, while she was anchored to him, she tipped her head back, surrendering to the feel of his whiskey laced breath against her mouth.

"Christ, how much I want you," he breathed.

"Yes," she replied, feeling his body almost fall into hers. And that was the moment, when someone like her, small and insignificant, could overpower a man who was well over six feet.

His head lowered to hers, blocking out the faint shaft of moonlight, cocooning her in his warmth and scent. His breath—hot mist—bathed her lips. Pressing her fingers tighter against him, she heard his growl of desire, and she raised her leg, making him think her wanton. When he moaned in approval, she lifted it higher, thrusting her knee between his legs. With a savage upward thrust, she forced her knee against him a second time, making him groan in agony.

But he did not let go of her like she supposed, and she tried again, but his hand found her knee, stopping her as his fingers cupped her leg, squeezing it.

"Jesus Christ," he rasped as he struggled to gain air

through pained breaths, "you've managed to kick my cods to my throat."

Time stood still, and the blood blanched from her face. That voice…she knew that voice.

"Your…grace?" she asked incredulously.

He gagged, doubling forward in pain, but never once lifting his hold on her leg.

"What the blazing blue 'ell are ye doin' 'ere," he gasped, his accent taking on a rougher, courser edge, surprising her.

"Were you following me?" she asked in relief and outrage. "Oh, I cannot believe this. Let me go this instant!" she demanded, but his fingers only tightened.

"Like hell!"

With remarkable recovery, he caught her up against him, and carried her in his arms into the deepest, darkest part of the alley. What he was going to do with her now, Lucy had no idea, and feared to guess. She only knew nothing good would come of it.

CHAPTER THIRTEEN

GOD HAVE MERCY, he was going to faint. Or cast up his accounts. He wasn't quite certain in what order, he just knew that both were going to happen. Never in his life had he anticipated Lucy would kick his bollocks up far enough to knock against his teeth!

Blackness edged his vision, and he struggled beneath her weight as he all but dragged her to the back of the town house.

Goddamn, he begged beneath heavy breaths, *don't let me faint.* Not now, of all the times and places to be rendered weak as a babe.

Dear God, what did she mean by traveling the streets alone, at this time of night? And kicking blokes in the balls? he savagely thought.

Rifling through his pocket, he pulled out the keys, watched as they jumbled in his shaking hand. Christ, the pain, it was all he could think about. And she was still going on, yapping to him about something, but he could hear of none of it, except for a curious swishing in his ears.

"What the devil are you about, strolling the streets at this time of night—alone?"

"I don't believe I need to answer to you."

"You damn well will, you little baggage."

"One might also ask what *you* are doing lurking in an alley?"

"Damn it, Lucy, you will answer the question, or I swear I will not be accountable for my behavior. This is not a game!"

She struggled in his hold and, still off center from the savage kick to his groin, Adrian temporarily lost his grip on her arm, and she escaped him for a second, before he reached for her hand, just missing and capturing the fingertips of her gloves instead, which left Lucy free and him holding the glove. She gasped, a terrified-sounding little noise that made him still in confusion. It was followed by the tinkling sound of metal hitting the flags of the foyer floor.

Lunging, she came forward, lowering herself nearly to her knees, but he was faster, despite his injury, and swooped down, seeing the shining object that had landed in the corner. He held it in his palm, studying it, then glanced quizzically at her. He thought her expression quite resembled that of a child's stealing a sweet from the kitchen.

"I suppose it would be superfluous to question where you got this coin?"

Chagrin melted away, replaced by the beginnings of fear. It irked him. What did she think? That he would do her some harm?

"Give it back."

He thought back to little less than an hour before, when Anastasia had showed him the same coin. *You give it to the doorman, and he summons a footman to take you up to the club. It's your ticket in.*

"You were going to meet him!" His gaze narrowed. "You've been there before, haven't you?"

Raising her chin in defiance, she replied, "I don't believe I owe you any explanations." Something snapped inside him, and roughly he reached for her arm and pulled her to him. He started to make his way deeper into the house, all but dragging her along, Lucy protesting bitterly. In the library he shoved her into the nearest chair and pulled his already loosened cravat from his neck.

"You will start speaking now, or I swear…" he threatened, unable to finish the sentence. His mind was reeling with information, the implications, and the terror of knowing that Lucy was alone on that bloody street, intent on meeting her lover at the House of Orpheus.

"I will not," she sniffed haughtily as she artfully arranged her skirts. "If you want to know, you'll have to drag it out of me—torture me with one of your Templar methods."

Oh, he'd love to, he thought as he stared down at her, mesmerized into pure idiocy as he focused on her mouth. He thought how he'd like to torture her—he'd start by unpinning that glorious mound of red hair. Shaking himself, he focused on the task at hand.

"I could use a Brethren Guardian tactic," he growled, unsure if the Brethren even had a torture tactic—certainly none that had ever been implemented in the past two or three centuries. "But you wouldn't like it." *Which was the entire point of torture—you idiot!*

"I am prepared."

With an arch of a brow, he reached for her reticule

and snatched it from her, causing her to jump up in outrage. "That is private! You cannot simply just open my bag and go searching through my effects!"

"Brethren tactic, remember?" She tried to wrestle it out of his hands, but he held firmly on to it, while forcing her gently back into the chair. "Why don't you just explain what you were doing out there, at this time of night, and why you have the coin with the mark of Orpheus? That will do nicely for starters."

"Never! You'll have to force it out of me!"

He laughed despite his foul mood. "Dear me, Lucy, this is not the Crusades, and I'm not going to strap you down on the rack."

She eyed him speculatively. "We're enemies."

"If I were to strap you down..." He shook his head and cleared his throat. Certainly he couldn't finish the thought because he knew she would not like to hear how damn much he wanted to lay her down on his bed and torture her with pleasure until she screamed and called out his name.

"Now, then," he muttered, after steadying himself. "You may tell me your tale, or I will go rifling through your reticule. Your choice."

With a shrug, she nodded to the beaded bag he held in his hands. "Do your worst."

Such a dramatic little thing, he thought with a smile as he pulled on the corded and tasseled strings that held the purse closed. Such fire. It made him want to bed her—*hard*—riding her into submission. She would burn hot beneath him, every expression naked for him to see, just as her body would be. And her hair, it would resemble a river of flame over his pillow, and he would reach for it, wrap the silken strands around his hand and tilt her face up to look at him as he thrust hard into her, making her accept him. And in her inherent dramatic fashion she would come beautifully—and loudly—*for him.*

Christ, he was hard as iron standing there, and he lowered the purse in his hands, trying to conceal the fact. He was supposed to be livid with her, not thinking of bedding her. He should be investigating her actions, discovering what the devil she was doing with this coin, but the image of her pale body arching beneath him, of her searching and reaching for the orgasm he masterfully held just out of her reach. By God, he would make her wait, make her teeter and fall, only to rise up again. He'd make her want…make her weep…keep her in an acute state of longing and aching need before he gave her what she wanted—just like she had done with him.

Get on with it, he reminded himself. And reluctantly he tore his gaze away from her face, and his mind from the fantasy of making love to her. He would—he vowed it. He would have Lucy Ashton, there was no mistaking that.

Drawing the strings, he opened the reticule. There was some money—some coins, a key, presumably to her father's house, which made him ask the asinine question, "Does your father know what you're about tonight?"

"Oh, certainly," she replied mockingly. "I shook him awake and informed him I was going traipsing through Mayfair in the dead of night to meet with the man who took my innocence."

It was as though an electric bolt lanced through him.

He had known what was in Lucy's past, and he had discarded it. But now, hearing it from her own lips caused a new ravaging in his soul. Was it insufferably hypocritical and priggish for him to wish that he could have been her first? He had dreamed of it for so long, how it would have been between them. He would have taken such good care of her. Would have made it beautiful, and tender—and slow, not rushing her, just allowing her to experience every nuance of pleasure he and his body would give to her.

With a savage oath, he picked through the bag until he came across a folded piece of paper. Her eyes widened, but their expression taunted him, dared him to unfold this bit of private correspondence, which did nothing to ease his riled, and feral—not to mention sexually frustrated—mood.

"So this is the damning evidence, is it?"

"I don't know what you mean."

"We'll see soon enough, won't we?"

Opening it, he read the contents, and saw red as every vessel in his head began to bleed, leaching blood from his brain, to his eyes, until his vision was swimming in crimson.

"Goddamn it!" he roared. "What the devil do you mean by obeying this summons? Alone? In the dark? My God, when I think of what might have happened to you. You're reckless…a danger to yourself," he huffed, quickly losing his control. "You ought to be tied up for your own good and safety and given to a man who will make it his life's purpose to keep you out of mischief!" He reached for the cravat that lay pooled on the table.

"What do you mean by this?" she snapped as he began to bind her hands.

"What does it look like?"

"Untie me at once. *Oooh,*" she stammered as she stamped her foot against the floor, trying to connect with his foot. The foot wouldn't hurt half as much as his groin still did. *"You cannot do this!"*

"I assure you, my love, I can. And I am doing a fine job of it."

He was done tying her, but his palm had caught her wrist, checking to make certain the cravat was not too tight. He had removed her cloak, and her arms were bare, the skin pale, beckoning as he made an upward brush of his hand along her arm.

"Get your hands off me," she gasped, struggling to free herself as she squirmed in the chair. "Cease your manhandling."

That did it. He stood in front of the chair, bent down to eye level as his hands wrapped around each of the chair's curved arms. He stared into her vivid green eyes, as glorious as a blade of spring grass, and said, "I am *not* manhandling you."

"Yes, you are."

"No, I am not. Trust me…you will be fully cognizant of the matter when you've been manhandled by *me.*"

"Oh, really?" she drawled haughtily. "And what distinction will you make, hmm? What difference will there be from now?"

His mouth came dangerously closer to hers. His cock stiffened, and his bollocks burned with a gut-deep ache, but he could not stop himself. Her lips were too close, her mouth so daring and tempting…

"You'll know, because I'll do it properly, and you'll beg me for more of my hands."

She frowned, crinkling her nose as though she was hit with a most distasteful odor, then her eyes went wide. "You are intoxicated, your grace."

The revulsion in her expression, the derision in her voice made him feel something more than a little dangerous. "Only mildly inebriated," he drawled with a sardonic air he did not feel.

"Disgustingly drunk." Her green eyes narrowed, a telling sign she did not find his repartee one bit amusing. "You are foxed. Ripping drunk, sir. *Sauced.*"

Something he had kept tightly tethered inside suddenly snapped. He straightened, putting distance between them, or else he might fall on her like a ravening lunatic. On the mantel, his glass of whiskey from earlier sat unfinished, and to settle the roiling emotions in him, he strolled to the hearth and reached for it. Taking a sip of the whiskey, he curled his lips around the crystal tumbler and studied her. The brandy did nothing to settle him. He wanted her with a power that would not be harnessed.

"*Sauced* is Cockney cant, Lady Lucy. Does your *lover*—" and he spat the word with such vehemence "—speak it to you?"

Her elfin chin tilted upward in defiance. "You insinuate that he is less than a gentleman, but he is more than you, sir," she said through gritted teeth.

"Oh, yes," he thundered, his hand gripping the crystal in a dangerously tight hold. "The very paragon of gentleman-like behavior. The man who shot and killed another in cold blood!"

"You have no proof!" she countered, and the passion in which she defended the bastard made him see red.

"I was there, damn you. I saw him point the gun and shoot Wendell Knighton in the chest from the rooftop. I am telling you, he did it."

"It…it can't be."

"Why? Because you don't want it to be true? Because you cannot bring yourself to ask a few very pertinent questions regarding the man you foolishly believe is better than me?"

"He *is* better than you!" she railed.

"Oh, really?" he drawled, the sound belying the depths of the darkness that he felt. "Well, I for one would never make you walk through the darkness of night to my carriage that I hid around a corner," he said with lethal softness.

Something like pain flickered in the depth of her eyes, and he almost despised himself for saying what he had, but jealousy and an unholy unrequited desire was ruling him now, and had been ever since he had read that damned missive.

Her gaze turned mutinous. "Well, I know for certain, that he would not bring me to the very place where he had only just completed fornicating with his mistress!"

Adrian knew he stood there with his mouth agog, and his eyes bulging. Whatever her response, he had not expected that.

"The room reeks of her perfume. That same overbearing scent that fouled the air at the musicale. I saw her," Lucy continued, her voice taking on a strange tone. "The tall blonde that kept sidling up to you, the one you made no pretence of showing interest in. For all your prudish, priggish ways, you quite forgot your head tonight, did you not? I was not the only one to notice the spectacle you made of yourself."

Something inside him fired to life, and he replaced the glass atop the mantel and strode slowly to where she sat, still bound in the chair. "She is *not* my mistress."

She snorted in derision, her eyes rolling. "You must think me a fool."

He caged her within his arms, his hands gripping each of the curved arms of the chair, making her jump, but he shortened the space between them, bending lower until he could look into her eyes, smell her skin, feel the rapid puffs of her breaths against his lips, and his body responded, wanting her, desiring to show her how it could be between them, what sort of lover he would be to her.

"I think you a maddeningly obtuse woman," he growled, and her eyes widened, either at his tone or the look in his eyes. "You could have been killed tonight—or worse," he said, reaching out to stroke her silken cheek with the back of his hand. "You might wonder at that statement, what fate could be worse than death, but I assure you, there are fates out there that would make death appear a blessing. And regardless of that, you walked blindly into the depths of it."

"Nothing happened," she whispered, shivering, his touch obviously repulsing her.

Abruptly his hand fell away, only to return to the arm of the chair. "We'll never know, will we? For I intervened, saving you from a certain distasteful end, I am certain."

"Thomas would never let anything happen to me."

"No? He let some stranger come out of the darkness and drag you into an alley before the night watchman could even lift his torchlight. Do you think he is still there, waiting for you? Wringing his hands with worry? Or do you think he muscled up and had the carriage turned around in the direction of your home to see if you were safe and sound?"

"You're crowding me," she sniffed, trying futilely to press away from him. He dipped his head, forcing her gaze to land on his face.

"Tell me," he said, his voice dropping low when his gaze lingered over her moist, pink lips, "why he is so much better than me? Is he handsomer? Wealthier?"

"None of that means anything to me," she spat. "If you knew me, you would never dare insult me with such innuendos."

"Then what can it be?" he asked, determined to be without mercy, even if it cost him his pride, a strip of his hide. Damn it, he could no longer go on wondering what this man was, how he could provoke her to such lengths of loyalty, when he would do anything—*anything*—for her, and yet she would not give him one glance.

"Your grace, this is not at all proper."

"But you don't like it when I'm proper. You think me a prig, remember?"

"I think the whiskey has made you say things that you will regret upon the morrow."

"You think this is all the work of liquor, do you?"

"Of course." She gazed at him with something like pity. "Obviously it has made you not in your right mind. If you were, then you would not be here. I would not be here, and we would not be having this conversation in this home, under these very peculiar, not to mention potentially destructive, circumstances. You do realize how this appears, do you not? If we were to be discovered—"

"I don't give a damn how it appears, and every demon in hell could descend upon this room and I won't give a farthing until I know if his touch makes your heart flutter. If his kisses leave you witless, breathless, aching for more."

She blinked, her lips parted, breath stilled for a fraction of a second. Adrian didn't dare blink, for fear he would miss some nuance of need. A flicker of desire. Her mouth opened, worked, but no words, no sounds were emitted from her beckoning mouth—she just studied him, and he moved closer, insinuating himself to stand between her thighs and loom over her, taking up the space between them.

"Do his hands touch you, caress you so softly you want to weep, to shudder in anticipation? Do you let down your hair for him? Does he brush it over your shoulder and allow his fingers to skim over the delicate curve of your arm? Does he kiss your neck, whisper in your ear?"

"Your grace…" she murmured as she stared intimately into his eyes, seeing something, something he didn't want her to know. But he was too far gone to think. To see the look of fear in her eyes. He'd been deprived too long. And yes, the whiskey was swimming in his blood, not intoxicating him, but giving him the courage to shed his reputation for politeness and solicitude, and give free rein to the darker needs and passions that were festering inside him—needs that had always been there, the ones he had been forced to hide from the world.

"Does he murmur all those naughty, highly improper things he had dreamt about? Does he tell you in a most ungentlemanly fashion of all the things he wants to do to you, wicked, wicked things involving beds and settees and darkened corners?" She gasped and color infused her cheeks. "How he wants to give you the greatest pleasure of your life, to feel you squeeze around him as he merges his body with yours?"

Tilting her chin up, he cradled her cheek, allowing his gaze to roam freely over her flushed face.

"Tell me, Lucy," he asked as his mouth descended in a slow slide, "does his kiss feel like this?"

The feel of her satiny lips against his made him moan. She did not pinch them together, but left them soft, pliable, and he deepened the kiss, mouth opening, tongue aching to reach deep inside, to lose himself to a place he thought never to go, a place to return to, where he had felt solace and warmth and love...

Lucy was caught in a sensual haze. She had never before been spoken to in such a brazen manner as the duke had just spoken to her. It caused a strange tingling in her belly. His mouth on hers only heightened the feeling, and she tipped her chin up, brushing her mouth against his, as he slowly widened his lips across hers. She wanted more of it, a deeper intimacy, and she pressed forward, her breasts thrusting upward, which made him growl deeply, an answering echo in her own body.

"Yes." His hand left the arm of her chair, only to wrap gently around her throat, his thumb placed directly over the pulse that beat hard and fast. "Reach for me," he murmured wickedly, as his palm smoothed down the column of her neck to the expanse of skin above her bodice. Her body jolted and she pressed in, her hands bound behind her back, making her spine arch, and her modest bosom thrust forward. His moan was deep, guttural, making her own body answer to it, while his lips caressed, teased, his tongue making decadent little sweeps across her lips.

His control was rigid, and she felt...so out of control, especially with the cravat tied around her hands. She mewled, tried to inch to the edge of the chair, to feel his tongue surge within her mouth, and his hand pressed deeper into her skin. But he was patient, making her wait, teasing her, and she would not cry out, not plead with him.

"Tell me," he murmured against her mouth as his palm slowly descended to the front of her bodice, leaving his fingers to trail lightly over her breastbone. "Does he inflame you like this? I've barely kissed you and I can feel you panting for more."

Oh, she wanted to hate him for that! Wanted to tell him to go to the devil, and if she wasn't a lady, she would spit in his face for that. But strangely, bound like this, with him looming over her, large, and masculine, and utterly controlled, the quip only aroused her more. He was dominant, she the supplicant, and it felt...strangely compelling, and sensual, and unbearably erotic. She, Lucy Ashton, cool, aloof and always in control, giving up her control, and...aroused by it.

"I will keep you here all night until you say it, Lucy."
His voice dropped to a seductive purr, and the cool of
his gray eyes was replaced with molten silver that made
his eyes glitter, and the scar in his dark brow all the
more alluring for the danger it represented. His hand, so
big and strong, slipped down until he brushed his palm
over the small rise of her breast. Closing her eyes, her
head tipped to the side, and she did nothing but enjoy
his touch. The soft but seductive way he flattened then
plumped her small breast.

Nudging her head back, his mouth sought the sen-
sitive patch of skin behind her ear. His tongue trailed
out and she jumped as he made little circles with the
tip. She was aware suddenly that he had hooked his fingers beneath the sleeve of her gown and was baring her
shoulder as his mouth descended in a series of kisses
and licks, a pattern that was making her writhe in the
chair.

When his mouth arrived at her shoulder, he licked
then sucked the rounded curve, making her moan out
loud, while the entire time he palmed her breast.

She couldn't remember what they had been talking
of. She was supposed to be answering something—a
very improper, smug question, but she couldn't think
clearly enough to remember it exactly. She was caught
up in a swirl of feelings that ranged from weakness to
strength to longing to fear.

She had never been this exposed—not even naked.
Thomas had excited her, had aroused her passion, but
never like this. This… What the duke was making her
feel was quite terrifying—and addicting, for she wanted

more, and more, to never stop feeling the heady sensations.

His lips were making slow progress to the center of her chest, his palm still a heavy, insistent presence. Despite the fact that he was so much taller than her, he did not drop to his knees, but loomed over her, his head between her breasts, the silken stands of his onyx-colored hair sliding against her chin and cheeks. She could feel the movement of his head—could watch but could not touch or clasp him to her. She was immobile, a supplicant for his pleasure. He would claim, take, press upon her kisses and touches, and she could do nothing to stop him. And it excited her to know it. To sit as still and quiet as a statue and watch him, study his face, how his eyes were closed, how his lips looked against the paleness of her shoulder and chest. And then suddenly—and she couldn't understand how or when he had done it—the bodice of her gown slipped down, leaving her in her chemise. She had not bothered with a corset this evening—the gown and her modest breasts had not required it. She was left sitting there helpless as the duke pulled back slightly and stared at the dark shadows beneath the fine lawn. Puzzled, he glanced up at her, then with a wicked smile, he lowered his head to her breast, turning his face to the side, so she could watch his every torment, and licked the straining tip until the lawn was more than damp—it was wet, and it was clinging to her ruched nipples.

"How interesting," he whispered as his thumb circled the small tip. Her body answered, her core clenching and dampening. His gaze had flickered to hers, and she knew she should look away, but she couldn't. Thomas had been disappointed when he had seen her. He hadn't said the words, per se, but she had seen it in his eyes. She wondered if Sussex would feel the same.

"Beautiful and dark," he murmured as he watched his thumb touch her nipple. "Such a lovely surprise when I have always imagined your nipples to be a pale pink or a lovely coral. But this…dark and mysterious, a dichotomy for one so fair."

She had always hated her breasts, small and insignificant with dark nipples that stood out against her flesh. "Please, don't," she whimpered when she saw him reach for the strap. His gaze flew to hers, she saw something there, he looked…stricken.

"I cannot leave tonight without seeing them. Touching them."

Cool air kissed her skin, and Lucy was mortified to discover her breast bared, a small little apple cupped in his hand, with a dark berry for a nipple.

"Cherries," he murmured as his thumb and forefinger gently pinched and pulled, making the nipple less rounded, and longer. Then his mouth lowered and she watched with shock and fascination as his tongue caressed the tip, circling around, making her hips move. Arched as she was, it appeared that she was offering herself to him, and he growled, noticing her position, too. He was still bent over her; she could still watch him pleasure her with his mouth, still unable to touch him—to only endure what he would give her. And he was taking his sweet time about, too!

Finally he kissed the tip, brought it into his mouth to suckle, and she watched, wicked creature that she was, she watched as her dark nipple was pulled into his mouth, and escaped with a little pop, only to be drawn back, and in the process repeated until she was moving her hips to the rhythm of his mouth. He was playing with her, and he seemed fascinated by it all. His eyes had stayed focused on her breast, and that one dark nipple he had made plump and big, which he toyed with mercilessly.

It was not enough. She needed more, and with her hands tied, she had little room, so she began to rock, the hardness of the chair, the slide of her linen chemise creeping between thighs eased, yet heightened some of the unbearable ache that was building as he worked his way to torment her other breast.

And before she knew it, her vision dimmed, and she cried out, terrified of what was happening. This had never happened with Thomas.

"What have you done to me?" she cried, and then began to shake. From a distance she heard the duke's voice. "Yes, yes, just like that." She was practically incoherent, but still she was aware when he told her to move her bottom closer to the edge of the chair—how she was cognizant enough to follow his direction, she had no clue. She felt his arm around her waist, pulling her forward, his knee nudging between her thighs, widening them, the hardness of his thigh riding against her sex—the chemise rubbing between her folds. His mouth was raining havoc on her nipple, his thigh creating release—and ecstasy—between her legs.

"Yes, like that," he was encouraging her in a deep whisper. "Shatter for me. Let me watch."

Her back was arching more, her rhythm—no rhythm at all, just fast, furious jerks of her hips that were uncoordinated movements, until his hand firmly planted on her waist, his fingers biting into her waist as he took over the task for her, moving her forward and back, onto his thigh as he commanded the rhythm.

"Damn, you are hotter than hell itself like this," he murmured over her breast. "Come for me, little Lucy, show me the fire that burns in you."

And then it happened: a feeling of utter euphoria, of floating weightlessly—not a care in the world. She was aware of Sussex there, holding her, keeping her safe, and then she was falling over a sort of precipice, shaking and trembling, and he was there, whispering in her ear, encouraging her to risk the leap. She didn't want to, didn't want to give that up, afraid of allowing herself to fall over that cliff where the future was unseen and unknown.

"Lucy," the duke whispered hotly in her ear, a beckoning voice that her body wanted to obey. "Come for me." He flicked, thumbed her nipple, the wetness of his tongue against her lips, the ride of his thigh brought her up once more to the point she couldn't think or see, only feel. "Yes," he whispered. "Give this to me—your first climax."

She didn't want him to know that, that Thomas had never brought her to this point. She hadn't known that this point even existed back then, but now that she did, she could not bear the shame of having Sussex know that what she and Thomas shared had actually lacked something so dark and complex, so elemental—so passionate. And then, she could no longer think, or dissect, could only allow him to coax her into taking that step over the cliff. She was alone in this, and she was afraid.

"Trust me," he whispered again. "I'll catch you when you come down."

And then she did something so strange, so frightening that she could only squeeze her eyes tight and let herself go as it happened—she fell, and all the while she was conscious of the duke's eyes upon her, watching her. "So beautiful," he murmured, awe in his voice.

"Adrian!" she cried. Not "your grace," or "Sussex," but his Christian name, and it terrified her that she even knew it. As she crested, and tumbled, she called his name again, only to find herself freed, her hands thrown around his neck as he lifted her from the chair, and moved with her so swiftly that she found herself pressed up against the wall, her legs wrapped around his waist, her skirts and chemise raised and the slit in her drawers opened wide, and the feel of Adrian's woolen trousers, his phallus hard and unyielding rubbing against her as his fingers pressed into her bottom.

"I want to come with you, to share this first time with you," he growled before capturing her lips and devouring them with a hard and demanding kiss as he rubbed relentlessly against her, thrusting her up against the wall as they shared lips and tongues and breaths. And then they were sharing something so intimate that Lucy could only breathe his name, and listen as Adrian's breath stopped altogether—the silence hung by a thread, and the world ceased to turn as their eyes opened and heat and wetness pooled between them, and they fell over the cliff together, her wrapped tightly around Sussex, a man she hadn't wanted to like, let alone trust. She looked into his eyes, and saw something deeper than she ever had before.

CHAPTER FOURTEEN

"YOU WILL NEVER believe the news!"

Lucy glanced up from the copper-colored satin that was piled on the worktable before her. It was early morning, and she had not slept a wink since Sussex had driven her home. What an uncomfortable situation that had been. Both had sat in the darkness of the carriage, silent, gazing out the window, wondering what should be said to the other. In mute agreement, they had decided that no words were necessary. For Lucy, she was still suffering from the effects of what Sussex had informed her was *la petite morte*. The little death. An apt analogy, for she had felt as though she was dying—the most pleasurable, earth-shattering death a soul could hope for—and it was all courtesy of the Duke of Sussex!

The sound of the chamber door opening and closing thankfully pulled her from reliving those moments in Sussex's house, and the brazen and shocking way she had so easily fallen for his touch, and his lips, and the way he had looked pleasuring her. She still trembled even just thinking of the way those black lashes caused shadowed crescents over his cheeks, not to mention how perfect it had felt to watch him, and feel the tiny movements in his body, the way his muscles trembled and flickered. She still hadn't the strength to think about the events against the wall!

"Issy," she remarked in surprise. "What are you doing here at this time of the morning?"

Isabella glanced at the wrapper Lucy was wearing. "Is that another creation? My goodness, all that lace—*stunning!*"

She pulled the wrapper a bit tighter around her modest bosom, her nipples still feeling slightly tender from the duke's ravaging lips and tongue. Frowning at the answering echo in her belly at the memory of his grace's exceptionally talented mouth, Lucy glanced out the window, then at the clock. "Issy, is something wrong? It's barely ten in the morning!"

"Of course not, silly." Her cousin breezed into the small salon that she used to sew her gowns and also where she kept her collection of dolls and dollhouses. "Oh, what a gorgeous color, such a beautiful burnished gold, and that black lace—how are you going to use it? As a flounce?"

"On the sleeve," she murmured, perplexed. "Really, Issy, you're making me uneasy. What are you doing here so early? Not that you're not welcome, but…but…"

"Yes, I know, Black has a terrible habit of keeping me in bed till noon, but today is different."

Lucy watched as her cousin pulled a side chair over to the worktable. Plopping herself down, Isabella began sorting through the assorted fabrics Lucy was using. "What will this gown be for, *hmm?*"

"Issy, what the devil is wrong?" Sudden suspicion rose in her mind. "Does Black know you're here?"

"Goodness, why does my husband need to know that

I've made an early call? I have my own mind, Lucy—I haven't quite given it over to my husband, yet."

"He'll worry if he awakes to find you've left without telling him."

Issy waved away her concern. "We shared an early breakfast and then he took himself off to Sussex's. I presume they are discussing the matter that I am trying to parlay to you."

"Well?"

Isabella looked to each side of the room for any un-noticed and obviously unwanted servants then leaned closer, closing the space between them and the table. "I have gossip."

Smiling despite still feeling confused and angry at the duke and herself, Lucy prodded, "About what?"

"The Guardians, this Orpheus fellow and the marquis, behaving very badly."

The soft hairs on Lucy's neck rose in alarm. "Orpheus?"

Nodding, Issy continued to fidget with loose threads of the silk. "Last night Black received a missive—from Sussex I believe—asking if Black would see to the task of assisting Alynwick."

"With what?"

"A duel," Issy whispered, her eyes wide with shock, and perhaps excitement. "With Lord Larabie of all people."

"No!" Lucy replied. But Isabella shook her head that she spoke the truth.

"Black left almost immediately, and naturally I could not sleep for worrying about him. I know nothing of duels, other than that they are a stupid means of assuaging a man's honor, and someone usually winds up hurt, or dead. So, I spent the remainder of the night awake and writing, trying to get my mind off the horrors of it all. Then Black returned."

"And?"

Her cousin's eyes were bright with excitement. "He told me everything. Apparently Alynwick was dead drunk, and Black feared the marquis wouldn't be able to hold the gun, let alone fire it. My husband said he was in quite a foul mood—a 'blazing rage' is how Black described it."

"Strange," Lucy murmured, "he didn't appear drunk last night when I saw him."

"Where, Lucy?"

It was Lucy's turn to lower her voice in case any of the upstairs maids might be walking by, or lingering about the hall seeing to their duties. "At the Sumners' musicale. He quite barged in and made a scene. Lizzy was strolling with the Earl of Sheldon, to whom she had only just been introduced, and then Alynwick came in, stalked over and quite tore Lizzy from Sheldon, and then proceeded to slam the poor earl up against the wall. Not only that, Alynwick thrust his arm against Sheldon's throat as if he were going to murder him!"

"Poor Lizzy!" Issy whispered. "What was that brute Alynwick thinking to have caused such a scene, and by putting Lizzy's reputation in jeopardy?"

Lucy thought back to the carriage ride home from the musicale. Elizabeth had sat beside her, tense and unusually quiet. They'd left the Sumners' house in a flurry, but the ride home had been quiet—too quiet, as if Lizzy hadn't trusted herself to speak, especially with

Sussex present. "I do believe that Lizzy was seething from it all."

"And Sussex?"

She would really rather not think of the duke, or speak of him. Her feelings were still raw and confused, and she was not yet ready to begin delving deep to sort them. "I cannot say what was going on in Sussex's mind. I do know that he pulled Alynwick off of the earl, but then the two of them disappeared, and I did not see Sussex again until he climbed up into the carriage with Lizzy and me. I have no notion what was said or what transpired between them. In any event, I was seeing to Elizabeth, who was quite distraught over the earl—I think she really fancied him, Issy, and was absolutely mortified by Alynwick showing up and acting as he did. She fears the earl will never want to see her or call upon her after this."

"Oh, dear. This is disastrous."

"Indeed. Now, the duel, was it a success? What happened?"

Isabella waved her hand in dismissal. "As is typical for this sort of thing—well, according to Black, at least—both Larabie and Alynwick counted their paces, turned and fired, both bullets going wide. No one was hit, honor was satisfied and the matter is now solved."

"Really? How anticlimactic. One would think that a husband catching another man ravishing his wife would be slightly more incensed, and would warrant more than a stray bullet in some farmer's field," Lucy mumbled. "At the very least, a sound pounding is in order, I believe."

Issy shrugged. "It does seem rather like a lot of effort

if one is not going to take matters seriously. I do agree,
a sound trouncing seems much more effective in preventing any future dalliances than firing your pistol
willy-nilly into the dawn sky."

"Men," Lucy grunted miserably. "They are all a
strange lot. I don't think I'll ever understand them."

"It's part of their allure to females, I think. They
are a puzzle that will never be solved, and as women,
we always want to put them to rights and fix them and
protect them from themselves."

Something about Issy's analogy struck her deeply.
She found herself shocked, thinking of Thomas, and
she couldn't understand why. For eight months she had
sought to find him, had mourned him, and now…now
she wanted…what, exactly? If it were true that she had
desired him in the physical, emotional sense, she would
have not fallen for Sussex's seduction so easily. She
would have railed and fought as best she could, but she
hadn't. What did that say about her? Was it just female
instinct to protect? Did she see Thomas as weaker than
Sussex, and was that the reason she was striving to
shield him? Frowning, she bit her lip and tried to make
sense of it all. Damn Sussex, she thought miserably, he
had confused everything, had made a hash of her careful plans and controlled emotions.

"Well," Issy continued on, barely pausing to notice
that Lucy had momentarily been thinking of other
things, "Alynwick has no right to get himself involved
with a duel, when this Guardian business should be his
first concern. But, more importantly, he has no right
to tear Lizzy away from anyone. Black is correct, Alynwick has become a liability—his drinking is out of

control, Black says, and his reckless ways might not only expose the Brethren, but get himself, or someone else, killed."

The image of the duke dead came unbidden and unwanted and she thrust it away, focusing instead on her conversation with Issy. "There was something unholy in Alynwick's eyes last night. I saw it—something very dark and troubling, as if he were possessed by demons."

"And that is just it," Issy whispered while she reached for her hand. Squeezing it, Lucy felt the anguish in her cousin's touch. "I was literally ill with fear last night. I begged Black to let me help with the Brethren Guardians but he says he won't expose me. But I'm afraid. I mean, dragging my husband to the scene of a duel? Appearing drunk and reckless? I'm afraid, Luce, that the marquis might do something to endanger my husband's safety. I won't stand for him being a Brethren Guardian if Alynwick is going to put him in danger."

Patting her cousin's hand, Lucy tried to find the right words to placate her. "Black is a smart, powerful man, Issy. He's been a Guardian all his life. I'm quite certain he can handle Alynwick."

"I'm certain he can, too, but this investigation and Orpheus has him distracted."

Lucy felt a measure of guilt by asking this, but she felt compelled to. Especially after what happened last night between her and Sussex. "What of Orpheus? What news is there?"

Issy glanced up. Lucy could see it in her eyes: Isabella was uncertain whether or not to tell her.

"Issy, I know that I cannot undo the past. I stole the pendant that Black and his family have kept hidden. I took the seed inside and it was wrong of me. I know you've been told not to say anything, but I swear to you, I do not want to bring down the Brethren Guardians." *Just discover once and for all if Thomas is really part of it all.* And that was the truth. Sometime in the past two days, the truth had become her focus. Thomas was alive, so why had he hidden from her? And Sussex, would he lie to her about what he'd witnessed? The blind faith she once had had in Thomas was crumbling, leaving too many questions unanswered—and too many perplexing feelings about his grace.

"Alynwick," Issy began, "has found a way to infiltrate the club. They'll be going in a few days to capture him. I don't know more than that. It's all Black would say."

A few days... Good Lord, she needed those answers, and soon. She must find a way to meet with Thomas. He wasn't Orpheus.

"What on earth is this?" Isabella asked suddenly with a little laugh as she held up a piece of wood. "My goodness, I doubt you found this at Albright's Toy Emporium."

As kindly as she could, she said, "Please be careful, Issy, please do. Just set it back down, it's fragile."

Isabella glanced at her quizzically as she obeyed Lucy's command. "All right then, there it is, back in its linen nest. But tell me, where did you get it? I've never seen it amongst your dollhouse treasures before."

Lucy stared at the adorably disproportioned doll piece. It was a four-poster bed that was knobby and nicked, one tester much wider than the other three. It was the dearest little piece she had.

"You've never seen it before," she said on a sigh, "because my father discovered that I had been given it as a gift by someone he deemed unsuitable, and he tore it from my hands and tossed it into the rubbish as if it were no more important than a potato peeling."

"That's what I think of your gift, girl, as well as the gifter. Not fit for naught more than rubbish. And as for you, boy," her father had railed, *"I'll teach you a thing or two about your betters."* Her father's hand had come down hard on Gabriel's head, his heavy signet ring slicing his face, the blood dripping down his cheek. *"Leave and never come back, or I'll have you hanging from the gallows and swinging in the wind for this. The impertinence of you, presenting something such as this to the daughter of a lord, thinking you might have her. Her future is with a duke, boy, not some filthy urchin from the parish stews."*

And then Gabriel had left, his sad eyes boring into hers. He had not said goodbye, and the fact still haunted her.

She had never seen him again; the toy bed was the only tangible connection she had to him.

"Oh," Isabella said. There was a wealth of meaning behind that word. "I see."

"The person who gave it to me—" the words were thick and choking as she tried to stem the pain that came with the memory "—was my one true friend. Before you came to live with me, that is."

Isabella reached for her, and for once, Lucy gripped her cousin's fingers, not the other way around. This morning, Lucy needed Isabella's calm, and her understanding. "After Papa punished me, I stayed up in my room and waited till night, and then I went outside and rifled through that waste bin to find it. A rat was nibbling away at a piece of meat that landed on it, you can see his teeth marks in the footboard, but I kicked him off and snatched the bed before the greedy rodent could run for it. I've hidden it away ever since."

"Lucy, what a terrible thing to have happen. I'm sorry."

"That was—is—my life, Issy. While you might have been raised poor, you at least had affection from your mother. I was raised in an institution. It's called the ton, and it allows a young girl with an abundance of dreams and hopes very little chance of obtaining them—not if there is any substance to those dreams," she added as an afterthought. "If my dreams were only to marry well, I could have had that my first Season."

"What are you dreams, Luce? I don't think you've ever spoken of them."

It must be the exhaustion that was making her tongue loose. Or maybe she was tired in another way— the way the spirit and soul fatigue from years of coldness and isolation.

"I've given up on them," she whispered, unable to speak in her normal tone for fear Issy would hear her voice break. "It doesn't matter now."

"Doesn't it?" Issy forced Lucy to look her in the eye. "I think it's never been more important, Luce. You've dragged this piece out of hiding for a reason."

Smiling sadly, she looked at the comical, misshapen bed. "It gives me comfort, I think. Makes me think back to a time when I was truly happy, when I believed that I…mattered to someone."

When she looked up it was to see Issy's eyes filling with tears. "You do matter, Lucy. You matter so much to me, and it is killing me, absolutely destroying me to see you in so much pain. Find your dreams," she whispered. "Resurrect the old ones, but please…find that place that brings you peace. The past cannot be undone, I know that. But the pain of it can be healed."

Swiping at her eyes before the tears could fall, Lucy looked down at their locked hands. "I used to dream of a garden, filled with roses and wisteria, and a lavender path and a lovely fence made of stone, with a white gate that creaked when you opened it. And beyond the gate was a white gabled cottage, made of ancient stones, and large windows that overlooked the rolling hills of the countryside. I used to imagine myself puttering in the garden, while children dressed in white dresses and white short pants played merrily around me. And then I would glance up and see him standing there, watching me…and I…and I saw the love shining in his eyes. The acceptance of his place alongside me. Silly, romantic drivel," she sniffed, as she waved her hand before her eyes. "Such a girlish, nonsensical dream."

"To wish for a husband who loves you? Children, made with the man you love? A home that feels warm and inviting, cozy and lived in, instead of a showpiece in the heart of Mayfair?" Issy asked. "Luce, it's not nonsensical, it's simple and warm, and it's the furthest thing from what you had as a child."

"It is the dream of a country-bred miss," she muttered. "Ladies of my class must aspire to a dukedom, a monstrosity of limestone and long galleries decorated with portraits of dead relatives. It is separate chambers, separate social schedules, separate lives, except for the matter of the heir—then we might meet and join in conjugal relations until I am with child. And then, after, my husband will amuse himself with his mistress until the next time a child is desired, leaving me to spend my days and nights alone, a lonely bird in a gilded cage. But I would live in a dirty old stoop if I could have a mate who regarded me with a little more than just a sense of duty."

"Oh, Luce, you will have that!"

Lucy smiled sadly. "No, I will not. I've gone cold inside, I had to. When you're cold, the pain doesn't penetrate, the sense of loss cannot break through. There are no dreams. Only realities. But I learned something that day, when my father broke my heart and shattered everything that I used to dream of in the night—I learned that I would not allow him to control me entirely. I know my duty, and I will perform it, but I will not just give up my life to a man he deems perfect. I won't give him that, allowing him to choose who I will wed, who I will lie in bed with and who will father my children. I will appease some of his dictates, but not all."

Issy bit her lip. "And the duke, Luce? Where does he fit into all this?"

She thought of Mrs. Fraser for some strange reason, and the eyes she had seen flash before her during the trance. She thought of her friend, standing in the door, crushed when her father had stormed into the kitchen and mocked the gift—then mocked her friend. She thought of Thomas, and what she had not shared with him—then allowed herself to think of Sussex, and what she had experienced with him.

No answer came, only confusion and the mad thumping in her heart. Reaching for the wooden piece, she cradled it carefully, allowed the peace and calm it always gave her to infuse her soul.

"I don't know," she said at last. "I...I don't want to know, really."

The door opened, and Sybilla barged in, carrying a letter. She was out of breath, Lucy realized, and she stood up abruptly, wondering if it was about her father. Why she thought that, she had no idea.

"A message boy just brought this around," she gasped, clearly out of breath from running up flights of stairs. "It's urgent, I'm told."

Reaching for the letter, Lucy scanned the contents, then felt her blood boil. "Sybilla, come along. I need you."

Oooh, he was not going to get away with this.

CHAPTER FIFTEEN

BLOODY HELL, HE'D done it now, lost his head. Groaning with the realization of it all, he wiped his palms down his face, trying to collect himself, and forget about those incredibly arousing moments when he was rocking his body against Lucy.

Lost his head, and then some, he thought. How could he have let it go so far? It was just bloody good luck he had happened to have an extra set of trousers at the house because his... Well, he just couldn't have escorted Lucy home in the state he had been in. He hadn't handled matters well. Hell, he hadn't even talked to her, but he hadn't trusted himself. He had wanted to hold her for longer, to sit her on his lap and whisper that he would take care of everything, that they would be married. Something had made him keep his mouth shut—tightly. Telling Lucy that they were going to marry wouldn't win her over to him—despite what they had shared. And asking...well, she hadn't looked in the mood to entertain an offer. She looked perplexed by the whole thing.

One thing he had been certain of was that *Thomas* hadn't bothered to pleasure Lucy to climax. Bastard! She'd been utterly shocked, and terrified of the experience, but it had given him such strength, such pride to know that he was the first man to pleasure her to such passion. The knowledge had made him reckless, and he had not thought of anything but making the experience nothing less than earth-shattering for her. Unfortunately it wasn't part of the plan for him to shatter in his trousers. But he could not regret it. Watching her come had been the most beautiful thing in the world to him. It likely always would be.

"What's with you?" Black demanded. "Are you ill?"

He had nearly forgotten he had company. He wished they would sod off and leave him in peace so he could relive every single second of last night with Lucy.

Nursing the effects of overindulgence was something the Duke of Sussex had very little experience with—and he was making a bloody hash of it, truth be told. But nursing said overindulgence while staring down his fellow Guardians was truly something he had no experience—or patience—with.

Black and Alynwick had barged into his study not more than ten minutes before, rousing him, perturbing him and downright irritating him.

"What the devil d' ye think ye were doing, fobbing me off at Grantham Field?" Alynwick asked indignantly. "Ye were supposed to be my second!"

"No," Adrian growled impatiently, "one of us was supposed to be your second, and because you showed up at the Sumner's musicale, drunk and itching for a fight, I had to bodily remove you from said musicale, and was, ergo, not able to perform as your second when I wanted to shoot you my goddamn self!" he roared.

"I wasn't drunk," Alynwick grumbled. "Itchin' for a fight, aye, but no' drunk."

"Careful," Black said with some amusement, "your

cultured English accent is giving way to your heathen Highland one."

Black was hardly helping. After sending the earl a glare, Adrian settled his dark expression upon Alynwick. "Surely you did not believe that it was the thing to do to be your second after the stir you caused at the Sumner's? Everyone saw what happened, and how I had to remove your arm from Sheldon's throat!"

"Get to the point, ye windbag."

He'd had it with Alynwick, and the events that had led to this impromptu early-morning visit and the disruption of his musings of Lucy. "My point, you infuriating brute, is this. We are not supposed to be anything more than acquaintances in the eyes of the ton. We're to pretend that our own private circles do not cross, so no one will suspect our true purpose—in ways we have all vowed never to reveal. And then you stroll in and force my hand, making my sister the object of ridicule and gossip, and you wonder why I didn't come and perform as your second! The reason, you Highland ninny, is simple, because no one would believe it! No one would think it plausible that we were out for a pint, met up, and I just merrily agreed to travel at dawn to some godforsaken farmer's field to aid you in putting a bullet hole in someone when not four hours before you were importuning my sister and nearly killing the Earl of Sheldon!"

Black's gaze volleyed between them then he groaned. "Alynwick, you didn't. Good God, you did, didn't you?"

The marquis was not chastened, and more to the point, he looked like he was ready to fight again. "You didn't force me away from anything," he sneered, "I *allowed* you to tear me off that piece of trash."

"And how do you know anything about Sheldon," Sussex growled, "when your face is constantly gazing into the bottom of a whiskey decanter?"

Alynwick lunged over the desk, but Black caught him by the coat, and hauled him back. "None of that, now," he grunted as he tossed Alynwick into the chair, who only tried to stand right back up. "Stay!" Black shouted, pointing at the marquis as if he were a biddable canine.

"I'm no' a bloody mongrel to heed your commands."

"Really?" Black straightened his waistcoat and resumed his seat. "You look like something that's been roaming the street for weeks. Where did you go after my carriage dropped you off après duel?"

"You don't want to know."

"By the stench of you, I think I already do."

Alynwick sent Black a glare, then slid deeper into his chair, his big hands rifling through his hair.

"Good God, Alynwick, what the devil were you thinking coming to the Sumners' and stirring up that scene? It'll be in all the gossip rags this morning, and we don't need that kind of exposure. Damn you!" Sussex growled.

Now sulking and brooding, and definitely looking capable of murder, the marquis stared out the window. "A provocation, I believe." He was under control now, his brogue banished. "I was never good at resisting taunts."

"Taunts?" Black asked, his brow quizzical as he looked between Alynwick and Sussex. Adrian just shrugged. He had no idea what Alynwick meant by that, and his head hurt too damn much to reason it through. All he wanted was a bit of sulphur tonic and his bed with cool sheets and his mind filled with lovely dreams of Lucy.

"I told you," Alynwick growled with quiet menace, "to leave her out of this."

"We're afraid, old boy, that neither one of us understands a damned thing coming out of your mouth."

"Elizabeth!" The name was said in a rage, making Sussex sit back in his chair. "Damn you both, don't you know the trouble she can get into? It could make matters worse for us. She has no place in this matter."

"Dear me," came a sweetly feminine voice from the doorway. "All this roaring and fighting, it's awakened the entire house."

Adrian saw the way Alynwick stiffened, but he kept his gaze focused on the gray streaks of daylight breaking through the rain clouds.

"Elizabeth, do come in," he said.

"I'll be on my way, then," the marquis muttered, rising.

"Really, Alynwick, don't be so childish. Do you think I am naive? I know exactly what you think of me, my infirmity and my limited skill in aiding your cause. You don't have to go slinking off because I've overheard you."

"My apolo—"

"I don't require that, either," she said. "Because it's a lie. You aren't sorry. It's what you feel. Don't bother to deny it."

"You have no idea what I fe—"

With a slight wave of her hand, she effectively cut him dead, and the expression on the marquis's shocked and indignant face gave Sussex his first grin of the day.

"Do carry on," Lizzy ordered. "I only came for a cup of tea. Mrs. Hammond claims to have brought you a tray, and I don't want to wait for another one to be sent up."

Black did the honors pouring, and would have carried it out for her, but Sussex knew his sister was too proud. So he watched as Black carefully passed her the cup and saucer, her fingers securely holding the handle. "Now then, keep it down, if you please, or the servants will be privy to everything. I heard two maids giggling as I approached the study, no doubt they were spying. As an aside, Lucy and I will be meeting today. It's likely she'll come here, so I hope the three of you make yourself scarce, because I plan on quizzing her about matters."

"What matters?" Alynwick demanded.

"That, my lord, is none of your concern. Seek your own clues and I will seek mine. Now, then, come along, Rosie," she said regally, and obeying her ladyship, the spaniel nudged Lizzy in the right direction, far away from anything that might impede Lizzy's elegant exit.

"Damned female," Alynwick grunted, "a curse and pox on headstrong women who won't be led by a man."

"I daresay you'll have half the women of London sporting pox marks and curses, Alynwick."

The marquis scowled at Black, but continued to watch Lizzy disappear beyond the door. Lizzy was a strong woman, Adrian always admired that about her, but lately he'd tested the waters with a strong-willed

female himself, and found it just as annoying as Alynwick was finding his sister. Yes, he thought, remembering the events of last night. Oh, yes, a curse and a
pox, and pounding head, not to mention a dull ache that
continued to throb in his nether regions.

"Now then, if you please, gentlemen," Black murmured as he sat in the chair opposite Sussex's desk,
sipping away at his tea as though he were a damned
prince. "The task is done, the objective reached and
our mission can commence," he said smoothly. "I acted
as second, performed a credible act and now it, to be
clichéd, is all water under the bridge."

"Oh, go to hell, Black," Alynwick muttered as
he sunk farther into the chair that matched Black's.
"You're being a self-righteous bastard, and I'd love to
shove my fist in that smug face of yours."

Black's black brows rose over the rim of his teacup,
and Adrian groaned, closing his eyes while attempting
to work out the kinks in his neck, caused by an impru-
dent night's sleep on the library sofa.

"Aren't we all pleasantness this morning."

Sussex and Alynwick both grunted. Black, the bastard, looked fit and rested—and was unmercifully enjoying himself.

"So, what is our next move? Sussex, have you
learned any more about the coins or Orpheus?"

"As a matter of fact I have, just last night—"

"Your pardon, your grace," his butler said from the
door.

"What is it now?" he groaned, sending his young
butler, Hastings, scurrying behind the door, only to peer
around the wood.

"You have a caller."

"What?"

"A caller. A visitor," Hastings clarified as if Sussex were a dimwit.

"Now? At this hour?"

Lord, he had a devil of a headache, and he hadn't yet shaved, nor brushed his hair. He was a hell of a sight and didn't seem to care, either. It was most unseemly for the highly proper Duke of Sussex to be in dishabille, let alone allowing anyone to witness the state.

It also wasn't like him to drink to excess, but he had, when he had arrived home after depositing Lucy off after their... What the hell did he call what they did? He'd drank half a decanter of his finest single malt scotch if he remembered correctly. Hell, after that much he should be facedown, unconscious. But here he was, hung over and taciturn and itching for a fight.

"Your grace?" Hastings asked after discreetly clearing his throat. "Shall I send her on her way?"

Her? His head shot up from his hands, making him bilious with syncope and blurred vision. Perhaps he was still drunk. *Disgustingly drunk,* the little redheaded pixie had hurled at him with frank disgust. Only then, he hadn't been this drunk. What would she think of him now? he wondered.

Before he could tell Hastings to put his caller into a salon to await him, a vision in emerald-green velvet trimmed with black satin glided through the door, making Hastings grow white with horror.

"And what is the meaning of this?"

Lucy was in a rage. And she was staring at him with barely contained loathing.

"I do not," she spat, "respond to this sort of black-mail. Oh, good day, Lord Black, Lord Alynwick." She dropped a quick but polite curtsey then turned once more to face him. Slamming a folded piece of paper on his desk, Adrian winced as the sound of her delicate hands hitting wood ricocheted around his brain.

"Good morning, Lady Lucy, might I offer you some tea?"

"No, you may not." Her eyes were wild, sparkling like precious gems in the daylight. "You, your grace, may offer me an explanation."

She pointed to the letter, and he followed her finger with his gaze.

"Good Lord," she murmured. "Have you even been to bed?"

Reaching for the letter, he grumbled, "No, more's the pity." With a wave, he ushered his friends away, but they were being obtuse, or rather playing at it. When he sent them both a glare, they took their bloody time rising from the chairs, as if they were both moldering old arthritics.

They were just strolling across the study when Mrs. Hammond, his housekeeper, screamed with such a bloodcurdling howl that Sussex dropped the missive and jumped up from his chair, banging his knee in the process, causing him to release a litany of expletives that no lady at all should be privy to.

"Your grace," Mrs. Hammond shouted. "Oh, good God in heaven! Your grace! You must come!"

All of them ran into the hall only to find the plump housekeeper, her white linen cap askew, running down the hall from the kitchen. She was breathless, her arms flailing.

"What is it, Mrs. Hammond?" he asked, catching the woman by the shoulders.

"There now, lass," Alynwick said. "Take a deep breath and tell us. It can't be as bad as all this."

The housekeeper's brown eyes were wild with fear. Shaking her head, she looked between the marquis and himself. "Oh, it can, your lordship. It can be worse. Oh." She cried into her apron. "It's over there, your grace, at the door of the kitchen gardens. A dead body—oh, I shall never recover from it."

Adrian was first to reach the kitchen. He could see upon entering the room that the garden door was open, and a wheelbarrow heaped with leaves and twigs sat on the flag path.

"What is the meaning of this?" he growled as his boots rang shrill beats with his steps. When he reached the barrow he stopped—frozen. Blue satin spilled from the barrow, and he closed his eyes, and whispered a plea that it was not true.

Brushing the leaves away, Anastasia Lockwood was revealed, pale, bruised, and, unfortunately, dead.

He heard a gasp behind him—Lucy. He reached for her, thinking she might swoon, but Lucy was nothing if not made of stern stuff. She passed him, headed for the wheelbarrow before he could reach her.

"Oh, good God! Who is she?" Alynwick asked.

Adrian's heart stopped. He could not answer truthfully; it was too great a secret, and he couldn't risk revealing it. He considered telling Black and Alynwick that she had been his mistress but he couldn't do that with Lucy present—not after last night and the progress he sensed they had made.

"She's still warm," Lucy whispered, and she crossed herself, shuddering. "And look." Lucy pulled a folded letter from Ana's lax fingers. Passing it to him, Lucy watched him read it then shrieked as he lifted her off her feet and carried her into the house.

It might have been the redhead. We crossed paths, but I thought I'd give you one final warning. Send another spy to my club, and the redhead will suffer a fate far more painful than this one.

CHAPTER SIXTEEN

ADRIAN WAS AWARE of the curious faces staring at him—especially Lucy's. Lizzy and Isabella had joined them, although they stayed far away from the body. Lucy, however, was still at his side, right where he had put her when he released her from his arms. The anger that was evident when she had burst into his study was still there, still simmering, but there was pity there, too. Why, he could not fathom—unless of course she truly believed that Ana was his mistress.

As he stared down at Anastasia's lifeless body that had been carried into the house and carefully placed on a settee in the salon, he quietly contemplated it, the marks she bore and the awkward angle of her neck. The sparkle of life that had once shone in her eyes was gone, hidden by eyelids that would never open again.

There were bruises around her neck—she had been strangled. She still wore the diamond ear bobs and necklace she had been wearing last evening, and a gold House of Orpheus coin covered each closed eyelid. Gently he took them, and studied them in his palm. In that moment, he decided he already had enough secrets from his friends—and from Lucy. He didn't want this one, too.

"Her name is Anastasia Lockwood," he said as his thumb passed over the engraving of the coins. The name caused Elizabeth to gasp in recognition. "She was my father's mistress, and unknown to anyone—to us, and to your fathers—my father let Ana know of his past, and his duties as a Guardian."

"That son of a bitch!" Alynwick growled. "He took an oath."

"That poor woman," Lizzy murmured, interrupting the marquis's tirade. "I didn't know her, of course, but I knew my father, and putting up with him for all those years, only to wind up murdered…well, it's horrible." And then something shone in her eyes. "Why is she here, Adrian? What has led her to us?"

Adrian could not look at his sister, or anyone else. "She is dead because of me. Because she met a man who seduced her into going to the House of Orpheus, and I allowed it because she knew she could do more than just infiltrate the club—she could give us a first-hand account of Orpheus himself. What he looks like, his weaknesses, his strengths—any information that might have proved useful in his capture. She wanted to be of use to us, to repay me for… Well, for not turning her away after my father's death. I allowed it, even when I knew I shouldn't have."

Ana's death was just one more thing he would feel guilty about.

"Let's see how she died, perhaps her killer left some evidence."

Black stepped in and examined the body; Isabella let out a shriek and cried, "Oh, Black, no, you mustn't."

"You needn't worry, Issy. All will be well. Death is gone, I assure you." They shared a private glance then Black went back to examining the body. Alynwick stood looking down, watching him.

Black pointed to Ana's neck. "She's got a curious mark there, amongst the bruising on her throat, below her ear."

"What is it, Black?"

Shrugging, Black brushed back the golden hair that had come loose from her coiffure to reveal her throat. Issy and Lucy both gasped. "I can't make it out. It's a mark of some sort, but the impression is fading."

Stealing a glance at Lucy, to see how she was faring in this sordid scene, Sussex was shocked to see her brows arched in…annoyance before she swept past him, her hem rustling against the floor.

"My lord, may I?" Lucy demanded.

Black looked over his shoulder, seeking counsel. As if Sussex could stop Lucy from doing what she damned well pleased. He shrugged then nodded, watching Lucy studying Anastasia's body.

"We met last night. She informed me then of her plans. She was wearing the same gown. I must assume she was taken shortly after." He shuddered, thinking of Lucy on that very same street only minutes later. And the note he held in his hand. *It might have been the redhead.*

"You're correct about that, Sussex," Black said. "The coins make it certain that it was Orpheus, or someone involved with him. This was not a random murder. No footpad would be so inept as to leave the diamonds. It was Orpheus."

Lucy stopped what she was doing and glared at him. "Your grace—" she started to say, bent no doubt on

extolling the merits and saintly virtues of her ex-lover,
a lover, he might add, that by all accounts had been a
rather poor one, but one who Lucy still felt the need to
protect.

"Lucy," he pleaded, his head pounding. "Don't start.
Christ," he growled. "I didn't want this for her, to get
mixed up in our business."

"It sounds like she wanted to be of use, brother,"
Lizzy said. "She understood the risks."

"My father was a hard, intolerable man, and used
Anastasia for his own goods, barely ever sparing her a
thought. He didn't take care of her like a man of good
breeding and fortune should, so when she died, I bought
her a house, and gave her a pension. She claimed it was
her way of repaying me."

"She knew him." Black's gaze darkened. "He killed
her because she knew something."

Ana had known many things that, if brought to light,
would ruin him. For some reason, this Orpheus killed
her, and brought her to him. He had either seen her
with Adrian, which meant he was being followed, or
he knew more—secrets from the past, his deeper connection to Ana. And that was far more worrisome than
being followed.

"When she came to me last night, telling me that
she had met a man who was high up in the club—he'd
given her a coin, a token to gain entrance into the club."
They exchanged a look, him telling Lucy that he had
not forgotten she was out last evening because she was
supposed to be meeting the man he suspected was Orpheus, or that she, too, possessed a coin. Her hand flew

to her reticule, and he knew that she still had it, tucked safely away.

"How did she even know about this club, and Orpheus?" Alynwick questioned. Lucy decided then to turn her gaze upon him.

"I sought her out one evening to ask if she knew anything about the club. Ana was born in the East End and was familiar with the area, the people, and we needed a clue. We had nothing. She came to me last night to tell me that she had a way in. She showed me the coin and informed me that there is to be a meeting in the next few days. Orpheus will be there, and she was certain that she would be able to ferret out information for us. I told her it was too dangerous, but she was insistent. She left immediately afterward. I assumed she went back to her lodging, but…" He pointed to her form. "I cannot be sure. She has not been gone long," he commented, "for she is just now growing cold."

"Damn it, this is the last bloody thing we need," Alynwick said. "Christ, a dead body that most of the staff have been witness to. How the hell are we going to cover this mess up? The police cannot be called. It would not only implicate you, but perhaps Black and myself. Normally I wouldn't give a damn, but the gossipmongers might decide to investigate us, and that will not do."

"An actress," Lucy said suddenly as she bent to study Ana's neck once more. "Cast aside by the duke. In a fit of melodrama, she ended her life because the duke would not continue their affair."

Alynwick gazed at her with appreciation. "Yes…that might work. Go on."

"I will not have myself implicated in an affair," Adrian growled. "It would cast aspersions upon you, Lucy, since I've made my interest in you quite clear, and rather public."

The room fell silent, all eyes on him, except for those of Lucy, who waved off his comment.

"Tell the staff it was a lover's quarrel," Lizzy added. "They're faithful to you, Adrian, and would not breathe a word, especially when they learn that she's fallen."

"It doesn't matter what sort of woman she is, for God's sake! She's innocent, and I'll not make up such a story to save my own reputation! She suffered enough in her life at the hands of our father. I will not have her death marked by lies."

No one seemed to be listening to him, it seemed.

"The wounds are not apparent," Lucy continued, "but he could suggest to the housekeeper that once the body was moved, the source of her death was revealed. I imagine that women—especially actresses and mistresses—must do themselves in all the time when their aristocratic lovers will not have them."

It was the only way, and he loathed it. There was more to think of here than his pride. Protection for the Brethren, for Lizzy and Lucy, were paramount in this matter; he curled his lips in disgust anyway. "Not a mistress. I'd rather keep my *priggish* reputation, thank you. Make her an actress, but make it so that I would have nothing to do with her, and that was the reason she 'did herself in,' as you say."

"Yes, the staff will buy that. They certainly won't question it as much," Black murmured. "Tell them you're taking her body to her family, that the police are not needed in this matter."

"Black and I will bury her," Alynwick stated.

"Not a pauper's grave, but someplace pleasant," he heard himself say. "Someplace fitting, for she was... important. My father's mistress, but she didn't deserve this."

"Aye," Alynwick replied. "We'll find a place, and when we're done, we'll search her room. Sussex, you're to have nothing to do with investigating her death, or what evidence she might have left behind—we needn't have her connected to you in any way."

"Agreed."

"She was strangled," Lucy said, her voice cutting through the quiet. "The murderer is a Freemason."

There was a ripple of excitement in the room before Alynwick asked, "On what grounds do you think this?"

Lucy pointed to the mark a few inches below Ana's ear, and just above the bruising. "Made by an impression—a Masonic ring. I can see the compass and square quite clearly."

"Impossible," Alynwick scoffed. "Even if the villain came at her from behind, a ring would leave no such mark."

"I assure you. Here, allow me to demonstrate. Which of you are wearing your ring?" They all were; on the little finger of their right hands as was the Templar tradition.

"It doesn't mean a Freemason murdered the lass," Alynwick insisted. "Anyone could have set it up as such."

"A cowan?" she questioned. "Possible, but I doubt

it. It is a Freemason's greatest possession, is it not, an instrument used in your rites? You're to keep and protect it at all costs. No, I doubt an intruder into the lodge would be able to acquire such a thing. And he wouldn't have borrowed one, either."

"You know much about Freemasonry," Sussex assessed. "Did your father tell you?"

"Not its secrets, the things that are to be kept private between members, but some things, yes. Such as the story of Hiram Abiff, how he was King Solomon's chief architect, and held a secret of the craft. When he would not tell three of his apprentices that secret, they set upon him, murdering him. It's symbolic, Hiram's death, and this woman's, linked only by Freemasonry."

"I still can't fathom it," Alynwick grunted. "There's no possible—"

Sussex froze as Lucy reached for Alynwick's hand, the ring turned so that the insignia faced toward his palm, and placed his fingers around her throat. "Press," she ordered.

"Like hell!" Lunging forward, Adrian pulled Alynwick away from her then wheeled on Lucy. "Have you lost your bloody mind?"

"I am only trying to show you that the someone who murdered this woman was a Freemason."

With a huff, she reached for his hand, repeated the same actions as she had with Alynwick, only this time when she placed his palm on her throat, she held him there, her hand pressing against her delicate skin.

"Don't," he whispered, aware of the tone in the room. It was unbearably intimate, and he saw how Black and Isabella, and Alynwick, too, looked away from them. "Lucy," he whispered as he stepped closer to her, her hand still holding tightly against his. "Don't."

Their gazes locked, and finally she moved away, and his hand fell to his side.

"Well?" Tipping her head to the side, she allowed him to touch her throat with the tip of his fingers.

"Yes, the impression is there, faint, but present."

"You weren't trying to strangle me. It was just a slight press of your hand. Imagine what might be left behind if you had taken my throat in your hands with the intention of harming me."

"Good God, the chit's right!"

Sussex growled, "Get away from her, Alynwick."

The marquis shot him a knowing smile. "Easy, your grace."

He was not in the mood to be placated. "So we do search for a fourth," he announced. "Or at least someone who wants us to believe that the legend of the fourth Templar wronged by our ancestors is true."

"I say we find Miss Lockwood her final resting place, and then we may discuss matters in more details," Black announced. "Now that the furor has settled, I am afraid staff might become...curious."

"A Lord Stonebrook, your grace," the butler announced from the door. "I don't believe I can put him off, he's looking for his daughter."

Black and Alynwick immediately placed themselves in front of Anastasia's body, concealing her from the marquis's gaze.

"What is the meaning of this?" her father demanded as he barged into the salon, waving a note. "I received this not more than fifteen minutes ago, telling me to arrive here, where I would find my daughter in a most compromising position."

"Good morning, Lord Stonebrook," Lizzy announced as she slowly made her way to the door to greet the marquis. "Such a lovely day, is it not? I can feel the sun shining through the windows."

Stonebrook watched Adrian's sister warily. "Indeed, Lady Elizabeth, it is. However, I have not come to discuss—"

"Oh, dear me!" Elizabeth shrieked as she tripped over her gown. Stonebrook reached for her, clasping her hand hard within his grip.

"I've got you," he said. "There, now, you're right steady on your feet."

"Thank you, my lord. Why, that would have been positively mortifying to fall at your feet. You might get the wrong impression of me!"

He chuckled, but Adrian saw the way his gaze jumped over every soul present in the room.

"What is the meaning of this?" Lucy's father repeated, more calmly this time. "I was just on my way to the lodge. Meeting Fenshaw and Nigel Lasseter for coffee."

"I have no knowledge," Sussex said, trying to appear amused. "It looks as though someone is playing a grand scheme, my lord. For I received a similar message, as well."

Stonebrook grumbled. "Lucy, what the devil are you doing here at this time of the morning? Your maid made no mention of you leaving the house."

"The day is so fine," Elizabeth interjected, "that I thought it might be nice to serve breakfast in the conservatory before Lady Lucy and Lady Black and I barrage the shops on Bond Street. Will you not join us?"

With a shake of his head, the marquis declined. "I will just have a word with my daughter. Lucy, if you please."

He motioned to the hall, and Lucy followed him. When the door to the salon closed, Lizzy made her way to them. "Adrian, look. Do you see what I feel?"

Unfurling her fingers, Adrian saw the mark made by the indentation of the marquis's Masonic ring when he'd saved Lizzy from tripping. A coincidence, he thought. Nothing more. *But this is not the first time you've caught Stonebrook in the middle of something you're investigating,* his inner voice reminded him. Stonebrook had been there, in the lodge, the night Wendell Knighton had been shot.

"Bloody hell," he muttered. "Alynwick, summon that valet of yours and have him trail Stonebrook today."

"Sutherland won't be pleased. Today I promised him the afternoon off."

"Something is not right about this situation," Adrian muttered, "and I intend to find out what it is."

"GOOD, THIS IS GOOD." Stonebrook nodded his approval. "Attending Lady Elizabeth's breakfast was a good decision, even though her having such an event at this early hour is rather unorthodox. But I suppose that a sister of a duke is allowed a little peculiarity from time to time."

Now was not the time for Lucy's father to have shown up to find her with the duke. He would jump to the wrong conclusion about her feelings, and right now, her feelings were rather in turmoil. She had just seen a dead body—of a woman she had witnessed flirting with the duke last night. Then she had received a letter, forcing her to come here—and now her father, mysteriously with letter in hand had arrived not long after. It was the work of someone connected to her and the duke, and she didn't like it—not one bit. She thought of Thomas, and could not help but think that he was the only person who seemed to fit this puzzle. She didn't want to think that way, but there were no other options left to her. She did not, she thought reverently, want to be wrong about Thomas, and the person she believed him to be.

"Now, my dear, you go on and enjoy yourself, and I will see you later this afternoon."

"Papa, wait. Where were you when you received this?" She pointed to the letter in his hand.

"Home, girl, where else?"

"You were not home when I left this morning. In fact, you never came home last night." And she should know, she hadn't been to bed all night.

"You…you aren't questioning me, are you?" he thundered. "A grown man, which I am, *Lucille,* has no obligation to inform his daughter of anything, much less his whereabouts in the evenings."

He was angry. Lucy couldn't understand why. "I only mean…well…" How could she say it. That she had received a summons to the duke's home and that she was uneasy, for both of them.

"Ah, Stonebrook. Lady Lucy, is all well?" Sussex appeared at the door.

"Just fine, your grace." Her father beamed. "Just

fine. Now, if you will excuse me, I'm meeting some gents in a few moments."

"Yes, Fenshaw and…" The duke rubbed his eyes, trying to recall, when her father helped him out.

"Lasseter. Nigel Lasseter."

"Is he new to town? I don't believe we've met."

"He's been about for a half a year or so. He's a philanthropic. Was instrumental in financing Wendell Knighton's expedition to Jerusalem."

"Really?"

Lucy's skin prickled with a chill, and she shivered at the mention of Isabella's dead suitor—the one who Sussex claimed Thomas murdered in cold blood. Thomas's name was creeping up too often for her comfort.

"Seems that Lasseter and I have a common interest. The Templars. Fascinating band of men, aren't they?"

Sussex didn't agree one way or another, but her father didn't seem to notice. "I've recently begun a study with him, you know. A learned man. Quite brilliant, actually. Well, then, I must be off. I'm to pick up Fenshaw and we'll meet Lasseter at the Ceylon Inn."

"The coffeehouse in Southwark?"

"Aye." With a nod, Stonebrook removed himself from their company and headed to the front door where the butler awaited him, top hat and greatcoat at the ready.

"We need to talk," Sussex whispered to her. "In my study. It cannot wait."

When she looked up, she saw how turbulent his eyes were, troubled, with ghosts flickering in them. She had seen many things in his eyes, but never this—never stark fear. It reminded her of… No. She was mistaken. It reminded her of nothing, and no one.

CHAPTER SEVENTEEN

PLANS, ONCE LAID, should not be changed. That was the way of revenge, but as Orpheus stood at the window, listening to the sounds of the street below, he reconciled himself with the fact that his plans had changed. He silently admired the brilliance with which he'd keep his revenge thirsty and strong.

He'd been a fool not to have noticed her before. He was slipping, becoming too anxious. She had seen him—too late—her gasp of surprise had shocked him, for he hadn't heard her enter his chamber. He'd been amused at first, their reunion so delightful. She'd fought hard, the little bitch, just like the little rookery whores who frequented the alley behind the theater. She'd fought, but lost.

It hadn't been his plan to kill her, but in the end, he had to. He couldn't allow her to tell the Brethren of her discovery. So, he had used her death to send a message to Sussex, to make him realize that someone out there knew of his connection with the whore.

He knew it all—that sordid secret Sussex wanted kept buried forever.

Make him sweat, he thought with laughter. The bastard deserved no less than that.

His revenge, when it came, would be so sweet. It mattered not that he had to change the events of his *plan; the letters had served their purpose. It would bring the redhead to Sussex—and leave him to eye the real piece of the prize.*

"How you gloat over there, my dear," his companion murmured. "I love to watch the supreme satisfaction cross your face."

His lover was no shrinking violet, he thought. They had been in bed together when the blonde whore had walked in. She had watched him murder the woman with his bare hands. She had laughed, and they had fucked after. No, his lover was every bit as evil as him. They made a good team.

"What is next?" she asked as she patted the empty spot in bed beside her.

He smiled. "You just keep performing your duties as I say and all will fall into place. You'll see, the Brethren will come into formation, and then we will watch them fall."

"START AT THE BEGINNING. Tell me how this letter arrived."

Lucy lowered herself into the comfortable leather wingback across from Sussex's desk. When she sat, the duke followed, all the time rubbing his temple.

"Does your head ache?"

"Like a packet of demons dancing merrily in my head, if you must know the truth."

"Have you tried sulphur tonic? I hear it works miracles."

"It does. But I have yet had an opportunity to use it—you see, it's rather difficult when one's Brethren show up unannounced, and then a young lady you've only just ravished the night before comes storming at you, and finally, a dead body arrives on your doorstep. Well, you can understand why I've had little opportunity to take care of my head."

"Do you suffer from headaches quite a bit?" Rising, she strolled to the bell pull and rang for a servant. Sulphur tonic was a fairly new remedy for headaches. She had been rather surprised that he not only knew of it, but had by all accounts tried it.

"Often enough, I suppose."

Lucy watched him as she rubbed her arms. His eyes were hollow, giving his appearance a startling image she couldn't countenance. "Where are the others?"

"Gone out the back of the house. They've taken Ana to her final resting place, and then they will proceed to her house."

"It's been a rather strange morning, hasn't it?" she whispered, fatigue straining her voice. "Even when I thought her your mistress, I did not wish such harm on her."

His head cocked to the side, his eyes lit with interest, forcing her to look away and curse her wagging tongue.

"You rang, your grace?" said his butler as he quietly opened the door.

"Yes, a sulphur tonic for his grace, if you please," Lucy ordered as she sat down once more and arranged her skirts. He was awfully pale again.

"Are you feeling all right?" he inquired, his gaze narrowed.

"I am feeling rather fit, in fact. At first when I arrived I was livid with you, and then when my father presented himself with a letter informing him that he would find me here with…" Heat crept up her cheeks. "Well, you know, you were present when my father told you."

"You thought it was me who wrote those letters."

Flushing she gazed down at her folded hands. The intense anger—and hurt—she had felt had melted away, leaving her quite uncertain exactly how she felt. The only thing she knew was she found it quite difficult to look him in the eye, and not recall what had transpired between them.

"Lucy…" His pause made her glance up. He was watching her again with eyes that still showed fear. "I didn't write the letter. I didn't write anything about you coming to me, or I would expose to your father what we did last night. I don't believe in blackmail, and I would never do to that to you—especially after last night."

Fortunately the tonic arrived then, saving her from having to reply. When he drank it down and grimaced, she quickly handed him the accompanying glass of water which he swallowed in one long gulp.

"Good God, that is a vile concoction."

"But rather effective, I think. Or so I've heard."

Rising, he walked around the desk, and turned the empty wingback chair to face hers. Then he sat, and carefully reached for her hand.

"About last night—"

"I would prefer we didn't discuss it right now."

"Lucy." He sighed, but she held up her hand, stopping him.

"I know the conversation must come—and soon—but today…today I'm reeling with thoughts and emotions, and I do not trust myself to speak openly about the matter. Do you understand?"

There was reluctance in his eyes, but he nodded his agreement. "There are other matters between us that must be discussed, perhaps ones that should be addressed first. Last night you had a coin from the House of Orpheus and a letter from…him."

"Thomas," she provided.

"There is a connection, Lucy. Anastasia…when she came to me…spoke of a man who seduced her. He provided her with the same coin, and the message that she was to come to him. Lucy, you are a clever woman, you must know what this is adding up to. I swear, I vow on my life—on my sister's life—that I saw the man who carried your handkerchief shoot Wendell Knighton."

She wanted to shout that he was wrong, that it was all just a coincidence. She was blind at times, but at this particular moment, she could not afford to indulge in foolish pride. "It would seem that yes, there are many things linking this Orpheus to Thomas—and to us."

Something like relief, and perhaps pride, shone in his eyes. "This is the letter that you pulled from Ana's hand."

She took it from him and read it, barely noticing when the paper fluttered to the floor. "My God." Her hands were trembling and she could barely breathe, her velvet bodice suddenly feeling much too tight.

"Lucy, look at me." He clutched and squeezed her hand until she did. "Promise me you will not attempt to see him, or go anywhere without an escort. I'm sending over one of my footmen. He'll protect you, and you are to take him everywhere, do you understand?"

In shock, she could only nod. "Who is this man?" she murmured. It couldn't be Thomas. It just couldn't be. She had not been that blind, that needful that she would have given herself to a murderer!

"You're tired, and chilled to the bone, I think," he said as his head lowered and reverently brushed his lips over her fingertips. "You need rest."

"I...I might have died," she said. "I can't believe it. It all seems so strange, as though we are ensnared in a spider's web," she whispered. "Our lives, they've become tangled somehow."

"I know, love," he said in a comforting voice. "And we can't let him pull us apart. We are tangled. Orpheus has found a way to do so. Perhaps in bringing us together, he sought to weaken us, and the Brethren Guardians. I do not know. I only know that you cannot be wandering about the streets alone. You must send word to me, or at the very least Elizabeth, about your plans."

"What will you do next?" she asked. "What is to be done?"

"Black and Alynwick will search Ana's house, removing anything that might link her, and her disappearance, to me or to my father. In the meantime Sutherland, Alynwick's valet, will track down the messengers who sent the missives, and follow the trail that led Ana here."

"And you?"

He looked pensive, and his gaze slipped to her neck where she had held his palm to her throat earlier. The mark was gone, but she knew he was seeing it as though it were still fresh. "I have something to do, and a few leads to follow up on. Lucy," he whispered, "promise me you'll not see him or go to the Adelphi Theatre. *Please*."

"I promise."

"Soon we must talk," he said again, and this time he cupped her neck in his palm and brought her closer till he could kiss her forehead, the corner of her eye. "We must because, Lucy, I cannot stop thinking of last night. Of how right it was between us. It's never been that way for me—never. And I…I can't go on like this. We are not enemies. There is something between us, and I hope you'll soon see that."

She did, and it scared her senseless.

"I'll see you out. Lady Black will travel with you, and I'll send the footman with you, as well."

"All right."

"I'll see you tonight, shall I?"

She didn't know what to say or think. Should she see him? She didn't know, didn't like being indecisive. She may have made some poor choices, but at least she had come to a decision—one arrived at by herself.

"I'll come around, then, and we can talk. How is your head?" she asked, trying to change the topic. But he smiled, and she blinked at the remarkable change in him.

"Not worth a farthing, but I'll wager one kiss from you would make it all better."

"I think you are moving too fast, your grace," she said with a shaking voice. "Time is what we need."

He looked disappointed, but reluctantly he agreed, and allowed her to pull away. "Till tonight, pixie."

LUCY HAD ALWAYS BEEN very careful about making promises she knew she could not keep—and really this wasn't technically breaking a promise. It was…bending it, perhaps. She wasn't seeing Thomas, and wasn't going *into* the Adelphi. The little rooming house across the alley from the Adelphi certainly did not count.

Bending, she told herself, and for a very good cause. She needed guidance, that was all.

"My lady, my instructions were very clear. I am to take you and Lady Black directly to Grosvenor Square."

"Which you did," she replied as the carriage turned the corner and made slow progress through the narrow alley separating the row house from the theater.

"I saw Lady Black 'ome, but not you."

"You will, Charles," she said, trying to placate the young man. Sussex surely had chosen the burliest of his footman to protect her. "I just need to stop here for a moment, and then we shall be on our way."

"His grace said I was to mind that I didn't fall for yer enchanting ways, miss," he said, blushing to the tips of his red hair. "He says ye have a mysterious way of making men's thoughts turn to mush when you smile."

"Did he? How delightful of him." Lucy felt an absurd sense of elation at that.

"I haven't been in his grace's employ long, ma'am, and I have three brothers and a mother to see to."

"You shan't be sacked, Charles. I vow it. Now, if you would only stop worrying, I could be about my business quickly, and be back in time to the house for luncheon. I'm quite certain you are famished. It is rather late for luncheon, is it not?"

"I am hungry, miss."

"Well, I will rectify that immediately when we arrive home."

The carriage came to a halt before the tattered door with its peeling red paint. She made to open the door, but a large white gloved hand came down hard upon her wrist.

"Begging your pardon, miss," Charles mumbled, withdrawing his hand. "I ain't to put my hands on ye, forgive me."

"No harm done, Charles."

"I'll see you up to wherever it is yer going."

"That's not necessary."

"Then you ain't going up."

He had a mulish, determined expression, which she supposed had encouraged Sussex to hire him as her personal bodyguard. It rather resembled Sussex's determined glares.

"Oh, very well, but I shan't need you to stay. You can wait in the carriage."

"I'll wait outside the door."

"No, that won't be necessary. My dealings are private."

"I won't tell his grace of your dealings," he said, and she could tell that the footman thought she was indulging in an assignation.

"Oh, for heaven's sake, I'm only having my fortune told."

His expression lightened. "I see. Still though, miss, I'll stay anyway. You never know, you might get told a fortune you don't like, and I might be useful to persuade the mystic to give you a better one."

Lucy couldn't help but laugh. "Come along then."

They climbed the stairs up to the door. With a knock the door opened to reveal Mrs. Fraser seated at her kitchen table with a pile of cards set out before her. Across the table was a teacup painted with white roses; steamy tendrils laced their way into the air from the deep cup.

"Hello, lass," Mrs. Fraser said as she began to place the cards at the empty place at the table. "I 'ad a notion ye would come today. Tea is 'ot and ready. Come an' 'ave a seat, and we'll get started."

FROM THE DARKENED CORNER of the coffeehouse, Sussex peered over his news sheet and turned the page. Stonebrook was in his sight; so, too, was Lord Fenshaw, a little sparrow of a man with yellowing hair and spectacles, and a third man whose image was burned in his memory banks. He had been there the opening evening of Knighton's museum exhibit. He recalled the fellow because he had been so odd. It had been late evening, the autumn sun gone, replaced with the moon. The gaslights had been lit, but were not overly bright. Nigel Lasseter had sat like a commanding pasha behind a long table wearing an expensive black suit, his long black hair reaching the middle of his back, and a pair of sun spectacles. It was the spectacles he remembered the most.

He was wearing them today, too, despite the fact the shades were drawn in the restaurant. He could not make out their conversation; it was too loud and busy in the shop for that. He hadn't come to eavesdrop, anyway. He had come to prove, or disprove, Stonebrook's claims he was meeting friends.

There was something secretive about the marquis. Adrian did not have the sense that the man was up to no good, but there was no denying that he was often reticent to speak of his whereabouts, not to mention the fact that he, his lordship, had an uncanny ability to pop up whenever there was something untoward occurring.

In this matter he was right where he said he would be, sipping coffee and no doubt talking about ancient Templars. Which was slightly alarming. Templars were a common fascination for all men—commoner or aristocrat. But it hit too close to home for Adrian—he'd never known of Stonebrook's interest before all the recent happenings. And there was something rather unsavory and unlikable about Nigel Lasseter. He couldn't pinpoint what it was, he simply didn't like the man, and most importantly, he didn't trust him.

The threesome rose from the table, and Sussex raised his paper, completely concealing himself. He did not see them leave, or which way they went, or if they even went separate directions, but he knew someone who would.

"Well?" he asked as Montgomery, his head footman, came up from behind.

"Stonebrook and the other gent went off together."

"Which one?"

"The little wasted fellow with the thinning hair. The black-haired gentleman went directly to a black town carriage that had just pulled up in front of the 'ouse. Strange 'ow it happened. One minute it wasn't there and then it was, and he was standing and strutting out with his fancy silver-and-onyx walking stick, making a grand show of leaving, he was."

"Follow him." Sussex placed a purse on the table. "It's noon, the streets will be choked with traffic…

it shouldn't be too difficult to trail him. I'll expect a report as soon as you're able."

"Aye, your grace, I won't let you down."

There was a sick feeling in the pit of his stomach. Too many years of heeding his instincts had made him attuned to such little things. Something was in the air. The hint of danger, the smell of deceit. He thought of Lucy, and felt relief that he had sent Charles with her. The lad was as strong as an ox, and as cunning as a fox. He'd been in the process of picking Adrian's pocket when he'd encountered those merits. He had almost lost against Charles, and knew that when he saw the young lad, and his desperation, that he would have use for him. Besides, he had a soft spot for the poor in the East End parishes. He'd save every one of them if he could, but it was an impossible feat, so he consoled himself with the fact he was doing what he could. Easing the suffering of Charles and his family was not enough, but it was a start.

Two familiar voices shattered his musings, and he lowered the paper to see Black and Alynwick take the seats across from him.

"A bit out of the way for conversation and coffee," Alynwick stated. "Far more comfortable coffeehouses in Mayfair. The midday traffic is atrocious on this side of the city."

"I echo your thoughts," Sussex said. "I've been pondering why Stonebrook felt the need for such intimacy."

"Women?" Alynwick suggested.

"None were visible. He barely even looked at the maid who delivered the coffee. What of Ana?"

Black turned his attention to him. "Nothing that will

link you or the title of Sussex," he vowed. "And we found a nice little spot in a meadow, heading out to Richmond. I am sure that in the spring and summer it is rife with wildflowers."

"She would have liked that. Thank you."

Both men nodded. "We talked on the way. We don't like this, Sussex. It's too personal. Orpheus knows us—or at the very least, you."

"I can't imagine how, but yes, I've been thinking the same." And worrying about Lucy, too.

"Now, Stonebrook. What are we to do with him?"

"I don't know. But I'm not finished him with yet."

"And the letters?" Alynwick asked.

"I haven't put it all together. I only know that whoever wrote them wanted Stonebrook to find me with Lucy, and for Lucy to believe that I was blackmailing her—and forcing her to wed me by having her father discover us."

"And the fact in the letter Lucy found on Ana, telling you the killer had crossed paths with Lucy?"

"To show us that he has seen us. That he's watching, and knows our moves. No one we care for is safe from him. He wants to hurt us. He wants to strike fear in us."

"And?"

Sussex slammed his hand on top of the table. "It worked."

CHAPTER EIGHTEEN

"Ye've come, lassy."

Sitting down, Lucy swallowed hard. This time there were no candles or pendulums or crystal balls surrounding her. She heard the door click and realized that Charles had left. No doubt he was standing sentry with his thick arms crossed over his chest. "How did you know I would be stopping by today?"

Mrs. Fraser laughed. "Ye told me I was a fraud the last time, lass. I had to prove me point, that yer wrong. I saw ye in my mind, clear as a Highland sky. You were coming, and I said to meself that it was time to put the kettle on for tea."

"Thank you." Lucy took a little sip and sighed at the comforting warmth. She had no idea why she had sought out the mystic once more.

"I do," Mrs. Fraser mumbled as she reached for Lucy's hand. Pulling off the glove she set the leather aside and turned her hand, palm up to face her. "Ye didna care for your future the last time, and now ye've come fer another. Only it doona work that way, lass. Yer future is your future, and you canna wish for it to be different."

"The man in it…" She swallowed once more and took another sip of her tea. "He was wrong."

"Nay. No' wrong, just no' the one ye let yerself believe ye wanted."

"Well, then, what can you tell me?"

"From yer hand, well, let's see." She crinkled her eyes and held Lucy's palm up to the dim light. "Ye've a long life ahead of ye."

That was a relief, considering the events of the day, and everything she'd seen.

"And you'll have bairns," she whispered, tracing little lines, "one, two, three, four wee ones. I doona know their sex, so doona ask."

A long life and four babies. Her spirits were lifting.

"And their father?"

"I doona know, I canna see him. But you can. Ye've just to open your seeing eye, is all."

"What if I can't?"

The Scottish Witch eyed her curiously. "Then it's because yer pride is blocking yer sight, lass. He's there, clear as day. Ye've a long love line—he's been there within yer heart for ages. Ye will 'ave one great love, and it will be unbroken. I doona even think death will tear it apart."

"One love?" she asked, and she half feared it might be Thomas. Had she loved him? She certainly had felt something for him, but last night, last night she had been forced to admit that what Thomas and she had experienced was barely lukewarm compared to the fire that raged between her and Sussex. Sadly, she thought of Gabriel. She had loved *him*. Perhaps not as passionately as a woman loves a man, but in her youth, that love had been pure and instinctual.

"Treachery lies afoot," Mrs. Fraser said. "It's no'

an easy won love. I see heartache and betrayal, and pride—oh, ye've pride enough to be a grand queen, my lady. It'll keep you safe, I s'ppose, but it could be yer undoing."

"Tell me about the heartache, the betrayal," she encouraged. "I must know. Who will it be from?"

"I canna tell, lass. You have the inner sight, ye ken who to trust, and nae to. You have the gift of knowledge, of being one with yer instincts. Ye must use them."

"Tell me this, Mrs. Fraser, the man I saw in my vision."

"The man in yer vision is yer future, lass."

"Yes, that one. Well, I saw his eyes, and…"

"They were no' the ones ye were expecting."

"No, they were not. Did I see them, Mrs. Fraser, because he will be my love, or because he will be the one to betray me?"

"I canna say. When I look into yer palm, and then into yer eyes, I see nothing but shadows and uncertainty. I begin to think that maybe yer future is not yet fixed, and that ye might be the fortunate sort to change what it might be."

Lucy glanced down, her fingers curling around Mrs. Fraser's gnarled ones. "I am…scared." Blowing out her breath, Lucy sighed, relieved at last to admit the truth. "I don't want to make a mistake and live with it for the rest of my life. I don't…I don't want to become like my parents."

"Ye had dreams once, I can tell that much about ye. And ye've had them dashed, leaving ye a cold and brittle soul."

Stiffening, Lucy did not lash out like she would have before. She accepted Mrs. Fraser's appraisal of her for what it was. The truth.

"Ye've a path to travel, lass. It may be fraught with dangers, and aye, some heartache. The dreams might no be what ye imagined, but they'll be dreams nonetheless, and yer future will unfold. Ye'll choose the right path, lass—in your own good time like any soul does when they've reached a crossroads and must choose their way."

Lucy smiled sadly. "What if I don't want to choose it alone?"

"Then look to the eyes that would guide you, lass. You'll know the ones. I see no more," she murmured, dropping her hand. "I canna tell you another thing, other than a future comes at ye whether ye want it or no."

"Thank you, Mrs. Fraser. About the last time—"

"Are ye sure ye doona have a lick of Scots in ye, for ye've the stubborn pride of one."

Lucy laughed. "No, I'm afraid I do not. Does willful pride allow me forgiveness for my past actions?"

"Pride is sometimes all we 'ave. That's the truth, and pride 'as gotten me along in life when I thought I'd be out in the streets, beggin' for me supper. Aye, lass, it excuses ye. And doona ye think to pay fer this."

"Oh, I must, this is your living. I couldn't accept tea and your time for nothing."

"Then bring 'im to me, when ye have chosen your path, and I'm right about what I'll see, ye can pay me then."

Slipping her glove back on, Lucy stood and considered the old woman. "I suddenly feel such tremendous faith in you," she said.

"Good lass, good. Now, I've one last thing to tell ye. The man, he 'as as many demons as ye. He'll find himself at a crossroads, too, and he'll have to choose a path—and I pray that the two of ye find each other where the path ends."

Leaving Mrs. Fraser, Lucy pondered everything she had learned as she descended the rickety steps. She was surprised not to find Charles in the hall, and she anticipated he was waiting anxiously in the carriage. She had been longer than she thought, and she knew Charles was worried about her safety—and she was worried that she might have bent the rules of her promise to Sussex a little too far.

Exiting the building, Lucy saw the familiar black carriage and frowned when Charles was not outside to open the door for her. She hadn't known him long but she assumed that he would be at his post, eager to get her inside. Maybe a doxy had lured him to a corner, she thought as she tugged on the carriage door. There were enough of them walking up and down this alley and the Strand.

Raising the hem of her gown, she stepped up into the carriage, seeing a pair of black glossy boots.

"Charles, did you fall asleep?"

When he didn't answer, she turned her head and saw his slumped figure. "Charles!"

She never saw whoever was behind her, or the cloth that came up to cover her nose and mouth. She struggled as hard as she could, but she could not fight the effects of the ether that cloaked her face.

Before everything went black, she fell limp, caught
in a masculine hold and dragged down onto the seat.
She thought of her father, of Issy and…Sussex, and
suddenly she remembered the fear in his eyes, and the
ghosts that danced in them.

ADRIAN PACED THE LENGTH of his study. It was dark outside, and neither Charles nor Montgomery had reported
in yet.

"Settle your feathers," Alynwick muttered. "They'll
be by soon."

"Something is wrong," he muttered as he paused by
the window and drew back the curtains. "I can sense
it. My gut churns with the sensation."

"There *is* something unsavory in the air tonight,"
Black insisted. "I confess I've been sensing the same
sort of feeling, as well. Something is not quite right."

"Black!"

The voice was Isabella's and she sounded terrified.
She burst into the hall before Hastings could announce
her.

"Bella, what is it?"

Black was standing with his wife in his arms before
Sussex could blink.

"Little love, what are you doing here? My God,
you're trembling."

"Lucy," she gasped, "she hasn't been home since we
left here this morning. No one has seen her. My uncle…
he's having pains in his chest, he's sick with worry."

"Shh, now, let's take it a bit slower."

Isabella nodded and gulped. "I called upon Lucy
this evening. We were going to have dinner, and…talk

about things." She gazed over her husband's shoulder at Adrian. "I know she was confused about something, and we made plans to discuss it tonight. When I called upon her, the butler answered, and Sybilla, her maid, came flying down the stairs stating that Lucy was not home, and had not been since the morning when we left to come to Sussex House."

Adrian immediately felt swamped with rage—and a bout of sickness. His gut was never wrong, and he knew that it was Lucy he sensed.

"Calm yourself, darling," Black cooed. "We will find her."

"Where?" she cried.

Sussex hoped to hell it wasn't where he thought it might be. If he found her at that damned club, he wouldn't be responsible for his actions.

"My lord, you'll want to come to the door."

"What now?" he barked, but Hastings did not back away. "Charles, your grace, he's in a bad way."

Before Adrian could move to the hall, Montgomery lurched into his study, Charles's limp arm draped over his shoulders. Blood dripped onto the carpet as Charles fell to his knees. Alynwick and Sussex leaped forward to catch him. Helping Montgomery place him on the couch, Adrian realized the footman was only half-conscious.

"I found him staggering down the street," Montgomery offered. "He was raving, said he needed to get to you."

"Miss Lucy," Charles moaned. "Failed her, yer grace."

"No, Charles, rest," Adrian said with a calm he didn't feel.

"Canna do that," he groaned, and Adrian saw the state of his face, battered and swollen, his eyes mere slits, his clothes filthy and torn.

"'Brought her ladyship to a place in the Strand. Pleaded with me, she did, just a bit of fortune-telling, she tells me."

"So you did not take her directly home as I ordered?"

The footman winced, tested his jaw. "No, guv, I'm sorry. She pleaded me, and well, I was thinking whot's a bit of fortune-telling. So I brought her and stayed with her. Only I got jumped in the hall. A punch to the side of me head and I was fallin' to the ground like a gullied animal."

"I think we can dispense with the descriptions," Black growled as Isabella hid a gagging noise behind her hand.

"And I wakes up in the carriage, in behind the Adelphi—all torn up and battered, and nothing to show for Lady Lucy but this." Charles pulled a green velvet reticule from beneath his jacket. "And this."

Alynwick reached for the linen that dangled from Charles's bloodied fingers. Bringing it to his face, he sniffed and grimaced. "Ether."

Rage boiled inside him, and the urge to run rash and unprepared into the night ruled him. He tried to move, but Alynwick shook his head. "No, Sussex, we need a plan, and we can't all leave and allow Elizabeth to be here alone."

He knew Alynwick was right, but his head didn't

seem capable of reasoning with his heart. Lucy was taken—alone, and afraid. Or worse, in that bastard's arms.

"Your grace," Montgomery said, the color now all gone from his face. "I followed that Lasseter fellow like you asked, and his carriage took him to the Adelphi. He took the back way in."

"Christ!"

"I have met Nigel Lasseter," Isabella said, shocking the room into silence. "Wendell introduced us. He was the patron that paid for Wendell's expedition. He said he had inordinate fascination with the Templars and the treasure hidden beneath Solomon's Temple. I remember him, because it was so strange, he wore sun spectacles and it was the evening, and he seemed so pleasant and then we began to talk of Yorkshire and he became quite insolent. Wendell ushered me away then."

"Do you recall anything else?" Black asked.

"No, other than I detected a faint French accent."

"Guv, ye can't go alone," Charles moaned. "Give me a moment, and I'll show you where it was, and where I think they took Lady Lucy."

"You will stay where you are, Charles. Rest, and know that I'm very grateful that you were able to give me this information. Montgomery, you will join us."

"Well, you had better dress for the occasion, your grace. I saw nothing but dominos and capes on the gents and feathered masks on the ladies as they went in. They were passing the doorman some sort of gold piece. I think they're having what you lot call a fancy dress ball."

"A masquerade," he said. "Ana said there was to be

an initiation party, and it was to be masked. It must be tonight."

"Black, I'm going with you," Isabella announced.

"No, you are not. You'll stay behind with Alynwick and Elizabeth."

"I will do no such thing, husband. I'm putting my foot down, and you will obey me."

Black arched his brow. "Will I indeed?"

"You will, or you will suffer the consequences later—when we are alone, and…well, you know what I'm about."

Black shot a grin at Alynwick. "A pox and curse, you said. I can understand why."

Sussex was already calling for a black mask, and didn't bother to stay to listen to the banter between his friends. He was consumed—possessed—and would stop at nothing to find Lucy, even if it meant exposing them all.

"Where am I?" Lucy was thirsty and groggy and her head spun as though she had imbibed too many glasses of champagne.

"Safe. With me."

Trying to open her eyes, Lucy fought through the haze, and the sleep that made her body feel heavy. She could not move her arms, or legs, or even lift her head from the pillow. The voice that cut through the fog pierced her memories. It was a familiar voice, from long ago, from dreams and nightmares.

"Thomas?"

Her hand was lifted, and this time she saw it was him. "You're safe now. That servant, he hit you, and drugged you with ether. I saved you from him and brought you here."

She stiffened. "Where is here exactly?"

"The House of Orpheus."

Her body jolted as fear slithered through her. The effects of the drug were weakening, and she felt her strength returning.

"Shh, do not worry, love. You've no doubt heard terrible things about this place, but it isn't bad. It is just a club above the Adelphi."

"Sussex," she groaned and she tried to move off the bed. She'd promised. And suddenly nothing seemed as important as keeping that promise.

"He kept you from me. I was there that night, I saw him take you into the alley. I tried to find you, but he disappeared with you, into the dark."

"Charles, where is Charles?" she asked, suddenly feeling frightened. She had barely glanced at Thomas, the man she had defended, whom she had wanted to find above all reason. And here she was, thinking of a man her father wanted to force her to marry, and his servant.

"Do you mean the bloke who was hurting you? Lucy, please, listen to me. He was going to hurt you."

"No." Not Charles. Something was wrong.

"The effects of the ether he gave you. I'm afraid it can cause hallucinations, love. It'll pass in time."

"I must get home."

"We've only just been reunited. We must talk—I must have you again, to know you're still mine."

Her sight was blurry but she tried to focus on his

eyes. She had forgotten their color. From what she could see, they were not gray.

"You're alive, but I thought you dead."

"I am very much alive. Can you not feel it?" He reached for her hand and placed it over his heart. "It beats for you, Lucy."

She frowned, tried to sift through the haze and organize her thoughts. "Why did you allow me to believe you were dead? You made promises to me, Thomas."

"And I meant every one of them," he whispered. "But I had nothing to offer you, Lucy. No money, no future. I had to make myself into something before I could return to you."

She was tired, slipping back into sleep and she struggled against it. "Did you kill Wendell Knighton?"

"Of course not. Sussex must have told you that, yes? He's lying. He wants to keep us apart."

"He saw you, and you obviously saw him," she whispered, alarm rising in her heart. "You were on the rooftop that morning."

She started to struggle, but he gripped her arms, holding her down. "I followed you, love, to the lodge. You remember, you broke into the building. I followed you and I wanted to make my presence known then, but Sussex and Black arrived, and I couldn't make them suspicious."

Sussex hadn't lied to her. It was Thomas he had seen. Thomas had been there.

"Were you on the rooftop?"

"Only to escape them."

She collapsed back onto the bed, unable to fight him, or hold her eyes open any longer. "You're Orpheus."

"No, I am not. But you will meet him tonight, and all will be revealed. Rest a while longer, and when your strength is returned and your head clear, open the door and step into the hall. A servant will direct you. Here, take a sip of this."

He was pressing a glass to her mouth, the green liquid tasted warm and bitter, and she choked.

"The Green Fairy," he said. "Absinthe. It will help. I'll be waiting for you. Tonight, we'll be together again."

"WELL?"

"All is prepared."

"You said that the last time. Sussex poked his nose in where it didn't belong."

"He won't tonight."

Orpheus pulled his minion closer, his fingers wrapping around the man's jacket collar. "See that he doesn't, or you and I will be through. Do you understand?"

"Yes, master."

"Now, see that the girl is prepared. My plan needs to be executed perfectly. It all hinges on this."

Orpheus smiled to himself—his connection with his minion was over. He had proved his usefulness, but that usefulness was at its end. He had brought the redhead to him, and the Brethren would soon play into his hand, and like a house of cards, it would all come crumbling down. And he could not wait to witness it. To feel the rush of power.

His plan was intricate. One needed to be patient and cunning. He'd waited years for this, and he would not ruin it by being rash. The end was in sight. He would have what he desired. His rightful place in the world.

CHAPTER NINETEEN

THE CLUB REEKED of sweat and perfume, cigars and alcohol, all mixed with sex and debauchery. It was cloying, a vaporous cloud that clung to every surface. The incense was heavy, the opium a bitter scent in the air that wafted and hovered, enchanting the revelers.

No one appeared to be in their right mind—if they were, they would not be acting out the scenes he was forced to bear witness to, but witness them he did. He was searching for Lucy, and he had not yet found her.

Adrian had no idea if Black and Isabella had made it to the club, or if they would come inside. He'd left with Montgomery before the others. He hadn't wanted to waste a second finding her. It had been easy to gain entrance into the club; finding her was proving more difficult.

"Over there, guv," Montgomery whispered. "There's a door, you take it and see where it leads, and I'll mull about in 'ere."

"Do not leave this room," he ordered, then he made his way through the bodies that danced, drank, and kissed, hoping he wasn't being observed. Discreetly he slipped beyond the door to see a vision in a green morning gown, with her red hair piled high, brush past him. She was wearing a black beaded mask, and his pulse raced. He was going to kill her for breaking her promise to him.

Adrian watched as a footman carrying a tray made his way over to the woman in the green dress, and she followed the servant. Adrian followed her. His head was thick with the scent of hashish oil and incense smoke. A heavy sensuality blanketed him, and he fought through it, forcing himself to recall where he was. Orpheus was here, there was danger, and he could not allow himself to take risks with Lucy, even when every fiber of his being made him want to reach out and claim her—here and now.

THE ATMOSPHERE WAS CLOSE, intimate. The gas lamps had not been lit—the light was provided by the cozy glow of dozens of candles flickering in their golden candelabras, casting shadows on the walls that were at once eerie and sensual. Wall sconces held incense sticks, their tendrils scented with spicy, heavy perfumes that clouded her thoughts.

Lucy had awakened and left the chamber, but still the effects of the ether and the absinthe made her head feel heavy, and almost dazed.

Standing by the wall, Lucy peered into the adjoining salon, and quickly glanced away, blushing furiously. There was every decadence in that room, and despite having once lain with a man, she was unprepared for the sight of what was taking place. Thomas had spoken of the house before—when they had been together, lying on the floor of his rental flat. She had thought it decadent and exciting, but in reality it was revolting. It resembled nothing of what she had shared with Sussex. In her mind, that had been beauty, needy and heated, true, but he was right; there was something there between them, binding them. It wasn't only lust. She wanted to tell him, but first she had something she must do.

Where was Thomas? Why had he not met her yet? She wanted desperately to leave. She needed to find Sussex.

Taking her mind off the antics she had just witnessed, she watched as a liveried footman approached her, carrying a tray laden with a glass, sugar cubes as well as silver tongs and a spoon.

"Will you follow me, my lady?"

"Where to?" she asked, fear and suspicion rising in her voice, especially when she saw the tray contained a bottle of absinthe and only one glass.

"To a place more private, and safe," he answered.

Reluctantly she followed him into a darkened chamber where only a few candles were placed. A sheer, gauzy curtain cordoned off a section of the room, separating it. What lurked beyond the curtain, she could not say, but she caught a glimpse of a shadow, and she stepped closer, realizing she was experiencing what the French called déjà vu. She had been here before, in a vision, a dream, or perhaps a trance.

"Who's there?"

No one answered, and she was left to walk the perimeter of the room until she came to stand once more before the wall and the curtain, to lean against it for support and to fight the effects of the incense, and the rise of fear that threatened her.

"Why are you here?" The voice was quiet, a whisper of darkness and sin.

It was not Thomas's voice, and she didn't dare speak the name to whom the voice belonged. She was afraid now. Very afraid, for she had broken her promise to Sussex. She had no idea where Thomas was, and if he was this Orpheus person they hunted. Only one thing was clear—his voice soothed her.

"Why?" the voice asked again. "Tell me." She felt his body pressing against her back, the brush of his warm breath against her ear, muted by the gauzy curtain that hung between them.

Closing her eyes, she allowed her head to tip back, but he moved slightly, allowing the curtain to cradle her into his chest. Behind her lids, she tried to conjure up his eyes—a pair of gray eyes flashed before her, and she tried to move, to reach, but the absinthe made her languid, liquid, while increasing her awareness. It was a strange drink, not like champagne that muddled thoughts. Absinthe was different in that it heightened one's perception, almost to a point of crystal clear realization. While the mind was clear and light, her body was heavy, as if she were trying to walk in water encumbered by the weight of a heavy ball gown. There was a sensuality to it, a languor, and a certain beckoning she must obey.

"Tell me, why now?"

"All this time," she whispered in an anguished voice. "I never saw you."

His body moved beyond the curtain, and she felt his arm slide along the soft fabric, as if trying to reach her hand—to touch her palm with his. Unbearably erotic it was, with only the filmy curtain keeping them apart.

"I have been here, waiting. But you refused to see me."

Sussex. It was his voice. His scent discernible amongst the incense. It was the large body that was so warm and inviting—familiar from last night at the Mount Street house.

This scene, this déjà vu, was the vision she had seen during Mrs. Fraser's trance. This was the purported future that held her.

Was this the crossroads she spoke of? If only she could turn around, and reach for the gauze, tear it down and reveal the man like she had in her vision. But she hadn't the strength, her body would not obey, would only allow her to slide her arm outward, searching through rippling water and darkness for a hand she felt, so close within her reach.

"I've seen you." Her voice wavered as her heart started to pound hard against her breast. Something was warming inside her, and in the dark, with anonymity, she felt an ease and confidence she had never experienced before. "I've…thought of your kiss, trying to recall those moments when…when something inside me changed."

"My kiss? Do you not remember it?"

She did. The memories of it had tormented her. She shouldn't want it, shouldn't be this inconstant creature who vacillated between dislike and passion, but something had changed between then and now. She had seen a different side to him, a side not ruled by pride and politeness.

"Shall I awaken your memories, then?"

"Yes."

"Do you not recall it? What it did to you, how it made you feel?"

"No," she whispered, trying to entice him to speak. "Tell me the power of it."

"The power of a kiss is a heady pleasure, one that teases the mind, warms the heart, lifts the soul and tempts the body."

Lucy let herself grow lax. Behind her closed lids, she saw him, and did not run from that image, or the knowledge that the man seducing her with words was not the man she had come to meet, nor was he anyone she would have ever dared to think might have this effect on her.

"One should feel a kiss deeply inside. It should melt them from the inner core of their being, to the outside, where the flesh burns for touches from lips and hands, and the caress of a warm, velvety tongue."

A breathless pant escaped her, and she knew she should be utterly mortified by it. But he only pressed closer, and she felt the tentative touch of his warm palm grace her fingertips.

"Words and kisses are so very much alike, they have the power to lure and entice, to arouse, and soothe—to punish in the most pleasurable of ways. Like words, a kiss should leave you wanting more—*needing* more."

Lucy gulped, unable to say anything. She wanted more. *Definitely more.*

"A woman's body should respond in the same way. Your pulse should race, a heavy drum in your veins, and beneath your chest. Your breath should catch, and your head tip back in anticipation." His voice dropped to a wicked, sensual, whisper. "Your breasts—" his fingers brushed along hers, the curtain still between them lessening the touch, yet heating her even more "—they should be heavy, growing with want. The tips sensitized, tingling, the dark cherry nipples, tight and aching—little points wanting to be freed from behind their steel cage."

Oh, God, her breasts were aching, and yes, her nipples were brushing against her corset, wanting to be freed, to be taken in his hands, between his teeth—to experience what she had last night.

"And your belly, it should be quivering, your womb aching, your thighs growing wet with desire. Inside, you should bloom, should open like the petals of a flower."

She nodded, squeezed her eyes shut and let his words rush over her. She was feeling all those things, and more.

"My mouth," he whispered, and this time he was right up against her, his head lowered so that his mouth, through the thin gauze, brushed her neck, "should make you open to me, to allow me to explore your body. And that body should welcome me deep inside, accepting the pleasure I could give it." His breath was hot against her ear, and she could barely stand, her legs feeling like gelatine. "I could give it so much pleasure, this body of yours. I could bring you to the stars with only my kiss. Did you know, I could make you cry out, and shatter—to come, with a kiss from my mouth on your core?"

Lucy hid her shocked gasp by steadying herself with a fistful of the curtain, but he must have heard, or sensed her surprise at the shocking image he just produced, for his next words were a dark chuckle, and a smile she could feel as he pressed his face closer to her neck.

"Would you allow that? For me to give you that pleasure?"

"That's…that's indecent," she murmured, trying to collect herself. The very thought was scandalous.

"I wouldn't take no for an answer. I would force it upon you, spreading your thighs, lowering my body between them."

Oh good God, she could see it, and she could not stop from wondering what he would look like, those gray eyes peering up at her.

"You would protest—not because you feared me, or because you didn't want it, but because you think you must—that it is the only thing to be done for a proper lady. But I would whisper to you that nothing is forbidden in love."

The smoke from the incense seemed to come faster, and the candlelight was beginning to dim. Perhaps it was all figments of her imagination, for she was breathing too fast—wanting too much.

"I would set my fingers to you, part you with my thumbs, stare down in wonder at how beautiful you are, and then I would lower my mouth to you, tasting, smelling, and then I would caress you with my tongue—slowly, thoroughly, until I felt your hips rise up to meet me—"

"Stop!" she choked. "Please…do not say more."

"A kiss," he said, "should leave a man aching and aroused. The woman should feel what she does to him, he should show her what her touch, her sighs and moans do to him."

He took her hand. The gauze came with them as he placed her arm behind her back, and rocked into her, filling her hand with the length of him that was pushing against his trousers.

"The promise of a kiss," he said, and his voice faltered as she gently brushed her hand up and down the steel length of him, "should make one feel as though they are dying, and their lover's lips are the only tonic to save them."

"I...I..." She tried to say it, to face the startling fact. Squeezing her eyes, she whispered softly, "I am dying."

The sound of fabric rendering jolted her, but before she could ascertain the cause of it, she was grasped and turned around and was staring up into the silver eyes of the duke.

"Dying. Perishing. Dissolving, and only your lips— your kiss—will save me."

His mouth captured hers—hard, demanding, his fingers threading into her hair, clutching as he ground his open mouth over hers. His tongue snuck deftly inside, and they both moaned at the feel, the taste, the heady intoxication of that shared kiss. Her arms came up around his shoulders; with her eyes tightly fused she allowed her hands to feel—to see him as he appeared beneath her fingertips.

She couldn't speak, could barely even breathe. His chest was pressed tightly to hers; she could feel through her watered silk gown that he wore no jacket or waistcoat. Only a linen shirt that allowed her to feel the incredible heat radiating from him, how the fine lawn clung to his muscles and smelled of him.

His lips moved from her, and she protested, pulling him closer, but he just tipped back her chin and nipped at her jaw, his hands leaving hers only to skim down her sides to cup her derriere.

She could do nothing but rest her head against his shoulder and savor the musky, male scent of him. She could not protest, only sigh as his lips skimmed her skin. His whiskered chin abraded her soft flesh as he moved his mouth lower, his tongue tracing a path down her neck—a neck that was surely glistening with perspiration—with desire and need. His hands…oh, the way his hands cupped and molded and cared for her, as if her pleasure was all that mattered to him.

"Kiss me," he commanded, his tongue finding its way into her mouth. He gripped her tighter as one hand left her bottom to cup her chin, holding and positioning her the way he wanted. It was as if he had known what drove her to mewl and moan against him, what made her restless in his arms.

"Put your hands on me." Taking her fingers in his, he slid them up his chest. "Let me feel them." He was breathing hard, and Lucy opened her eyes, seeing how his eyes were pressed shut, feeling his fingers, which curled around her waist, tremble. "Awaken my body, Lucy," he said, his gaze narrowing on her.

Her fingers swept over a muscled chest until they reached the starched cravat and folded collar that shielded his throat. A rivulet of perspiration trickled down his neck, and she followed its path with her fingertip until it disappeared beneath his collar.

His breathing was harsh. She could hear it in the quiet, could hear his beating heart over the hum of the theater and the debauchery in the adjoining room. She could smell the maleness of him despite the earthy, humid air in the chamber.

Lucy couldn't suppress the shiver that snaked along her skin as he twirled his fingers along her curls. He brought her closer to him and she felt his lips nuzzling her hair.

"Such beautiful skin. I want to touch every inch of you. I *have* to touch you." The tip of his finger trailed down her throat, slowly, inexorably, to rest at the junction of her breasts. His lips met her skin, gently brushing the swells of her breasts.

He grasped her waist and brought her tightly up against him. "I want to look at you. I want to touch you and kiss you and feel your body beneath mine—to make you open for me like an exotic, heady hothouse flower."

"Sussex—"

He groaned. "You want it, too. That kiss was everything I said it would be. Everything I told you you would experience, you are feeling now. Aren't you?"

His cravat came undone in her hand, and she pulled it from his neck, exposing a small patch of his throat that was notched, and hollowed—a perfect place for her to fit her tongue. Before she could, his palms cupped her breasts, and lifting them, he traced the small swell as they pressed against her bodice. "Little cherry nipples," he murmured. "I thought of them all day, how I want to stare at them, all red and glistening from my mouth, and then I want to play with them, savoring them as if I were savoring the most decadent dessert in the world.

"You tremble?" His smile was pure male wickedness and satisfaction. When he pressed into her, found her ear and whispered, "Are you wet for me? Your body is aching for what I can give it. When you fill the ache, it feels so damn good—so good."

His hand reached for her skirts and she felt him slide his fingers up along her stocking-clad thigh. "Let me fill it, Lucy. Tonight, let me part these sweet thighs, plunge deeply inside, making that ache burn and grow, and then you can shatter like you did last night, but with me inside, and I can feel every tremble and shake."

"Your grace," she said, fisting her hands and forcing them against his shoulders. "We shouldn't. We might be discovered. We can never go back once this happens."

He became more eager, unable to be thwarted. He seemed to sense her pulling away, her reluctance that was steadily building. She was not ready for this. Not when she had just realized the extent of the desire they had both shielded from the other.

"You should have never accused me of being passionless." He swooped down, capturing her mouth in a searing kiss that robbed her breath. His tongue touched her, his pace frantic—carnal. His fingers tightened around her thigh, squeezing as he rocked against her.

Her desire might have temporarily waned when she thought of getting caught, but if anything the duke was more aroused, she could feel his erection pressed unrelenting into her.

"No, by God, you've accused me of coldness, but how can you, when you can feel how hot my body is against yours? You've said I have none of the red-blooded passion of my sex, but you don't know. You," he gasped, pressing against her with a hard thrust of his hips, "you will know it—the depth of my passion. But you will." He whispered hard as he moved his hand between them and unfastened his trousers. "Tonight I will show you, so that you will never, ever again accuse me of being less than a man. To hell if we are found, it will only expedite the inevitable."

There was a shocked silence, and Lucy's gaze widened with the dawn of understanding. A shield fell over his eyes, but he would not release her, and the heat of sexual frenzy still encompassed them.

"You are shameless," she spat, struggling in his arms. But he wouldn't let go. "You are no gentleman, sir."

"You don't want a gentleman," he replied but his voice had lost its fevered edge, and was once again the sound of control, and carefulness. "Admit it, you wanted this. You were writhing and moaning in my arms."

"This was all to prove a point, wasn't it?"

It was his turn to show horror. "Lucy, no! Good God, no."

"I taunted you, and you thought to get me back, is that it? Or did you hope someone might wander in and recognize us in such a scandalous position?"

"No," he snapped. "That isn't it at all. If you only knew how many times I have gone to bed in this condition—" he motioned to his trousers "—then you would know that this…" He paused, ran a wildly shaking hand through his hair. "This isn't what you think. This isn't why I came to you—"

The sound of a door slamming cut him off and, horrified, Lucy looked up to see her father barreling into the room, his face a mutinous shade of crimson.

When he saw her, the way she was being held in Sussex's arms—because he would not let go—he stopped in his tracks and shook a finger at her.

"By God, girl, this is the last straw. Your rebellion, your hellion ways…I've had it to the back teeth. You will marry Sussex, and I won't hear anything from you about it."

"Papa!"

Her father raised his hand, but the duke stepped in front of her. His shirt was untucked, his neck was bare and his hair was a mess from her fingers. "I would contain yourself if I were you. Lay a hand on her, and you'll answer to me."

"What in God's name is the meaning of this? Half the ton is outside this room. What if you had been seen? Christ, Sussex, when you assured me you would find a way to make her agree to this marriage, I never assumed a man of your stature would lower himself to a tumble in a public domain. The floor of my library would have been sufficient!"

"Oh!" Lucy cried, tears stinging her eyes. It was then that she saw Isabella and Black standing beside her father. Black was studying his boots, and Isabella's delicate gloved hand was covering her mouth.

"And to ensure the deed would come to fruition, you brought witnesses to my humiliation!" She whirled around and slapped away the duke's hand.

"There is nothing else to be done. Who knows how many have seen you enter this room? By even entering such a place, you've put your reputation in danger—but to be found here, in this room…well…" her father grumbled. "There is nothing to stop it but a wedding. Sussex, I entrust you have the necessary documents for an event such as this?"

His gaze never left hers. "It was not my intent for it to happen this way."

"What? By entrapment? Betrayal?" Her voice caught and she fisted her hands, determined not to cry. "Of course you did, because you knew it was the only way."

"I never wanted this—"

"Oh, do not lie now, your grace. This is exactly what you wanted."

"Not like this." His voice had grown so soft, so pained, that she could have almost believed in his sincerity—almost.

"I may have to marry you, your grace. I may have to become the Duchess of Sussex, but there is one thing I will never be, and that is your wife!"

She had her answer now. The man who owned the gray eyes would not be her lover, but the one to betray her.

HE WATCHED THROUGH shadows, the murky play being acted out before him. Yes, his plan was unfolding—spectacularly well.

"You lied to me!" His minion was angry, his voice rising. "When I agreed to your madness," he hissed, "it was because I wanted her—she was useful to me, for making my way in the world. You promised me if I delivered her to you and the others followed, she would be mine."

"There's been a change of plans, I'm afraid."

"You lying bastard! I killed for you!"

"And so you did. But things have a way of changing, Thomas. It's a pity, I'm afraid, but my course never wavered. Now, I need for Sussex to take her out of the city. My goal has been accomplished. My other assistant has been so good about getting the letters out, so that everyone would arrive here, ensuring that the right thing be done. Sussex will marry Lucy as he desires. They will leave the city quietly to decrease the rumors, which is what I desire. You see, we're all happy.

"It doesn't really matter, does it, because what you desire is no longer a concern of mine. You see, your part in my plot is over now."

He heard the hitching of breath, and he smiled, right before he pulled the knife from his vest and thrust it into Thomas's chest.

"I never did give a damn about what you wanted. The girl was always meant to be a decoy for something I wanted more."

CHAPTER TWENTY

"THE DUKE OF SUSSEX, milord."

Lord Stonebrook glanced up as Adrian entered the room and shut the door. He shook his head when the marquis motioned to the decanter of brandy.

"Tea then?"

"Just answers," he said, his voice cold and hard as he stared at Stonebrook, so confident, so smug in his world. The old anger swelled up, and he glanced away, not wanting to see the man who reminded him so much of his father.

Stonebrook looked up sharply then sat back in his chair. "Answers to what questions?"

Sussex took a chair and crossed his legs. "To some questions that have plagued me for some time."

"And do my answers hinge on you marrying my daughter?"

"No, in fact, I came to make certain that tomorrow is still certain for our wedding."

"It is."

He was in a devil of a mood this morning, not quite in control of himself, which must have been the reason he asked, "Are you quite certain you wish her to have me as a husband?"

"Why wouldn't I?"

"Because I ravished her in a public place. It wasn't

well done of me, and says nothing of being a gentle-man."

"Bah, you're a duke, for God's sake."

"Does that mean my actions are acceptable to you because of my title?"

"Of course." Stonebrook agreed. "You're a man of honor and you upheld your oath to protect my daughter's reputation. That is all a father may hope for in situations such as this."

His gaze narrowed, and a violent rush of anger swept through him. "What if I were not a duke, or even a mere sir. What then?"

It was Stonebrook's turn to glare. "Why then, I would have beaten you to a bloody pulp for having such designs on my daughter, and the tenacity to think you might obtain her through such scandalous means."

His lips curled. "It is fortunate that I am a duke then, and quite outrank you, isn't it?"

"You're in a strange mood today, your grace. What is it?"

He waved his hand. "Questions, I'm afraid. I've been plagued with them. Wondering why a father would allow his only child to be tied for life to a man who might have made her a public spectacle."

"Look, Sussex, I've wanted you to have her for years. You were fifteen when the idea caught my fancy. Nothing would make me happier than to call you my son-in-law. You're the man I've always wanted for her."

"Is that so?" he asked darkly. "Well, then, here I am, prepared to face my bride."

Stonebrook assessed him, and Adrian knew his mood was perplexing to the old marquis. He didn't understand the recklessness that seemed to seethe beneath his skin.

"I am pleased to see you here this morning. Although that daughter of mine will not make it pleasant on you. Sulking about, she is…it's most vexing."

"No doubt. Having you find us in such a way was not a stroke of luck for either of us."

"Bah, the girl is a dreamer. She wants a cottage in a sleepy little English village where she can play house like she did when she was five. Nonsense."

Adrian contemplated the marquis. He didn't understand his daughter, that much was certain.

"Now then, questions you had. I suppose you want to know about the marriage settlements, and what my daughter is to receive from me—and your son, too, since he will bear my title when I'm gone."

"No, that's not it," he said impatiently. "What I want to know is what is it you do, my lord, when you are away so long from home? You are never here in the evenings."

Stonebrook was taken aback by the question. "All you have to do, Sussex, is send around a missive. I would ensure I was home to entertain you."

"But what of Lucy? Who should entertain her?"

"Why, you will, I suppose. You're marrying her."

"The night Wendell Knighton was killed you were at the lodge. This morning you received a missive instructing you to come to my home, but it did not find you here, did it? How then did the messenger find you when you were not where you should have been?"

"My valet, if you must know. He's very discreet."

"Why does he need to be?"

"Why are you prying?"

"Because I am under the distinct impression that something is afoot. I'm marrying into this family, and I have the right to know before we go ahead with any of this."

With a groan, Stonebrook reached into his desk drawer and pulled out a stack of letters, which landed in front of Sussex. "Read them if you want, if it will appease your infernal curiosity."

Adrian thumbed through the letters. "Why don't you tell me?"

The marquis lunged upward, tipping his chair. "If you must know, I'm carrying on with a young woman, the housekeeper at the lodge. She's less than half my age, and I don't want my daughter to discover it. I was there that night…with her. Last night, too. We meet at the lodge because I cannot afford to be seen with her."

Whatever Adrian had thought the old man was up to, that was not it.

"A housekeeper from the lodge? She's obviously not of your class—makes her home in another part of the city, I'd wager."

Stonebrook flushed. "I have a penchant for doxies then, is that what you wish to hear?"

No, it wasn't. But it was so typical of men like Stonebrook and his father, to use those less fortunate to exploit their own desires and pleasures.

"There is no harm in it. Besides, she gets much more from me than she would any customer she might service in an East End alley."

"Is that so?" Adrian could hardly stomach the notion of the young girl who was being subjected to Stonebrook's lust and his proclivities for playing out Master and Servant.

He had always disliked Stonebrook. There was something there that always ate at him. But he had tolerated him—only for the reason that he had wanted Lucy. Today, though, he found he could barely stand to stay in the room with the man, let alone talk to him.

"Do have the decency to keep this from Lucy, will you? She thinks her mother and I were in love, and it would destroy her."

"I don't think you'll shatter any illusions."

"Well, I don't want to hear that I am a hypocrite. Years ago—" he sighed "—I put an end to a friendship that had blossomed between my daughter and a filthy street urchin that came 'round with the butcher on deliveries. Lucy has such a kind heart, a soft heart—it was damn frightening knowing she could be taken advantage of because of it. So, I put an end to it, and told her it was because a lady of her station didn't associate with the lower orders. She never forgave me, and she has never let a moment pass by to allow me to forget."

"So she would not take kindly to the fact that you are enjoying the charms of *your* lesser."

He had the decency to flush, whereas Adrian's father never had. His thinking had been much like Stonebrook's and Adrian had despised his father for it.

"Fair enough, I'll keep your secret. But you must let me see Lucy."

"Good heavens, why? She'd as soon scratch your eyes out than see you. No, wait till the morrow when I'll drag her down the stairs. See her then, in front of the vicar."

"We need to resolve matters before tomorrow."

"All right, third door down on the first level. She's in her curiosities room."

Rising, Adrian bowed. "Till tomorrow, my lord."

THE DOOR TO LUCY'S private chamber creaked open, and she glanced up from the copper-colored satin only to see Sussex appear around the door, his expression grim.

"I hope I'm not interrupting."

"Indeed you are." She indicated the disarray in the room, the heaps of clothes, the dollhouses one of the footmen was busy carefully dismantling and packing safely away. Sybilla was wrapping her porcelain dolls up in linen cloths, filling trunks upon trunks with them. Lucy was busily putting the finishing touches on the gown that was to be her wedding dress.

"My apologies, then." Clearing his throat with a little cough, he glanced awkwardly between Sybilla and the footman. "I have your father's permission to speak to you."

"Oh?"

"Yes. Might I?"

"I suppose. James, Sybilla, will you give us a few minutes, please?"

"Of course, my lady. Shall I arrange refreshments in the parlor then?" James asked.

She glanced at the duke—*her fiancé,* she corrected herself.

Shaking his head, he declined the offer. "I won't be staying long."

With a bow the footman took his leave. Sybilla was slower to vacate. As she passed by Lucy she sent her a look that read *ring if you need me,* before dropping a curtsey in front of Sussex. Strangely enough, when she left the room, her maid closed the door tightly.

"Your father told me I would find you in here," he murmured as he studied the contents of the room.

"No doubt he called it my Den of Eccentricities."

"Curiosities, actually, but now I see it's more a chamber of collections. I had no idea you collected dolls."

"And houses. I have since I was a child." They had been her only friends, except for Isabella, whom she rarely was allowed to see.

"You made their gowns. I am familiar with your craftsmanship."

"Yes." She was flushing, not from the compliment, but from the embarrassment of having her secret pastimes known. Only Issy had been in this room and had seen the things she had collected over the years.

"Marvelous collection," he murmured as he walked around the room, studying the dolls, and what remained of the houses. "I have a room at my estate that would be perfect for you to showcase your collection. Lots of space to continue it, as well."

Lucy shifted in her chair then turned her attention to sewing a black lace cuff to the sleeve of her gown. She did not want to hear of his estate, because it reinforced the fact that she would become his wife. Something she had still not reconciled herself to.

It had been two days since that disastrous night at the House of Orpheus. This was the first time that she had laid eyes on him since running from the chamber. Seeing him now brought the memory flooding back, and she could not look at him. Could not think of the words he had whispered to her. How she had believed it all, falling into his act. She had been so wrong, thinking she had misjudged him and that he was indeed a deeply passionate man. He *was* passionate—ruthlessly passionate was what he was.

He cleared his throat again. His boots thumped against the floorboards as he came up behind her. She felt him reach over her shoulder. "What's this?"

"Don't touch it!"

But already the object was in his hand, his fingers carefully pulling away the linen wrapping. When their gazes met, he was smiling. "What the devil is this?"

"My most treasured possession," she snapped while taking the delicate piece of dollhouse furniture from his hand.

"Most treasured possession?" he asked, incredulity making him sound as if he were laughing at her. "There are heaps of beautiful gowns on the settee, a jewelry box over on that table that is spilling with diamonds and gems—all of which are not paste. There must be a king's ransom in that box, and yet, this oddly shaped…"

"Bed," she sniffed as she lovingly wrapped it back up in its linen blanket.

"This bed is the most treasured piece you own?" He watched her most intently, his gray eyes boring into hers. Shock registered in them.

"I don't expect you to understand," she said as she gently placed the piece in a trunk.

"No, I don't. But help me to. Help me to know who you are, Lucy. It's all a man desires of his wife, to know and understand her as no other man ever has."

She bristled and whirled around. He was looking at her again, those eyes that saw too much. The gaze that penetrated so deeply. She shrunk back from it. She had allowed him a glimpse that night, and he had betrayed her. Never again. Never would she allow herself to be vulnerable before him.

"Did my father not also inform you that I have been sulking in petulant female behavior for the past two days?"

"He did."

"Then why did you bother to climb the steps, knowing I was intent on being taciturn and pigheaded, and an ungrateful female who doesn't know the good fortune that has been bestowed upon her?"

He winced, glanced away. "It sounds like your father has climbed these same steps, as well."

"He has. He adores lectures, and I have been forced to listen to the same one uncountable times since he discovered us."

"And what was your reply to this lecture?"

"I informed him he might as well not exert any further energy on the matter, never mind stair climbing, for I am quite deep in my desire to sulk and pout, as is so common for my sex."

"I agree."

She froze, glared at his back. "I beg your pardon?"

When he turned, he was smiling. It was a strange smile, at once wistful, but sad. "It is the only avenue open to you at the moment. The only way to make us pay for the marriage you are about to embark upon."

"That is a pretty speech, your grace, but seeing things from my viewpoint will not save you from my plan to make you utterly miserable, and filled with regret for this marriage."

"For how long will you wage this war, then?"

"That depends, how long do you intend to keep breathing?"

He smiled. "I plan on enjoying a very long life— unless, of course, you are plotting to plunge a knife into my back."

"I am not planning murder. It's too expedient. I was thinking something along the lines of prolonged torture."

"Indeed? That thought is rather interesting. Makes me wonder what sort of counterattacks I might be persuaded to implement."

"I do not find your amusement endearing, your grace. The truth of the matter is I planned on making you absolutely miserable in your choice of wife until you are an old moldering arthritic."

"There is the spunk," he murmured.

"It is not spunk, but pure, unadulterated loathing. You betrayed me in the worst possible way, and I will not be swept up into this marriage and forget that the entire reason I find myself chained to you is that you arranged for us to be found! I will never trust you." She took in a deep breath, her bosom rising in her gown. "I will never accept you and I most certainly will never love you. Now, if you are not sufficiently put off by my idiotic female melodrama, as my father calls it, you may have a seat and discuss whatever it is that drove you up here. Otherwise we are done."

To her shock, he pulled out a chair and sat down at the worktable. When he met her gaze, she could tell he was settling himself in for a while. Rather like digging a trench in preparedness for their impending warfare.

"I'm certain my father informed you that I would be quite unmanageable in my present state of selfish indulgence."

"He did." He released a long, heavy sigh. "I don't want to manage you, Lucy. I want…I want—"

"Yes, I know. A wife and broodmare. It's what any aristocrat desires, is it not? Perhaps we should get on with it, shouldn't we? Lay the ground rules, so to speak. What do you require of me in my role as your duchess?"

He frowned, but his gaze was watchful. "I know you are indulging in a fit of outraged womanly honor. I can appreciate it, actually. I'll even accept it—for now. You have made your views clear, and despite all this, I would have you know that I vow I will take care of you. You'll want for nothing."

Just a different husband, she thought viciously, just for the pure enjoyment of being hurtful.

"Well, that is something, your grace. But I cannot be bought. If your plan is to buy yourself out of my petulance, you may save your coin. As you see, I have little care for trinkets and baubles. Every man attempts to placate a woman's ire with some piece he orders a shopkeeper to wrap up." She glanced at the doll's bed tucked lovingly in the chest. "No," she murmured, "I have long ago learned to look past a glittering surface." His gaze followed hers to the trunk.

"Tell me about it."

"Why do you care?"

"Because I find myself wondering how you came by it."

She shrugged off the pain of that long-ago day, and refused to meet his determined stare. "It hardly matters now, does it?"

There was an odd wistfulness to his voice. "It matters to me."

Closing her eyes, she hardened her heart around that soft voice. She didn't want his kindness or understanding. Despite her attempts to remain aloof, she started to speak. She had not even told Isabella the true story of that misshapen little piece of furniture.

"My…my friend. At least I would like to believe we were. I was only twelve when I met him."

Sussex's hand tightened around her wrist, as he watched her. "Him?"

"Yes, Gabriel. He was the butcher's boy. He must have been a year or two older than me, but he was so much bigger that he looked older. He had such a fierce expression—almost wild. He came every Tuesday with the butcher."

"And why were you in the kitchen? It seems a strange place for a young lady to find herself."

She shrugged. "I always played in the kitchen. I used to get under Cook's feet, but she wouldn't scold me or send me to my room. She would laugh, and feed me, letting me help sometimes with the bread and cakes. You see, my parents never noticed me, unless it was to their advantage."

Here is a new dolly, my dear. Now, you must be a good girl, and come to tea and behave yourself. You must be on your best behavior and make Mummy and Papa proud.

They had bought her—always. Never had they come

to her empty-handed, and never had they given her anything that did not have some hidden catch behind it. In truth, the gifts meant nothing. She had only wanted their affection, an embrace, and perhaps for them to come to her at night and tuck her in and tell her a story. But those were her governess's duties and she had been every bit as frosty as her parents. The isolation had destroyed her, making her retreat into a hard shell. She had been a quiet, withdrawn creature, a gentle spirit with feelings that were easily hurt, and a heart that was just as easily broken. She knew she must harden it herself if she was going to survive.

"There's more to it."

She paused—stilled as she listened to the conviction in his voice. He would not pull this out of her—not take it away from her like her father had. Tears began to burn her eyes, and she forced them back. "There is nothing more to it. He came, and then weeks later, he presented me with this bed he had made for my dollhouse. Then he left, and I never saw him again. He's probably dead. No one lives long in the rookeries."

He wouldn't release her hand, wouldn't let her look away from him, either. "Why didn't he come back?"

There was a darkness in his voice, and Lucy's breath caught at his expression, the way his eyes watched her so carefully. The scar on his brow made her pause and she almost reached out to touch it, but she didn't. His voice, insistent in the quiet, made her go on.

"Why did he leave?"

"My father forced him to," she whispered. "He said he was nothing, treated him like rubbish and then…" She closed her eyes and told him. "Papa took the bed from me, said I wasn't allowed to have anything made by his filthy hands. He threw it in the rubbish bin—so carelessly—and it had been the only thing ever given to me that was not intended to buy me—and then...then papa struck him. He was bleeding. I can still see the blood running from his forehead. I tried to go to him, but Papa caught me, and Gabriel looked up at me and then left. I never saw him again."

There was something that sounded very much like shock, and perhaps awe, in his voice when he said, "You took this from the trash and hid it, knowing your father would be livid with you for doing so."

"I couldn't be parted from it. It meant everything to me. He left, believing me to be like my father. I can't bear to know that, to imagine him alive and thinking the worst of me."

His gray eyes flashed. "He doesn't. He couldn't possibly think ill of you."

There was stilling of that moment, when their gazes met. Fear mixed with curiosity shone in her eyes. "How could you know such a thing?"

"Men, from whatever walk of life, are not so different, Lucy. We all have honor and pride, and I know this butcher's boy you talk of would be honored to know you saved his work. I know this duke is."

"I don't want your pride, in fact, I want nothing from you. But you desire something from me, or else you would not be here, would you?"

His jaw clenched and he hesitated. "About Thomas... The police found his body floating in the Thames. He carried identification on his person. I thought you should know."

"Thomas," she whispered, trying to sort out her feelings. She had been devastated the first time she had believed him dead. Now she was left feeling numb. She had her answer—he *had* been involved with this Orpheus. It had been him on the rooftop with Sussex—most definitely him the duke had seen murder Wendell Knighton.

She'd been so wrong about him—in so many ways. He'd made promises that he never meant to keep, and she was left with only one conclusion, that he had never really desired her in the first place.

"Black and Alynwick will continue to investigate how he came to be under Orpheus's command, and how they both discovered the Brethren Guardians. I'll share what I know with you. You deserve the truth, I think." His head hung low, and Lucy watched as his hold slipped from her wrist, to her fingers.

"And is that all you have to say to me, your grace?"

"I must ask one thing—that you do not bring him up again."

"Why, your grace, does it shame you to know your future wife has lain with another man?"

She was being intentionally mean, but she had to locate the coldness inside her once more. To hide behind it, to forget about both Thomas's and Sussex's betrayals.

His glare was furious, and she jumped as he unexpectedly reached up and captured her chin firmly in his hand. "No, it does not shame me. But mention of him makes me insanely jealous and provokes me to distemper that makes me want to unravel and smash things." The violence of his words surprised her; so, too, the way he looked deeply into her eyes. "I trust you will remember that, and not seek to intentionally provoke me. Jealousy is a very new experience for me, and I am just learning how to manage it. Although, you may rest assured I would never lay my hands on you—not in that way."

He held her captive, while they looked into each other's eyes. "And what later, your grace? Will you seek to find ways to invoke my envy?"

"What do you mean?"

"You won't, you know. For I don't care what you do."

"Ah, so this is my carte blanche to take a mistress, is it?"

She flinched at the word, at the very thought of some woman rutting beneath him. Why she could be affected by it, she did not care to examine. It was too soon, she told herself, much too soon since that moment of un-bridled passion they had shared.

"I will grant you one night, your grace. You may have access to my body to consummate this marriage."

"Once? You owe me an heir."

"One night," she repeated. "That is all."

"Ah, I see, I am to have you as many times as pos-sible in that one night. You will lay there dutifully, with your prim white linen night rail raised to your waist, your gaze cast up upon the canopy while I grunt and work atop you, filling you with my seed until I am drained dry, and all in the attempt to consummate this marriage, and conceive my heir."

His gaze flickered to her mouth as he reached out and brushed her bottom lip with this thumb. "And what am I allowed, Lucy? What pleasures will you endure in the name of wifely duty?"

"You have me. For one night."

"So you will endure anything I force upon you, is that right? Even suckling your nipples till they resemble dark cherries? What of indecent kisses between your thighs?"

She blushed, reminded of their exchange that night. "I will endure what I must."

He smiled. "Oh, no. You will not endure. You'll enjoy. And perhaps even beg."

"I will not."

"Then I will wait until you do. For I am not the sort to lie atop a woman and take my pleasure—it will be my pleasure to pleasure you, as well. Did you think I would not? I know you believe me cold and indifferent, but I would never just take, Lucy. I want to give, and I want you to take—and to give to me as well."

"Then you will be vastly disappointed, your grace. For I want nothing from you, and I certainly have nothing to give you." Her glare was mutinous. "Now, have you said all you wished to say?"

"Ah, you wish to continue your pursuit of sulking and petulance, is that right?"

"I wish to get on with packing. My father informs me that tomorrow morning we are to be married, and then you plan to depart the city for your estate in Yorkshire."

"Yes. I think it best for the start of our marriage."

"As you can see I have a great deal of work to do before that. So, if that is all?"

He stood, reached into his pocket and withdrew a

blue box, tied with a white ribbon. Placing it in front of her he said, "A wedding gift."

Leaning forward, he reached across the table, pulled the ribbon free and opened the box. Pressing in, he lowered his face to hers. "Ear bobs, for I have been thinking of how very nice they would look dangling from your ears while I nuzzle your neck."

Lucy glanced down at the pearl earrings with gold filigree. They were lovely and she tried not to be swayed.

"Pearls, because your skin is as smooth and luminescent as one, and because the first time my lips caressed your throat I thought your flesh as opulent and lush as one. Gold," he whispered, moving closer, "because it reminded me of how your hair looked in the dying candlelight, how it burned and glistened, and how badly I want to lie in bed, in our chamber, and watch you at your dressing table, unpinning it for me. I will have that, Lucy, the rights of a husband to enter his wife's room, to see her at her toilette, to watch what no other man will ever be granted. You do understand that? That I won't settle for less?"

"You have made your line in the sand very clear."

He grinned. "You can cross it anytime you wish, you know. You might even like it on my side."

"I don't think so. But thank you for the earrings. They really are lovely."

His smile was pure devilry. "I didn't simply order a shopkeeper to pick something and wrap it up. I went to several stores before I found what I was looking for, and I thought of you the entire time I was choosing them. It's not a poor replica of a hand-carved bed, but the sentiment is no less worthy. Till tomorrow." His breath was a whisper across her lips. He didn't try to kiss her, and Lucy was left to follow him as he departed the room. He turned back one last time.

"This is not how I wanted it to be, but I'm too ruthless and determined to regret it. I wanted you, and now I have you. I intend to keep you, Lucy. And I will do anything to make certain that you stay where you belong—by my side."

"Is that all that matters to you? Am I some prize to be won?"

"No. But Lucy? *You* are my most treasured possession, and I will keep you just as safe as you have kept that little piece of carved wood."

CHAPTER TWENTY-ONE

ADRIAN HAD NEVER anticipated seeing anyone more than he had his Lucy on their wedding day. She looked beautiful in her copper gown, her ears adorned with his gift. He was saddened to see that her eyes held nothing but coolness in them. He had hoped that somehow she might have found their union more agreeable, but apparently she did not.

When they said their vows, hers were repeated in a quiet voice. He had shuddered when she had repeated "with my body I thee worship." He could hardly think of anything other than how he was going to endure this night—his wedding night—without being lost inside her.

She would not relent in her proclamation, and he would not give in and take her. One night was a farce. He needed to tread carefully where Lucy was concerned. He had believed she was thinking differently of him. Believed she might even return his feelings after that night in his Mount Street house, but then this had happened, and she believed him a coldhearted bastard, reduced to clandestine meetings in order to get what he wanted out of her.

"Shall we?" he asked as they walked arm in arm down the hall. "I thought we might have a word."

"Of course."

There was no warmth, no fire in her, and he thought he might die if he never felt that again.

They stepped into the salon, and she sat, her wedding gown spread over the cushions, reminding him of a crimson sky at sunset.

"You're beautiful."

She said nothing, but looked at him—or rather, through him.

"I… Things did not get off for us as I hoped. I wanted to win you fairly, not…this way."

"Well, you have me. Whether you will still want me is another matter entirely."

"I understand you're hurting, Lucy."

"No, you don't."

"I do. I know what you're feeling."

Something inside her snapped, and everything bottled up inside came crashing down. "You know nothing! Not me, not my feelings, nothing!"

"I have felt much the same before you. I know the feelings, Lucy."

She began to rail and rage, to show him how pompous he was to even begin to think he understood the depths of what she was feeling.

"When have you ever done anything against the grain, your grace?" she demanded. "When have you ever broken the mold, or gone outside your unbearably proper and stuffy organized little world to risk anything?"

Oh, how she felt like striking him. The world and her future loomed heavy and lonely before her. She was filled with anger—and rage. The injustice of it all, the pain of having her life managed for her as if she were too weak and feebleminded to manage it for herself. And while the anger she felt seethed and grew and all but consumed her thoughts and body, the duke stood silently, towering over her with his implacable granitelike countenance that betrayed nothing of what he felt—if indeed he even felt at all.

"What do you know of what it is to live, to take a risk? You can have no understanding, no comprehension, because you live your life ordered and distant and controlled. You're nothing but a title," she taunted, baiting him, waiting for some flicker of *something* from those glacial eyes of his. When he would not rise and meet her challenge, she jumped from the settee and took a step toward him, the anger inside now a living, breathing thing, making her restless and destructive. But she must obey it. From childhood, she had ignored the pain, the heartache, hoping it would go away, but it hadn't, and now…now her heart was shattering into a million little shards while her new husband looked on— remote, unfeeling. Not giving a damn, only caring that he had secured himself a rich, blue-blooded bride.

"You can have no idea what it is to risk all for happiness." She took another step, and then another, heedless of the fact her body was trembling, and her bottom lip quivering, and her eyes—how they misted with the scalding heat of tears. One slipped down her cheek and she tasted it, the bitterness of betrayal and pain, and the engulfing melancholy and despair that filled every fiber of her being. Another fell, unchecked, a testament to her sorrow, the pain of having every last one of her hopes and dreams dashed by one negligent, selfish wave of both her father's and the duke's hands.

"What?" she demanded, taking another step toward him, until her burnished-golden gown brushed over his trousers, and shoes, and she was forced to tilt her head back to glare up at him. "Damn you, Sussex, what do you know of risking all for the one thing you want most?"

The seconds ticked by, marked by the delicate clicking of the mantel clock. Between them, the air, which had been settled, seemed to change. It was a subtle thing at first, but then it seemed to crackle, to take on new life, to hum between them as Sussex lowered his gaze to her face, letting it travel over her tearstained cheeks, then to her mouth, where it lingered, robbing Lucy of breath.

"What do I know of risk?" he murmured, his voice deep and velvety, as luring as the nap of expensive velvet against her fingertips. "What do I know?" he repeated, this time his voice darker, more compelling, and when he stepped closer, and the heat from his body, and the scent of his cologne washed over her, he seemed to take the air straight out of her lungs—the room—possibly the very Earth.

"I know risk," he said, and she heard the rustle of her gown swishing around his legs as he moved closer. "I've tasted it. Felt its heady call."

"You've never heeded the call," she accused.

"Oh, but I have. I know what it is to take the greatest risk of my life, for the one thing I want most."

He had backed her up against the wall, and the marble pillar that stood on either side of the salon door pressed cool and unyielding against her shoulders.

"The greatest risk of my life was today, when I made

you my wife. When I vowed to love and protect and stay faithful to you. When I vowed to worship you with my body."

To remind her of that, he brushed against her, his body melding and pressing against hers in an erotic reminder of what would happen between them. Another brush, another waft of his skin, and hair, and everything that made a man a man, told her that he would use this body against her to subdue her, break her—worship her. The whispered reminder—in his voice—made her skin grow warm and taut, her breasts swell as her body seemed to grow weak and willing beneath the subtle erotic pressure of his.

He was crowding her, his big, tall body encompassing her short one. Surely that was the reason she had suddenly reached out and grabbed the lapels of his jacket; why his hand was wrapped around her waist, his strong fingers squeezing, pressing into the bodice of her gown.

"Today, I tasted that risk when I made you my wife, knowing that you might never feel the way about me as I feel about you."

His hand, so hot and strong, was sliding up her midriff, his fingers gliding over her ribs. The tip of his index finger lingering beneath her breast. Their gazes were locked, and she felt some inexplicable force pull her to him. But she would not give in to that power.

"I am but a pawn in the game of powerful men. A possession to be bought and placed on the shelf for your friends to admire."

"No." The word was a deep whisper against her flesh as he lowered his head to hers.

"A duchess to play hostess for you. A wife to see to the running of your household, and your social and political ambitions."

"No."

"A…a…" She floundered, trying to find another analogy for his purpose in marrying her, but he stopped her with the delicate brush of his mouth above her jaw.

"A friend. A companion. A beautiful, passionate lover to spend the days and nights with. A woman to carry my children, a partner to share the triumphs and failures. A woman I can share my dreams with, and who will share hers with me. A woman who I can comfort and hold in times of need, and who will hold me when I am weak, and sorrowful, and in need of the sort of succor only a wife can give to her husband. A woman who I want so desperately to make love to. You, Lucy, you are that woman."

Their gazes met, and she could not resist asking him the question that burned in her mind. "H-how…" She wet her lips, tried to speak again. "How do you feel about me?"

His eyes, those cold, mysterious eyes, stared down at her, haunting her with their ghosts and mysteries. But they were not the eyes of the duke, she thought in wonder as they grew warmer—almost silver. These were the haunted, troubled eyes of the man behind the title, the man who had known pain and coldness. The man who was her husband and who held troubling secrets deep within.

"My dearest Lucy," he said, his gaze never wavering from hers, "I would die for you."

THE CARRIAGE TRUNDLED amongst the streets of Mayfair, before making its way out of the city along the old
North Road that would take them to Yorkshire. The
November sky was gray with the promise of snow. He
had debated taking the train, and perhaps now, looking up at the sky, he should have made arrangements
to do so. But then, he had not been thinking clearly
these past days.

He studied Lucy from beneath the brim of his hat.
She was gazing out the window, and he could not help
but wonder if she was thinking the same thing, that
he was a fool to drag them to North Yorkshire in this
weather. Did she think her new husband inconsiderate?
he wondered.

His *wife*. Air stuck in his lungs as the word whispered in his mind. They'd signed their names, and the
clergy had blessed the rings they now wore on their
fingers. She belonged to him in the eyes of the law and
God. But she was not his. He was acutely aware of that
fact. She was a wife in name only, and would remain
so until he found a way to break through the icy shield
she'd built around her.

She had said little that day—nothing but her vows,
and a quiet goodbye to her father and Lady Black. She
hadn't spoken to him since her explosion after the ceremony. There was so much to be said, so many words
that needed to be shared, but he was at a loss to begin.

It was strange how uncomfortable he was with the
silence between them. How he longed to hear her voice
in the quiet of the carriage. He'd never been one for
talking, and yet he craved the sound of Lucy's voice
enveloping him.

Day by day he learned more about her. Today, he was discovering that his wife was at peace with the quiet. Strange. Every female he had ever known had chatted away, barely stopping to draw breath. They had tried to coerce and lull him into their web with words, but he had never been lured. But there was something in Lucy's voice that made him draw near to her. Perhaps it was the fact he knew it might be the only thing he had of her—her conversation.

"It's going to snow."

His gaze darted from the lead-colored clouds to his wife. "You're right. I suppose I should have arranged for the train to take us north."

Dismissively she waved her hand. "People have been traveling north in the winter by coach for centuries. I'm certain we shall endure and survive the ordeal."

"I shall see to it that we do."

If she detected the smile in his voice, she did not let it show. "My father and I traveled by train to Whitby in March when we brought Isabella back to London. There was a sudden snowstorm, and we were stuck for days. You see, there really is little difference between track and road—both must be cleared for safe passage. At least by road, you're more apt to come across someone who might be of a mind to help, or a little roadside inn that might have a room to spare. On a train, you're stuck in the carriage on a track, with nothing around but open air. I'd rather take my chances on the North Road."

"I imagine that it was somewhat more comfortable to be on the train than in a carriage."

"No. It was just as cold in the train carriage as it

would have been in a coach. And I was rather irritated by the other travelers, always grumbling about the situation. What more did they wish the conductor to do? The snow was blinding and the drifts so deep over the tracks that the train was utterly immobile."

That was Lucy. Practical. He never would have thought it but there it was. She might be a forerunner in fashion—a slave to the ways of the ton. She might have been pampered and spoiled but she was not the sort to carry on and indulge in theatrics. Hell, she'd had every right to do so when they had been discovered at the House of Orpheus, but she hadn't. She'd borne it all like a vigilant little soldier, when he knew that her hopes and dreams had been shattered.

He probably should have felt remorse for being the one who had dashed all her hopes—it was the gentlemanly thing to do, after all—but he was no gentleman. Nor could he summon up the regret and remorse. He wanted her. Had wanted her from the very first moment he'd seen her. No, he was not one bit remorseful that the beautiful woman who sat across from him was now the Duchess of Sussex.

There were so many mysteries to her, so many complex layers, that he wondered if he would ever truly discover them, and know her as a husband ought to know his wife. Had she allowed Thomas to discover her? To learn her as a man learns his lover?

The pain of that thought made his expression blacken. He'd told himself that it no longer mattered. Thomas was dead, and Lucy knew the sort of man he had been. Besides, she was his now, and they were traveling far away from London for their honeymoon, a chance for them to get to know one another, to start anew.

There was melancholy in her; he could see it brimming there in her green eyes. She wasn't happy and he'd give everything he owned, everything he was, for just one chance to change that. To bring a smile to her lips, and a glow to her eye.

"I need to apologize."

The words cut through his thoughts, and he stilled then sharply gazed at her. She was wearing the dark green velvet cloak, and the white fur muff lay on her lap—her fingers warm and safely out of grasping range.

"Oh?" he mumbled, perplexed at her abruptness.

She swallowed and he followed the fluid line of her throat, the paleness of her skin. She looked so small sitting across from him, dwarfed by the heavy velvet squabs. He wanted to lift her up and haul her onto his lap, and hold her in his arms. He wanted to be the big brutish ruffian she had accused him of being, and show her that this big, brutish body could offer safety and warmth—and pleasure.

"Isabella confided in me before we left that she was the one to tell my father about the House of Orpheus. In fact, she and Black brought him in their carriage. I assumed, well…"

"You thought I had staged it."

"Yes. I may be prideful but I am one to admit when I'm wrong. And I was wrong. It is over now, we're married. And I've discovered that it's too much effort to exert to sulk and be miserable all the time."

"Lucy…" She looked at him and he reached for her, wishing she would yield a bit more so he could pull her from the carriage seat and kiss her. "Pixie," he murmured, "if we could do it over again, I would win you fairly."

"And you might have succeeded, too."

"You talk in the past tense, as if now it is not possible for me to win your affections."

"Affections are not required in a marriage such as ours. Breeding and money are all that one needs—and an heir."

They were out of the city now, making their way north. He was feeling tired and miserable, and ready to fight with her. Her jabs were well-placed, hitting him where he felt guilty.

"Perhaps now is not the time for this. We should both rest."

Closing his eyes, he meant to feign sleep, but actually succumbed. When he awoke it was to the sound of the footman pounding on the carriage door, and a raging blizzard outside.

CHAPTER TWENTY-TWO

"YOU CANNOT MEAN to go outside in this weather."

They were forced to find shelter within the walls of a small inn. Something heavy hit the scarred wooden table, and Lucy turned from the window to see Sussex tossing his overcoat onto it.

"I must."

He was rifling through the pockets, pulling something out and placing it to one side, paying no heed to her concerns. "You will freeze out there. Besides, you won't be able to see a foot in front of you. The snow is blinding."

He grunted something, and carried on about his business making Lucy's temper flare. Strange how easily he could provoke her into a temper—or any rash feeling at all. She had thought after all these years, she'd conquered the emotions that had threatened to rule her as a child; she had easily found them once again after she thought he betrayed her.

"Go then," she grumbled and turned her back to him. Wrapping her arms about her waist, she watched as the innkeeper and his wife ran out into the ravaging snowstorm.

"There's not enough help for them and the animals. They must be brought into the barns, and I must see to the horses and the servants."

Why did she care? she thought churlishly. What concern was it of hers?

"You'll be safe here."

She whirled around, her skirts in a rustling flurry about her. "It's not my safety that concerns me!"

Her cheeks flamed, and she darted her gaze away, refusing to look at him. What the devil was wrong with her? Let him go out in the snow; she would not allow herself to care.

She could feel his gaze boring into her back, and she refused to respond to it, to that beckoning call of his mysterious gray eyes.

"Lucy—"

"Go." She swallowed and squeezed her fingers around her arms in an effort to cease the sudden storm of emotions that suddenly swirled as violently inside her as the storm beyond the windowpane. "The servants need you."

There was a very long pause, and then she heard the retreat of his boots along the weathered floorboards. His fine clothes would be no barrier to the harsh winds and blowing snow. The bitter chill of the lashing winds would rip through the fine linen shirt and wool jacket he wore. "Your grace?"

He stopped and turned. Lucy went to him, pulling her cloak from the back of the chair. "Take this. It's lined with fur and will fit well enough over your coat."

"It will be ruined."

"Far better that it be destroyed than to have you freeze to death out there. I don't know where we are, let alone how to find my way back to London. I'm afraid I need you alive."

Oh, wicked, wicked thing to say, but she could not stop it. He was looking at her in that way again—the way that made her heart ache to know him, to discover the man behind the sad, gray eyes. She couldn't have that.

He smiled, damn the man, and took the cloak. "Oh, I think I have a far greater chance of freezing to death in this room than out there."

Her mouth was still hanging open in shock when he closed the door behind him. Arrogant man! He thought it chilly between them now, wait till he returned frozen and chilled from the weather. She would do nothing to help him! Not one thing! Let him freeze to the very marrow, she thought. She would not thaw him.

Strolling to the window, she gazed out, watching the chaos as the small handful of the inn's employees struggled with the horses' harnesses. Rosie stood on her hind legs beside her, her front paws balanced on the windowsill, docked tail wagging in happy little circles.

"Stupid man," she said, and the dog glanced at her, tongue lolling to the side. "Well, we're well and truly trapped here, Rosie. We might as well settle in and make do. This weather will not let up for some time."

Rosie jumped down and headed for the fireplace where she snuggled onto a worn mat and immediately fell into a deep, sonorous sleep. Would that she could sleep for twenty-two hours of the day. Then maybe she could avoid her husband, and the unwanted marriage she now found herself in.

She could unpack their things, she supposed, and was about to do so when Sussex came into view. He was shouting to the others, and they stopped, gathered around him as he took control of matters.

He was very good at that, taking control. He was a born leader; people gravitated toward him, listened to him. Soon, he had the flow of help turned to specific tasks, and Lucy could not help but notice that he did not simply order people about, but assisted in the task of getting the animals sheltered and their servants settled.

How long she stood there and watched him, she could not say. His hat had blown off, and his ebony hair was now heavy with snow. His greatcoat swirled around his boots, and she noticed that the innkeeper's wife now wore her cloak over her threadbare shawl.

And another frozen corner of her heart seemed to chip away and melt into her chest.

I would die for you... Those words crept into her mind, and unconsciously she began to touch her fingertips to her lips, remembering his kiss, the tightly held control that swiftly slipped away, consumed then by a frantic devouring.

I would die for you...

She was lost in that memory, his words. The lonely isolation she saw in his eyes. Inside she warmed, the ice thawing further. Feelings she didn't want to acknowledge sprung forth and she buried them, but they rose up again as she watched the man she had married that morning rush about the inn yard.

I would die for you... But would she for him? The ice began to form again, and she reached out, pressed her fingers against the iced windowpane.

She was afraid. So damn afraid of the feelings inside her. Conflicting thoughts and emotions. Passion. That was all she had wanted. But this… What she was feeling had nothing to do with passion, and she wanted to run from it, to hide behind the veneer she had erected.

Empty, soulless creature. You want only passion because it's all you can feel. Because it makes you forget that inside you there is nothing.

"No," she gasped, pressing her palm against the window. But she could not force herself to look deep within. She didn't know what resided there. Maybe the voice was right. Nothing dwelt within her. Nothing but her pleasure-seeking impulses.

You wouldn't die for him.

And she felt the burning sting of tears behind her eyes. Biting her lip, her fingers curled tightly against the glass, as if by squeezing them she could somehow keep the tears from spilling.

She had cried in front of him today. But that had been in frustration and anger. But this was something else. This was self-reflection, a moment of discovery, when one looked deeply within and realized that one was a horrible human being who cared only about her own wishes.

Oh, God, what had she allowed herself to become?

A sob strangled in her throat was about to break free when the door to her chamber opened. The cries of a babe screeched, and she whirled around to see a young woman carrying a bucket of coal in her hands.

"Pardon, your grace, but his grace sent me to fetch ye some coal and build up yer fire."

The young woman's hair was clinging to her neck, wet with melting snow, her fragile fingers reddened with cold. She shivered as she curtsied and rushed to the hearth. In moments the fire was roaring. Rosie sighed contentedly, stretching out before the warmth as the babe continued to cry.

"Shall I bring you some warm water for a bath, your grace, or tea perhaps?"

She was cold, this poor girl, and here she was catering to a woman dressed in heavy velvet and wool, with layers of petticoats and lace, and warm, fur-lined boots.

"No, stay. Warm yourself by the fire."

The girl's eyes went round, before her gaze darted to the hall, and the now frantic wails of the baby.

"I mustn't tarry," she said shyly. "We're full to bursting now, and I've got to get to the kitchens to get the dinner started."

"Abigail," a voice roared. "Where is that gel?"

Nervously the maid glanced at her then curtsied. "If that is all, your grace."

"Abby, get that bairn to bleedin' stuff it, and get yerself to the kitchens!"

The maid rushed past her, and Lucy reached out, stilling her. "The child is yours?"

Wincing, the girl nodded. "I've done me best to soothe her, but she's getting teeth and, well, she wants ta be held. I'll move her to another part of the inn so your grace isn't disturbed by her ruckus."

"Abby!" the innkeeper roared again. Abigail rushed to the door.

"Bring your child to me," Lucy said. "I will mind her while you see to your duties."

"Yer grace, oh, I couldn't—"

"You'll be busy with the cooking, and once those men come in they'll be famished. My husband in-

cluded." *How strange that sounded, her husband.*
"Come, bring me your child."

The sound of heavy footfalls clambering up the stairs
sent the maid into action. In seconds she had returned
with a red-cheeked and tearstained infant and threadbare blanket.

"My father and mother run this inn, and once things
get settled, I'll be back to fetch the child. I won't be but
a minute," she said as she fussed to soothe the child.
"Oh, yer grace, she's gnawing on your lovely pearls."

Glancing down at the chubby baby she held in her
arms, Lucy couldn't suppress her smile. "So she is. And
what is her name?"

"Fiona, your grace."

"Well, Fiona," she said as she jiggled the baby in
her arms. "Let us watch the storm. Have you ever
seen snow like this?" she murmured to the child as
she turned toward the window. "No, I don't expect you
have. You're not above half a year, are you?"

Lucy held the baby and watched as she settled. Together they stood by the fire, and soon little Fiona was
asleep and Lucy was staring down at the baby she held.
She wanted one of these—not out of duty, but created
out of love. She wanted its father to love it no matter
whether it was a boy or a girl. She wanted this, this
sense of family and home and warmth.

She could find this with Sussex, something told her.
She just needed to choose the right road.

ADRIAN STILLED when he came into the room and saw
Lucy asleep with a babe cradled in her arms. What the
devil?

He looked about the room, finding no one else there. The babe stirred. Adrian inched closer to the bed, peering down and studying his wife and the babe nestled to her breast. What a sight. One he wanted more of—one he wanted to see when it was their child.

"Lucy, love," he whispered, and she came awake with a start. She clutched the child protectively.

"You're soaked to the bone," she whispered. "And you have ice in your hair."

"Yes. I'll sit by the fire and let you sleep. What have you found here?" he asked, smiling as the baby stretched.

"This is Fiona, and she's cutting teeth. She was in quite a temper when we arrived and I took her from her mother who was needed downstairs."

"Ah, I see. Shall I take her from you so you can sleep?"

"Oh, no, certainly not. I feel much better. Here, help me up and I'll set about getting you dry clothes. I assume your valet is boarded up at the other inn down the road."

"Yes, but Lucy…" He stilled her. "You needn't wait on me. I can be quite self-sufficient." He had been for years, he reminded himself.

A knock at the door interrupted them, and she called, "Come," and saw that it was Abigail.

"Oh, your grace, I'm sorry. Here, let me just—"

"There is nothing to worry over, Abigail. The child is fine, and as we are newly married we are both marveling at her, wondering when it might be our turn to have one."

Their gazes met, and Lucy looked away, her cheeks red. How he couldn't wait to get her with child.

"Well, they're lovely, but not when teething."

The babe fussed, but her mother soon quieted her.

"I think I'll bathe now. There's a tub room down the hall. The owner's wife was going to see about setting it up for me."

"I'll just unpack," Lucy murmured.

He wanted to kiss her, to tumble back with her onto the bed, but he couldn't. One night, she had said. He had to make her wait.

CHAPTER TWENTY-THREE

"Is this room satisfactory for a few more days, do you think?"

Stiffening, Lucy gasped and jumped.

"Apologies. I didn't mean to frighten you."

Her husband—good Lord, would she ever get used to that?—was lounging in the open doorway, fresh from the tub, his shoulder pressed against the frame. He had a bright red apple in his hand and she watched how he raised it to his mouth and bit off a large chunk. The crispness rendered the air, sharpening the quiet. They had already been married two days, and still she found herself jumping and starting at the sight of him. He hadn't touched her, certainly hadn't bedded her. He'd only given her a brisk kiss good-night, and she was taut and nervous because of it.

"Am I disturbing you?"

"Not at all, I am merely going through a few of my things."

His head tilted to the side as he watched her. "May I stay?"

A frisson snaked up her back and her fingers trembled, fumbling with the cloth-covered object she held in her hand. Why, she wondered, would he be content to stand in the doorway and watch her unpack? Because he always watched her, she reminded herself, with those mysterious knowing eyes, with their long black lashes that hid so much of his own thoughts.

"I am merely unpacking, my grace. It will hardly be entertaining."

"It takes very little to entertain me," he mumbled as he took another bite of his apple. "I must apologize for the room. If I thought we would run into such weather, I would never have left London."

"Really, it's fine. I rather like it, and the rooms are clean and the linen fresh. It's amazing that this inn had a suite of this size."

"You do not mind this room, despite the fact it adjoins mine?"

She did not look over at him, but continued unpacking the leather trunk. "We are husband and wife. Naturally I assumed our chambers would adjoin—just not in an inn."

"Naturally."

"You need not make use of the separate room again tonight. At least not on my account."

He paused, and he caught her gaze. "Is that just a polite way of saying that you understand and accept your duty?"

"I've been raised properly, your grace. I do know my duty."

He nodded, and she saw the light in his eyes dim. How strange his moods were. She had thought him utterly devoid of feeling when they had first met, but these past days had shown her that he was a man possessed of strange fits and starts. Lucy didn't think she would ever come to understand him.

"I am not interested in duty," he said as he tossed the

browning apple core into a wastebasket that sat beside
the rosewood dressing table. He then proceeded to
make a slow but calculated entrance into the chamber.
"At least not in the bedchamber."

He came to the bed and stood beside her, and she
smelled him, felt the incredible heat that seemed to
radiate off him. He was wearing only a waistcoat and
shirt, and the shadows from the hearth danced along
the black silk, illuminating the flesh of his muscular
arms beneath the soft linen.

"Is that why you have not yet consummated this
marriage?" she asked, finally getting up the nerve to
inquire about the matter. She had thought of little else
these past days. He had appeared eager enough at the
House of Orpheus, but then, that was when he was attempting to secure her hand in marriage. Now that he
had it, perhaps he found her lacking in some way?

"You...this," he parroted as he ran his hand along
the cotton wrapping that protected her most treasured
item. "Why is it not 'we,' or 'our'?"

He must have been drinking when he was down in
the taproom talking with the men, for he wasn't making
a whit of sense. He also possessed that strange tautness
in his body as he had that night he had abducted her
from the street. There was something dangerous lurking just beneath the polished veneer.

"I beg your pardon?" she replied. "I am not following your line of questioning."

He looked at her then, and she took a step back, astonished to see such deep emotion in his gray eyes.
"Why is it you only ask why *I* have not consummated
this marriage?"

"And what would be a better turn of phrase, then, your grace?"

His voice was deeply masculine when he replied, "Why have *we* not yet consummated *our* marriage?" He moved a step closer, reached for her and, stunned, Lucy could not move, could not breathe for the spell that was wrapping itself around her. Not even when he grazed the backs of his fingers along her cheek did she move. Just stood there, silent, watching, looking up into his face, which was austere now.

"You should ask, 'Why haven't we made love?'"

Her breath was coming too fast now, her mind whirling. "Why?" she whispered, not knowing if she meant to say it aloud.

"Because it is a duty to you," he murmured. "A task to be completed."

Swallowing hard, she met his gaze. What was there to say? It was indeed a task. A wife had a duty to allow her husband to bed her. It was a fundamental act in the marriage contract. A simpleton knew that. But that was not the question he was asking. Instinctively she knew that.

"I want you to want it," he said. "I want you to need it." Wrapping his arm around her waist, he pulled her closer to him. *"I want you to ache for it."*

"Beg you, you mean."

Closer he pulled her, the warmth of his hand seeping through the material of her night rail and wrapper. "No, that would not bring me pleasure."

She rolled her eyes. "Then what would?"

"A mutual desire. A mutual need. You see, I want you to actually want to lie beneath me. To want to feel

my mouth on yours, my hands on your body. I want..."
he said, his voice lowering until it was just a husky
whisper. "I want you to accept me into your body not
out of duty, but out of pure, carnal desire."

She was breathless now, her hands gripping the edge
of his waistcoat, holding him to her. She was dizzy with
the effect of his words, his nearness, the passion she
felt just beneath the caress of his breath as it whispered
across her cheek.

"When you take me inside you, I want it to be because you need me—not just inside your body, but in
your soul. I want to be there, Lucy," he said, his voice
pained as he pressed a kiss to the shell of her ear. "I
want so badly to be in your heart, your soul, and yes,
in your body. I want to show you pleasure, the real sort
of pleasure that you can experience with someone who
cares, who gives a damn about what you need. But..."
He swallowed, and Lucy felt the faintest tremor flash
through his big, strong body. "But you have to want it
as much as me. You have to want it like I want it. I...
won't take anything less. I won't let it be duty, when I
know it could be so much more than that between us."

Lucy shivered, and he pressed against her, molding his body into hers. "I'll feel you shiver like that as
I lay you onto the bed and follow you down, covering
your body with mine. When we finally come together,
not as man and wife, but woman and man, we will
be performing more than a duty, Lucy. It will be the
most sacred of acts, a union, a future for us. We might
even create a life. No child of mine will ever be con-
ceived out of duty. Never. So, I will wait." He kissed
her again, pulling away in slow increments that only

made her want to reach for him and grab him back. "I think I'd wait till the sands of life run dry for one night with you that was nothing but hot, slick need, grasping hands, searching tongues. Your hips rising to meet my thrusts."

She wanted to whisper his name, wanted to relieve the pressure that pooled within her, but she couldn't. She was held hostage by his words, the look in his eye—the deep-rooted passion in his gaze.

"Our first night together is too important. It can't be anything less than what I've described. And for that reason, I'll wait, and I might even pray, that one day—soon—you'll see this marriage as something more than a duty forced upon you. And me, you'll see me as a husband who could give you everything you need, a man who only wants to give to you, not take. Who wants to share everything he is with you, and have you do the same."

HE WAS DREAMING—a nightmare. Lucy heard the cry, followed by another. Creeping from the bed, she padded across the cold chamber floor and to the connecting door. Peeking in she saw him tossing and turning and she went to him, touched his shoulder.

"Adrian?"

He jolted and turned over, his eyes wild. He was frightening like this, and she took a step back, but he reached for her and grasped her, tugging her into bed so that she was sprawled out on top of him.

"Adrian, you're dreaming."

"I must be," he said, his voice dark and sleepy, "because you're saying my name, not 'Sussex' or 'your grace.'"

His lips pressed into her, and he pulled the ribbon free that held her hair in its long plait. His fingers threaded through the strands before he pulled her head down and kissed her hard. Melting into him she kissed him; let him explore her mouth with his tongue, her body with his hands.

"Dark, cherry nipples," he whispered. "I've been fantasizing about them since I first saw them." Tugging the night rail over her head, he exposed her. Her naked flesh pressed against his, and before she could revel in it, he hooked his hands beneath her arms and lifted her up so that her small breasts dangled above his mouth. His eyes were dark, and she could feel the insistent pulse of his phallus against her core.

"Perfect," he whispered, then tongued them.

She moaned, fisted her hands on his shoulders and allowed him to fondle her with his mouth and tongue. She was obscenely wet, aching, and she would have sat astride him if he would have allowed it, but guessing her plan, he lifted her off him and placed her on her stomach. His chest came down to her back, his lips nipping, searching, caressing, his fingers stealing around to her front, lifting her up so he could pluck at her nipples, pulling and tugging.

"I've wanted you forever," he breathed hard against her. Her nipples were scraping against the pillow, making them harder as he rolled and played with them. "I wanted you before I even knew what sex was."

"Adrian," she moaned as he nipped at her neck and sucked.

"You thought me passionless," he growled, "but you're wrong. I'm full of it. Bursting with it. My gut has ached with it, and it's all for you. The first time I saw you I knew I would have you."

His hands left her, and she protested, but then he plumped up the pillow and lowered her until just the tips of her breasts grazed the cotton. He was rubbing his phallus against her bottom, and his hands were squeezing and pulling, letting him slip against her wet core.

"He didn't even make you come," he growled as he lowered his mouth and kissed her hip. "Didn't even take the time to taste, when I would have died for just a lick of you."

And then he was on his back, his shoulders between her thighs, and his hands parting her, smoothing and spreading. His breath was hot against her and she was shaking with desire and mortification.

"Lower," he ordered, and she couldn't, just could not do as he asked. But he growled the order again, and as she obeyed, his tongue came up to meet her, pushing deeply into her flesh.

She moaned, allowed his hands to curve her hips, his fingers to direct her movements, the rolling movements, the slow back-to-forward motions as he pleasured her.

"My God, I love the way you respond to me."

She cried out when she felt him insert one, then another finger. *"Please,"* she gasped and begged, not knowing what she needed. It had never been like this with Thomas. It was all new, this frightening need to feel him moving inside her.

"Adrian, please, please," she moaned.

"One night," he teased, "you promised one night, and I promised to make it worth it."

Oh, that silly taunt, she thought, then shivered as his mouth and fingers found the perfect rhythm. What a fool she had been to deny this, to ever think him incapable of this.

"I am dying," she begged, increasing her rhythm, wanting more. "I need you inside me."

Never had a woman made him so aware of his virility. Everything about Lucy pulled and tugged at the primitive urges buried deep inside him. The desire to take and plunder was strong, almost impossible to resist. All his senses cried out to take her, to sink himself inside her tight welcoming body and claim her for himself.

But it wasn't enough. He wanted more. He wanted Lucy at his mercy, begging him to fill her, to take her as no other man ever had, or ever would. He wanted to hear his name uttered in her husky voice when it was full of passion.

She rocked against his hand, his mouth, and he felt her reach behind her, touch him, try to grasp him, and he moved away, knowing he would never last.

He watched as she learned and responded to the rhythm of his touch, her hips moving seductively in time to his fingers. It would be even more erotic to watch her move when he was inside her, encouraging her to take all of him, watching her lush thighs encase his waist as he stroked her deeper with each thrust.

"Come then," he whispered, pulling her down. Turning over, he said, "Open to me."

Her tongue came out to wet her lips and he captured it with his mouth, imitating what his body would soon be doing inside her. She mewled and struggled and slowly he entered her. His stroke was light, slow, purposefully not enough to give her release, but enough to make her plead for what she wanted.

"Is this what you desire?"

"Yes— No!" She twisted beneath him.

"No?" He removed her legs from his waist and rested them against his shoulders. "What about this?"

The minute Adrian set his mouth to that part of her, Lucy wished to scream. It was decidedly indecent and wicked, and decadent, and oh, she couldn't think anymore, she didn't want to concentrate on anything but the pleasure his mouth was giving her.

"Ah, this is it," he said between flicks of his tongue. "Yes, this is definitely what you want."

His words were arrogant, assured and laced with a lethal sensuality that Lucy was unable to resist. He was very male, and he made her feel very much like a desirable female.

Her body began to shake, splintering her thoughts. And then he was inside her, filling her as she continued to tremble, his strong hands fitting her thighs against his waist as he pushed farther and farther into her body. Lucy moaned his name, unable to help or disguise the desire in her voice.

"Come for me, Lucy," he begged, and she clutched his hair, his hips pumping wildly into her. "I want to be the last thing you see, the last thing you feel."

She was close, so close, and he was whispering in her ear, dark erotic words, his accent looser and more guttural—gone was the politeness. The indifference. The respectability.

"Yes. I can feel you clamping around me, squeezing me, milking me. Take me in you…let me come inside you, Lucy, hot and deep."

Feminine power infused her, and she reached down to snake her hands down his chest. They were staring into each other's eyes, her hands clasping his cheeks, the ghosts gone, the gray warm and vibrant.

"What do you see?" he gasped.

Shaking her head, she couldn't say, couldn't form thought or words. She saw a past, a young girl staring across the kitchen at a feral, frightening male who would not stop watching her with his cold, emotionless eyes.

"Adrian, stay with me!" she cried as she clutched at him, and brought her mouth to his shoulder, which she made horribly indecent noises into.

"I will, love. It's all I've ever wanted—to be at your side, protecting you, making your dreams a reality."

The little death wasn't little this time—it was impossibly long and beautiful, their skin slippery with slick heat, the musk of their bodies rising up, their lips and tongues and hands devouring, clutching, never letting the other go. Holding on to him, she fell off the cliff, holding him tight, listening to his primal sounds as they filled the room, and her soul.

CHAPTER TWENTY-FOUR

THE BED HAD grown cold and Lucy shivered, wanting her husband's arms around her once more.

"Adrian?" She had been awake for a while, watching him standing at the window, holding the carved bed in his hand as he stared out into the night. The snow had subsided; now only sporadic light flakes floated in the night, a brilliant white on a canvas of black.

He stiffened when she spoke and, reluctantly, he met her gaze. "Rosie has begun to pace. I'll get dressed and let her out."

This was not the man she had come to know. This was someone else, someone much darker, and it scared her.

"What is it?" she whispered. Had she been too brazen, too eager for the marriage bed? Had she disappointed him? She felt like cowering in the bed, the bed where they had just made love, where they had become man and wife in the true sense of the word.

"You're frightening me," she found the courage to say. "I want you to talk to me, tell me what you're thinking, because your eyes shield your every thought, and I am left with only my own conclusions, none of which, I may assure you, are at all comforting at the moment."

Wiping his hand over his face, he sighed deeply. "Go to sleep, Lucy, it's late."

"Don't shut me out," she demanded, but it sounded more like a pathetic plea. "Please don't. I…I know I've been difficult, but I'm trying. I'm trying to make this work."

His gaze flickered to hers. "That's the problem, you shouldn't have to try. It should just be."

She was starting to feel panicked now. "I don't understand what happened between then and now. I thought, well… I thought you enjoyed yourself."

He half turned, his gray eyes studying her. "I did enjoy it. I lost myself in you."

Heart skipping a beat, she wiped her hair out of her face and studied him from the bed. "Then what is wrong, Adrian?"

"It's Gabriel." He gazed back at her, his eyes remote, full of ghosts. The only reminder of what they had shared was the dampness of his hair and the slick sheen on his chest. He had wrapped his lower half in a sheet, leaving her with the blanket. He was big and muscular and beautiful, and she had utterly lost her heart and soul to him. It was so confusing that it had happened—how it happened, but now seeing him standing there, pulling away from her, well, she wanted to cling to him and hold on for dear life.

"Luce," he whispered. "Did you hear me?"

Shaking her head, she struggled through the images of what they had done, and tried to focus on him—his needs, which by all accounts were rather large at the moment.

"I'm not who you think I am."

Alarmed, she sat up and rested back against the headboard, making certain she was covered with the blanket.

"I'm quite certain that you're my husband. I don't think there are any loopholes left." She grinned, but he didn't return it, instead stared down at his hand, and the bed he carefully cradled.

"I thought you might have reasoned it out—seen it— seen *me* when you clasped my face in your hands and looked into my soul."

Time seemed to stand still as she thought back to that searing moment of intimacy, when she had felt at one with him, when he had stolen her heart and soul. When their gazes locked, held on—she had seen something, and felt it, too. A searing connection that was profound and beautiful, and soul-shattering.

And then the memory changed into something less sexual, but just as visceral—a connection in another lifetime, with another soul, with someone who knew her, her deeply held secrets, her girlish dreams and insecurities.

"My God," she whispered while she watched him, his eyes as haunted as she had ever seen them before. Her hand flew to her mouth and trembled against her lips as she looked him over, her gaze lingering on the scar that marred his eyebrow. "You are…you are…"

"That arrogant little gutter rat who thinks himself equal to you."

That was what her father had called him—the butcher's boy. *Gabriel.* Adrian had whispered it so softly, so painfully. She saw him as a boy, standing in the kitchen, his clothes tattered and torn, his dark hair in need of a cut and taming. In his dirty hands he held out the bed to her, his only words, *"For you."*

"I'm a bastard, Luce. Born in the stews, raised in the alleys of St. Giles amongst rubbish and animal offal. I am that gutter rat who came to your house and watched you. Who accepted your friendship because it was the greatest gift ever given to me."

"Adrian— Gabriel—" She paused, unsure of how to go on. "Dear God, I don't understand. How this can be?"

"Don't you? It's my deepest, darkest secret and I cannot go on lying to you. Not after tonight—after that." He motioned to the bed, to her, and he closed his eyes. "I thought never to tell you, but it seemed a sacrilege to me to make you think I'm something I'm not. I'm a fraud. An impostor—well and truly beneath you. I never wanted you to know, not because I feared you would not keep my confidence, or that I might lose my title, but because I didn't want you to look at me the way your father looked at me when he cut me from your life. What we shared tonight…it was beautiful, and all I could think of was that I would never lose you, never give you cause to leave me.

"My God, I've never felt anything like it, and all the time I was watching you—taking me deep inside you, thinking how damn arousing and humbling it was the way you were giving yourself to me—a filthy by-blow. And then I began to think of how many years it had been that I've wanted you. How I never forgot you and swore when your father turned me away that one day I would come back, and you would look at me, and think me worthy of you—that *I* would know I was worthy of you. I was branding you, making you mine, making you forget everyone but me, every place but our bed, and finally I realized you were mine and I was worthy of you. But then…" He glanced away. "A bead of my sweat fell on you."

She recalled that moment, still tasted the salt of it as it dripped from his brow and landed on her lips. It had been him, his essence, and it had not repulsed her, but aroused her, made her feel feminine in his masculine arms.

"It reminded me of the first day we met. I was filthy, and you took me to the water pump and washed my hands and face so that I could eat a tart with you. I was conscious then, as I was in that moment tonight, that I was so far beneath you. Rutting on top of you like a wild animal—like the gutter rat I was born to be."

"Adrian, Gabriel," she cried. "What do I call you?" she pleaded as she tried to get her limbs out from beneath the weight of the blanket.

"I have no identity."

"You must explain," she whispered as she came to him, pressing up against him, trying to hug him. She was naked and vulnerable and cold, but she would weather it all; this moment was the crossroads—his crossroads.

"Don't walk away—not again. Please not again." Taking his face in her palms she forced him to look at her. "I never forgot you, whenever you would look at me these past few weeks, I would think of him—my friend—and how your stare reminded me of his—intense and determined, silent, but knowing and seeing. I should have known it was you, so often you made me think of him—that boy I fancied…the one who listened to my dreams."

She was crying and he was brushing her tears away with his lips.

"I just wanted to be yours—for you to be mine." He sighed, caught her lips in his and kissed her, robbing her of breath as he held her close.

"Tell me all of it, everything," she murmured between kisses.

"I can't," he choked, pressing his face into her hair. "I can't confide in you because the secret is so dangerous, so…I simply cannot."

He pulled away, and reached for his trousers. "I'll be back. I need to clear my head."

She understood the need to run, but she was still afraid. He had turned away from her once, and disappeared amongst the humanity of the city. She had lost him once, and she wouldn't do so again.

Reaching up, she cupped his face and kissed him.

"It's fear that makes you run, but I understand it. I have done my fair share of running, too. But don't run because you think I cannot look upon you with anything other than acceptance. I don't see what my father saw. I don't see that young boy. I see a man, Adrian. A man who is strong and passionate and honorable. A man I want to be married to—I want it," she said, kissing him. "I want you. Please come back to me soon," she whispered, and stepped back. It was the only thing she could do—for now.

Watching him nod and walk out of the chamber was like a blow to her middle. She felt sick and frightened. Memories of the last time he had walked away made her run to the window, to stand watch as he emerged from the inn, Rosie slowly walking behind him.

Gazing up, he saw her in the window, and stood there watching her. What a sight she must be, with her red hair wild from his lovemaking and her nude body covered with nothing but a sheet. She pressed a hand to the frozen glass, and he smiled: a slow, sad smile that broke her heart. How had she not realized she saw her friend's eyes in the duke's beautiful face?

I love you. She wanted to say the words, but he turned away before she could. She stood there for a long while, searching into the black night for any sign of him and the liver-and-white spaniel that walked at his heels. But he did not return, and she collapsed onto the bed, exhausted from worry and crying, and fell into a deep sleep.

"LUCY, I NEED YOU!"

She came awake with a start, only to see Adrian kicking the door closed. Rosie was in his arms, mewling and whimpering. Blood soaked his hand, and he placed the dog on the mat before the hearth.

"What's wrong?" she gasped. She had donned her night rail, and ran across the floor in her bare feet. Rosie was whimpering and kicking her back paws.

"She's whelping."

"Oh, no!"

"Of all the damn times," he said. "I've nothing here, nothing prepared. My breeder is in Yorkshire, of all places."

"No, don't use that," she said when she saw how he

was making a bed with his coat. "It's the only one you have. Wait."

Running to her trunk, she reached for her extra night rails and wrappers, and tore them up then handed them to her.

"They're ruined."

"It's only linen, for goodness' sake. I have plenty more. Now then, tell me what to do."

He smiled. The darkness was still in his eyes, but he seemed lighter, and the ghosts were not there—at least not at the moment. "Ring the bell pull. We'll need some water and blankets, and something comfortable for Rosie to lay upon. The fire needs building up, too."

Abigail answered the summons and immediately ran down to gather the things they had requested. In the meantime, Lucy came to kneel by Rosie's head and petted her. "There now, it will be over soon."

Adrian glanced up at her. "She hasn't even begun."

"It's good to offer hope. I hope you'll do the same for me when my time comes."

Lowering his head, she saw his grin before he hid it. "Let us hope your time does not come while we are stranded in a country inn far from home."

"I wouldn't mind," she said thoughtfully as she sat down on the ground and placed Rosie's head into her lap. "I've always dreamed of a nice little cottage on a beautiful winding country lane."

Rosie let out the most mournful sound, and the first puppy was born in its sack. Lucy was rather horrified by it all. Especially when Adrian instructed her to release her hold on Rosie so the dog could break the sack and clean the pup.

"It's the way of animals," he said as her face scrunched up with distaste. "Her licking will stimulate the pup to breathe, and when it does, we'll help to dry it, then place it by the fire and wait for the next."

"How many will she have?"

"Up to seven. My God," he groaned as he watched Rosie with her baby. "I hope it's not that many, I can't stand much more. Her crying is making me feel damn guilty for bringing her along."

Lucy placed her hand on his arm. "It's the way of Mother Nature, Adrian. Rosie will do just fine. And we're together," she said. "We'll do it together, and then I will write to Lizzy and let her know how wonderfully Rosie did—and you, as well."

It was a long process, but by the time the morning light crept over the horizon, Rosie had delivered four little puppies: one male and three females. She lay by the fire exhausted while Lucy stroked her ears, and Adrian placed the pups at their mother's teats, making sure the warmth of the fire blanketed them. Their eyes were fused, and they were the most adorable little things in the world.

"You did it," she murmured.

"No, Rosie did it."

"Lizzy will be pleased. I don't know why she didn't come along with us. She would have been present for Rosie's big day."

"She wanted us to be alone. I tried to persuade her, but she wouldn't hear of it."

"You're very good to her, Adrian. She told Isabella and me once, that you were not always so kind to her. But that you became deathly ill, and upon convalescing you had changed and that you had become the ideal brother to her."

"I'm a fraud," he said quietly. "There is nothing ideal about me—but my love for her is real. I care for her and wish only the best for her."

"Does she know?"

Shaking his head, he opened his mouth to talk, but stopped instead and reached out, stroking his hands over the puppies' little bodies, which were only the size of a mouse. "They're nice and warm. We should make sure the fire doesn't die out. They need heat and Rosie is exhausted, she won't awaken if the room becomes chilled."

She allowed him to distract her—for now—and got up from the floor and walked to her trunk, where her velvet traveling cloak lay folded. "This will keep them warm—and Sybilla can clean it when we're done using it."

She covered the pups, and stroked Rosie's head. "It was really rather wonderful, wasn't it?"

He reached for her, pulled her down so that she was sitting in his lap. "Harrowing and exhausting," he corrected, "and I found myself wondering how men watch their women lie upon a bed suffering hour after hour, feeling helpless and inept."

Lucy smoothed her hand down his cheek. "You weren't inept, Adrian. Besides, when our baby is about to be born, I hope you'll stay by my side and whisper the same encouragement to me as you did to Rosie."

He smiled then. "Men don't attend their wives in labor, Lucy."

"My man will," she said, and she kissed him, only

to groan when a soft knock on the door was replaced
by the sound of creaking hinges.

"Shall I clean up here, your grace?"

Lucy hid her face into his chest, and he wrapped
his arms around her, rubbing her back as the servants
worked quickly to pick up the bloody clothes and blankets they had used.

"Ah," the housekeeper cooed. "Look at the little
loves."

Both she and Sussex beamed with pride, as if they
had had some hand in the whole matter.

"Well, you've been up the night through, yer graces.
I'll have breakfast ready for you and sent, and a fresh
tub of hot water."

"Will you draw a bath in here, please? My wife re-
quires the tub, as well."

Abigail curtsied, and it seemed within minutes that
the tub was full of steaming water. Adrian pulled her
gown over her head and helped her to step into the
water. She groaned at the feel of the heat that soothed
her muscles. She had been sitting on the floor for hours.
But she wouldn't have missed it for the world. There
was such a sense of accomplishment, she thought as
she glanced over at Rosie and her contented, sleeping
puppies.

"Don't fall asleep," he warned, and Lucy nodded.

"It feels nice, that's all. I'm relaxing." But she was
sound asleep in seconds.

ADRIAN CAUGHT HER and stepped in behind her. Lowering himself into the tub, he brought Lucy back against
him. Her head leaned back to cradle against his chin,

and he held her like that, just watching her, taking in every rise and fall of her chest. The way she smelled and felt beneath his hands was a balm to his soul.

Her breasts were small—perfect handfuls. Her nipples, God, he couldn't get enough of them, the color, such a contrast to her skin. They beaded perfectly, and they were so responsive. He couldn't help but stroke his thumb against one, watching as it puckered for him.

He shouldn't be doing this, not after what he had done to her in that bed—what he had confessed. He was a bastard, a filthy urchin who had no right to touch her, but his hands wouldn't listen to his brain, and he caressed her, needing to touch her, to watch his palm possessively roam over her body.

He was hard, and she was soft, her plump bottom cushioning against him, and he rocked, experimenting with the sensation. He was a wretch for doing this, but he couldn't stop. He slipped inside her, stretching her wide, and she moaned, raised her arm and wrapped her hand around his neck as he slowly pushed inside her, her body awakening in slow increments with every thrust, every one of his breaths in her ear.

"Lucy." It was a benediction the way he said her name. So full of awe and wonder. He couldn't help it. He watched as he touched her, parted her sex and stroked her, his cock filling, hardening even more at the sight of her breasts, her pale body spread out along his.

There were no words, just the sound of the water lapping and sloshing against the copper tub. Occasionally Lucy would moan, and he would encourage her with a touch, or a different stroke to do it more, and louder.

"I want to see you," she whispered, and she turned to the side, and dislodged him, and he felt…empty at the sensation. He noticed she did not use his name, and wondered at the omission, but thought of it no more as she straddled his hips and lowered her body onto his cock.

"I've never done it this way before," she whispered as she kissed his lips in a slow drag and pull. "Teach me?"

Resting his head back on the lip of the tub, he let his hands roam over her breasts, the flat of her stomach, as he watched the water bead over her skin. He shook his head, denying her.

"Learn me," he said simply. "Learn our rhythm."

Slowly she rose and fell, and he watched, loving every nuance of her dance, how she made love to him.

"Take as much as you want, as fast or as slow as you want," he encouraged. "Just don't stop."

"I won't." She captured his lips again. "I won't give up until you cry out my name and stare into my eyes."

Their loving was slow, close; she pressed against him, her breasts scraping against his chest, their lips constantly touching, their voices whispering, their fingers locking. She took her time, listened to his sighs, felt the way his body grew taut and insistent. And then she pulled back and watched him, their gazes focused on each other, and he wondered what she saw—a duke or an urchin from the slums. He wasn't either, and it terrified him to think that perhaps the man he was did not please her. She was young when she had fancied her little urchin friend, and when he had returned to her, he was a duke—rich, cultured and successful. What did she see when she looked at him, when she was taking him into her body and loving him?

Her eyes were misty as she loved him, and he reached for her, kissed her, felt her say against his mouth, "I want a place to belong."

"You have a place to belong. Here with me, Lucy. As my duchess."

"No!"

Lucy could no longer contain her thoughts, the emotions that filled her just as strongly as Adrian's body did. She bit her lip against the sudden pain she felt searing her breast. She'd been bred for this duty. She could run his ancestral home, and the other three estates he owned as well. She could plan balls, and country house parties, and dinners for fifty people. But that wasn't all she wanted. She wanted the sense of belonging—of being needed. Not her skills as a duchess and hostess, but as a woman. A wife. She didn't want to be just a duchess. She wanted to belong as Adrian's wife. Gabriel's wife. Whoever he was, whatever he was, she wanted to belong to him in the most elemental way.

She trembled, her whole body quaking. "I...I want to belong—somewhere, to...someone..."

Blinded by tears, she saw him gazing up at her, and the ghosts in his eyes shone brighter. Through lips that trembled, she braved the fear she felt, reached for the center of her soul which he had slowly thawed to a warm liquid during the days of their marriage and weeks of their strange courtship. A fat, hot tear fell from her eye, falling onto her lip.

"I saw Fiona again today, adorable and chubby and squealing with laughter. Abigail looked at her with such love, and I wanted that, Adrian," she said, her voice breaking. "I wanted that sense of belonging, of warmth and acceptance. And I imagined it, what it would be like to sit in your library, with our children laughing around us, and I...I'm sorry for everything. For being cold and heartless."

"What are you saying, Lucy?"

"That you've broken me," she gasped through large gulps and sobs. "You've taken everything from me, my shields, my defenses, and broken them down until I can feel the rawness deep inside me. You have made me want this marriage. Made me want to be your wife in every way. I don't care who you are, I only know that I cannot be as I once was with you, distant and cold. Even then, you drew me in."

"You do belong somewhere, to someone, Lucy. You belong to me as my lover, my wife—my entire life."

"Show me, then," she whispered, "make me feel it."

And he did, until she was gasping and crying and clinging to him, and he was whispering her name over and over, spilling inside her, realizing for once that he, too, had a place to belong.

CHAPTER TWENTY-FIVE

FINALLY THE ROADS cleared and the Duke and Duchess of Sussex made their goodbyes, with promises to return. Their servants had already headed north, and they both laughed at how well they had managed to get along without a lady's maid and a valet. Of course, Lucy had taken to wearing her hair down. It seemed her husband had a fixation with brushing it and pressing his face into the silken mass.

Lucy discovered she rather enjoyed lounging in their marital bed, the sheets rumpled from their lovemaking as she watched him shave. It was fascinating to her, the intimacies of a marriage—outside the activities of the bedchamber. They had talked, had shared their meals together, and an evening drink by the fire. He had written correspondence, while she sewed a new sweater and bonnet for Fiona—and refashioned a cloak for Abigail. They had taken the puppies, all healthy and strong and bundled warmly along with Rosie for the ride home.

Waving to the gathered staff, Lucy watched as the stone inn disappeared into the horizon. When she glanced at her husband, it was to discover that he was watching her.

"We'll come back—yearly," he vowed as he lifted her hand and kissed it. "Do not cry, my love."

"Silly, isn't it? We barely know them, but I will have

such fond memories of that inn, and what happened there."

"We found each other there, didn't we?"

She smiled shyly. Yes, they had. They had discovered each other's bodies, what pleasured them, what inflamed them with passion. They had made love so many times, and each time it was better, more intimate, because Lucy knew without a doubt that she loved him. He hadn't said the words to her, but sometimes she would catch him looking at her, and she knew that his feelings were deep, every bit as deep as hers were, but he still held back—his love, and his secret.

"When will you tell me?" she asked in a quiet voice. "We have two days yet before we'll reach Yorkshire."

"I should never have spoken it to you, but when I saw you with that doll's bed, and listened to you talk about the boy you knew, something inside me broke. I wanted to show you I was alive, and I was there, and that you only needed to reach out and I would be there whenever you needed me."

"So how did it come to be, Adrian?"

He looked away, swallowed and remained silent as he watched the rolling countryside go by outside the carriage window. Just when she had given up all hope that he would tell her, he spoke.

"My mother was a Scottish maid in the ducal town house. Her name was Mairn and she was... Well, I hardly knew her. She died when I was about six. But from what I remember, she was conniving and ruthless. My father, drawn to her spirit so he could tame it, found her intriguing, and they began an affair. She became pregnant with me, and used the pregnancy to bribe him." He snorted with disbelief. "My father was not going to pay for her silence, so he packed her up, threw her out and forced her to find her way on the streets. I was, quite literally, born in a gutter. And I was called Gabriel."

Her heart actually ached for him—for his mother forced to live in the streets, to deliver her child amongst the cruel elements. "Did your father know of you?"

"I haven't a clue. I didn't know him until I was six. He already had Elizabeth, you see, and a son—his rightful heir, who was little more than a few months older than I was. I don't know how I made it there," he said, his gaze distant and fixed, and far, far away. "But when you grow up in the stews poor and hungry, you grow up fast and learn to make your way around. Somehow I found myself in a rainstorm knocking on his door. The butler slammed it in my face. So I waited in the cold and rain, and eventually he did come out, and when I stood before him, he froze, his cruel gaze narrowed on me."

"So you're alive, are you? Remarkable."

"My mother is dead."

"Is she?" he said, my father's voice so cold and full of mockery. "Well, boy, the first thing you must learn is that whores have a very short life span—they're only needed for so long, and then they become a nuisance— something to be tossed out when they become tire- some."

"You're my father."

"No. I sired you, there's a difference." He laughed and came down the steps until he could touch me, and then he cruelly picked me up by my dirty coat collar

and lifted me so that he was looking into the same silver as his eyes. "Astonishing, you've none of her in you, that little Highland hussy that birthed you."

Adrian remembered his father's eyes…how they looked at him with pure repugnance.

"Pity that my wife couldn't do the same. My children—the legitimate ones, that is, are the very image of their mother. French weaklings, both of them. There is no York blood in them."

"What will you do for me?"

He dropped me then, and I landed on the steps.

"Do for you? Boy, I shall do nothing for you. Men make their own way in the world. Come to me when you make yourself into something that interests me."

"And then he left," Adrian finished, "but not before he tossed me a few coins, and laughed at me as I scrambled to find them in the dark."

Lucy was crying, tears making tracks down her cheeks. She had thought herself miserable as a child, but her childhood was glorious compared to what her husband had endured. She thought of her father, the way he had hit him, scaring him, and she reached out to kiss his brow and give him comfort.

Straightening, he seemed to push away that memory, and forged on to the next. "A butcher—you recall Mr. Beecher? He caught me sleeping with his pigs the next morning. I thought I'd have my hide stripped from me, but he and his wife were childless and they took me in, fed me, clothed me and cared for me as best they could, and they taught me a trade."

"I still remember the day I first saw you, standing

in the kitchen. You refused to talk, or take the tart I offered you."

"I was fourteen and I was awed by you. You were pure and innocent, and I wanted to touch you, to see if you were real."

"You didn't even speak to me."

"I had a Cockney accent, and when I heard you speak you reminded me of my father, that night I went to visit him. I felt inferior, and I didn't want you to think of me like that. So I didn't talk—not that first time, at least. I was content to watch. But then I couldn't resist, you were such a chatterbox, and I realized how lonely and sad you were, yet how you were content and happy with the staff—and with me. I saw you sewing your dolls clothes and once I saw you in town looking in a toy store window at a fancy gilded bed with blue bed curtains. I wanted to buy it for you, but I knew that I would never be able to afford something like that. It just reinforced what I knew was the truth—I wasn't good enough for you.

"So, I did my best to make you the bed—I cut myself so many times." He laughed and shook his head. "It was all I could give you, and when your father took it away, when he called me those names…I was six all over again, chasing after those damn coins. I vowed when I turned away from you that I would find you again, and I would be someone worthy of you."

The pain of his father's words echoed in the carriage, and Lucy struggled not to sob. She could see the pain in his face. He didn't need to comfort her—it was him that needed her comfort.

"To know you treasured it, you can't believe what

that made me feel that day. It made everything worth-
while, every pain, this secret, the horrors of my father,
it made it worth it, because I did it for you, Lucy. For a
chance to be yours."

"You did what, Adrian?"

"Took my brother's place," he whispered, and the
darkness descended once again.

"Tell me, all of it. I need to know, and you need to
unburden yourself of this secret."

"I was working late. The butcher shop was across
the street from a notorious bawdy house. The blokes
from the West End used to come and cause trouble
there, and one night, when I was cleaning the street of
animal offal, I heard a commotion. A young aristocrat
came out of the house, drunk as a lord." He grinned and
shook his head. "He *was* a lord. There was a fight, another man came out and the young man engaged him
in a fight, despite the fact he was so drunk he couldn't
stand. The other man beat him to a bloody pulp and
left him for dead in the gutters. When I went to him,
he was barely alive, his face a bloody mess. I searched
his clothes for any identification, and that's when I noticed his ring—it was the ring of the heir to the Duke
of Sussex, and as I looked down upon him, I realized
he was my brother. I don't know what possessed me,
but I hailed a hackney and drove to my father's house.
He was alone, and the butler let me in. I can still see my
father sitting at his desk as I walked in, his heir hung
over my back like a sack of flour, his blood running
down my clothes.

"'Good God,'" he said. "'Are you still alive, after all
this time? Ten years?'" His gaze never once strayed to

his injured son. 'Ten years in the stews without a damn farthing, and here you are, alive and hearty—big as an ox.'

"I said nothing. I placed his son on the settee and told the duke what I had seen. His mouth sneered as he looked at his heir.

"'Waste of a man,' he said. 'Effeminate, weak, I cannot believe he sprung from my loins.'

"'He needs a doctor.'

"'Does he? I don't think so, he's getting exactly what I told him he would get if he continued on in these unnatural ways.'"

Lucy knew not to question what unnatural ways he spoke of.

"You can imagine the duke's disgust. He was quite willing to allow his son to die on the lounge as he studied me. And then, before I knew it I was ushered to a room and locked inside. I was left there for hours, until he came back for me, and then he snuck me out of the house by way of the servants' staircase. I was brought to a house—my father's mistress's house."

"Anastasia."

He nodded. "My father allowed his son, the true Adrian, to die, and he wanted me, his *strapping bastard,* to play his part. It didn't matter that my mother was poor, without a drop of blue blood. All that mattered was that I was hearty and I knew how to survive—and fight. He had admitted to worrying over how his son would handle the duties of a Brethren Guardian when he was weak in mind and body."

"He stole your life from you."

Shrugging, he smoothed his hand down his pants.

"It wasn't much of one. As kind as the Beechers had been to me, I wasn't their son. I worked for them and Mrs. Beecher fed me and washed my clothes."

"How old were you?"

"Sixteen."

While she was flitting about Mayfair shopping and going from tea to tea, Adrian had been struggling to survive.

"My father thought it a grand plan, you know. He would see to educating me, to have me take on the role of an heir to an ancient dukedom. But I was an alley rat. Illiterate. Uncouth. I resisted the notion, but my father said that there would have been witnesses to his son's beating, so he put it about that he was taking his son to convalesce in the north. We were of the same height, the same dark hair. He informed me then of his family's legacy. How Adrian would never have been able to carry out the duties of a Brethren Guardian, but me, I survived the London rookeries with nothing but his scorn driving me! He was impressed by that. And I wanted to show him." Lucy saw his fist curl. "I wanted to prove to the bastard that I was better than him, and better than his legitimate son.

"At first I was revolted by the suggestion, by his utter callousness for the loss of his child. But then I began to think. I had seen you, you know—had never forgotten you. I watched you from afar. Sometimes I would walk from St. Giles to Grosvenor Square and wait for a glimpse of you. I began to think of what I could have if I was the Sussex heir. I would be a peer, of your world and appropriate rank. I would be rich, educated, everything I thought you would want in a husband. And it was for that reason, for you—and to show my father that bastards could succeed in his world with nothing— that I became Adrian York, the heir to the dukedom of Sussex. We left London, Ana accompanied us. Everyone believed that my father had finally decided to take his degenerate heir in hand and shake some sense into him. My father educated me in both reading and writing, and literature as well as math, and the ways of the Brethren Guardians. Ana taught me about the ton, and how to behave like a duke. It is my father's model that I am fashioned after."

"Adrian, I don't know what to say…what to call you."

He looked at her, and from the brim of his hat she could see those beautiful eyes watching her. "Adrian. Gabriel, the boy I was, is gone. I never really knew him, anyway. And what to say? Lucy, say I haven't turned you away. Say you do not think me less of a man for what I was born into. I'm not a duke—"

"You are, and a rather well-respected one at that."

"It's a sham."

"Adrian, you are everything the word *duke* conjures up. You have not turned me against you. How could you?"

"Because I'm a bastard."

"I for one am glad your father kept you. You make an excellent duke, and you're a wonderful loving brother to Elizabeth."

"She was already losing her sight, you know. My father kept me up north for months while she stayed in London. When she was due to come up to Yorkshire my father took Ana and I to Europe, on the pretence of giving his son a grand tour—and I did have one—but it was also where I began to learn more of the Brethren Guardians. In all, it took eight months to mold me into the heir. And when I finally met Elizabeth she was blind, and had thought me changed and matured after my tour."

"Her brother had been a perfect toad to her, hadn't he?"

"Indeed. She was shocked at the change in her brother. I had never had any family to speak of, and I cannot tell you, Lucy, how much I cared for Elizabeth. She was everything a boy could want in an elder sister. And it was not long before I saw how my father utterly ignored her. He was a hard man, cruel and cold. The only reason I was even allowed in his home was to continue the Brethren Guardian duties. He'd made it perfectly clear that I was useless to him otherwise."

Lucy studied him. "You were branded."

He nodded. "It's the way of the Guardians. But I cried out, and my father demanded that I be branded again till I became a man."

"Cruel, cruel man. You have suffered more than your fair share."

"I have been given more than most, Lucy, and I shall never take it for granted. There is one thing that I am most thankful for—it led me to you."

Reaching across the carriage, she grabbed his hand. "Yes, it did. Funny," she said, smiling. "I distinctly remember telling Isabella at the ball, the night she met Black, that you were too 'shiny,' rather like a brilliant and pure archangel—and your name was really Gabriel."

He laughed. "Imagine my horror when I thought how

easy it would be to stroll into the ballroom and claim you—finally. But you thought me cold and passionless. How that hurt, Lucy my love, because my gut had burned for you for so long, and my body—I ached with the want of you, and my heart…it was so full of love for you, that I could not countenance how you could not see it. How you could not want what I could give you."

She gasped, and felt her eyes begin to water. Raising her gaze from their hands to his face, she whispered, "And is it still, Adrian? Is your heart still full of love?"

He pulled her to him then lowered her onto his lap. "Lucy," he murmured as he tipped her back and stroked her cheek, "I love you more than life itself. You are the first thing I ever loved—you'll be the last, too. I never knew kindness until I stood in your kitchen and you tried to make me feel welcome. I never knew what it was to crave another human being. I never knew that love could hurt like the devil until that day when I gave you back that scrap of lace and you declared me cold and unfeeling."

She tried to talk, but he placed his fingers gently over her lips.

"I never knew ecstasy—or the deepest, truest meaning of the word *love*—until we made it that night. Do I love you? Yes." He kissed her damp eyelids. "Yes." His mouth moved to her cheeks. "A thousand times yes." Finally his lips brushed over hers. "Forever, and always, nothing could change it. *Nothing*."

"Promise me you always will, Adrian."

"I promise, little love."

He swooped down to kiss her, but she stopped him

with a hand over his chest. "Don't you want to know how I feel?"

"I already do, I feel it in the way you touch me."

She smiled. "Do you? Well, then, you don't need the words."

"I would die for the words."

"I love you, Adrian. Not the duke, not the memory of the friend I once had, but the man you are, the man that is right here with me in this carriage—my husband."

He kissed her, softly, lovingly, and when he pulled away, she looked at his eyes. "The ghosts are gone at last."

"I'm glad."

"It feels good to have the secret out. To know it is safe with you, and no one ever need find out. As far as society and Black and Alynwick are concerned, I'm the only duke—the true son of the previous duke."

"Secrets are dreadful things, aren't they?"

He nodded. "It's cleansing, just talking to you. I don't have to hide anymore. The words come easier now, because I don't have to worry about mucking up things, or losing my accent and slipping back into my cant. I can just be me. There're no more secrets, Lucy. Nothing between us. A fresh start, I think."

"Yes," she purred, "with my very own fallen angel."

CHAPTER TWENTY-SIX

THERE REALLY WAS nothing more revolting than Alynwick whispering to a lady, Elizabeth thought—and a
married one at that. Something was going on with him.
He'd been a constant presence at her side for weeks
now since Sussex and Lucy had left for their honeymoon. She was coming to know him, his moods and
his brooding presence in her salon. Tonight they were
at the opera, and he'd taken her for a refreshment then
promptly abandoned her to speak—no, *whisper*—with
this other woman.

"You haven't been to see me," she heard the woman
say in pouting tones. "I'm heartbroken, my lord."

Alynwick's reply was a mumble, intentional no
doubt, for he knew Lizzy's hearing was far more acute.

"Darling, you must come by the club."

Lizzy's ears perked up at that. What the devil was
Alynwick up to? she wondered. Her brother should be
informed. There was no telling what he might cause.
And there was no denying that the marquis had been
acting strangely—even for him.

There was a shuffling of bodies, followed by a
demure little purr, and Lizzy was tempted to dump the
contents of her punch glass over Alynwick's head.

When he came back to stand beside her, she was
positively fuming. "Take me home."

"We just arrived."

"I don't give a damn, take me home."

He heard the intake of her breath. "Lizzy, calm yourself."

"I will do no such thing, my lord. How dare you make a mockery of me like this, talking to that…that woman."

"That *woman*," he hissed in her ear, "is Guardian business, and I need her cooperation."

"I don't care what you're getting from her, take me home."

"I think you do care what I'm getting, and perhaps giving," he whispered huskily in her ear.

Pinching her lips together, she turned, sought to find a way out of this hell that was forming around her, but he was there, quickly latching on to her arm. "Where the hell are you going?"

"To the carriage. This was a mistake. I should have known better than to have trusted you."

"Why?"

"Because you're a rake, and a bloody heartless one at that."

"When I agreed to allow you to help in this Brethren investigation, I assumed you were a brave enough girl for the task."

"Brave, yes, idiot, no. You brought me here to flaunt your latest conquest in my face. She has nothing to do with Brethren Guardian business, and everything to do with slaking your lust."

They were outside now, and Lizzy felt a measure of relief as the cool air kissed her cheeks.

"I am through discussing this with you. Call for the carriage, if you please."

"As your ladyship demands," he said in mocking tones. "Waste of a bloody night."

"I couldn't agree more. We discovered nothing but the fact that your mistress misses you in her bed. Hardly a startling revelation."

"Oh? Do you miss me in yours, Beth?"

She would not answer that. She couldn't. "Perhaps in your fantasies, Iain," she grunted.

"Isn't that the truth?" he grumbled as he helped her up into the carriage and slammed the door. They were off, and the silence in the cab was overbearing. She couldn't stand it, the way her mind kept drifting back to that woman, and her voice.

"I will check the locks and windows before leaving you," he said as his foot slid across the floor of the carriage, coming to rest between her legs. "My gut is on the alert tonight. Something is in the air."

"Yes, I smell it, too. It's called unfettered debauchery."

She could hear the grin in his voice. "Are you offering, Beth, because I would, of course, be more than happy to accept such an offer from you. You've turned into such a plump armful that I couldn't resist."

"Go to hell," she snapped, hating how he made her lose her cool elegance.

"Already been, my dear. The service was not up to my standards."

She ignored him after that.

When they exited the carriage, she barely waited for his assistance. When Hastings opened the door, Maggie was there waiting for her, and she took her companion's hand, anxious to be away from him.

"Well, how was your evening?"

"Insipid. Uninspired and downright intolerable."

"Oh, dear," Maggie whispered as she steered them to her chamber door. "As bad as all that?"

"And then some. Maggie," she said. "Fetch the writing box. I have a letter to write to my brother, and it needs to be posted first thing on the morrow."

The sound of the writing implements on the desk told her that Maggie was preparing for her dictation.

"Dear brother, something of alarming import has come to my attention. I need you to return to London posthaste, for Alynwick, that horrid man, is bent on destroying the Brethren."

There, she thought. That should get her brother's attention.

Lucy was learning what it was like to be a duchess—and a wife. The Yorkshire weather had cleared up enough that Adrian had taken her into the village and introduced her to the tenants. She had admired babies, visited the ill and took notes on the needs of the village. Her husband was genuinely well-liked and respected, and she couldn't have been happier.

The vicar and his wife came over for tea, and some of the surrounding gentry came to call and to offer their congratulations. But for the most part, their days and nights were spent together, quietly—touring the grounds, or the house. Adrian was a patient tutor, helping her to remember names, and what rooms were used for entertaining for tea, or for reading.

"I don't like to be such a stickler about such things, Lucy. I don't really give a damn if you serve luncheon in the front room, or the back room. It's for Lizzy's sake, you see. She's so damn insistent on being independent, but when things change, she trips, and could hurt herself."

"Absolutely. I wouldn't want anything to happen to her. By the by, has she written to you? What did she say about our puppies?"

He had frowned then, and murmured that he had not yet had a letter from her, and he was worried.

"Perhaps Maggie has been ill and has not been able to write it for her," she had suggested. Adrian had nodded, but he remained quiet the rest of the evening.

Today they were strolling hand in hand down the long portrait gallery.

"I shan't bore you with the names. My father beat them into me, and I thought it all rather useless. But there are a few portraits I would show you."

They strolled a few yards more and came to a portrait that stared down at them. "Sinjin York—the infamous Templar."

She smiled up at the man, thinking how Adrian had inherited his eyes—and perhaps his crooked smile. "He was a rogue, I can tell."

"Yes. There is a rumor that he seduced the Marquis of Alynwick's daughter, got her with child and promptly abandoned her. There's a curse, they say, that it is forbidden for any of the House of York to take a lover from the House of Alynwick."

"Or what will happen?"

He frowned. "I'm not certain. Locusts or floods or something equally horrifying, I think."

She laughed. He had spoken a bit of his ancestors and only a touch more about the Brethren Guardians. Like Black, he was loath to involve her, but Lucy decided not to pry. He would tell her, in his own good time—just like Black had done with Isabella.

Tugging her along he brought her to the next portrait. "My father."

Lucy could not hide the little gasp of shock. This is what her husband would look like in ten years. He was handsome, very masculine, but his eyes lacked the warmth of Adrian's, and his mouth wasn't soft and lush, but firm, pinched into a hard line.

"I have stood here so many times wondering how it could be that I have so little resemblance to the woman who bore me. It is as if he created me out of some black magic."

"Adrian—"

"He made Anastasia into what he wanted for a mistress—something common to assuage his deep-seated fantasies, but something he could boast of to his cronies, someone who would flatter his pride. And he made me, too."

"No," she said, rising on tiptoes so she could kiss his lips. "He made you a duke, a Brethren Guardian. He did not make you the man you are. You did that, Adrian."

Clasping her to him, he hugged her for a long while and she felt his guilt and fear subside. "Do you want to see something very special—something magical?"

Giggling she whispered, "You already showed me that this morning."

He swatted her bottom. "Minx! Not that!"

Following him, Lucy gave him her hand as he guided her from the portrait gallery, to a maze of corridors with stone walls and doors. "If you take that door, it will lead you to the cellars and a way out over the moors. There is always a horse there, ready to be ridden. Only the groom knows of it, and he takes excellent care of it."

"I can picture it now, a knight in armor with his Templar tunic riding hell-bent over the moors with his sacred relic."

He laughed. "What a romantic dreamer you are, my love. It makes me want to wake you up in the middle of the night and put you on horseback and take you riding over the moors beneath the moon and stars."

"And what of the chalice, your grace? You have forgotten an integral piece of the story."

It was dark. How he could even see to lead her, let alone where she stood next to him, Lucy could not believe. But he found her, pressed against her. The cool stone wall was suddenly against her back and her husband was pressing up against her.

"I haven't forgotten the chalice. I would take care to fill it," he whispered wickedly, "to put my lips to it and savor what flows from it."

It aroused her, at the same time it made her laugh. "That is a very naughty analogy, your grace."

"I'm a gutter rat," he whispered against her lips. "We're known to be crass and licentious. Shall I show you?"

"Not in here," she said. "I fear this is a wonderful place for spiders, and I'm not fond of spiders."

"And I thought you an adventuress. What of your séances and the occult, there was no fear then, and a little spider saps the vinegar out of you?"

"Indeed."

"Come along then," he said on a sigh. "If we cannot dally here, we will where I take you."

They climbed a set of steep stairs—in utter darkness.

"How the devil can you see?" she asked.

"My father's training. He made me learn how to get around in the dark—a Brethren Guardian task."

"The man sounds perfectly horrid, Adrian. I thought my father cold and uninterested, but I have learned that I have little to complain about."

"He taught me things I would never learn otherwise. In a way he proved useful to me."

The door creaked open, and Lucy found herself in a tower. It was medieval in design and smelled of mildewing artifacts and dusty antiques.

"The only way up here is through that tunnel. There are never torches in case the place gets invaded—by whom I haven't a bloody clue, but there you go. It's a virtual castle, and you, fairy lady, are the princess, caught in a marauding knight's lascivious hold."

"I wonder if I should scream?"

"Only in wicked delight."

"I thought you had something to show me?"

"Later, I think. I'd like to show you something different now."

"And what would that be, good knight?"

"How much I love you," he said, pulling her to him. "How hard I am," he whispered wickedly.

Adrian captured her face in his hands and brushed his lips softly against hers. Her lips parted beneath his and her soft breath caressed his mouth. He kissed her, long and slow and thoughtful, showing her without words how he felt about her.

Lucy moaned and wrapped her arms around his neck, bringing him against the little mounds of her breasts. His body tightened and he brought her closer as he deepened the kiss. His fingers skimmed along her bodice to brush his thumb against her hardening nipple.

She tugged him ever so slightly closer to her and before he realized it, he was closing the door. Their kiss was unbroken and he felt Lucy's body restless against his. Her fingers were clenching in his hair in an eager, almost wanton fashion that made him long with a desire that burned deeply in him. He would never get enough of her—never.

The kiss, despite his best intentions, turned more carnal and Lucy returned it with exuberance, matching his rhythm and allowing her tongue to playfully dance with his. His finger traced the delicate line of her collarbone and shoulder. Without thinking, he lowered one sleeve, exposing a small perfect breast to his hand. He cupped her, skimming his thumb along her hard nipple. She moaned into his mouth and he broke off the kiss only to slide the remaining sleeve down her shoulder, revealing her fully to his gaze.

She was perfect. Filling his hands with both breasts, he watched the expression of pleasure cross her face. Their eyes met and he very purposely skimmed both thumbs across the taut, dark nipples. Holding her gaze, he went to his knees, all the time watching her, seeing how she followed him with her beautiful green eyes. Unable to resist the temptation she offered when she filled his palms with soft flesh, he pressed forward, nuzzling the valley of scented skin with his lips.

She whimpered and clasped his head to her chest and for a second he was content to press the side of his face between her breasts and listen to the rapid rhythm of her heart. Then he flicked them with the tip of his tongue, first in short flicks, then in slow, languorous circles, relishing the taste, liking the way her nipples puckered for him.

Her knees gave out and she slid to the floor in a puddle of blue watered silk. He held her tightly, stroking her nipple, feeling it firm and quiver beneath his fingers.

Then he was laying her back onto the floor, raising her skirts. She was spread wide and inviting, and Adrian closed his eyes, as he plunged deep inside her.

She arched perfectly, taking him all; he never wanted to leave. "How perfect you are," he said as he reached for her hand and brought it over her head. Their fingers were locked, and he watched her body accept his. "Perfect," he thought. This was a marriage in the true sense of the word, and when he finished, he lay with her, entwined in her arms, listening to her heart beating rapidly.

"Shall I get the chalice then and show you?"

"Later," she whispered, "just lie with me here, and hold me."

Her suggestion was far nicer and more pleasurable than his, and he indulged her. It was hours before he showed her the ancient chalice, and he did not regret it. There was peace between them. In the beginning, at the inn, there had been a sort of truce, one based on cool politeness. But this feeling, this contentment, was peace and acceptance. They were married now, man and wife. He knew her, what she desired, what made her wet and moan, but most importantly he understood how she thought, her fears, her desires.

As a child she had thought of a picket fence and cottage. Wildflowers and a country lane. She had thought of children, of gardening and looking up to find her husband standing there. He wanted to give her that dream. Wanted to be part of it.

"I'll follow you into your dreams," he murmured to her. She slept deeply, and he kissed her ear. "I'll be your very breath." And he meant it.

THE WINDOW RATTLED, stirring Lizzy from her sleep. Was it the wind? she wondered. She thought of calling for Maggie, but her companion had been unwell that day, so instead she tossed back the covers and padded across the floor. The breeze blew in, robbing her of breath. Strange how the window, which had been locked, suddenly blew open...

"Don't make a sound."

Her mouth was covered in an instant and a cloth pulled down firmly over her face. She fought, her cries muffled as a second person reached for her feet.

"Wait till she's out, and then we'll bring her to the carriage and collect our wages."

"She's strong," the other grunted, letting her foot slip from his hold. She fell to the floor, her body uncoordinated from the ether. The side of her head hit, and she heard nothing else as she slipped slowly into a state of mental darkness.

"Check her," the voice said. "If she's dead, Mr. Lasseter will have our bullocks strung up."

"Alive," his partner announced. "Let's load her up before someone comes to check on her."

Minutes later she was in the carriage.

"She's nothing much to look at," a woman's voice said sourly. It was so familiar...

"She's worth more to me than you can imagine."

"What now, my love?"

"Alynwick. He's the next piece in the puzzle. Bring him to me." Too drowsy to react to what she was hearing, Lizzy finally gave in to the blackness.

THE NEXT MORNING the sun was shining, the snow was melting and the air seemed to promise a bit of warmth. Inside, Adrian was cold—freezing. Tossing the letter onto his desk, he got up and strolled to the window, contemplating the grounds and tried to gather his self-control. It was never a difficult task for him, but this morning he was finding it nearly impossible to harness.

The door to his study opened, and he heard the soft tread of his wife. "You sent for me, darling?"

"Yes. Have your things packed. We're leaving."

He half turned from the window, with a wave of his hand he motioned to his desk. "I've had a letter from Lizzy. Something is wrong. She claims that Alynwick is acting out of sorts. Plus, she has been hearing strange things in the night, doors opening, windows unlocked, when she is certain they had been locked. I don't like it. She's alone, and I have only Alynwick to rely on to take care of her. I knew it was a mistake not to drag her into the carriage myself."

"I can be ready at once, Adrian."

He reached her and held on to her tightly, as if he wouldn't let her go. "You'll not leave my side, do you understand. Not while we're traveling, and not in London. I want you with me every minute."

"All right," she said as she smoothed a hand down his back. "I won't go anywhere without you."

"I dread what I will find when we arrive."

So did she. She just hoped it wasn't a heartbroken Elizabeth.

"Goddamn Alynwick, he was always reckless and impulsive. If he's put my sister in danger, I'll kill him, Brethren or no."

THE CARRIAGE RIDE had been grueling. They had barely spoken to one another; Adrian was lost in his thoughts and worries for Lizzy. Shadows were beneath his eyes, and she felt a measure of peace when he allowed her to hold him.

They were within the city now, and the sky, as if sensing their turmoil, had turned gray and leaden.

When the carriage pulled up in front of the house, they both jumped down and ran up the steps where Hastings waited uneasily.

"Tell me the worst of it," her husband demanded.

"Lady Elizabeth has been gone for three days, your grace, and the Marquis of Alynwick with her."

CHAPTER TWENTY-SEVEN

"I DON'T LIKE this, Adrian," Lucy said the next evening as she watched her husband from across the table. "Is there another way?"

"No, there isn't. Where else would she be but there, at the damned club? It had been his intent all the time, to take Elizabeth—to steal the artifacts for himself while I was out of London."

"Alynwick is many things, but he's not a kidnapper or a thief."

"He's in league with Orpheus. We found the evidence at his house, letters with the seal of Orpheus. Outlines of plans. Mentions of a fourth Templar. He was in league with Orpheus all this time. He knew our every move, and he betrayed us," he growled. "Black and I will deal with him in a way that is fitting to his betrayal to us and my sister. I entrusted him with Lizzy, and the bastard lied to me."

"I still cannot believe it."

"I've shown you the proof. You've read it, their correspondence. Orpheus is the descendant of the fourth Templar the legend speaks of. It's been Alynwick all this time."

"I realize that the information looks that way but, Adrian, think. You've known him forever. He wouldn't hurt Elizabeth, and he would not betray you or Black. This is much too tidy, don't you think?"

"I can't think! Not while Lizzy is out there alone, unable to see or help herself. Damn it, Lucy, I can't form a single intelligent thought."

"I understand. I feel the same way, thinking of you entering that club with nothing but a gun. He killed Ana, and Thomas, too. He won't stop till he kills you."

"I won't let him."

"How will you prevent it? Please," she begged. "You're jumping to conclusions. Your passions are ruling your head. You need more time to rationalize it all."

Adrian glanced up at his wife. On the eve of one's potential death, it seemed most fitting to be sitting across the table from one who was your very life.

He had thought quite a bit about that today, the possibility that he might be returning home in the morning in a casket. It was a strange sensation, to feel your impending death while staving it off by gazing into the eyes of the woman who made you want to keep breathing.

"You know I must do this. Lizzy's life depends upon us finding her—tonight."

"I'm so afraid," she whispered. "I don't want to lose you."

It was strange, he had never worried about death before, but tonight he was consumed with it. He'd even sent for his solicitor this afternoon to amend his will to ensure that Lucy would be properly cared for. Orpheus was a bastard, and he knew the man wouldn't fight fair. Both his and Black's lives would be in danger.

"I will see you at breakfast, my love. You'll see...all will turn out well."

Such an innocent statement, one that had a profound effect on him. He couldn't imagine it, not being able to see her again, not staring at her over tea and toast, and the morning paper. Not sharing a tray in their room after a night of lovemaking.

By God, he could stand this thinking no more. Standing, he tossed his napkin onto the table and walked to her end. Without a word, he took her hand and helped her up, put his arm through hers and steered her out of the room.

"Adrian, don't go. Please?" she said. "Not yet."

Opening his study door he ushered her through, closed the door, locked it and shoved her against it. "Forgive me," he said, his mouth descending to her throat. "I can't be soft. I have to have you now. Tonight, before it's... Well, before it's too late and I must go."

He was frantic with his need for her, his hands searching over her gown, the bodice, inching the hem up her thighs.

"Adrian—please," she whispered, her voice breaking down into tears.

"No words," he moaned into her mouth as his hand cupped and squeezed her thigh, then her bottom. "Let our bodies say what needs to be said. Actions speak louder than words."

She accepted him, kissing him as frantically as he kissed her. He needed her, to be inside her, possibly for the last time. He wanted to give her something of him to remember in the long nights without him. He wanted to spill deep inside her and give her his soul—his child.

She might already be pregnant and he might not ever see him or her. Which only fueled his need and fear.

"Yes," she moaned as he lifted and wrapped her legs around his waist. He had nearly taken her like this the first time, and there was beauty in it, symmetry. That night had catapulted them into a discovery of one another. It had been the beginning, and this moment would be a new one.

"Lucy," he growled as he struggled with the fastening of her gown, the chemise, and thank God, she had forgone the corset. It felt like forever before she was bared to him, her tiny breasts teasing him.

"Perfect mouthful," he murmured before capturing her breast while his hand cupped her bottom, holding her. He suckled and licked and she cried out, her fingers raking hard through his hair. He had already freed himself, and he slid hard and fast inside her, stretching her, and she cried out, clutched him and rocked against him, encouraging him with her kisses that were all over, that were raw and uncoordinated. It was messy and loud, and frantic, and it was better than anything they had shared.

The way he slammed inside her taking her against the door spoke of his need, his wildness, the way she accepted him, encouraged him for more, told him what he needed to know, that she was his. She had always been his.

"Adrian, now," she begged, and he obeyed her, only to collapse against her. They sank to the floor, still holding each other, panting and whispering, caressing and kissing each other with soft, loving mouths.

"I'll come back to you," he whispered, not meaning to say it out loud. "And I will ravish you over breakfast, and I will never leave you alone another night of my life."

CHAPTER TWENTY-EIGHT

How HAD HE gotten here? He had no clue. His head still pounded and the taste of ether made him gag. The pain in his shoulder where he had been stabbed ached, the wound stiff and crusted with his dried blood.

The steps to Sussex's town house seemed an enormous mountain to climb, but he endured it. Beth was gone, and he couldn't find her. He'd been out for days searching for her when he had been accosted, stabbed in a fight with none other than Nigel Lasseter as he'd come silently upon the man known to him and his Brethren as Orpheus.

He'd almost had the bastard, too, thanks to Lady Larabie, who led him straight to his nemesis. But as he cornered Lasseter in his room, another had come out of the shadows, bashing him over his head until he crumpled to the floor. He had awakened in a back room of the Adelphi, Sutherland had discovered him, only because he had sent his valet to follow Nigel Lasseter. By the grace of God he was still alive, alive and relieved to find Sussex returned home from Yorkshire.

He did not have to ring the bell. It opened as if by magic and the sound of a gun being cocked and pointed between his eyes greeted him.

"You've saved me considerable trouble, Alynwick," Sussex said with deadly calm.

"Where is Elizabeth?" he demanded, trying to figure out what the hell was happening.

"You tell me...what have you done with her?"

"Goddamn it, Sussex, if you think you can just take her from me when I've been all she's had these past weeks, you are sorely mistaken."

"You traitorous bastard," Sussex snarled. "I'd shoot you dead right now if I didn't need you to tell me where my sister is."

"I don't know, damn you!" he snapped. "That's what I'm trying to tell you. Orpheus is Nigel Lasseter. I've been to the club, I've seen him."

"We know what you've done, and who you have been with, Alynwick. Betraying us. Betraying me. We found the correspondence between you."

"What!" This couldn't be happening. It just couldn't. Sussex was wrong, there was a mistake.

"No mistake. It was all there in your study drawer. You should have been more careful, but then you probably never imagined Lizzy would write to me to tell me of your bizarre behavior."

He couldn't think; the world was suddenly spinning. "Damn you, Sussex, it's a trap. I'm not one of them. I only want to find Elizabeth. Someone has taken her, and it sure as hell wasn't me!"

Something flickered in Sussex's gaze, and he slowly lowered the gun.

"I swear," Alynwick vowed, falling to his knees, "I do not know where she is. I want only to find her. We're wasting time, Sussex, time we don't have—time that is running out for Elizabeth. If you cannot believe me about anything else, then believe me about this. I love your sister."

Lucy appeared at her husband's side then closed her hand around Sussex's arm. "Come inside, it's late, and there are people about. We don't need to perform such a show."

Sussex gathered her close and rested his head against hers. She brought him closer until he was covering her with a tight embrace. "She's alone, in the dark…afraid," he whispered. "What if I can't find her…"

"We'll find her," she whispered, "we will."

"Stay, Lucy—" he gripped her tighter "—stay with me at all times because I can't lose you, too."

"I will. I promise."

Pulling away, he turned back to Alynwick. "Finding Elizabeth is paramount. The rest, Black and I will deal with. Hastings," Sussex ordered. "Send Lord Black a message to meet here."

Alynwick looked distraught. "I can't waste any more time knowing she's out there all by herself. I have to keep searching."

"We have nothing to go on."

"You gather the clues, with Black," he called as he started back down the stairs. "I'll tear that club to pieces searching for her."

"The hell you will. I don't trust you, you bloody bastard!"

Lucy reached for Adrian. "Let him go," she whispered. "He'll prove no use to you in this state."

He stared at her, his expression perplexed. "He said he loved her."

Her eyes were wet, she loved this man so much, and

she loved Elizabeth, who she was truly frightened for. "He does. And I believe him. No man could look so wretched if he was lying about such a thing."

With a nod, he reached for her hand and brought it to his mouth, pressing it softly to his lips and holding it there.

"Promise me, Adrian, you'll find Lizzy and bring her back home."

"I will, love. As you know, I always keep my promises."

IN THE DARKNESS, Lizzy listened to the distant echo of water dripping onto stones. She was quite alone now, with only her thoughts. Fear had long since left her, and she was left to lie upon the cold, damp stone in nothing more than her night rail.

She had no way of knowing how long she had been gone, if Sussex had received her letter and was even now on his way back home. She didn't dare hope that Alynwick knew she was missing—they'd fought, and he swore never to grace her door again.

Oh, stupid, pigheaded fool that she was! She had let her pride get the better of her, and now she was trapped here, quite alone and at a madman's mercy.

She began to twist and cry, to claw at anything around her, searching fruitlessly for a way out of this tomb she found herself in.

Laughter echoing off the walls made her still.

"It's quite useless, you stupid chit," the voice said, and she stilled, cocked her head to the side. She knew that voice.

"Yes," the voice said again. "You thought it was

over? Well, my dear, I'm here to tell you, it's just begun. And in the end, I will be back where I should have always been."

* * * * *